Pr...
COSM

"May be the most enthralling science-fictional portrayal of how actual science is done since Benford's own Nebula Award-winning 1980 novel *Timescape* . . . his highly believable characters have little in common with the unrealistic scientists of so much SF."
Publishers Weekly (starred review)

"Nobody writes harder hard-science fiction. Yet Benford's story is grounded in compelling character."
Columbus Dispatch

"[Benford's] skill as a writer gives this literary science-fiction thriller the edge and pacing of a suspenseful bestseller."
Des Moines Register

"The science underpinning COSM is intellectually intriguing and superbly woven. Benford's writing skills and personal insights are just as impressive."
Newport News Press

"This is neat SF, with realistic characters, genuine dialogue and some very, very interesting problems posed."
The San Diego Union-Tribune

"Solid . . . No one is better at depicting scientists at work than Benford . . . It's hard not to react to the image of a tabletop universe, with galaxies aswirl and stars in collision."
Locus

Other Books by
Gregory Benford

THE STARS IN SHROUD
JUPITER PROJECT
IF THE STARS ARE GODS
(with Gordon Eklund)
FIND THE CHANGELING
(with Gordon Eklund)
SHIVA DESCENDING
(with William Rostler)
TIMESCAPE
AGAINST INFINITY
ARTIFACT
HEART OF THE COMET
(with David Brin)
A DARKER GEOMETRY
(with Mark O. Martin)
IN ALIEN FLESH
MATTER'S END
FOUNDATION'S FEAR

THE GALACTIC CENTER SERIES
IN THE OCEAN OF NIGHT
ACROSS THE SEA OF SUNS
GREAT SKY RIVER
TIDES OF LIGHT
FURIOUS GULF
SAILING BRIGHT ETERNITY

COSM

GREGORY BENFORD

AVON · EOS

This is a work of fiction. Names, characters, places, and incidents either are the product of the author's imagination or are used fictitiously. Any resemblance to actual events, locales, organizations, or persons, living or dead, is entirely coincidental and beyond the intent of either the author or the publisher.

AVON BOOKS, INC.
1350 Avenue of the Americas
New York, New York 10019

Copyright © 1998 by Abbenford, Ltd
Inside cover author photo by Joan Benford
Visit our website at www.AvonBooks.com/Eos
Library of Congress Catalog Card Number: 97-29652
ISBN: 0-380-79052-1

First Avon Eos Paperback Printing: February 1999
First Avon Eos Hardcover Printing: February 1998

AVON EOS TRADEMARK REG. U.S. PAT. OFF. AND IN OTHER COUNTRIES, MARCA REGISTRADA, HECHO EN U.S.A.

Printed in the U.S.A.

WCD   10 9 8 7 6 5 4 3 2 1

To the younger women,
Alyson and Vanessa

PART I
GLITCH

If you don't make mistakes, you're not working on hard enough problems.
And that's a big mistake.

—FRANK WILCZEK, PARTICLE PHYSICIST

1

Alicia was irked, not exactly a rare event. She glared at the thin man across the desk from her and wondered if he was being deliberately irritating, or whether this was just his best-of-the-menu personality.

"A *stop* order on my experiment?" She repeated his words scornfully.

"On any uranium run."

"They're gonna stop the whole damn Collider?"

"There's the final A-3 safety review—"

"Done!"

"But not completed and filed."

"What? You want all the paperwork?"

"Hey, I don't wanna rain on your parade . . ."

Had this man actually said *rain on your parade*? He should be in a museum. "It's the lawyers, right?"

A Long Island judge had leveled a stay order on the Lab, active until yet another environmental impact report got done. Suffolk County was a hotbed of worriers; they had once shut down a five-billion-dollar nuclear power plant.

He gave her a smile like wilted lettuce. "I've got to certify on it, then boot it over to Legal, and they certify to the judge."

"I thought that was all a done deal."

Hugh Alcott held up a thick packet of paper. She recognized the safety report from the manila jacket. "There's some technical detail missing."

"The background data? I was told the Lab would pony that up."

"That's your job, I think." He was known as the Safety Nazi for his unshakably banal, hedgehog manner and now he gave her the blank safety operations officer gaze. "I suppose I could check with—"

"The whole damn report was supposed to go through yesterday."

He stirred uneasily in his standard-issue desk chair. She could tell he did not like being seated while she stood, especially since she was taller than he was anyway. He scratched absently at his ear and she noticed that today's hairpiece was a demure Tom Cruise '95 model. She had seen so much of this guy, he was repeating on rugs.

"I think we've really got to dot the *i*'s on this one."

Alicia turned, crossed her arms, and made herself look out Alcott's window. Eastern Long Island, early spring, grass just peeking out of the brown mud. Truck ruts rather damaged the view of pine trees and soft, cloudy sky. She had lived in the East and a familiar sensation came over her whenever she visited from California: here was a place with its edges worn off. And she preferred edges. Still, she was close to blowing up all over Alcott, so she let five seconds of stony silence go by in hopes that would help. Ever since she had moved out to California, she found it harder to work with East Coast types. Her home campus, the University of California at Irvine, worked in subtly different ways. When she flew back to Brookhaven to work, she had to retune her social responses. She turned back, arms crossed tightly across her blue work shirt, and said clearly, slowly, "Look, I've—we've—planned for years to use uranium on this run."

"Yeah, I know all that, but my point is, this suit—"

"Uranium is the *point*! The review committee said, 'Put all the details in and we'll get it cleared.' In one shot, they said."

"Then you've got to expect delays."

"But we're ready to run! My team's all set up—"

"That was a mistake by Operations." He blinked owlishly. "Not my department."

"You said this would all be done a month early!"

"That was before the Friends of the Earth filed their suit. Again, not my department."

Not my department, said Wernher von Braun, she thought skittishly. *I just shoot them up. Who cares where they come down?*

"I *have* to start running. If I lose my time—"

"You should have anticipated delays in agreeing to your scheduled run time," he said, another standard phrase. "You're getting a one-week window, the only experiment operating, while the big detectors do maintenance away from the beam. You understood—"

"It's *your* fault, damn it." She bit her lip to stop from saying more, but the tone in her voice had already done the damage.

Alcott's jaw hardened until she half-expected to hear his teeth burst one by one, like enamel popcorn. "It's a poor workman who blames his tools."

"Even your clichés don't make it!"

His lips compressed to a white line. "Look, this isn't about anything else, just regulations, follow-through—"

"What 'anything else'?"

"Your being black, I mean."

Silence for two heart thuds. "I didn't think it was," she said more stiffly than she had intended.

"Good. You're just another facility guest, see? And until your tech detail is complete—"

"I never expected otherwise," she murmured carefully, noting that he said "guest" rather than "user," which was the common term.

"I mean, you got bumped up some because of those minority scientist points that got added to your group's proposal."

"Okay, okay!"

Then she was out of there, before she could say anything more and louse things up even further. Her lab boots clicked on the concrete, *tick-tick*, wasting time.

2

She worked off her anger by biking the whole distance from the health, physics, and safety building to the collision hall. On top of the administration building loomed a vast satellite dish, like half the discarded bra of a giantess. It carried the data link to physicists around the world, those who could collect measurements and analysis from the accelerators, archived here and available over the Internet, without ever leaving their snug offices. It saved a lot in airline tickets.

A cool breeze whipping by reminded her that spring was still laced with chilly air skating down from Canada. The gust unfurled her bun and sent tendrils playing about her face. She felt she must look even more peculiar than usual, a big black woman with the classic African bulging bust and rear, a blob bobbing along on a spindly bike. Definitely out of place on Long Island. She had never entertained the slightest hope of resembling the willowy models of *Vogue*; those she regarded as aliens from another world, whom all true human females hated.

She zoomed on her beat-up bike alongside an enormous grassy berm, nearly four kilometers around and buried in the sand and stone of Long Island. Slanting morning beams highlighted the immense curve of the Relativistic Heavy Ion Collider, a giant swollen wrinkle. She had used the acronym RHIC, pronouncing it *Rick*, for so long that she thought of it as somehow male. Taking in deep breaths, she coasted amid pine trees just showing the light green tips of new growth.

Patches of the berm were bare, the residue of gasoline some vandal had sprayed. When the damaged areas were found, the more vocal environmental groups had publicly wondered if they were due to radiation from the accelerator. Page one stuff indeed. Chemical analysis killed that theory a week later, back on page twenty-eight of *The New York Times*. Still, the Lab had a continuing problem with hot-eyed ''enviros'' who wanted the Lab closed forever, even though it did a great deal of medically directed research using high-energy sources.

Gray concrete framed the delivery bay of her experimental station, one of the six where particles collided along the circumference. Teams of resident scientists and outside users combined here to study the myriad effects of particle collisions. Threading among huge apparatus, she went past the Northrup Grumman magnets, long sleek cylinders. No humming, only the chill of cryogenic cool. RHIC needed nearly two thousand of these superconducting particle guides, and it had turned out that an aerospace company knew best how to make so many. With half a billion bucks of building budget, RHIC had entertained many industrial suitors.

She weaved among the necessary clutter of ongoing experiments. Most people envisioned labs as tidy and clean, with white-coated scientists working alone, making careful, meticulous movements. Experiments in nuclear and particle physics were big, often noisy, and where neatness didn't matter, fairly sloppy. Big steel racks packed with instrumentation crowded together, some out of alignment. The odor of oil and shaved steel hung everywhere. Makeshift wooden housings covered thick bunches of wrist-thick electrical cabling. Some cable bunches were so fat that little ladders had been passed over them for foot traffic. Necessary chaos.

Through her pique she reminded herself that she was damned lucky to even be here. A lot of talented physicists were selling stock options over the phone or pursuing exciting careers in sales management. She had gotten in on the ground floor, working as a graduate student in the UC–Berkeley team that helped build one of the detectors. When the accelerator fired up for the first time in 1999, she had staked claim on her own patch of conceptual turf, and now that was paying off.

Of course, in 1999 they had just turned the Collider on for a few hours at low intensity to meet the schedule, then shut down. That let the Lab accountants use the operations budget to finish actually building the machine. Nobody dared run overbudget, not after the Superconducting Supercollider debacle in the early 1990s.

Even now, the place had a slapdash feel, with pipes wrapped in metal foil held by duct tape. Nothing worked or looked better than it had to. Results mattered—period. This was one of the few spots in the world where any big physics got done any longer.

Brookhaven had its own rugged spirit. All the major race-track accelerators in the world went clockwise, except Brookhaven's "feeder" accelerator; the full RHIC was a Collider, with beams running in both directions. Still, people from Fermilab and CERN joshed them about their "backward ring." So someone regeared the Lab clock so *it* ran the other way. Then they could boast that they had the only accelerator ring that ran clockwise—by their clock.

Granted, Brookhaven National Laboratory was stuck in a pretty boring part of Long Island. This far out from the city, people thought of quality entertainment as a six-pack of Coors and a bug zapper. Not that surroundings mattered to her or the other Lab physicists; all people did here in the Physics Gulag was work, anyway.

Example A: her postdoctoral student, Zak Nguyen, hunched over a screen. "Got those calibrations done," he said by way of greeting.

"Great, great," she said uncomfortably. He was ready to fly on his first run, had chattered incessantly about it on their flight together from California. Among the seasoned technicians and physicists here, he was an awed neo. She had to let him down softly.

"Source conversion is nearly finished, the ion guys say."

"Good, good."

Zak grinned. He looked eager and thrilled but trying not to show it, like a puppy in a new home where nobody had much time for puppies. "They're giving us plenty of cooperation."

"Asking for plain old uranium, we're low-budget." A weak joke, but Zak nodded dutifully.

When congresspersons had heard that a bunch of snooty physicists were throwing *gold* around, there had been some headline-grabbing hearings. It all blew over when even the lawyers realized that during the entire lifetime of the facility they would not sling enough gold to make a visible speck.

She didn't want to break the news to Zak, but she made herself say, "There's . . . a delay."

"Huh? We only got a week-long slot as it is."

"Safety again."

"Damn, I thought we'd dealt with that. I mean, the radiation's trivial!"

"This is paperwork, not logic, Zakster."

His face fell. She wanted to comfort him somehow, but she didn't know how to not be obvious about it. Zak was actually named Phat by his Vietnamese parents and had taken the improbable name Zak—not Zachariah, he reminded people, just the short, zippy Zak—as a gesture of his distance from them. One side of him wanted to be totally American, drove a Chevy, and had an eagle eye for nuances of hip fashion that eluded her. Another side emerged in his earnest, often troubled expression, eyes always squinting a little when he concentrated; there lurked a devotion as strong as hers. He had the nuclear/particle physics bug, an obsession that had opened a deep cultural chasm between him and the small tailor shop his parents ran in Garden Grove. She was fond of him perhaps because, like her, he was struggling with an identity imposed by others' expectations. That did not prevent her bossing him around, of course; such was the world of competitive science.

"But after that stupid gasoline business," Zak said earnestly, "how can any judge even *listen* to some lawyers and their trumped-up—"

"Nuclear *anything* scares people. The Lab's security blanket is more paperwork."

The Collider normally smacked gold ions together at speeds razor-close to the speed of light. Alicia had gotten her hard-sought few days on this colossal machine by proposing an ingenious experiment, one that could yield higher net energies than ever before attained, simply by speeding a heavier nucleus around the racetrack.

Trouble was, the heavier nuclei wanted to fall apart into radioactive debris. Nature built a nucleus by gluing in several uncharged neutrons for every proton, to overcome the electric repulsion of the charged protons. This strategy worked up to Creation's prettiest triumph of stability—gold, with 79 protons, needed 118 neutrons to force things together. With a total of 197 nucleons—the term for neutrons and protons alike—it was among the heaviest of elements. Nuclei not much heavier than gold eventually fell apart. Some of them were always dying, so those elements were radioactive.

Alicia had decided on uranium as the best compromise between the lust for mass and the troubles of handling radioactives. Uranium's most stable and abundant form had a nucleus with 238 nucleons and a curious property shared by the heaviest elements: it was not a sphere, but cigar-shaped. The struggle to remain stable—lost, ultimately, by U-238, with a decay time comparable to the age of the Earth—stretched the nuclei, protons edging away from each other.

That was the crucial fact driving Alicia's method. Rarely, two U-238 nuclei struck each other exactly front-ended along their axes, like trains colliding. Such an aligned crash might be more energetic. *Might*—theorists were not sure.

"What do they want?" Zak asked in the blank way that meant he was irritated. The only sign in his lean face was a slight tightening around his eyes, shadowed by a wedge of thick black hair.

"A better estimate of the shielding and radioactive products."

Spraying high-energy nuclei into a chamber yielded a shotgun blast of decay particles. Those in turn collided with the surrounding detectors, walls, floor, iron—all leaving telltale radioactivity. Most of it cooled off within minutes, but the heavier the nuclei used, the worse the effect.

How much worse? The Friends of the Earth had argued for

greater certainty in court, as soon as they found out about the shift to uranium. After all, *uranium* meant *bombs*, right?—to the crowd that pronounced nuclear "new-killer." The Lab had passed the buck to Alicia, as principal investigator. That meant more calculations, a numerical simulation, then writing up pages of graphs and jargon-heavy charts—

Alicia snapped her fingers. "I think I see a way."

3

Hugh Alcott worked his mouth around but said nothing. Alicia sat at one end of the polished walnut table gazing steadily at Hugh and at Dave Rucker, the director of experiment operations. Her stomach rumbled, not merely from hunger. It was 11 A.M. and in the last twenty-four hours she had eaten just one meal and slept only four hours.

Hugh's office looked across the majestic sweep of the Collider's huge ring, a pleasant grassland dotted with pines, but the vista did not help her relax. She had asked for this special audience to speed up matters. With only one card in her hand to play, the maneuver was either going to work immediately or not at all.

Hugh put one finger on the cover of her completed safety report, pressing down on it as though he could penetrate to the heart of matters. "You sure did this job fast."

"I had it in pieces. I just pulled an all-nighter."

"You had these numerical simulations? The Monte Carlo codes?"

"Yes," she lied.

Dave Rucker smiled wanly. "Great. You've always been a go-getter. This damned lawsuit hit us out of left field."

"I'm just glad I had the backup work nearly done." Her stomach lurched with guilty fear. What if they found out this was a bluff? Well, now it was out. Too late for afterthoughts. She willed her gut to relax.

"Indeed," Dave said neutrally.

She made her expression earnest and modest. She didn't have to fake the fatigue lines. It had taken plenty of hours to make the results look plausible and authoritative. One of the beauties of involved numerical calculations was that if they looked reasonable, nobody was going to check details. Among people always a bit behind where they thought they should be, tedium was a useful repellent.

Dave slid his gaze to Hugh. "Seem okay?"

"These count numbers," Hugh said judiciously, "they're done with an optimized integral?"

"Yes." Curt nod of the head. Best to be clear and simple. She had done a quick cut at the complicated sums. The order of magnitude was right, but no more.

"Spallation rates—"

"All included."

Hugh nodded, twisted his mouth a little in his standard skeptical reflex, let the pause play out. Then he carefully looked at Dave, not Alicia, let two more seconds squeeze by, and said reluctantly, "I'll . . . boot it to the lawyers."

"Great! Alicia, you may proceed as soon as we get to the judge."

"Which will be . . . ?"

Dave picked up his phone. "I'll have this messengered over."

"Lawyers never do anything fast."

"Yeah, or cheap," Hugh said sourly.

"These will. Tom Ludlam has been riding their asses about this."

She got up with an odd, giddy feeling. *So quick, so easy.* Technically she had finessed here, not lied. Fatigue blended with guilt, a potent mixture. She would have to learn to live with both. Sleep would work on one of them, anyway.

Dave gave quick instructions in the clipped, slightly aggressive style the better managers used and then said cordially to her, "Come on, I want to have a look at your setup."

"Mind if I stop at the cafeteria? I skipped breakfast."

"Could use some decent coffee myself," Dave said.

Hugh left and they biked over to the cafeteria, Alicia feeling bulbous and awkward. She was not fat but muscular and the ride made her perspire. Usually she was so busy that she ate from the coin-operated vending machines; she equated the cafeteria with luxury. With teams working all hours, breakfast was always available, even if it was steam table stuff. She got some virtuous Lite Granola with nonfat milk and then splurged calories on the works: eggs, bacon, toast with butter.

The early lunch crowd half-filled the cafeteria. A lot of science gets done in the coffee shop. The management provided little notepads at each table.

The customary social order played out in the geometry of table placement. The librarians, administrative assistants, and secretaries—all women, most in pantsuits and a few wearing dresses—clustered in groups of four. Engineers and senior technicians sat together in groups of six or eight. As Alicia threaded her way toward a small table, a troop of experimenters from the big PHENIX particle detector trooped by, pulling tables end to end to sit as a body. Theorists ate in smaller bunches. Nobody ate alone and people scanned the room often, noting who ate with whom—or didn't.

She was used to this pattern and could pick out the physicists by dress alone. They looked like a middle class suburb on a weekend, disdaining any distinguishing details: jeans or anonymous slacks, down-market shirts with sleeves rolled up, cushioned shoes. Alicia wore black jeans, a minor deviation, with a broad black belt and a pale yellow blouse, the understated feminine offset by steel-shanked work boots. Admin types wore classic business garb, even suits, but left their jackets in the office, wearing them only in meetings with outsiders.

Dave took pains to never look like an admin guy, signaling this with his tan slacks and lumberjack shirt. Still, he was as earnest and hardworking as any coffee-driven obsessive one could find in the Lab. The sort of man, she mused, who would go to a T.G.I.M. party. He bit into some low-cal crackers and sipped coffee while she dug into her eggs.

"Cereal comes after?" he said.

"That's how I like it. I'm a nutritional pervert."

He watched her putting away bacon and toast. "I remember breakfasts like that."

"First Law of Thermodynamics still applies. If you eat it, and you don't burn it off, you sit on it."

"You burn it, looks like. Exercise?"

"Worry. Saves time and you don't have to shower."

"I know you're wound pretty tight about this first trial, but don't be." He leaned back, elaborately casual as he got to the point of this little interlude. "It's just a first shot. Nobody's going to frown if you don't get anything."

"Thanks. Not that I believe it, of course."

He smiled. "Okay, you caught me giving the standard rookie speech."

"My dad says it's better to be underestimated."

"He's right. What's his line of work?"

"Op-ed."

"Uh . . . ?"

"Sorry, family jargon. Opinion-editorial writer, Thomas Butterworth."

"Can't say I—"

"He's a small-time columnist, runs mostly in the conservative papers."

"Which nobody here would read, right?"

"Only the malcontents."

"You and he don't usually agree."

"How'd you guess?" An edge in her voice?

"Conservatives have been better supporters of physics than the liberals." He gazed around, automatically checking out the seating configurations. "But I'll bet there aren't five confessed Republicans in the room."

"Dad's a libertarian."

"Oh, then all bets are off." He eyed her as she dug into her Lite Granola. "Y'know, we do have high expectations here from everybody. RHIC has to show performance, make a splash."

She nodded, noting that this contradicted his this-is-just-a-first-shot speech a moment before, designed to put her at ease. "Congress sank nearly a billion in, wants some headlines?"

"Well, we're not quite that bald about it."

"Maybe we should be."

"Plenty of people think we're way beyond the point of diminishing returns in particle physics, and for nuclear—well, they confuse it with reactors."

She arched an eyebrow. "All that stuff about science running out of gas?"

He sighed ruefully. "I had dinner last week with a congressman. He seemed to halfway believe it."

Fashionable skepticism about science had risen around the turn of the millennium, when every pundit and amateur philosopher was pronouncing the end of eras. There was some worthwhile argument to the position, which had kept it alive until now, five years later.

Some felt that the big, solvable issues were largely done, and the unsolved ones *couldn't* be settled. That left smaller, manageable, naggingly boring science, like sequencing human DNA. Of course the implications of that knowledge could be vast, but no one expected grand syntheses to emerge. Mostly, it would be endless detail. Fascinating particulars indeed, but smaller in scale than the heroic era that had followed Crick and Watson.

Some observers foresaw a style of sardonic science emerging—a blend of speculation, ironically oblique points of view, reinterpretations of the same data. Sardonic science's luminous figures were those like Richard Dawkins, Mr. Selfish Gene himself, unable to add any new data or brilliantly turned experiments, but arch and arrogant in a fetching way, sarcastic and insightful rather than original.

Often sardonic science came from figures who had retired or gotten bored with the humdrum world of grinding, everyday science and so had entered a "philosopause" of armchair rumination. But not all. Even some luminaries of particle physics saw the great era closing. The essential outlines of the universe were done, they said. A physics devoted to minutiae would follow.

Alicia sniffed in derision. "Lack of imagination isn't an argument."

''It affects the budget.''

''So do all the geezers sopping up their Social Security.''

''Hey, we compete with a lot of social needs.''

''I'm not arguin'.'' She gazed at him levelly. ''Just want enough beamtime to get something done here.''

''You're the first to try uranium, so you can't expect to get a lot of time. We're fitting you in between stand-downs at the other detectors. For example, on PHENIX—''

''I know, this is just a trial run. In a week you go back to hunting.''

The promise of the Collider was that using heavy ions might—just might, no guarantees—for the first time cross a fundamental threshold. Slamming whole nuclei together might create a new state of matter, one ruled by the jawbreaker-named Quantum Chromodynamics. The resulting high-energy densities could conjure up a spitting particle fog called the quark-gluon plasma. Gluons were particles which held together the lumbering protons and neutrons, until a collision broke them open like egg sacs, spraying wreckage. Such a miasma of subnuclear particles resembled how the universe had looked in the first millionth of a second of the Big Bang. Collisions at the RHIC focus could be like a ''Mini Bang,'' as the Lab publicists liked to put it.

Only that hadn't happened yet. The first five years of running at RHIC had failed to provide clear evidence of any such state.

''Your idea is neat,'' Dave said, still inspecting her face. (Or was she just feeling guilty?) ''I mean, go for the most total energy, jumping to the highest mass nuclei available.''

''I'm going just a bit above gold.''

Though gold was a lighter element, it could be accelerated to over one percent higher energy per nucleon than uranium. But uranium had 41 more nucleons than gold. That might count in creating a particle fog. Some theorists thought that the total punch of a nucleus was the key. A majority didn't.

She shrugged. ''It's just a small chance.''

''One worth trying. And I'm glad to see it for other reasons, too.''

"The black thing."

"The black woman thing."

"Hugh brought up those minority scientist points that got added into UC–Irvine's proposal. How much difference did that make?"

His mouth pinched at the edges. "Not much."

"How much?"

"I'd have to look it up."

"Come on, Dave, that's a standard administrative dodge."

"Nobody thinks you're here because of anything other than ability, Alicia."

"I want to be sure of that. These minority scientist programs—"

"You have the full support of the staff here, believe me."

She shrugged and smiled ruefully, feeling awkward for even bringing it up. Getting time on RHIC was a lesson in diplomacy itself, never one of her great skills, and self-doubt dogged her still. "I'd kinda hoped all that hype had blown away. Black woman particle physicist, one of a kind, a zoo animal—"

"Find the quark-gluon plasma and that'll look like nothing."

"Your publicity people, the last time they made out like I was the only person on the whole experiment."

He held up a placating hand. "That's media-biz. People don't want complicated stories."

She nodded ruefully. "One of them said to me, 'The best technical journalism cooks up a pound of personality and an ounce of content.' Sheesh!"

"True, though." His face sobered. "Uh, there's one more matter. We're having data storage troubles, as you probably heard."

"No, I hadn't." Though this was no surprise. The stream of numbers spat out by the myriad RHIC diagnostics was a Mississippi compared to all earlier machines.

"We're going to have to keep all the uranium data and process it here," he said flatly.

"What! I want to process it at UCI, too."

"We're not going to have it in a form you can use."

"I can do it in BITNEX—" And they were off, trading acronyms for computer systems and software, DAQ and PMD and CPU, voices sharpening as their disagreement worsened. She finally said, "Damn it, we agreed that I would get a fair, equal crack at the data."

"We just don't have the resources of people or machine time," Dave said stonily, "to translate the masses of uranium data into your machine language."

"You should have told me!"

"We've been barely keeping our noses above water on this. When I went to the central counting facility, they just shook their heads."

"But it's in our contractual—"

"There's a clause about the Lab getting to do first-pass processing of the data—"

"That's just a default term. We have an agreement—"

"Not really. It's up to our discretion."

"Damn it, it's my data!"

"You'll get it, too."

"When?"

Dave's eyes drifted away from hers uneasily. "We'll let you have representative events, say one out of every hundred. Getting it all, though, will take a few months."

"Months! We're due to have a second run here in half a year. We'll have to come back without enough time to think over our first results."

He shrugged, angering her with the gesture more than he had with his words. She blurted, "It's *my* experiment!"

"It's *our* experiment. You're a guest."

She wanted to snap back but realized it would do no good. The Lab would eventually get her a filtered, compressed data set, sure, but she and her research group would be cooling their heels until then. Struggling to be civil, she limited herself to: "I don't like this."

"I'm sorry, but there it is."

She could see that he was embarrassed by this reversal. Was this a side effect of the continuing division at Brookhaven between the nuclear physics people and the rather more lofty types who called themselves particle physicists? With RHIC the nuclear guys had annexed another neglected piece of the particle physicists' landscape, and Alicia was definitely a member of the particle tribe. The edgy relationship of the two fields produced spats and squabbles; this smelled like one. As a visiting particle type, she went to the end of the line when data-processing computer time got handed out. She sighed and tried not to show how angry she was.

Dave smiled tentatively. "So now, how about showing me your setup?"

4

Alicia took a deep breath to fight her nerves. The oily reek of big machines, the sharp bite of cleaning solvents, the dull dry smell of electrical insulation—all conspired in the earthy mustiness of the underground world.

She could not sit still before the data screens that filled one wall of the operations and counting center. Instead she paced in a short orbit determined by the length of her headset wire. Every time she made her turn, Alicia looked at a poster of horses plunging along a racetrack. There were a dozen people in the room, the RHIC team plus the UCI team, Brad Douglas and Zak and herself, but she had eyes only for the screens.

"Dispatching the run now" came a heavy voice in her headphones. "Tuning beams." That meant the Booster had done its job.

She kept her voice flat and restrained as she said to Zak, "The ponies are away."

Since the Collider was a miles-long ring racetrack, their joke was to translate accelerator jargon into horsey talk. Zak's eyes widened. "Out of the gate?"

"Hitting the track now," she relayed.

The room's electronic displays gave few hints of the drama occurring, but she could see it in her mind's eye. The Alternating Gradient Synchrotron was handing off its particle ponies to the controlling magnets and pulsing electric fields of the big track. Specially designed strippers had ripped all the electrons from the uranium atoms until they now coasted unprotected, their total nuclear charge of 92 protons exposed to the shove of electric fields.

Into the ring racetrack came 57 bunches of nuclear uranium, stacked around the circumference boxcar fashion. Each bunch held a billion nuclei. In ten-millionths of a second a bunch shot around the track. In a separate stream an equal number of bunches accelerated the opposite way. They could cycle for a day if unneeded, coaxed and herded by electromagnetic fields alone.

''Incoming,'' Zak announced.

The uranium nuclei had already stacked into the Collider to the running density. Now they were focused at the experiment nexus. With a twitch of electromagnetic fields, the two counter-streaming currents of nuclei suddenly met each other. The counting room staff sent her images.

''Getting hits!'' she cried.

Alicia envisioned two streams of cigar-shaped uranium nuclei, focused against each other in the beam pipe. Nuclei would strike each other at odd angles, shattering themselves into tens of thousands of particles each second.

In her mind's eye she saw the myriad extinctions as flowers. Gaudy, with lines zipping in and out, forming a pattern of garish, baroque growth. Oppositely directed, the nuclei had no net momentum in the laboratory. Their fragments would blossom in tiny, fierce explosions that sprayed debris into narrow cones fore and aft of the collision. The flux perpendicular to the line of flight was the crucial zone where diagnostic sensors sought the Grail: a quark-gluon plasma.

Cheers from the technical staff. Somebody was slapping her on her back. A woman was cheering in a screechy voice and only when she stopped did she realize that it was herself.

A cork popped and bounced off the tiled ceiling. An electronics tech handed her a plastic cup of cheap champagne. Alicia thanked everybody, grinned, said words that she forgot the moment they escaped her mouth. She gulped some champagne and it was really awful and she didn't mind.

The whole while she was there with them and also not, a portion of her always focused on the screens. Flowers blossomed there, their glossy vector traces color-coded for particle types. The harvest of her detectors, the intricate measuring slabs she had toiled over for most of her adult life.

She hugged Zak and gave him a quick peck on the cheek. Somebody flipped a switch and the audio boomed with Brahms's *Second Symphony*. Her detector group was the Broad RAnge Hadron Measuring Spectrometer, or BRAHMS. The grand chords hammered in her ears, but she didn't ask for it to be turned down.

And still the flowers bloomed.

She managed to spill champagne on her classic white lab coat, worn in self-mockery over jeans and a frumpy, oil-stained blouse. A standard radiation badge clung to the pocket. She thought abstractly that she had always felt a bit silly wearing it. If by some bizarre chance she were exposed to the beam while it was running, the badge-measured dosage would make an interesting notation on her tombstone.

Again she thanked all the people who had labored to make the shift from gold to uranium, who had kept the BRAHMS system working, the many expert hands it took to keep one of the most complicated machines in the world up and running. And she watched the screens, entranced.

"And Zak. C'mere, you." She hugged him. "It's not love that makes our world go round—it's postdocs!"

Laughs, cheers. "And grad students," she added, pounding her own grad student, Brad Douglas, on the back.

She remembered stories about the old bubble chamber detectors at Brookhaven. They were pressurized bottles where particles left bubble trails which cameras read by arc lamps. A famous story told how when a propane bottle exploded, the grad students fled. A postdoc realized he was going to lose his data and ran back inside. A second blast blew him out the door, data in hand. Nobody was surprised that he had gone back in.

"Data, gorgeous data." She gazed at the screens like a little girl admiring a Christmas tree.

The uranium nuclei were gliding right on through. *No glitches. Wonderful.* The nuclei started off in an ordinary electric field accelerator, then passed through the Booster ring, then to the big, circular Alternating Gradient Synchrotron. It was the destiny of Nobel-winning machines to become the mere handmaidens of later accelerators; these once-grand devices now humbly handed energetic nuclei into the RHIC.

Once upon a time, in the now-fading Golden Age of the field, such machines had dazzled the physics community, working ever-deeper into the fabric of reality with ever-larger hammers, smashing ever-smaller walnuts. A long march, from the tabletop cyclotron to the aborted Superconducting Supercollider—which had proved to be not so super when it got canceled, sucking over three billion dollars into a useless racetrack hole in Texas. A pricey condo for fire ants and prairie dogs.

Still, the faith of the field was that every new, bigger accelerator would yield up a gratifying plethora of new particles, fresh physics. Now the Standard Model predicted that the particle zoo was nearly complete. From fat protons down to tiny leptons, then on to more exotic quarks by the mid-1990s, the particle species obligingly turned up on cue, at higher energy levels. RHIC was hunting bigger game, though—a new regime of matter itself.

"Logging is going right," she told Zak crisply.

"Right, right, great, hey?" He had never been at a run initiation before and his eyes danced.

"Your Core Element? Logging right?" a technician asked her.

"Dead on," she said proudly.

The Core Assembly was the University of California at Irvine's contribution to the Brookhaven Lab's BRAHMS detectors. Alicia had worked on nothing else since her arrival at UCI three years ago. Following up on her UC–Berkeley thesis, she had designed and built it with her small team of graduate students and postdocs. Running it now gave her an inexpressible sensation of lightness, like flying on joy alone.

A particle detector that ran beautifully was either obsolete or hadn't been designed close enough to the cutting edge of the technology. But in the months of getting the Core Assembly up and running right, her team had beaten all the problems.

Now data acquisition computers tasted the data stream, regularly reporting back with pictures of interesting collisions. Every single collision event got stored onto big spinning laser disks, holographic optical platters. Colored lines showed incoming U-238 nuclei, which then shattered each other into showers of lesser lines, curving off in mad confusion. Events bloomed into gorgeous bouquets. Numerals at the screen's borders reported energies and times, remorselessly dissecting the beauty as bluntly as a biologist sectioned a frog. All these splendors were frozen from a slice of time so thin that no living thing could register even a million of them, laid in order.

Humans lived too slowly, too crudely, she reflected. Sloppy, slow beasts they were. Yet they reached down with electric scalpels and cut into the heart of tiny moments.

Then things started going wrong.

"Event rate is down," Zak announced an hour later, calling her from the counting room. She went over there to find trouble brewing.

Zak was proud to be left to monitor beam performance, thinking it an important job. In truth nobody expected RHIC's beam to burp or stray; the Collider had been performing well above expectations ever since its shakedown runs. But postdocs seldom got a chance to feel significant around here.

"Huh?" one of the technicians said. "You're probably reading it wrong."

Alicia peered at the data stream. Her face stiffened. "Counts are off thirty percent," she agreed.

"It dropped all of a sudden," Zak said.

"Got to be a glitch," the technician said.

"A big glitch," Alicia said, her voice tight and high.

By now the room had calmed down for the long haul of the run. Heads turned as operators murmured.

WE LOSING A BEAM? Alicia typed on her console and answered herself, "Nope. They're coming in steady."

"This a normal failure mode?" Zak asked.

"Sure," one of the operators said. "Could be any of a dozen causes."

"Like what?" Zak persisted.

Alicia smiled. He was learning to extract information, prying it loose if necessary.

"Module mismatch, detector failure, plenty of possible malfs," the operator said. "We'll find it."

But they didn't.

The net number of collisions in the beam intersection region kept dropping. Uranium nuclei streamed steadily into the BRAHMS. Magnetic fields in the vicinity were constant. Yet somehow the beams were not finding each other. At these collision rates, they would not get enough good data.

They ran two more hours before Alicia ran out of patience. By then the collision flux was only a few percent of what they had been seeing four hours earlier. Technicolor flowers seldom bloomed on the big screens. She paced, slurped bad coffee, used the elaborate detector monitoring programs, paced some more.

The operations director called her. Beam managers disliked losing flux, fearful that the whole massive system was somehow damaged. "I think there's something wrong in the BRAHMS," he said delicately.

"Seems like," she said, not wanting to concede more than the obvious.

"This is a new show. I'd say you need a close-up of your apparatus. We'll stop the beam while you do."

"Nominal running time is ten hours!"

"Only if things are going right."

"But we haven't really gotten started and—"

"Look, you people can get in there, maybe find a quick fix. We'll go back on the air right away."

"Quit so soon?" Alicia said, knowing that there wasn't a damn thing she could do about it.

5

BRAHMS could look over a wide range of angles for evidence of a quark-gluon plasma. Nuclei meeting head-on made a hot "gas" of gluons and quarks. This tiny violence squeezed matter, compressing it to a hundred times the density of the incoming nucleons.

This debris cloud then expanded, cooling. BRAHMS watched the swelling central region and sampled the virulent spray, seeking fleeting evidence of a new state of matter. It somewhat resembled trying to discover steam by hurling water droplets together.

Alicia, Zak, and a technical team came into the BRAHMS bay pushing carts laden with diagnostic gear.

"Let's start with the forward spectrometer arm," Alicia said. This device sifted among particle energies with fine resolution, a vital role.

It seemed a good idea and they spent an hour on the nineteen-meter-long bulk. There was nothing wrong with it.

"Should we do the tracking elements next?" Zak asked one of the team. They nodded. Usually one would sit and await the verdict of the remote readouts, but Alicia worried that the problem might be a failed power supply or blown gas lines that they couldn't sense from the counting room.

As "users" Zak and Alicia didn't know the ins and outs of those who had spent a decade building BRAHMS. Alicia knew that a lot of users would sit in the control room and wait it out, trusting to the Collider team to find the glitch. But she had trained here as a graduate student herself, helped build the BRAHMS multiplicity array, the beam-beam counters, and all the rest of it. She wasn't just another user, she told herself. Some of the team didn't quite see it that way, but she glowered and barked and the work moved faster because of it—or so she thought.

The tracking elements were all right, too.

No trace of radioactivity in the bay.

"I'd say we look at the ring-imaging Cherenkov detector," Alicia said to them all. "Could be it's giving us a faulty feedback signal and—"

"I don't think so," one of them said.

"What?" she demanded curtly.

"Look, let's go to lunch," the team leader said. "We been at this awhile and it's past time."

She blinked. In her skittering, superheated attention time played no role; there was only the job, the puzzle, the infuriating mystery.

"Oh, okay. Look, thanks, you guys have been great."

As they left, she took a deep breath. "Zak, help me look over here . . ."

She wasn't about to knock off for food and Zak knew it. He did not even sigh as he walked with her over to the central assembly.

Down the axis of BRAHMS ran the beam pipe. The nuclei streamed through it in opposite directions, held to the straight and narrow by powerful magnets. The wreckage of their collisions spewed out into the detectors clustered close around it. The pipe was only a few centimeters across, strikingly modest for the energies it contained.

As distant users they brought their own special, home-built gear, the Core Element, to the experiment, augmenting the rest of BRAHMS. Those who had built the main body of BRAHMS tended to think they owned the facility. Alicia's doctorate had been mostly devoted to designing and building a cylinder covered with flat, dead black surfaces. Concentric slabs of silicon held millions of tiny detectors, electronically linked, fabricated the same way commercial electronics firms made integrated circuits for computers. A charged particle passing through the dense slabs set off electrical impulses. The sum of many such pixels gave a picture of the glorious smash-ups.

Other detectors were long slabs in black plastic jackets, stacked shingle-style and trailing bundles of color-coded wires or optical fiber.

She typed commands into the keyboard and studied the screen, where scintillator arrays were sheets of numbers, all softly glowing green: OK. "Damn!"

Zak jerked his head up from checking connections. "What's up?"

"There's nothing *wrong*."

"Gotta be."

"The uranium is shooting through the beam pipe, but nothing's coming out!"

Zak frowned. "How could the two beams miss each other?"

"They can't. The magnets are all working fine, focus is sharp . . ."

She felt ridiculous shouting out the obvious, but it felt better to do it. And there was nobody here but Zak. Transgressions of the calm, sure façade were allowable in front of postdocs and graduate students.

Embarrassed, Zak said, "Uh, well, guess we just keep—"

"Let's look at the ring imager."

She had recovered her cool and now marched toward the big assembly at the far end of BRAHMS. Zak dutifully tagged along. She was virtually certain nothing in the ring imager could louse up the flux count, but the innate perversity of Nature could—

A loud bang. It rang from the concrete walls.

Startled, she tripped and sprawled. Fragments clanged against the walls and peppered the metal casings.

The explosion had come from behind her. What—?

"You okay?" Zak called.

"Sure. Fall down, go boom."

Zak seemed to be trying to knock a bee out of his ear. "Wow, that was *loud*."

"How in . . ." A hissing rose. "The vacuum system is breached!"

They hurried back to the beam pipe at the BRAHMS central focus. A big hole gaped in the pipe.

The rupture was near the center of their own detector, in the bore of one of their strongest magnets.

"I'll call Operations," Zak shouted, voice shrill, the adrenaline starting to hit. He ran toward the wall telephone, boots clomping. The hissing rattled her concentration.

"It'll automatically shut down at the next lock . . ." her voice trailed off as foreboding clouded her face. Disaster lay all about. Shards and twisted metal lay everywhere.

Alicia stepped gingerly among the usual tangle of cables. Fragments crunched under her boots. The Core Element built by her group at UC–Irvine was a cylindrical array of special sensors, webbed by cables. She swallowed hard. It was a wreck.

A particle experimenter had to know a detector intimately to strip away the noise and find the kernel of data. That usually meant you had to have built it, gotten married to it in long nights of frustration and tedium, all invested for the all-too-brief moments of insight.

She had tossed in fevered dreams about this instrument. Now its smooth surfaces, its buried microchips, its painstakingly knitted circuits . . . all lay shattered.

She sagged against a gray steel support. She had put years into the Core Element, as the detector diagrams termed it. It was her intellectual child. She had entertained the complete physicists' fantasy, from the runs at the Collider, then the job of convincing your colleagues that your beloved detector was a transparent lens, passive and objective, through which Science gazed upon the Real.

In particle physics the typical talk opened with fifteen minutes of loving detector description, known by theorists as the "Scotch tape" part of the seminar. Theorists were Platonists, trusting detectors to peer coolly into reality. Experimenters were Cartesians, endlessly worrying over the reliability of their senses.

For a long moment, head hanging, Alicia lost all senses. She plunged down a pit of despair and felt her trembling knees threaten to buckle. The hissing brought her back. Was it getting louder?

She edged her head between two big magnets and into the bore of the Irvine detector. The beam pipe was split. A whole raw section of it had blown away. Twisted shards of tough beryllium had dug into the faces of the detector and blasted whole chunks out.

The force had to have been huge. And all the bent steel and curled-back sections nestled around something quite impossible.

Sitting in the beam pipe's rupture was a shiny sphere.

It was larger in diameter than the pipe. She approached it carefully. In its glossy sheen she saw her own reflection loom, face distorted and mouth open.

The chrome ball fizzed with light. Images seemed alive with a speckling glow.

Not a flower, but a thing of eerie beauty. What the hell?

6

High in the ceiling a horizontal steel beam whined along on wheels, riding heavy rails. "Back it off a little," Alicia called to Zak.

The beam hoist inched backward until the permanent iron magnet it held was directly above the strange chrome ball. "Okay!" she said.

Zak called from the hoist control panel. "Look, don't you think—"

"They'll be back from lunch within minutes. Help me get this thing trapped."

"But what if—"

"*Now*." She kept her voice flat, commanding. Her jittery nerves came out as bossiness. She did not like the implicit hierarchy of professor/postdoc, but at times it was handy. Still . . . "Uh, please."

The sphere had not moved, despite her prodding it with a wooden two-by-four. A steel bar would have stuck to the magnet poles. Then she noticed that the sphere made no contact with the beam line sheath. It floated a millimeter away, nothing visible supporting it.

That left only one possibility. The focusing magnetic fields held it firmly lodged in the middle of the detector complex. Two chilled superconducting magnets bracketed the focus point. There were smaller U-shaped magnets kept in a reserve bay, made of permanently magnetized steel.

If she could bring the U-shaped permanent magnet directly

down upon the sphere, then pulse the other magnets in the configuration, she might get the sphere hung up in the permanent magnet's fields. A handoff using invisible, rubbery forces.

"Okay, let's fiddle with the current controls," she said.

The nearby magnets could be overridden through the keyboard she carried. A few keystrokes turned down the strong fields surrounding the region of beam line rupture. Did she see the sphere bob, as though responding to the grip of unseen fields?

She had been cautious, never touching the sphere herself. Poked with a rod, it seemed solid. Yet the way it reflected images with a speckled pattern was unsettling. Laser beams had that odd quality, as the light matched wavelengths and made bright patches alternate with dark hollows. How could this thing do that?

It must be a conductor, because the beam line's strong magnetic fields held it in place. A rock, say, would have fallen straight through. When she realized that, she saw an opportunity.

"Careful . . . bring the permanent down . . ."

She eyed the big U shape as the poles of the magnet neared the sphere. If she pulsed the other magnets just right, she could force the sphere into the magnetic web of the more powerful permanent iron magnet.

"Lower . . . little more . . ."

The sphere wobbled again. She typed in more commands to adjust the surrounding focusing fields. The sphere rose into the air, toward the magnet's poles. It moved as if against a gummy resistance, sluggish.

"How much does that thing weigh?" Zak called.

"Plenty." These were the strongest fields one could get and they were barely moving the object.

She trimmed the upper fields slightly. The sphere bobbed into the space between the permanent magnet's poles—and stopped.

She carefully let her breath out, as if the slightest breeze might upset things. "Okay, I think we've got it."

"Think this'll hold?" Zak wore a worried frown.

"That's a half Tesla field between the poles. It can hold plenty."

The sphere hung still between the poles when Zak delicately raised the hoist. Slowly he lifted it to the ceiling. Alicia came over to the control panel.

"Careful now," she said, taking over. She couldn't leave the tricky part to him. If anything went wrong, it should be on her shoulders.

Servos whined as the hoist pulled back, running on rail lines back into the recesses of the big concrete walls. It carried the U-shaped magnet into the shadows.

Zak nodded. "Neat idea, getting it out of the way like that. Where in hell did that thing come from? Some part of the mechanical assembly?"

She realized that he thought the sphere was simply a big, shiny ball bearing. "I dunno. Best to get it out of the way of the crew, so they can seal the beam line."

"Hope we can get back online soon."

"Zak, the Core Element is beyond hope."

"I know, I know, but the other detectors . . ."

His voice trailed off. He was still dazed. Had it been cruel to hustle him into action, set him to wheeling out the permanent magnet? No—she was sure the best way to absorb a shocking disappointment like this was to work on through it.

She clapped him on the shoulder. "There'll be plenty of data from the rest of BRAHMS."

"Think so? The midrapidity spectrometer—"

"Sho 'nuff." Her fake Southern accent always made him smile, like a private joke between them. "Let's roll."

By the time the work crew came back from lunch, she had a makeshift pressure patch on the beam line. This they didn't like; repairs were their province. Alicia had counted on that to direct their attention away from the tarp she had thrown over the permanent magnet, stuck back into the wall recesses.

Maybe Zak was right, the thing was just some oddly blown bubble—but she didn't think so. Her gut instinct was that the shiny ball was something utterly unexpected. Until she had a chance to study it, best not get the staff involved in the riddle.

So what could it be? An accident, but of what kind? Something in the experiment had made a metal sphere form? Blow up a panel or something, like a balloon? Not likely. Who said it was metal? A conductor, sure, or the magnetic fields couldn't hold it. Shiny, yes—but the fizzing light was a powerful clue that something else was at work here.

From the trash heap of theoretical physics she knew plenty of hypothetical particles. Some were too bizarre to decay into everyday particles, so they might hang around—but as shiny bowling balls?

7

That night she lay awake and wondered why she had done it.

The sphere was plainly connected to the vacuum failure. When the crew had returned, there had been plenty of cleanup, and a lot of worried BRAHMS physicists turned up to survey the damage. She had hovered nervously, worrying that someone would spot the tarp and say, ''Hey, what's that?'' But no one did. There was plenty of scenic wreckage to catch the eye.

Her snap diagnosis had proved right. The UC–Irvine Core Element had absorbed the momentum of the splintering beam pipe. Designed especially to look at uranium by-products, its layers of silicon were riddled with steel fragments. Gray shards like sharp sand lay everywhere. Building a second one from scratch would take many tedious months. And money. At least they had ample backup silicon sheets, so the cost would not be huge.

Nobody had any plausible ideas about what caused the explosion. Typical vacuum failures came from tiny cracks or badly fitted seals. Even a complete collapse sucked components inward, not out. Yet the interior beam pipe was bare of steel slivers.

The sphere had to be the answer. And she was concealing it.

Well, she thought grimly, it was *her* detector that had paid the price.

And her guest user contract covered data about microscopic particles, not macroscopic ones.

And . . . She grimaced in the dark and abruptly laughed at

herself. "Face it, girl, you *wanted* the damn thing," she told the darkness.

If this was a mere oddity, fine. If it was something fundamental, then she wanted to know what it was *first*. In her gut she knew it was that burning curiosity, not the ambition stuff.

There were four basic reasons why physicists did experiments, her thesis professor had once told her, and the list had remained chiseled in her memory.

First came *I want to know*. Her driver now. Prying into Mother Nature's secrets. Well, the old Mother had made it hard to ignore.

Next came *Theory predicts*. The committees who approved beamtime applications liked that one. Experimenters awed by theorists felt it was the best reason of all. Alicia wasn't one of those.

Among the older experimenters there was a lot of *This is what I do*. Habit, often rather mindless. More deeply, it meant *This is who I am*.

And another, one that had drawn her into using uranium: *A sweet experiment*. Maybe the best of all reasons. If uranium worked out, it could give them a key to the early universe. She liked the weird symmetry of using the element that had ushered in nuclear destruction to open the central mysteries of Creation itself.

The sphere might turn out to be sweet, too. She itched to find out. Alicia sighed and banished her doubts. She had acted on impulse, tucked it away—so be it.

Knowing that, what next?

The BRAHMS group was small in comparison with the big PHENIX machine, over which several hundred Ph.D. physicists labored. Still, "small" in the congested sociology of particle/nuclear physics meant that even BRAHMS had over thirty physicists contributing, from Strasbourg, New York University, Texas A & M, UC–Berkeley, and the Chinese Institute of Atomic Energy in Beijing. They all had been very sympathetic about the accident, tut-tutting at the shattered Core Element.

But they had been restless to clean up and get running again. The big detectors, PHENIX and STAR, lay in other bays around the racetrack. At the moment they were staged down for some repairs, but quite quickly they could make detailed studies of debris trajectories coming out of the uranium collisions. They could yield data—for those groups, not hers. The Core Element had been the leading instrument for this run and now it was down, like an injured horse while the race goes on.

Uptime, downtime, beamtime—these were the currency of particle physics power. In six days the Collider would switch back to throwing gold and the teams of detector tenders would change. This gang wanted all the data they could get. Too bad about the Core Element, but there it was.

"And the bastards are going to keep the data—my data—for months, too," she said aloud into the darkness. "Damn!"

She let herself feel the anger and then managed to get a grip on it. She told herself the usual homilies. Their goals were hers, after all. Uranium might yet whisper wonderful secrets, if you cupped your ear just right.

She knew with a leaden certainty that revealing the sphere would conjure up the competitive rat race that she so disliked about the field already. Standing in line for her own data! In this era of few big machine facilities and squeezed beamtime, the merest odd spike in a graphed plot could bring about a feeding frenzy. "Gang-bang the data," she sighed to herself.

Ah yes, the data, she recalled. They had waited until the last minute to tell her that she wasn't going to get to crunch the data herself. Instead, they'd savor it at their leisure, here at Brookhaven. Anything really startling, they'd thoroughly chew through first.

Well, she thought vengefully, this was tit for tat, then. She wasn't just saying, *Okay, then I'll take my ball and go home.*

She immediately felt a pang of remorse. This wasn't going to sit squarely with her own inner voice and she knew it.

Still, what was it her father used to say? Into the gloom of the small Lab guest room she recited, "If you keep your eye on your goals, you're not keeping it on your ass."

8

The prep area was too damn busy. That became obvious in the first hour.

With the help of Zak and Brad Douglas, she had gotten the U-magnet lowered onto a motorized cart, then hauled it out to the prep area. Zak had already told Brad that they had found ''something funny'' in the beam pipe and that Alicia wanted to study it a bit. With solid Middle America good looks, Brad was a quietly ambitious student, even more awed than Zak by Brookhaven's high-powered atmosphere. He had a way of working in sudden bursts of energy, as if an idea had caught fire inside. He respected Zak's professionalism, with a hint of envy.

There was no immediate need to tell Brad anything and Zak's dedication would keep him from mentioning the sphere to anyone. That would buy the time she needed.

She sent both of them off to help with the new start-up. The beam pipe section was replaced, the vacuum pumped down, and the BRAHMS group was starting up the uranium flux again. She should be in the control room to see the data come in again; she was still a team member, after all. At 10 A.M. the accelerator managers had started stacking uranium bunches into the RHIC ring again. Physics goes on. With the Core Element dead, she felt none of yesterday's zest.

A look around; nobody watching. Gingerly, she pulled the tarp away from the magnet poles and examined the sphere. It reflected the hard ceramic fluorescent lights of the big prep room and Alicia's squinty-eyed face, peering at it from two feet away. No radioactivity. The apparently smooth face of it had a slight blue tinge.

Alicia sniffed. Ozone? Could be the spark gaps firing nearby on a test rig.

She prodded it with a two-by-four, just like yesterday, with the same result: a hard surface, no give. She rapped it hard. No ringing, just a thump as it absorbed the impact. Solid?

Quickly she glanced around again. Good. No one seemed to pay her any attention. She studied the end of the two-by-four. A small dent, no other sign.

Her nerves jumped, fingers fidgeted. What more could she do here? Teams were busily checking out their gear all around her.

Physics prided itself on its international nature, but often it split into microscopic tribes. At Brookhaven each detector group had its own coffee urn; when one was "down," they would not borrow coffee from another group, just grumble and wait for the repair. Alicia got around the Lab more than most, since the switch to uranium from gold affected every part of the Collider. More than once, people would ask her how things were going in the other groups, if there was any news—even though they were only a few hundred meters away.

Now physicists and technicians from several groups, the STAR and PHENIX and PHOBOS detectors, came around to offer commiseration for the loss of the Core Element: "A real puzzle, it is," and "What you figure could do that, eh?" and the usual sympathetic noises. She nodded. They really were kind, but she had trouble concentrating on what they were saying.

She sighed. There were too many people around here to set up any diagnostics without arousing interest. And which diagnostics were relevant? She needed to get this thing into a quiet lab where she could think. Brookhaven was a particle factory, not a place for scrutiny.

Maybe we've discovered a *really big* particle, she thought crazily, the *bigon*. A particle the size of your head—no mess-ing around with complicated microchips and imagers, just study it up close, by hand.

Physics had been like that just a century or two ago. Hertz measuring his waves by walking across his lab, because their wavelengths were as long as his arm. Roentgen discovering X rays using ordinary photographic plates and a steel paperweight. Maybe particle physics *needed* a bigon.

"Hope that field can hold on to it," Zak said over her shoulder.

"Uh, how is the run going?" The rest of BRAHMS was still functional; the Core Element had been a special device custom-built for uranium.

"They're getting plenty of events in the midrapidity arm."

"Great." They had spent the previous afternoon pulling the remnants of the Core Element out of BRAHMS. They would have to be content with the few hours of data they had on disk, analyzing the compact clouds of subnuclear debris, in the months it would take to rebuild the detector.

"That's what, a half Tesla field in there?" Zak checked the side stenciling of the permanent magnet. "Yeah. Hope it's enough."

"To hold that sphere? Let's see . . ." She wrote quickly on her clipboard. The flux of magnetic field crossing the sphere, multiplied by the sphere's cross section area, had to exceed the acceleration of gravity, so . . . , "As long as it's less than a hundred kilograms, no problem."

"For steel, that's probably okay."

"It's holding steady," she said. Let him think it was steel. Zak wrinkled his nose. "What's that I smell?"

"Ozone from those spark gaps over there, I think."

"Ummm. Say, you get the word on that safety board hearing?"

She froze. "Uh, no. When?"

He glanced at his wristwatch. "In 'bout two hours. Didn't you check your e-mail?"

The section of ruptured beam pipe sat on the table between her and Zak and the safety board. The ceramic fluorescent clarity of the conference room gave the torn steel the air of a cadaver laid out for an autopsy.

The preliminaries were methodical. Description of procedures, review of evidence, plenty of Cover Your Ass detail. Her stomach lurched, but she did not give way to the usual impulses of insecurity, especially her specialty, talking too much. If only nobody had noticed the sphere . . .

The TV monitoring cameras had views partly obstructed by detectors but showed the pipe blowing in one blurred frame, Zak's shirt visible in the distance. Alicia felt an undertone of uneasiness; engineers never liked the unexplained, whereas physicists lived for it.

Minutes tiptoed by, frowning. Hugh Alcott went over the facts in a monotone. "Note clear signs of a pressure rupture at segment 148. Some burnishing of the inner lining, as if from photon damage. Dave?"

Nodding, Dave Rucker gave her a wobbly, rueful smile. "I saw the mess it made of the Core Element. Sorry, Alicia, but I believe I can assure you and your team that this was not due to any foreseeable Lab oversight."

She said, "The natural place to rupture was the focus, since the beam pipe is thinnest there. Some anomalous energy deposition in the pipe wall created a fracture, I suppose."

The engineers had already thought of that, she was sure. A thin pipe let the decay products through well, but that carried a price.

"We've never had anything remotely resembling this," Dave continued. "Clearly, some energy release created a pressure on the inner lining."

"I understand," she said.

"Point is," Hugh said, knitting his fingers together, "did this happen because of something specific to using uranium?"

"I can't imagine how." She spread her hands. "It's true the total energy released in a collision is higher, over 200 GeV per nucleon times 238, and times 2 because there are two nuclei. But that's not a lot more than we had with gold."

"Unless you crossed some crucial threshold," Dave Rucker said quietly.

She was ready for that. "This is my postdoc, Zak Nguyen. He and I checked the signatures in the Core Element and the surrounding BRAHMS detectors. We looked at the count rates in the time just before we shut down. Show them, Zak."

Zak rose and handed out copies of an energy graph. He was grinning to cover his nervousness, she saw. He gave the specs and described methods in a flat, small voice that got stronger as he got into the detail. "These show no unexpected excess in counts in any detector," Zak concluded firmly.

"Ummm." Dave pointed to a descending curve. "Looks like the base rate was low already."

"We had a slow erosion of flux for several hours before the incident," Alicia said. "The system was underperforming."

Hugh Alcott looked attentive. "You're suggesting a system failure?"

Alicia shrugged. "I'm not a Collider expert."

"It's worth checking into," Dave said. "I'll recommend a look-see to Tom Ludlam."

Alicia nodded. Ludlam was the highly respected research director.

"Let me get this straight." Hugh leaned forward. "You saw nothing else on the Core Element signal?"

"No, nothing." Not her fault if they didn't ask the right question.

"If this blowout had occurred at the focus of one of the big detectors, PHENIX or STAR," Dave said in a slow, troubled monotone, "we'd have a catastrophe. It would've peppered all the microcircuitry and made the detectors useless."

"Scary." Hugh nodded. "I'm still not convinced this hasn't got anything to do with using uranium."

Alicia had nothing to add to that. She watched the board and waited. As a graduate student she had learned that among physicists, unless you were pretty damn sure of what you said, best not say it.

Dave said soberly, "Until we figure out what happened, I think we'd better not do any more uranium experiments, Alicia."

She had expected this. If they found nothing, a few months

of frustration would make the whole matter recede. By that time she would know what had happened and could make her pitch for resumption of uranium runs. "I understand," she said.

Dave's lips parted a bit, as if he were surprised. The confrontational style of the field virtually dictated that an adverse ruling be argued against and then appealed. Her simple acceptance would probably work better, she calculated. When she came back with an explanation and cure, they would be better disposed to go along with her.

To break the pause Hugh said, "I sure hope this doesn't get us a fresh lawsuit. An explosion, even though unrelated, during the first time we use uranium . . ."

"The rabid anti-Lab folks, like Fish Unlimited, they don't have to hear about it, do they?" Alicia asked.

"Good point," Dave said, brightening. "Let's see that nothing about this gets into a Lab publication."

"Yes," Alicia said. "Those people scare me more than any blown-out pipe."

Particle physics was rich in imagery of change—annihilation, disintegration, fluctuations, decay—and counterposed with phrases of stability. Experiments began from *simple initial conditions*; particles assumed their *ground state* from which experimenters perturbed them; all in pursuit of the new, of signal over noise.

But such thinking assumed careful preparation. The mystery suspended under the trap was raw reality, unprepared.

In the five running days remaining Alicia helped the BRAHMS team monitor the uranium results. Data streamed in and flickered onto the big laser disks for later digestion. BRAHMS strummed with purpose. The pursuit of the particle fog that signified the Quantum Chromodynamic plasma state was never going to be a "eureka moment," as Alicia thought of it. Rather, careful diagnostics had to fathom the spray of debris emerging from the beam focus point. Detailed backtracking would tell if they came from a compressed mass over ten times more dense than a proton.

It was like reconstructing a massive traffic accident by counting the shards of steel that peppered the roadway. This the particle physicists shared with those at RHIC who thought of themselves as nuclear physicists, because they dealt with the convolutions of many-body interactions. Their ancient rivalry was mostly an argument over boundary fences, and for once at RHIC the two communities were united, probing the complicated wreckage made by complex, fundamental particles smashing together.

Whatever label they labored under, tedium was the lot of particle and nuclear physicists alike. Only the relentless could weather through to their reward.

At the shutdown they all toasted each other again and started the breakdown of special gear deployed only for this run. Then came the packing up and checking out, an inevitable letdown.

Except for Alicia and Zak. With Brad Douglas they filled crates with the carcass of the ruined Core Element. When Zak and Alicia wheeled out the already crated permanent magnet, Brad asked few questions. Alicia had gotten the magnet consigned to her on a loaner basis, her request rubber-stamped without a murmur.

But they had to get it past the usual exit examination. The inspecting team looked over the crates while her heart pounded. One stopped at the sphere's crate, studied the paperwork, tapped the crate absently. She held her breath. Then he just sauntered off.

So they came to stand watching their crates loading at Islip Field, a regional freight-hauling airstrip nearby. Transporting an object she did not understand troubled her, but she brushed aside misgivings. She had plunked down her ante solidly now and might as well play her hand out. Probably it would all come to nothing anyway.

She had a farewell supper with Brad and Zak and others of the BRAHMS collaboration at the usual Long Island indifferent Italian restaurant. Months of data analysis loomed ahead of them all as they tried to ferret out evidence that something new and worthy had happened at the focus of the two uranium beams. They had a certain bravado about them, this tired crew, because they were trying an idea outside the conventional.

Most of the Brookhaven staff felt that if the quark-gluon fog was to be seen at all, it would come from the many runs using gold nuclei, carefully building up statistics. Uranium was a cute idea, they would allow, but a long shot. A very long shot.

The whole time a clock ticked in the back of her mind. She had done something based on pure gut intuition, but that did not keep the anxieties away. She found herself tapping her belt nervously, even biting her fingernails—habits she had long ago mastered, she thought.

Somebody proposed driving into Manhattan to walk around and sniff the Essence of Big City, but Alicia begged off, saying she was tired and had an early JFK flight in the morning.

All true, but she did not mention that underlying her leaden fatigue was a high jittery eagerness.

PART II
MAY 2005

How often have I said to you that when you have eliminated the impossible, whatever remains, *however improbable*, must be the truth?

—SHERLOCK HOLMES IN *THE SIGN OF FOUR* (1888)

1

The University of California at Irvine was the youngest campus in the system, founded in 1965, but it had lost its raw look long ago. The original planners had laid out the campus around a wooded, circular central park. Framing it were tall tan buildings done in droop-eyed windows and graceful curves. Two decades later a biology building had infiltrated, proudly flaunting its bare metal conduits and pipes on the outside. It stood out like a pimple on a princess. Back then biotechnology had looked as though it would inevitably dominate the research companies growing up around the university. That idea didn't look as good now and neither did the building.

Asphalt parking lots and a clutter of buildings in the stuck-together style of the late Twen Cen now seemed to jostle each other, trapped in the original circular layout. Angular and knobby, the newer buildings with their glued-on steel afterthoughts made the stately Moorish edifices look like elderly aunts brooding from their heights over the antics of unruly children.

Fanning out from the rim of the central park, the physical sciences complex sported five buildings. Pale wooden trailers were wedged into available crannies, more ratty each year as their "temporary" status looked more permanent. Students sat on the hard concrete benches and slurped coffee as they studied. Nobody looked up as a truck pulled into the utility parking lot and edged around an illegally parked car.

Alicia Butterworth carefully backed the UC–Irvine truck

into the receiving bay of the Physical Sciences Research Facility. Zak jumped out of the cab and waved her in. At 7 A.M. the air held only a promise of the moist spring heat to come and there was nobody in the facility, which was the way she wanted it.

With the ceiling crane they got the crate off the truck bed. Alicia had plenty of experience with moving heavy gear from her years at Berkeley and RHIC. The cubical crate lowered into position on the polished concrete floor and she and Zak used a forklift to get it into one of the smaller subsections of the bay. Out of the way, they could work without anybody kibitzing. She picked up a crowbar and popped a steel packing band off. The shipment had come into John Wayne Airport late last night, May 3. She and Zak had been there when the gate opened this bright Wednesday morning. Nothing had gone funny with the shipment, or so the manifest said. Still, she wondered if the sphere was still anchored in the magnetic field. Had it shaken free? No sign of damage on the outside, at least—

Her wrist alarm went off. "Damn," she muttered. "Zak, hold off. We'll finish opening when I get back."

He nodded a little foggily and went in search of coffee. She went by her lab desk and picked up her viewgraphs and notes, left there three weeks before so they would be tidily close to the lecture hall. She sorted through them, trying to recall where the class should be in the progression of ideas and homework problems. The ideal in such introductory courses was to give an illusion of science's steady march, systematically searching the perimeter of an ever-expanding horizon. She crossed the courtyard into the main lecture hall. Five hundred faces greeted her.

She slapped her first viewgraph down, a sketch of a quantum mechanics effect. That would give the hired note-taker from the Clone Factory time to copy it lovingly and sell Xeroxes of her lecture by tomorrow morning, relieving some of the class from showing up today. The classic lecture-and-notes system had started with medieval Irish monks and was staggering badly into the twenty-first century. Audio hookup on, tap the mike, check. She glanced up at the audiovisual booth where an attendant recorded her lecture, also offered for sale tomorrow. Was the rest of their med school preparation this packaged and passive? She sighed. Adjust the focus and begin—

She apologized for having to bring in a substitute lecturer for the weeks she had been gone. To get Clare Yu to take over had cost Alicia a substantial trade: three weeks lecturing in an upper-division class Clare would teach next fall, plus dinner at the Four Seasons, where they had enjoyed a fine, long, silly conversation about the antics of their colleagues.

Launching into a description of quantum mechanics, Alicia knew the cost was worth it. It had been only three weeks on chilly Long Island, but it felt like three months of fresh air and sunshine. Teaching was all very fine, but research made the heart sing.

She finished her eight o'clock—students hated the hour, but it gave her the rest of the day to get something done—and checked in with the department office. Her pigeonhole mail slot was crammed and at the factotum's front desk she picked up another whole box of mail, the fruit of three weeks. She was heading out to the lab again when the department chairman came ambling down the main corridor of the department staff offices. Apparently the management services officer (nobody had ordinary titles anymore) had told him she was back.

"Oh, Alicia," an unconvincing brightening in the voice, "I have a small favor to ask."

Martin Onell wore his usual uniform of full three-piece suit, gray today, with a sea blue button-down shirt and muted amber tie on a bronze clasp, all set off by a lime green decorator handkerchief peeking out at the scruffy world.

"Martin, I just got back last night from Brookhaven—"

"As I know." He gestured at the white board where faculty names were listed with destinations and dates. Four faculty strewn around the world, in Kobe and Geneva and Cambridge and D.C., a typical roster. "You made your 3-B lecture?"

"Sure." What was he edging up to?

"The head of Gender Education—"

"Not that again." She sighed.

"—called and well, they really would like to talk to you about—"

"I haven't got—"

"—just showing up for their board meetings—"

"—any time right now—"

"—because you *did* agree, since they wanted a minority woman, to take the post—"

"I got asked and said yes, but that was last year—"

"—knowing it was a two-year appointment—"

"And the vice chancellor said it would be no real work." A quizzical expression flickered over his face. "It isn't, is it? I mean, just vote on measures—"

"You have to listen to them first. That's what I found out I couldn't stand."

Martin Onell gave her a raised-eyebrows stare that was supposed to make her feel guilty but only made him look stupefied. "You did say you'd do it."

"I'll call them." That got her off the hook and took the problem off his desk, which was what he really wanted.

"Good, good." An audible sigh. "Uh, how did your run go?"

"Disappointing. We broke down early in the run."

"Really? I thought RHIC was reliable."

"It is, but . . . well, I'm looking into what happened. The beam pipe vacuum failed."

"That's odd." Onell was a solid-state physicist, but he had broad interests.

"I'm taking some space in my lab to look at the damage. It pretty well wasted my detector."

"Too bad." He shook his head.

"I'm keeping it quiet because Brookhaven wants it that way."

"Ummm." A knowing pursing of lips. "Not unexpected. The big accelerators are closely watched these days."

"I don't think it's a major problem," she said to deflect further interest. Onell was a terrible gossip and an old foe of the particle physics group. Probably had cronies at Brookhaven, too. She turned away and retreated down the hall, waving goodbye.

The stock room had a delivery for her. Down to the basement, into the wire-caged office, sign the paperwork. The bill of lading said they were circuit elements for the Core Element, which she had fax-ordered from Brookhaven. Good. She could use them in the pep talk she would have to give her graduate students when she broke the news.

Back up to her office on the third floor, taking the steps two at a time, usually her only form of exercise. She fidgeted her key in the balky lock to her office. Her desk was a sea of paper. A stack of phone messages, but they could wait. Clare Yu had left the results of the latest quizzes given in the discussion sections for Physics 3-B. Alicia scanned the curves provided by the grading program and sighed. No better performance than usual. In fact, a bit worse, though within the expected quiz-to-quiz variation.

She had really *tried* with this class, too, holding extra problem sessions and carefully going over examples in lecture, the works. Had her three weeks at Brookhaven badly damaged their opinion of her? Feeling neglected, ideas of disloyalty if the prof was gone for too long? They should be grateful, actually; Clare Yu was the better lecturer. Physics 3-B was for nonmajors, which meant mostly biology students. Which meant, at a ninety percent confidence level, those who wanted to go to medical school. They saw the 3-B professors as hurdles they must leap on their way to respect, status, and a Mercedes-Benz.

She had given them the nose-in-it speech on the first day of the quarter, too: "Look at the student on your right, then the left, then in front, then behind. On average, only one of you five will get into med school. Your grade in this course is a major sheep/goat separator used by admissions committees. I don't like that and I'm sure you don't, either. But as physicists are fond of pointing out, facts are facts. I'll try to help you all do your best."

Glumly recalling that speech, she was startled by a knock on the door. It was a 3-B student, a demure young Vietnamese woman. Office hours; she had completely forgotten laying on an extra load to make up for her absence. The student came in and voiced the usual worries over her grade and Alicia let her run for the usual two minutes. Then she coaxed her into concrete talk about what the student didn't understand, which after a few more minutes seemed to be just about everything. Alicia sat back and eyed a little poem she had stuck to the leg of her desk, out of view of students.

> Cram it in, jam it in,
> Students' heads are hollow.
> Cram it in, jam it in,
> Plenty more to follow.

Cynical, but won from experience. The sheer pace of 3-B demoralized quite a few. Some realized that this might be the most important aspect of the course as a filter: med school would be the same, only worse.

Students ate up her morning. She headed over to the Phoenix Grill for one of the chicken curries they did reasonably well. The walk was crisp and warm in the advanced spring here and the grill supplied knots of diners enjoying the lancing sun. Clare Yu was there, sitting outside with the solid-state group at a round table, easy to find because they all wore hats; the undergraduates around them did not apparently worry about skin cancer. Alicia thanked her for taking over the 3-B lectures and listened to a postdoc excitedly describing an effect he had predicted. She had trouble following his point.

When Alicia got back to her office, her secretary intercepted her with messages. A phone call from her father, some academic business she could put off, and a *Call me!* from old buddy Jill. All for later; she beat a quick retreat to the lab.

In a working laboratory's necessary chaos there is often an island of order, scrupulously clean and clear. In Alicia's lab this was the assembly room where graduate students and diligent undergrads followed intricate plans, piecing together the myriad sensors of the Core Element. Here Alicia also labored, taking most of her research time in cross-checking, puzzling out problems, and patient encouragement. Such hard-slogging attention to detail was boot camp for any experimenter.

Zak was in the assembly room, unpacking the ruins of the Core Element. They had come in on a later freight shipment and without even mentioning it to Alicia he had gone to the airport and picked them up. But then, she thought sourly, how could he have found her? She had been buzzing around all day.

Brad Douglas was helping, along with two more junior graduate students who were eyeing the mess carefully packed inside the box with fallen faces. They had all put in long months building, testing, and optimizing the Core Element. They gave limp greetings.

She stopped them from taking any more pieces out of the crates and sat them down around an assembly table. Time for the pep talk. Not easy, especially after losing the first game, and in the Brookhaven Super Bowl.

First she said that the Core Element had worked perfectly and it was a tribute to all of them, up and running with no trouble, got a lot of data on disk to analyze, until . . .

This was the hard part. She blamed the damage on an explosive failure of the vacuum system and left it at that. "The whole matter is under investigation," she said. She hated using the passive voice, but here it did the right job, describing without actually showing who was acting. They would assume she meant Brookhaven, not her, so she let the subject stop there.

"Let's get the unpacking done, then knock off. The whole tedious business of figuring out what we can salvage and what we've got to fabricate again—we'll leave that for tomorrow."

They nodded, a bit numbed. She made a show of energetically taking out some smashed boards and sorting them into categories. Pretty soon the whole team was working reasonably well in the big bay. They cleared space and carefully unfolded the white foam packing sheets and there were even some smiles here and there.

Time for the finish. "And here"—she held up the shipment of circuit elements—"we have the first replacement parts. We're on the way back."

It sounded lame to her, too staged, but the kids brightened.

Brad would be the key here. He said little, but she noticed that he casually dropped by each laboring figure and buoyed up spirits. He was the best of the graduate students, quiet and ambitious, but good at handling people. In fact, better than she was. He had been the obvious choice to go with her and Zak to Brookhaven.

After two hours, during a break, she took Zak into the separate space where the big crate stood. They made quick work of the wooden frame. The gray U-magnet had foam packing sheets and bubble wrap around it. Gingerly, they peeled it off. The sphere was still there.

"Came through okay," Zak said.

Alicia stuck her head into the magnet gap and eyed her warped reflection in the mirror spherical surface. The fizzy quality of the reflected light was . . . gone.

"Zak, does it look the same to you?"

His head poked into the other side. "Um, pretty much."

"There was a kind of, well, coherence to it."

"I remember. Maybe the lab light at Brookhaven was different?"

She pursed her lips. "That smell again."

Zak sniffed. "Ozone. We smelled it back in the Brookhaven prep area."

"Must be the sphere itself." She backed away and the smell faded. "That's the source, all right."

"Funny. Takes a lot of energy to make ozone, doesn't it?"

"Yes, but *how* can a solid object do this?"

"Ozone forms around transformers and power lines."

"Electrostatics?" She frowned. "If there's a big potential on this thing—"

"How would it get charged?"

"Who knows?" She got a shielded cable and brought it over, using work gloves. "If this discharges to ground . . ."

But it did not. "Okay, no electric effect." She wrinkled her nose at the smell. Was it stronger than it had been at Brookhaven?

Zak frowned. "How can a metal bubble . . . ?"

Time to be frank. "Zak, you've been pretty quiet about this."

Discomfort flickered in his normally impassive face. He shrugged. "I figured you knew best."

"I took this because I think it may be important, very important. Some new physics may be going on and this is a big, fat clue. But I know what I did—and I'll take the blame here, not you—is out of bounds. I just . . . had to."

Zak nodded. "I didn't come to UCI on a postdoc because my parents live nearby. I came because of you. You're a really good experimentalist. Everybody says that. I'll go with your judgment."

She had wondered a bit at Zak's silent compliance. By now she would have filled the air with questions. They were both outsiders in the scientific community, but of quite different personalities—so be it.

"Anyway," Zak said to fill the silence between them, "we should get something back in return for losing the Core Element."

"A kind of cosmic balance? Yeah, I kinda feel the same way." They smiled at each other, some unspoken understanding passing. Alicia sighed and stared again at their reflections, two quizzical frowns. "I wonder if that surface is solid."

"Well, sure it is."

"Let's check."

They got a drill from the machine shop and mounted it on an equipment frame. Zak fished a diamond tip from the rack and put it in the chuck. He advanced the whirring tip as Alicia watched from the side. It met the sphere. Nothing gave. A high thin scream of metal in agony, but the tip did not advance.

"Good grief," Zak said, pulling the tip back.

"Wow," Alicia said, rather an understatement of her feelings.

"A tip like this should cut steel, even a really tough alloy. I can't get it to advance any."

There was no mark on the sphere. "Let's try to chip it."

That failed as well. Zak snorted in exasperation. "What kinda super-hard material can this *be*?"

"Maybe it's not material?"

"Huh?"

"Just a thought."

Irked, Zak jabbed a finger at the offending sphere. "Sure feels solid. More likely, we're doing something wrong."

Maybe so, she thought, *but not in the way you mean.*

For the first time she felt a cold trickle of apprehension, peering into her deformed reflection, which seemed to be leering back at her.

2

Laguna Beach was the sort of town where a stack of tiny apartments clinging precariously to a hillside on the Pacific Coast Highway could call itself The Villa and nobody would laugh. Alicia slipped her blue Miata into the last long-term parking space left on Lower Cliff Drive as dusky fog edged in from Main Beach, only a hundred meters away. She had taken a two-bedroom, the largest in The Villa, because she wanted to live in the middle of the village. Most people fled here from the Orange County sprawl to hole up in the narrow, steep canyons, living on streets where it was impossible to walk but crawling might work.

She had wanted just enough urban pulse to remind her of Northern California, where she had done her graduate work, but without the People's Republic of Berkeley upscale slum atmosphere. On an assistant professor's salary most chose to live in the university-run condos on campus. Alicia's skin itched at the idea. Rents would have been cheaper inland, but there lay the lairs of cotton-topped elders wearing fruit-colored comfort clothes, the men with legs ghostly pale above the black socks they always wore in their sandals, and the women in pastel golf visors with super-size sunglasses.

She made her way down the tricky steps, letting the flowers welcome her home. Sweet jasmine layered the moist beach air as it climbed up the trellises at doorways. As she teetered down steep steps between jocular blue-and-white tile walls, a hummingbird darted around some fuchsias in baskets. It paused and gave her a look and then moved away so fast it just vanished. On the next level petunias cloyed the mood with their thick sweetness. The apartments here were tiny and The Villa joke was they were reserved for New Yorkers so they would feel at home. The petunias alone would have driven her away. But just further along, between narrow tiled walls, the air gave way to the cutting acidic aroma of golden marigolds. On the left her apartment had a commanding view of Broadway and the Pacific Coast Highway with the whitecaps beyond, all wreathed in a halo of magenta bougainvillea, mercifully scentless. She was feeling better already, putting the lab puzzle behind her, when she noticed that her front door was ajar.

She went in cautiously. There was a heavy lilac smell in the living room. "Come out or I start shooting."

"My my, you're so butch," came a light voice.

"Jill, that's a new lock."

"Yeah, took me maybe thirty seconds with a dull nail file."

"The new perfume is overpowering." Alicia walked through the archway into a room of spare rattan furniture covered in tweedy gray. Jill lay on the couch reading *Natural History*, feet up, open-toed sandals off, blue silk shirt tucked into white duck slacks, her blonde hair spread around her head like a halo.

Jill grinned. "Giving it a trial run. A guy at work likes it."

Jill had been famous for picking locks at university, some kind of high school prankster talent. "They teach that as part of investigative journalism?" Alicia dropped her briefcase in a corner and Jill bounced up and hugged her.

"Just in case I get assigned to the White House and hear about some funny stuff at the Watergate. Got my special tools all ready."

Alicia smiled wanly and eased into her bare mahogany rocker—good for the ache in her back. "Girl, I'm pure, plain, kicked-dog tired."

"Hey, we're supposed to celebrate your experiment, remember?"

"It crashed."

"Like, bang?"

"Big bang."

Jill blinked. "Then you really weren't kidding in that phone message."

"You keep thinking everybody's as ironic as you are."

"It really crashed? Why?"

Alicia launched into the story and within a solid minute Jill got the familiar blank look, so she capped off the tale with a quick reference to the sphere and then just rocked a bit in silence. Jill respected her work but had little interest in its intricacies. Come to think of it, Alicia thought, maybe that was one of the reasons they got along.

Jill looked relieved. "Uh, save the details for the appetizers. Ready?"

"Lord no. I'll open something. Red or white?"

"Go for white. I'll probably spill it."

Alicia fished a sauvignon blanc out of her tiny refrigerator in a kitchen only marginally bigger. The small kitchen had appealed to her, a ready excuse for not whomping up five-course dinners. She came back out under the archway, poured the wine, and plopped back down in the rocker.

Jill eyed her and said, "Y'know, that's your best frame. When you have a guy over, always sit there."

"It's good for my aching back."

"No, really, it sets off your skin very well."

"Mahogany lady? My ambition is to be thought of as what my dad calls a 'high yella.' "

"Yellow? How can black people be yellow?"

"Mix in some white, which is really pink."

"Ugh. Don't take up oil painting."

"In this town I'll be the only one who doesn't."

Jill flexed her fingers and Alicia knew she was thinking about a cigarette. Well, they both were. Three months now and not an hour passed without the urge; they were helping each other quit. A flicker of a frown, then Jill said brightly, "Three guesses."

"New guy."

"It's that obvious?"

"C'mon, we've served together through a decade of the Sex Wars. You were going out with that computer guy—"

"*Him?* Turned out he had a rag for a gas cap."

"So spill."

Jill rattled off name, job, physical highpoints, all with an accountant's speed and accuracy. Alicia interrupted with: "So he looks like a potential Mr. Right?"

"No, just Mr. Right Now."

Alicia shook her head. "The utilitarian approach. Maintenance sex."

"Hey, I'm just voyaging through the six stages of life: Birth, Childhood, Hideous Adolescence, Midlife Crisis, Plastic Surgery, Death or Whatever." Jill nervously flexed her fingers again and her upper teeth bit into her cardinal-bright lipstick, as if searching for the filter tip that wasn't there.

"Those are the choices? Think I'll sit this one out."

"Oh, you're infuriating!" Jill leaned forward toward Alicia. "You said after this experiment's up and going, you'd get back in the game."

"No finger-pointing. There's trouble with the experiment—"

"Sheesh! Look, as far as your romantic life goes, don't bother thinking for yourself. Get a pro to do it."

"Like you?"

"I've been around the track a lot more times."

"A real Olympic athlete."

"As I recall, that's called judgmental."

"Factual."

"Hey, drop that. This is Jill. I've seen you with your dress caught in your panties, 'member?"

Alicia smiled wanly. "Okay, okay. Maybe I need some encouragement."

Jill eyed her meditatively. "A remake is more like it."

They had met in Berkeley. Jill was two years younger with a master's in Communications and a law degree, which meant that she freelanced in what she called TV Land and got big-time bucks for it. Fast-track stuff, compared with Berkeley's Lite Granola and Birkenstocks. Alicia could see the effects.

Still, it beat UCI, where one could appear in an outfit with just the perfect muted shades and downright witty tailoring and the academics would look right through it. Of course, the secretaries would say something, a little awkwardly because she was a professor, but that was thin gruel indeed.

Alicia sighed and finished her wine. "Where's for dinner? Someplace we can walk."

"Don't change the subject! Look, I'm not saying make this a major campaign or anything, doesn't have to be the Normandy invasion."

"Last time you got me so dolled up, I had that hundred-dollar hairdo ruined by a ceiling fan."

Jill held up both hands, palms out. "Okay, a tactical error. I was trying for the retro Diana Ross look."

"The Eva Peron look, you mean."

"Okay, but you're wearing it hopelessly short now. With just a bit more length—"

"Look, I got reasons not to date right now. Work—"

"No work, not allowing work anymore. You've used that one up."

Alicia smiled. The only way to get Jill off her favorite topic, Let's Save Alicia, was something in her own style. "Okay, reasons not to date." She ticked them off on her fingers: "I can't make myself share in Chinese restaurants. My ideal man hasn't been invented yet—in fact, may be anatomically impossible. I need to be in bed, asleep by 10 P.M., or I become quite cranky."

"You're cranky already."

Alicia nodded. "Woman need dinner."

"You need a date. I may have mentioned this a few hundred times before."

"Date? Could you spell that?"

"Hey, is no man an island or what?"

"Most of them should be."

"Don't go insulting the prey."

"And I'm the cranky one?"

They went to Las Brisas, both liking the feeling of making a virtuous, healthy choice with the soup, ignoring the dollop of artery-clogging buttery potatoes that made it delectable. Already nearly packed, it was a Southwestern Mexican joint, upscale touristy in a nice way, pricey but still reasonably hip. No interesting guys loitering at the intense singles' bar, which is how one knew it was a real restaurant and not a watering hole with appetizers.

Jill displayed her full range of neurotic restaurant behavior, ordering everything on the side, asking for her food on smaller plates to make it look bigger, hauling out her own ultralite salad dressing, counting calories with a calculator at the table, pretending to find sprouts just yummy. Once on a double date Alicia had listened to her long soliloquy on whether to eat just a little something before they got to the restaurant, so the guys wouldn't think she was a pig.

The menu listed every single ingredient in the dishes, the full cinnamon-apples-drizzled-with-clover-honey-*crème-fraîche* sort of thing. They were most of the way through a shared entrée (a delicately negotiated point) of chicken mole with white asparagus, an unlikely combination that didn't quite work out, before Alicia could get a word in edgewise about the sphere. Jill listened intently, nodding and snapping off chunks of celery sticks.

When Alicia's tale finally dribbled off into details about diagnosing the sphere, Jill yawned and poked a finger at her. "So what can Brookhaven say? You took something that ruined your experiment. Well, you were owed."

"Physics doesn't work like that. It's not horse trading."

"You'll have to split it some way?"

Alicia chuckled loudly. Maybe it was the wine. "We tried that. It won't split."

"You can say you didn't know what it was."

"True. But spiriting away an important result from an experiment—"

"You don't know it's important."

Alicia found that her hand had knotted into a fist. "I can feel it in my gut."

"Your honor, witness is unresponsive."

"Okay, I don't know. But if they ask, truth is, I had a feeling from the beginning—"

"Just say, 'your honor, I refuse to answer on grounds of insufficient database.' "

Alicia shook her head and said nothing.

Jill frowned and leaned across the narrow table, pushing aside her decaf espresso to hold Alicia's hands. "You're worried more than you let on."

"Yes. I . . . I don't know what the hell this thing is and I've done this crazy thing on impulse and I can't really turn to anybody or word will get out and I'll have to answer—"

"I'm no rocket scientist—God, don't you hate that phrase? As if engineers who launch rockets are real smart? Try sleeping with one of them!—but listen, having a consuming curiosity and following your nose is what people like me *expect* a scientist to do."

Alicia looked surprised. "From the outside it doesn't look like I've committed a cardinal sin. I like that."

"You're absolved, kid. Doesn't the Pope get his ring kissed? I'll have another espresso."

They went along the sloping beach. Jill narrowly escaped a big wave hissing up to and nearly over her new green sandals. Alicia walked her to her top-of-the-line BMW, which, because the tourist season was already picking up, was parked on Legion Street.

Walking home, Alicia looped by the beach to listen to the crash and slither of the waves some more. Sitting on the rocks for a while made her feel better about everything. Coming back along Coast Highway, the town lay like strings of Christmas lights wrapped around looming hills of coal.

She yawned and then saw another black woman coming toward her. Jill's pressure was working; she instantly began sizing up the woman as competition. Not bad, no, but not that good, a little hefty and certainly not in her class of looker. Then she blinked and saw that she was looking into a store window reflecting her own backlit image. She walked the whole rest of the way home unsuccessfully trying not to think about it.

3

Most scientific research flows along well-charted channels. Within a recognized framework it seeks to discover minor eddies and byways, expanding knowledge without breaking boundaries. It strums with the tension between the known and the half-seen.

Alicia had always scorned such conventional, safe approaches. RHIC, after all, was a bold stab into new terrain; its failure to yield any eyebrow-raising discoveries so far did not deny its initial ambition. But she had worked within a community, using time-honored approaches. She saw now the comforts of those boundaries. At this juncture she had to voyage into territory wholly unknown.

Of course, this thing hovering a few feet away from her could be a mere oddity of explosive metallurgy. Zak still thought so. And making a fuss about a poorly understood result could be fatal.

Once at the Stanford Linear Accelerator, a famous story went, an off-site user who was a professor elsewhere was watching fresh data emerge in a late-night experiment. He jumped to the conclusion that he was seeing a new particle. Right away he started talking about setting up a new group to study the effect and asked a postdoc to come work with him as soon as the group was formed. The postdoc kept quiet when a few days later the professor called a big meeting of all collaborators of the in-house group, plus users, and dramatically showed the data, claiming that he—not "we," the postdoc noted—had discovered a new particle. The data didn't look sound to some. *More noise than signal*, the standard cut said. Within a few weeks the professor was out of the collaboration, gone, flushed from the field. Overclaiming was a permissible flaw, the familiar vice of ego, but beating a drum with no parade behind you betrayed poor judgment. A big mouth was more dangerous than anything but a bald error.

She was going to keep hers well shut until she figured out what was going on. Midmorning, students working nearby, a whole day beckoning. Nerves a bit jittery, but work would cure that.

Alicia turned away from the magnet poles. What next? The problem with the unknown was its lack of road signs. Yesterday they had tried the diamond-tipped drill and gotten nowhere. She started taking the drill apart on a workbench, thinking about using a laser, when she noticed a glint from the drill tip. It shone brightly in the lab's fluorescent glow.

Under a low-power microscope the diamond tip seemed fresh. Had its contact rubbed away the slight layer of oxidation all metals develop?

She tried a higher-power microscope borrowed from Walter Bron's lab in another building. The sphere had no discernible structure at that level of magnification. No cracks, abrasions, flaws. What *was* it?

She felt a tingling, curiously pleasurable: her "curiosity reflex," she had called it in high school, when she had first glimpsed the serene certainties of physics, starkly contrasting with the world's raw hubbub.

The drill bit had made a high keening sound when pressed against the sphere. It had scraped the diamond tips clean.

When in doubt, do the obvious. She arranged calipers and carefully measured the radius of the sphere. Getting everything centered properly, she brushed against the sphere, the first time she had touched it. The surface felt slightly warm, smooth. Not cool, as she had intuitively expected; metals feel cool, even if they are at room temperature, because they conduct heat readily, and skin reacts sensitively to heat loss rates. She stroked it a few times while making the measurements, then

averaged her numbers: 37.8 cm. plus or minus about 0.3 cm.
A small bowling ball.

She thought awhile about ways to weigh it. If she knew the
magnet's mass, she could weigh the assembly and subtract—
but she didn't. A direct measurement would require easing off
the magnetic field and lowering in onto a scale. She felt uneasy
at the idea. What if the magnetic restraint were somehow important to its structure? Her intuition was to leave matters as
they were, even if working on the thing was a bit harder in a
magnetic field. She did not like the picture of losing control
of it in the lab.

She frowned. That ozone smell. A damned big clue, but
pointing at what? When in doubt, get some numbers.

She went up to the chemistry department and looked up a
simple test for ozone concentration. Oxygen was two atoms,
she remembered, and with enough energy added it became
three: ozone. It was heavier than air, so if the sphere were
giving it off, the stuff would drift to the lab floor. Silent electrical discharges made it, and the *Chemical Rubber Handbook*
said that ultraviolet radiation around 250 nanometers could,
too. That was an energy of 4 electron Volts, equivalent to a
temperature of about 40,000 degrees.

Was the sphere emitting radiation up in the ultraviolet? She
couldn't see anything. It took a moment to walk around the
bay switching off the high fluorescents and local spot lamps.
After her eyes had adjusted, she peered between the magnet
poles. The human eye could see over an enormous range of
sensitivity, better than photodetectors, but it could be deluded,
also.

A glow there? Try looking at it out of the corner of the eye.
The desire to find something could provoke what she called
"wantum mechanics," fishing a result out of nothing but
noise. To prevent that she turned around in the pitch darkness
and looked again. Where was it? There? She put her hands
out and felt a lab bench. No, she wasn't fully rotated. The
faint light she thought she saw had been in the wrong place.
She turned her head but saw nothing. Try again. Nothing. After more fruitless trials, she quit.

Perhaps try looking in a darkened room with some high-sensitivity photodetectors? That demanded quartz lenses . . .

Maybe later. Right now, try something simple.

One of the atmospheric testing labs in the geophysics department had a compact, computerized meter just sitting in their cabinets which measured ozone, for atmospheric pollution studies. She quickly wangled her way through a postdoc, then had to properly consult the professor in charge, of course, and he cheerfully let her swipe it for a short while. He even came by the lab, wondering what she was doing with such an ordinary instrument when she worked at ultrahigh energies. She was so jumpy she at first tried to stand between him and the U-magnet, then realized he couldn't make anything out through the close-packed instruments, anyway. Seldom can a nonspecialist divine the function of gear. "Just looking for a funny source," she said, trying to sound relaxed.

She spent the middle of the day taking readings at varying distances from the sphere, neatly penciling them in her lab book. It was a sweet device, user-friendly. The ozone concentration fit an inverse square relation pretty well, just as though it were being created at the sphere's surface and then diffusing outward.

She sat and frowned at the thing while her graduate students worked on the Core Assembly in the other half of the high echoing bay. She had told them she didn't want to be disturbed and went over every hour to see if they needed help with the excruciatingly tedious work on the replacement Core Element.

Should she try to cut it with a laser? That required quite a powerful laser, a big job to even get it in here and set up. Also, attention-getting. Who had one? Toborek? Bron? No, too much trouble and risk.

How about asking a metallurgist? Not much help there if it wasn't metal, and something in her gut now told her that it wasn't. Also, another way to launch rumors.

Just to be doing something, she fetched the low-power laser they had for general use in the bay. She set up some simple optics and trained the laser on the sphere. Then she made the resulting beam fall on a simple white screen, which she made out of the plastic backing from a Core Assembly shipping crate.

She had some trouble lining everything up right and getting the screen between the magnet's poles, close to the sphere. When she reflected the beam from the surface at a steep angle, it came off nice and tight, a single ruby spot a millimeter across, scintillant on the screen.

Then she shifted the angle so that the beam struck the very right-hand edge of the sphere, just skimming the surface. The spot spread into an ellipse several centimeters long.

"Ummmm?" she murmured, puzzled. She fooled with the setup for awhile, but there was no way she could be wrong.

That should not be. The curved edge should scatter the beam into a smear, but not nearly so broad as the ellipse that hung on the screen a few centimeters from the sphere. To get a broad ellipse meant that the sphere *refracted* the beam, not just reflected it.

She twisted her mouth, not liking this conclusion. It was as though the steady laser beam went *into* the sphere a bit, then got refracted back out.

She thought of another test. She edged a wooden ruler into the laser beam from the left and watched the elliptical spot. A dark border crept into the *right* side on the screen.

"The left side is refracted most," she whispered to herself.

Light coming in on the left edge of the tiny laser beam went farther . . . into the sphere? . . . and so suffered more refraction, so that it came out on the right hand of the spot. The refraction reversed left with right.

So this thing reflected light, all right, but it refracted, too, proportional to how far the light went in. But that made no sense. *In?* The sphere looked like a hard reflecting metal surface. As though light bounced off one single layer. But this refraction result plainly said that light penetrated to different layers of differing refractive strengths.

Her head hurt, not from the ideas but from staring at the laser beam. Her mind refused to budge any further. Brad Douglas called to her from the far end of the bay, where students were laboriously assembling the new Core Element. Something about a part he could not find.

Somewhat gratefully, she went to help him. When in enough doubt, let your subconscious work on the problem.

4

At the end of her Physics 3-B lecture she happened to look down at the textbook. While the students emptied out of the deep bowl lecture hall, she paged through it idly. She used this moment, rather than struggling through the inadequate doorways, as an implicit invitation to ask questions; some, particularly the Asians, were terminally shy about coming to office hours.

Her approach in lecture was to give her own slant on the material, assuming the class had read the textbook to get a different flavor. This always rankled a faction, she knew, who wanted lectures that combed through the material in exactly the same way they had read it, salted with heavy hints about the exam. She much preferred students who cared for the physics itself, of course; her job, then, to show them some of the sublimely simple beauty in it.

The textbook pages were dotted with black-and-white photos of Physics Greats, typically in portrait pose, head and shoulders only, wearing jackets and ties, gazing off in lofty meditation. Only Richard Feynman and Einstein came across casually, Feynman playing bongos and Einstein wild-haired and sad-eyed in a sweatshirt. Great men—she did not think, *Great white men*—abstracted out of their time and place and assumptions. That too was an assumption, of course: that physics rose above the stormy swamp of culture.

Well, maybe. Some of her first love of physics had come from that hope: that humanity could loft above the dark plain of incessant strife and passion, glimpse a serene beauty hovering beyond the veil of tribe and language. Such visions came to the great, soaring intellects, who passed them down to those struggling below.

Alicia had no illusions that she was going to be a lofty monolith like Einstein or Faraday or Fermi. There came a time in the lives of physicists when they realized that they would be spear carriers, not prima donnas, in the grand opera of science. But she felt a delicious tension as she left the lecture hall and headed straight for the lab. Let department tasks and paper grading wait; she had gotten into physics for exactly this pulse-quickening sense of Being on the Chase.

No students had stopped to ask a question; they rushed off to memorize. With a decisive snap she shut the textbook, gathered up her viewgraphs, and went off to her lab.

Zak had been following her instructions from yesterday. He had carted in a gaggle of photodetectors rounded up from hers and other labs. Nobody had a lot of instrumentation in these days of ever-dwindling funding. Borrowing was common. She reviewed the gear, noticing that it had been bought on grants from the Air Force, NSF, Navy, Department of Commerce, and NASA. Did these agencies know to what diverse uses their dollars went? Sure. They just looked the other way. Only senators and simpletons thought science took place in neatly drawn boxes.

She and Zak finished getting the photodetectors set up and linked to computers. First they would study the sphere's properties in light it reflected. Then they would work in the dark and look for emission. Rather than move the magnet and sphere, they wanted to hood the magnet with light-shielding cloth and then kill the lights for good measure. Her graduate students usually worked in the afternoon, after class, so mornings were best. They were nearly ready to start when her lab phone rang. She answered, despite a strong temptation to ignore it. Her secretary knew better than to disturb her here except for something important.

"Alicia? Hugh Alcott, Brookhaven?"

"Oh. Ah, yes." A sudden, keen apprehension.

"We've been reviewing the accident? And were wondering if you had anything to add."

"Uh, like what?"

"Anything about the debris?"

"I don't think so."

"Well, I'd like a description from you of the whole thing, the incident, in writing."

"I thought you recorded the safety meeting."

"Well, we've got to dot the *i*'s on this thing, you see."

"Why?"

He paused, as if surprised. She wished they were on one of those Net systems that carried a visual still, refreshed every five seconds. But then he could see her, too, and she was not sure what her expression might give away. Good grief, he could even have seen the magnet behind her.

"To be sure it doesn't happen on your next uranium run."

"Oh, sure." She had completely forgotten that she had a run penciled in for half a year from now. Could they get the Core Element ready in time?

"Then you'll e-mail it to me?"

"That might take awhile. I'm coming up on finals here—"

"Well, I'd kinda like to see it pretty soon."

"Okay. I'll do what I can."

They danced around it a little more, then Alcott finally hung up. She closed her eyes and reviewed the whole conversation, holding the phone and listening to the dial tone so that Zak wouldn't get a look at her face before she composed herself. It seemed pretty ordinary, a bureaucrat covering his ass with paperwork. Nothing more. So why was her heart thudding?

She went back to help Zak finish hooking everything up.

"Where shall we start?"

She clicked on some illuminating lamps. "Look for some spectral lines in reflected light."

"Iron? We could look for spectral lines."

"Sure," she said and rattled off two line frequencies in an

easy-to-see range. She didn't think this thing was steel, but they had to start somewhere.

It took half an hour to be sure that there were no iron lines. In another hour they failed to find any other lines, except those already present in the illuminating lamps. When Zak wondered what that meant, she exploited Professorial Mystique, a technique she had observed often. "Ummm," she murmured mysteriously and started setting up for the studies in the dark.

It was nearing noon, but they hooded the magnet and the photosensors and doused the lights. Carefully they patrolled through the spectrum displayed on a computer screen, looking for emission from the sphere. There were the usual goofs and errors, quickly corrected. Light leaking through a doorjamb reflected into one of the photodetectors and they had to mask for that.

After a long while, Zak said, "We're getting photons . . ."

"How much?" She checked the hood to be sure nothing was leaking into the magnet area.

"Very, very few. Right at the edge of detectability."

She checked the 'scope traces. "I don't see a line."

"There isn't any."

"No lines? There must be."

"There aren't."

"Something wrong with our setup, then," she said firmly.

So they went over the entire arrangement again. It was straightforward and she was sure they would find a loose cable or shuttered input somewhere. They did not. So they looked again and still did not. Finally she sighed and said, "Okay, maybe the spectrum is right. But how can it be?"

Zak looked at her blankly. "I don't know."

The light was distributed all across the spectrum. Atoms emit precise frequencies, corresponding to the jumps that electrons make between their quantized energy levels. In a solid the atom-atom binding interactions smeared these lines somewhat, but not enough to yield what they saw. This dim glow was spread everywhere, not concentrated at all.

"That's crazy," Alicia said.

"Maybe we'll bring the lines up out of the noise if we accumulate over a longer time," Zak said.

If they simply added up all the light—in camera language, keeping the shutter open for awhile—then errors would tend to cancel themselves out and they would see the persistent radiation.

"Fair enough." Alicia was pleased. Zak was a quick, absolutely competent student, always thinking one step beyond, able to adapt. A natural. Professors educate those who are capable, but they treasure the students who go beyond that level, who make working with them exciting, not a job at all.

They let the optical-processing system work on the emitted light for twenty minutes. Alicia felt both elation and worry as they waited, checking the system as it counted photons of light over the full width of its spectrum. Elation, that the sphere *did* seem to be giving off some light. Very, very faint, but it was there. Worry, though, because possibly this entire result was just a mistake. Maybe their makeshift rig, set up in a big bay not designed for this sort of sensitive spectral work at all, was letting in an unsuspected source of light. Well, they would have to repeat it all, of course. Nobody trusted a delicate measurement on the basis of one trial.

"Let's have a look," she said when she could restrain her curiosity no longer.

The digital readout took a moment to compile and then wrote itself in a blue curve on the screen. They both reacted at the same moment. "Huh?" said Zak. Alicia drew in a quick breath, mouth gaping until she remembered to close it.

"Looks a lot like a blackbody spectrum," Zak said.

"It does indeed." The smooth curve peaked and fell away in the classic slope known for a century. Any dark object— the ideal *blackbody*—radiated such a spectrum; as it heated up, the peak shifted to the right, to higher frequencies. "No lines, for sure." Alicia read the horizontal frequency axis and scribbled on a pad. "It's radiating very faintly, all right . . . but at an equivalent temperature of over 40,000 degrees."

Zak shook his head. "Crazy. Got to be wrong."

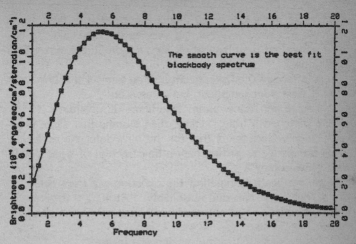

The smooth curve is the best fit blackbody spectrum

"Ummm, probably. Let's inspect everything again." She was quite sure nothing was wrong with the spectrometers or the rest of it; this was a standard measurement, after all, nothing more than standard Advanced Lab 320 fare. But there was always some chance of error, and it would give her time to think. They reversed their usual procedure, following the logic backward from the computers, and it all looked right. Puzzling . . .

Alicia set everything up to do another integration over time, checking the light hood, and started the experiment again. Then she led Zak to one of the small assembly rooms, cluttered with odd elements of the Core Element. She gazed at the parts as if they were from an archaeological site, far back in her past. One wall held a blackboard covered with fragments of old chalk talks. She erased it all and noted down their results:

BLACKBODY, T $= 40,000$
FAINT EMISSION
REFLECTS AMBIENT LIGHT
DIAMETER 37.8 CM.
MASS ~ 100 KG.

"We've got a shiny ball that seems to emit in the ultraviolet. As if it were very hot, but very weak," she said. "It can also reflect our light back at us, so it's more like a mirror than a window."

Zak's face twisted skeptically. "You know I'll follow your lead, I trust your judgment, but—come on!"

"You're not following *my* lead here—it's Nature's."

He stiffened a little. "Okay, then assume that same property, high reflection, is true for the ultraviolet we're seeing. That means we're getting only a tiny fraction of what's emitted. How come?"

She shrugged. "Somehow the radiation can't get out."

"Come on," Zak said reasonably. "At 40,000 degrees?"

She nodded. "But put your hand on it, it's room temperature."

"So the radiation's from whatever's inside?"

She fidgeted, trying to enumerate possibilities. "I suppose so. Radiating at us, very weakly, through this . . . window?"

"A window we can't see through." Zak paced, face twisted with concentration.

"In visible light. The ultraviolet comes through, for some reason. It reflects ninety-nine percent of the visible light we give it, remember? And it's *not* a metal." She folded her arms.

"It refracts, too—hell, it does everything!" Zak was agitated. "We must be getting just a tiny fraction of the ultraviolet that's emitted from inside, or otherwise this ball would burn everything up in the lab. That makes no sense!"

"And it weighs as much as a person," she added. "A fat person."

"What's that imply?"

"I don't know. But it's another fact." Alicia plopped down in a lab chair, laughing at herself. "Usually making a list suggests something."

"Not this time," Zak said laconically.

"Anything this hot . . ."

"Yes?"

"Should be glowing, burning a hole . . ." Her hands fluttered uselessly.

"Well, it is, sort of. Burning a hole in the air, I mean. Making ozone."

"Hole. Right, I left that out." She got up and wrote on the board:

REFRACTION PROPORTIONAL TO PENETRATION DEPTH

She explained her earlier observations to Zak. "It looks like light coming in at slightly different angles to the sphere penetrates to different layers and gets refracted more strongly the farther in it goes."

"Huh," Zak said.

"Exactly." They sat some more and stared at the list and agreed that little of it made sense. She remembered hearing once that research types had a tolerance for ambiguity, for not knowing where they were headed while still keeping going. A curious view, she thought, for this was the part she most enjoyed: the mystery.

Usually in particle physics the biggest puzzles were *Why doesn't this damned thing work?* or *How can we get any meaning out of this confusion?* but beneath those lay deep imponderables. Was this thing such a fundamental object? She felt a tingling, pulse-quickening expectation.

When in doubt, sharpen the data. "Let's clear up the uncertainty in that blackbody measurement," she said, slapping her hands on her thighs to break her drifting mood.

"That'll take a darker lab." Zak looked around at the bay. "We're getting leakage."

"Agreed. Probably means running at night."

"I can set that up."

"Good. Let's sketch out what to do and then I've got other business. I was thinking, too, that perhaps we should look in the journals, see if any anomaly like this has ever turned up."

Zak's mouth twisted skeptically. "I doubt it."

"Me too. But we should look. I'll do a quick literature search."

Particle physics postdocs seldom read the journal literature except to find out whom to talk to and get the real dope. In seminars they rarely asked questions, not wanting to seem out of it. If they knew the subject well, though, they would challenge and probe. Talking about their own work convincingly was crucial, and a bit of bluster often worked. Nearly all experimenter postdocs had a favorite story about how they made a piece of gear or software by unstinting labor, just in time to keep the experiment going. Even as they told their tales, a rueful note crept in, for mere skill was not enough to get them up the next ascent in the profession; for that, they had to show independence, insight, intellectual grace. Nobody told them so, of course; it was part of the unspoken subculture of particle physics. Some never quite realized this; others caught on after their grunt labor went unrecognized, while a risk-taking postdoc got all the smiles.

Zak was different. Her grant could afford only one postdoc; he had stood out because, while he had many typical traits, he also showed intense loyalty. To succeed at RHIC demanded that a small outside team function like a well-oiled machine, quick with the ideas and ready to work harder than others.

She left the lab and headed for her office. Students thronged the physical sciences plaza, in their faux-casual, pricey splendor: sweatsuits, tube socks, glossy windbreakers, big-heeled white marathon shoes, warm-up jackets advertising designers' names, tank tops, baseball caps worn in the new style, bill forward. Mostly gear for working out, not as in working out a problem but as in sweat. She wondered why this generation knew terms like *deltoids, pectoralis major*, and *triceps* better than the names of the outer planets, while they walked little, thronged the campus elevators and escalators, and packed the parking lots with comfortable cars.

The Asian students were the best-dressed—or at least the most expensively. Often now the simple, hand-lettered signs stuck to campus walls and kiosks were in foreign, usually Asian, languages. Advertisers wanted only their own ethnicity, especially in the ads for rooms for rent and houses to share.

She had heard UCI sourly referred to as the University of Indochina. "Diversity" had come to mean Balkanization.

But in the divisions among students lay a deeper strategy. The administration practiced tactics of divide-and-conquer, turning each student faction into a client, supplicants to the ever-expanding executive corps who thought of themselves as "management," of faculty as workers and students as captive customers. In this they merely mirrored the national political style, a legacy of the Twen Cen.

She got to the fourth floor as the department afternoon tea began. She meant to snag some cookies and a cup of tea and keep going, but several of the particle experimenters wanted to hear about how the Core Element blew. She gave them the standard story, using the opportunity to feel out their reaction. A circle formed around her. They were sympathetic and probing, seeing it as a new unsolved problem, i.e., fresh meat. Postdocs and faculty joined in equally, but graduate students kept quiet.

The particle group considered itself an elite, a meritocracy in which everybody had a fair start. Underscoring that were their similar offices, use of first names even for the senior figures, and rigorously informal dress code. When she once pointed this out to a full professor, he shrugged and said, "Well, sure, naturally," in a tone implying that to think of social and psychological forces was un-physicist-like. Nobody spoke of such matters, but everybody learned the fine structure of the profession well before they took their final places in it.

Jonas Schultz, the grand old man of the experimenters, took her aside and asked, "How's this going to affect your observing schedule?"

"I'll try to make the next run, six months away."

"Is there anything I can do to help?" He was a handsome, graying, mild-mannered New Yorkish man, from the more genteel days of the field. She had a momentary impulse to tell him about the oddity she had in the lab, but caution prevailed.

"My team seems up to it, but thanks for asking. I might need to borrow some equipment."

"Just let me know," he said warmly. "We don't want this to hurt your progress toward tenure." The flip side of particle physicists' intense competition was their tribal loyalty.

Tenure: the Holy Grail in an age of dwindling science funding. To venture into particle physics in such an era was to court ceaseless anxiety. Undergraduates secretly feared that they weren't good enough compared to the giants of yore. Grad students feared burning up their time on experiments which would only marginally work out. Postdocs had to peer several years ahead, guessing the rewarding questions upcoming, then betting with their hours. In such rough weather she had (surprisingly, to her) gotten a faculty position. Not a single sniff from Stanford or Harvard, of course, so she had interviewed at three less prestigious universities, getting an offer from UCI alone.

Once here, Alicia had found that her anxiety level increased. The next height to scale was the wall of tenure; fail and there was nothing left but to quit, or try for a slot at a national laboratory. Even if she made tenure, beyond it lay the long climb through the ridges and crevasses of funding, getting your share of beamtime, and, as always, pursuing chances to network, network, network. Of course, she had liked every step of the way. Anybody who didn't would not be as good at the game and so was by now pursuing a productive career in stock analysis or routine technology.

Ignoring knocks on her door, she hammered away on her office computer, writing the report for Hugh Alcott. His questions seemed a long way off, somehow, the entire matter fading into the past, in comparison with the sharply outlined mystery she faced in the lab.

She quit halfway through and got some more tea from the cart on the fourth floor and came back, sat down, stared at the screen. She had learned while writing her doctoral thesis to back away when she got blocked writing, so she called up the UCI library data services menu. For an hour she negotiated through the labyrinth of reference sources, emerging triumphantly empty-handed: there were no references in the published physics literature to an eccentric object remotely like hers.

Yes, she thought, *hers*. Might as well be possessive about it. Then she got back to work on her report, e-mailed it to Alcott, and went back to the lab.

5

She wanted to stay home, read, maybe veg out before the TV, but Jill wasn't having any of that.

"You *said* you'd go to this mixer." Jill plopped down on Alicia's couch and tossed her microscopic abalone shell handbag aside. "I'm going to sit here and fume until you get ready."

"But I've got work to do and I'm tired and—"

"If you're tired, you shouldn't work. Boy, you intellectuals have to have everything spelled out for you."

"This is another singles' meat rack," Alicia accused.

"An unfortunate choice of phrase. We're just trying to meet likable strangers." Jill jabbed a polished maroon fingernail toward the bedroom. "Cover your body."

Alicia spent fifteen minutes searching for some clothes that did not Make a Statement until Jill intervened. She ended up in a blue dress, complaining, "But it's not really my best color." To which Jill shot back, "Who cares? It's men's favorite color. Don't you read *any*thing? You're not trying to date your*self*."

Alicia then dithered over jewelry, a choice not helped at all by her being unable to find most of it. This seemed like a general law: as soon as you moved something to a more logical, orderly place, the only thing you could remember was where it used to be and that you had decided to move it to a much better, really obvious place.

She finally "got herself presentable," as her father used to say, and Jill inspected the result. "Black shoes? You have a good red pair."

"Those are my fuck-me shoes. Not the signal I want to send."

"Ummm, granted. Let's go."

Alicia said, "Remember when gals we knew took condoms to these things?"

"That was way before our time, a mid-Twen Cen thing. Now I just rely on my personality. Keeps that dangerous semen where it belongs, in its container."

"Containers."

"I keep forgetting, there are two. I wonder why? They make a gazillion each."

"A guy thing. Always carry a backup."

They got to the mixer in good order. The social whirl south of L.A. was strung along the power ZIP codes of coastal towns, from Huntington Beach's 92649 to San Clemente's 92672, with Newport's 92660 the surest path to favor, and Laguna Beach's 92651 holding the All-County title for collective weirdness, artists, and media fame. Tonight's collision of anxieties was at Fashion Island, just inland from Newport Harbor. Lining the drive in from the Coast Highway were spindly phoenix palms with blue-tinged floodlights buried in their boles. The radiance picked out their green fronds swaying like great hula skirts in the salty, ocean-flavored breeze. A pus yellow searchlight poked up into the usual marine layer fog that hovered like gauze over the Four Seasons Hotel. They handed Alicia's Miata off to the valet and made their way through the usual obstacles, a sign-in barrier with stick-on name tags, singles' organization tables, and—as they rounded a corner—a body. The man lay faceup, shirt disheveled, something splashed over his hair.

Alicia gasped. "My God, is he dead?"

"Only socially. Drunk, I'd say."

Without hesitation Jill stepped over him. Alicia followed, and by the time they got down a long corridor, some men were trying to get the man to his feet. Apparently none of this excited much comment.

"Wait a sec." Alicia stepped out onto a patio.

Jill followed. "Classic anxiety smoker" was all the criticism she would voice, though her slanted mouth said the rest.

Alicia waved away the objection. She could *feel* the phenols and pyrenes raping the tender epithelial cells and the laboring cilia of their bronchi, the carbon monoxide and cyanide latching hungrily onto innocent hemoglobin, her virtuous hardworking heart heaving and lurching in chemical panic. They sang fruitlessly of her body's fragility in a world of malicious molecules, but *she needed it*, and who, after all, was in charge here?

Alas, it evaporated into the dry air all too quickly. She closed her eyes, sighed. Into the fray. Alicia had been to several of these, though not lately. This gave her some separation, and she found herself sitting back, two centimeters behind her eyes, taking in the show.

Women greeted each other in high-pitched, singsong voices, stretching their words into extra syllables: *Hi-i-i-i-e-e-e, h-o-o-o-w-w are yo-u-u-u?* Men reversed this, dropped into basso profundo, staccato grunts with curt nods: *Hey, hey. How ya doin'?* Women tried to connect, emoting and overshowing emotion. Men meeting each other were setting the pecking order, maybe throwing a mock punch or friendly insult. With their handshakes men overcame their urge to defend personal space; after all, centuries ago it came from showing that you weren't carrying a weapon. Alicia got both barrels as she came into the big, babble-filled reception.

"Alicia, where've you been *keeping* yourself?"

"Missed you, kid."

"My God, I figured you were either married or dead!"

"Or both," she replied flatly, but nobody paid any attention. The longer women had been apart and the closer they were, the higher their greeting tones. They leaned toward each other, talking face-to-face. Alicia saw the pattern, all right, and muted her own, but the strut and howl carried a compelling pleasure.

Men watched this as if witnessing a banshee ritual. Pointedly, they stood at angles to the greeting pairs, glancing around the room, hunters alive to the game.

Greetings done, everybody reverted to approximately normal tones. It made sense, she realized abstractly. Greetings were anxious, so the defensive move was to go back to your gender role. Women infantilized their voices, saying, *I won't harm you*, while men's deep tones said, *Don't make trouble.*

She surveyed the crop. Men in Orange County too often came in bright blazers, beltless slacks, shiny loafers, and cheerfully colored socks. Or else the George Will look. Mostly Caucasian men, of course, with a sprinkling of Asians. Some Brahmin-style Indians, a bit out of place. Three black men she could see from here, near the door. They all looked away from her when they noticed, the usual signal. They were patrolling for Caucasian women; if they'd wanted black, they would have gone somewhere farther north, maybe all the way to L.A., where there was a bumper crop.

"Hey, good to see you again," a reasonably well-dressed man two inches taller than her said.

"I'm sorry, I don't remember . . ." Which was the truth, but it at least served to get her off into a predictable conversational trajectory. In the first five minutes his conversation was quick, bright, easy. In the next twenty minutes his conversation was like somebody trained to sound very good for five minutes. His polished quips made you think he was quoting somebody else—and he probably was.

Suddenly hungry, she worked her way through some appetizers and swore that she could feel the blue dress get tighter. Jill was working through the crowd, but loyally circled back every quarter hour to check on Alicia's progress and give mini-pep talks. About the blue dress, which now seemed to be inching up Alicia's thighs like a sentient fungus, she said sardonically, "Look, men say, 'I wear a thirty-four,' but we say, 'I *am* a size eight.' What's that tell you?"

"That I'm probably a size nine," Alicia said grimly.

"Having any luck?"

"I wish people wouldn't steer the black men over to me. They have a trapped look in their eyes as they approach."

Jill nodded. "I'll put the word out again. I just wasted half an hour on a guy who thought the Styrofoam cooler was as great an invention as the wheel."

"Veins in the nose?"

"Yup, a drinker." Jill frowned. "Why do I attract them?"

"These socials are like climbing Mount Everest in a cocktail dress. The party carnivores smell weakness."

"Maybe the telltale beads of perspiration on the upper lip give us away?" Jill eyed the crowd.

"That, and we're not Class A lookers." Alicia had never thought of herself as even Class B. "Beautiful women know less about men than us, the uglies. They treat us differently."

Jill's mouth twisted sardonically. "It doesn't count that I can whip up a quick meal, nothing fancy, say, veal *aux champignons*, in two minutes?"

"Only after you're married, when of course it's too late."

"Why do we always come here full of optimism and leave depressed?"

Alicia said thoughtfully, "Because the men don't fit our dreams. We keep trying to see into them at first glance—"

"And instead we think we see through them." Jill sipped some wine and made a face. "See that guy? If I was in a mean mood, I'd say just from the expression on his face that he probably thinks a Volvo is part of a woman's anatomy. But he might be just fine."

"So go talk to him."

"See who he's chatting up? The black leather skirt and nose ring? Too bad Henry Ford put the buggy-whip makers out of business. They didn't stick around long enough for the recent lucrative market in S&M."

"You're not in the mood for this, are you?" Alicia said gently, hopefully.

"Okay, I'll go hit on him. As soon as the nose ring goes for another appetizer."

This took another quarter hour, but within another Jill was giving Alicia hand signals, smiling furiously, and ended up going off to dinner with the man. Alicia had no such luck. She stalled a bit, then left, stomach soured on cheap Chardonnay. She wasn't any good at this at all, she realized yet again. Something in her did not fit with the usual academic sort of man, so she succumbed to Jill's unsubtle poking and went to these awkward affairs.

A severe mismatch indeed. She was seriously out of step. Evolution had designed primate thought for effective socialization, the biologists said, but she was a dead flat failure at it. It was a marvel, really, that the same minds which caught the intricacies of mating and avoiding predators could fathom reality at all. Science was a recent human invention, difficult for all but a few; why was it now her principal refuge from a world she could barely understand?

6

Brad Douglas blinked and said with genuine shock, "Why didn't you tell me?"

"The fewer who knew, the better," Alicia said. Inevitably, Brad had wandered over to the U-magnet area in search of a tool, gotten interested in what was going on under all the tarps and screens, and seen what was up.

"Why? We could've studied as a team—"

"That's what we are doing," Zak put in.

"Brookhaven isn't a place to do open-ended research," Alicia said mildly. Zak had found Brad puzzling over the sphere. Without saying a word to him, Zak had called her in her office, and she had come right down. "It's a big tool made for a specific purpose."

"Yeah," Brad said, "particles. Plenty of people to help—"

"And get in the way," Alicia said.

"We had—*you* had—an obligation to show the other members of the BRAHMS team," Brad said firmly.

"Our agreement is to share data. This thing wasn't detected—it destroyed a detector."

Brad's hands cut the air in exasperation. "A lawyer's argument."

Alicia felt startled. Friends of the Earth, lawyers, mounting frustration, her first run as principal investigator, the safety shortcut, the smashing of the Core Element, the sphere—all linked, bringing her to this.

"I'm principal investigator on this research grant and I set policy," she said, hearing a wobble in her voice. *Be firm. This guy is just a graduate student, after all.* But her throat wasn't working right.

Zak came to her rescue. "We were thinking this through, didn't want to look stupid, making a big deal out of nothing."

Not really, Alicia thought, but okay—that element was there, too. She nodded.

Brad shook his head, a not-having-any expression hardening his face.

Zak persisted, keeping his voice light and casual, "Hell, we thought it was a fresh steel bubble."

Again, not really, but she could live with that. "Our working hypothesis, yes. An interesting solid-state effect. No big deal."

"Then why not just toss it?" Brad eyed her defiantly.

"We had to move it out of there anyway. It's heavy, hard to get a grip on. The magnet seemed a good way to handle it, keep it isolated." The logic sounded weak even to her, but her voice was firming up now.

Brad looked skeptical. "Hum. So . . . what is it?"

She shrugged. "Nothing about it makes sense."

"It's not iron, though," Zak said. "We did a spectral reflection analysis using the gas laser."

"So what is it?" Brad's tone was still flat, no-nonsense.

"Nothing clear. No lines for any metal I know." Zak bobbed his head, a gesture she recognized as mild modesty, one he must have picked up to conceal his own confidence in his ability. She recognized something of herself in that small nod, a nominal bow.

Brad's mouth twisted with frustration. "What if it's dangerous?"

She allowed herself a small smile. "Why would it be?"

"It blew open the beam line, didn't it?"

"Perhaps. Maybe this sphere wasn't the cause but a side effect."

"Of what?" Brad shot back.

She shrugged. "We don't know. It's important not to jump

to conclusions when you haven't a clue what's going on.''

"But caution—"

"Research is when you don't know what you're doing.'' Alicia took refuge from his intent gaze in an ancient cliché.

Zak said, "It's probably no big deal. Plenty of things turn up that are hard to explain but not exotic.''

"Were there any others?'' Brad asked and Alicia saw that he was stalling for time, trying to figure out where he should go with this.

"No,'' Zak said.

"You looked?''

"Hey, it was right at the focus of the Core Element, where the beams intersect.''

"So?''

Alicia said crisply, "Occam's razor—prefer the least hypothesis. At the focus, because that's where the energy was to drive the formation process. We'd seen a drop in collisions for more than an hour before we finally shut down and went to look. Probably the sphere formed and blocked most of the beam flux. One sphere alone explains that. Plus, with people checking everything out on BRAHMS, they'd have noticed another even if we didn't.''

Brad twisted his mouth again, as if taking distasteful medicine. "I still think you should've told the rest of them.''

"That's a policy decision. I make those.''

Brad sat on an assembly table and shook his head. *Time for some carrot. Stick won't do it alone,* she thought. "Zak, thanks for your help. I'll handle it.''

"Huh? Oh.'' Zak had been shuffling uncomfortably from one foot to another and now looked relieved at a plain invitation to be missing. He left by the side door.

"Brad, I wanted to clarify the problem before I took up your time with it,'' she said mildly.

"I suppose I can understand that,'' he said guardedly.

"As well, you are vitally important in rebuilding the Core Element.''

"Yeah, but it's, well, getting kind of boring.''

"Tedium goes with the territory.''

"Well, there's more interesting stuff . . ."

Was he hinting at something? "Let's get you some more pay for doing it, then."

"How?"

One of the minor features of the University of California system lay in its rituals and examinations, whereby a student working on a doctorate could pass his candidacy examination and then be eligible for a higher grade of research assistant. Brad had finished all the required course work and was doing research full-time now, supported by her Department of Energy grant. Usually graduate students delayed taking the candidacy exam until they were very nearly through with their thesis, out of a mixture of stage fright and laziness. The closer one was to a solid result, the less the chances of flunking the exam.

She explained this to him, trying to not make it sound like any kind of payoff for keeping quiet. Though, of course, it was for his doing as he was told. To her surprise, he shook his head. "I'll take the exam, sure. Point of it will be what?"

"I was thinking that your thesis would be a description of the technical problems in building the Core Element."

"I want some more physics in it than that."

"We'll get more data at Brookhaven—"

"Sure, if they let us come back."

"What do you mean?"

"That." He pointed at the U-magnet. "It could mean a lot of trouble, for all we know."

"You're exaggerating—"

"I'd like to work on it with you. Do something different for a change."

So, the exam *and* the sphere. The kid knew how to bargain. Fairly subtle, too. "We can use the help. But that doesn't mean you can slack off on the Core Element."

"Oh, I won't," Brad said with sudden eagerness. His cagey reserve vanished and he peppered her with questions about the sphere. The list of experimental points she had chalked on the board three days before was still there—a startling lapse of security, she realized ruefully. She took him through it and could see the fire of curiosity kindle in him as she spoke.

"Wow, this is *strange*."

"Strange and secret," she said carefully. "We want to have a clear understanding of whether this is something truly new before it, well, gets away from us."

He took it metaphorically, but she meant it literally. A note from Hugh Alcott in her e-mail, when she got back to her office, sharpened the issue.

> A review of the video monitor tapes shows you and a postdoc doing something with a permanent magnet. Could you explain this? It looks like you're lifting something out of the beam line. Nothing in your report about this.
>
> Hugh

She went and got some tea and generally milled around the department, chasing details and paperwork, letting her jittery mind subside. Best to answer fast, she saw. Casual, dismissive.

> I think you're looking at Zak Nguyen and me freeing debris from the beam line. There was Core Element debris in it. We decided to pull it out with the permanent magnet, since some of it was heavy and we didn't want to waste time taking it all apart.
>
> Best to Tom and the gang,
>
> Alicia

There, that might put them off. Might. Those damn cameras! She had completely forgotten about them. Better not try to start a sideline holding up banks.

7

Zak twiddled with the knobs on the computer display, then typed commands into the keyboard. "This dashed line is the newest data, from several days of data accumulation. Our earlier result is the solid line."

Alicia bent closer. The two curves were very similar, to her relief; at least they hadn't made some foolish mistake. Zak had run the experiment for five solid days, carefully capturing every glimmer of ultraviolet from the sphere, allowing no contaminating light in.

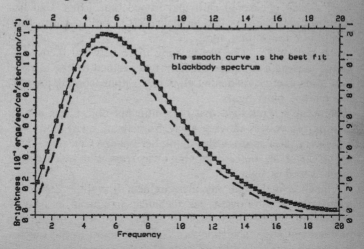

The smooth curve is the best fit blackbody spectrum

But there were differences. The newer, dashed curve was shifted slightly down toward the red end of the spectrum and was shorter, too. "Something wrong with our first curve," Alicia muttered to herself.

"I don't think so," Zak said.

"It's offset from the later one."

"The difference is real." He looked at her intently, as if he had to quell her doubts with a steady stare. "I checked into the sources of error. None is big enough to explain this."

"The whole second curve is moved to lower frequencies. Lower temperature."

Zak gave her the believe-me stare again. "It's real. I've got it all here." His lab notebook lay open, offering meticulous inked entries in several colors: blue for data, black for calculations, red for conclusions, a few crossouts in an ugly bile green.

"Suppose it's true. The temperature of this black body distribution is falling?"

"Yes," he said, pacing despite his obvious self-control. He wore a neat checkered shirt and ironed blue jeans. Had he spruced himself up for this moment? "It's cooling down. But it could be red-shifted, too."

"A red shift?" The words hung there between them. An object moving away gave off light that seemed to lose a fraction of its energy, reddening all colors. Atoms coming toward one emitted bluer light.

But Zak's result said that the entire hot object was either cooling off or was moving away from them, away from the laboratory, at a speed—She shook her head. "Can't be. That would mean the source is moving away from us at two percent of the speed of light."

"Right. But I think my measurement is right," Zak said adamantly. He followed her technical judgment in nearly everything, but he knew when to defend his own work; good professional style, she thought. "It's not warm to the touch. But *inside* it there's a black body at 40,000 degrees K."

Some blunder, she guessed. "I've got to go over this."

He relaxed, sagging onto a work stool. "Nothing could make me happier."

She smiled. "Thought you were crazy for awhile?"

"Something like that."

She felt a burst of affection for him. "Living with ambiguity, Zakster," she said, patting him on the shoulder. "Sometimes it's a bitch."

The shift in the curves was real. She spent two days going over the data, sometimes calling up the raw returns from the counters and counting photons one at a time, looking for some mistake. Maybe in tabulating the individual counts far out in the wings, where the effect was largest but the flux of light was smallest? This was where an error would hurt them most.

She looked hard, then looked again. There were none.

Zak worked beside her and said little, but she could sense his rising excitement. Finally he said, "That's all the data."

"Congratulations."

"I would feel better if I understood anything."

"Sometimes understanding is the booby prize. Having found it, that's the thing."

They both knew that and for a moment they simply stood and looked at the two curves. She gestured at the list of puzzling results, still on the board. Brad had come in and kibitzed but knew that this was, for the moment at least, their show alone. Nobody had ventured any explanations.

"Y'know, this could conceivably be a red shift. There's the Hubble shift, of course . . ." she said distantly.

"But that's a cosmological shift." Zak sat on the edge of their work table beneath the pale luminesce of the high bay lamps. "Caused by the expansion of space-time."

"Maybe this has some such explanation?" she ventured.

"A ball that's cosmological? If it were something like a black hole, well—" He strode to the blackboard and scribbled an equation for the size of a black hole below their list.

"See, a black hole with a mass of 100 kilos would be smaller than a proton!" Zak tossed the chalk from hand to hand. "Nope, nothing cosmological here."

Alicia had considered the same idea and rejected it, but it was good to let Zak run through the same logic. "We need help."

"I am afraid so." His elation was burning off, his face sobering.

They had also tried to get an image out of the accumulated light, getting only a smooth glow. That was consistent with a hot object with no features.

Alicia said, "What was it Newton said? 'I frame no hypotheses.' Good advice when you haven't got a clue."

"Who can we ask? I mean, we don't even know what field to ask about. I'd say it must be some weird condensed-matter phenomenon."

She ran through the list of her colleagues at UCI. Good, solid physicists, true. But a trifle too conventional for this weirdness. Some, she knew from departmental politics, instinctively awaited all new ideas with three nails and a hammer. More important, she didn't want word of this to get around.

"Think I'll take a little ride to clear my thoughts," she said.

8

Shortly after she had first moved out from the East, one morning without thinking she went down to the beach to watch the sunrise. As the truth literally dawned on her, she saw how far she had come, to a place that was the end of America. It had taken awhile to get the feel of this raw land lying compliantly in alkaline, probing light. L.A.'s horizontals mocked and oddly mimicked New York's verticals, each framing humans in pressing, insistent geometry. The only true constant here was the rate at which California disappeared beneath concrete, ushering in its own sequels. Classic strategy: subdivide and conquer. Maybe it was no accident that just as the frontier closed, the movie studios opened their doors, taking possession of the national imagination, the future.

Now the slumbering natural world lay hidden beneath the hurry-scurry. Driving up the 5 Freeway, she dodged off on the 57 and carried out a flanking movement toward Pasadena along the 10. Not direct, but fast. She ran into jams, even though it was only early afternoon. On part of the 10 that looked like an infinite parking lot stretching to the Pacific, she slid down an off-ramp and onto a "smart street" that monitored flow and intricately adjusted traffic lights and freeway-entry meters. She did not have one of the "pathfinder" systems inside cars that gave drivers the latest data on jams ahead; half of all congestion came from accidents or breakdowns. All effective, she supposed, but nobody had figured out where to park all that traffic once it arrived.

She parked illegally and walked into the heart of Caltech. Spanish galleries framed the long grassy promenade. The stretching perspective was dotted with pepper trees sighing in a hard dry breeze that whispered in from the desert baking to the east. Two Californias collided at the end of the grassy ribbon, where a rectangular library reared like an exclamation point above the nostalgia of early days, announcing with its severe Euclidean smoothness the no-nonsense present. Inside a long Moorish building marked EAST BRIDGE the arched motif continued in high white segments above floors of big brown tiles. She passed under wrought-iron gratings that accented the atmosphere, framing a room of the latest journals. The ceramic scent of aging plaster and tile, with its absorbing hush, reminded her of a chapel. She needed some fresh illumination, all right, but not the kind that comes through the west window of a church.

At Caltech physics was about attacking fundamental problems. Useful, correct, but ultimately unsurprising work was scorned. This was the citadel of Richard Feynman and Murray Gell-Mann; legends stalked the halls. She stopped, teetering on the brink of retreating to UCI. What if the sphere was just some metallic oddity? She could have made some simple mistake somewhere, a dumb way of fooling herself. To bring in others could open her to harsh derision.

Get a grip, girl. She walked on.

Just beyond the Theoretical Astrophysics Interaction Room, with its coffee machine and stacks of recent preprints, lay the offices of well-known physicists: Thorne and Blandford and the rest. She hesitated. Bright types, authorities, but what would they make of her story? Implausible on the face of it, and with her quick-and-dirty at Brookhaven on top of it all . . . She had jumped in her Miata and zoomed up here without thinking it through.

Maybe somebody a bit more humble? At Caltech that would be hard.

Rooms were clogged with big computing systems. Every profession now had its "quants," people who could handle the dizzying digital wilderness, interpret it for their peers.

"Crossover" was the hot buzzword. Computer hackers worked with organic chemists to study molecular structure. Medical school graduates worked with electrical engineers to design neural networks that worked something like the brain. The new technologies dissolved disciplines.

From the corridor she could hear people talking to their computers in customized pidgin. At its best, the new tech devoured complication and delivered simplicity. Telephone answering machines were so programmable and "smart," they now projected the listeners' style, not the machine's design contrivance. They could sound like a stodgy British butler's reserved politeness or a brisk secretary asking snappy questions—or even like a robot, which it was.

She walked around some corners, into the section where Thorne held sway. Two-to-an-office postdocs peered out at her curiously, probably wondering what a black face was doing here, she thought. Beyond was an assistant professor's office, Room 146, Max Jalon.

She peeked around the doorjamb and saw a thin, tall man in steel gray slacks and soft, button-down blue shirt. Wire frame glasses perched on a narrow nose and he absently brushed long brown hair back from his high forehead as he wrote on a yellow pad. The office was not the usual piles-of-paper theorists' haunt. Magazine boxes held crisply labeled papers on STRING TH, MATH BKGND, and OBS.

Well, at least he knew something about style. She had always rather liked men who were neater than she was, though that was not difficult. At UCI she had taken a moment to look up the Caltech catalog, which listed Jalon's specialty areas as "gravitational waves, cosmology, astrophysics." OBS probably meant observations, a sign that he was not another totally abstract math type. Okay, stop dithering. Take the plunge.

"Uh, Dr. Jalon?"

He didn't even look up. "Go away."

"I have something that might interest you."

"Ten minutes." When she stepped inside the door, he added, "I'll see you then," eyes still on the page, hand scribbling.

She spent the ten minutes irritably stalking the corridors, touring the journal library, taking in the obscure joys of recent published papers displayed on gray steel racks. By the time she came back she was fuming but made her voice say dryly, "Do I get ten for ten?"

He finally glanced up at her, then glanced back. Surprise at seeing a black woman here? His mouth broadened into a half-smile. "You're a student?"

"Thanks for the unintended compliment. No, I'm a professor from UCI."

They got through the usual sniffing-out of each other in a few minutes. Her edgy opening move, "Can you keep a secret?" he countered with "Can you keep a promise? Tell me *all* of it."

She had opted for a here's-a-mystery strategy, showing him pictures of the sphere, listing the same properties she had on the blackboard at UCI, finally springing where she got it. He sat with his Doc Martens-clad feet up on his desk the whole time, hands behind his head, asking nothing until she got to the uranium collisions. Then he quickly sucked the relevant facts and assumptions from her with clipped questions, finishing with a small smile. "And you got this away without telling anybody?"

"I figured it for a metal bubble or something, just an oddity—"

"Nope, that story won't play."

"What?"

"You smelled something interesting and swiped it. 'Fess up."

"You're jumping to conclusions without—"

"Tell me I'm wrong and I'll apologize."

Despite herself, she laughed. "My God, you're annoying."

He abruptly sprang to his feet in one fluid movement, Doc Martens slamming down on the tile floor. She looked up into an amused face with one sardonically arched eyebrow. "Then I have my answer. Come on over to the Greasy for coffee and then let's have a look at this thing."

9

She had imagined this moment, when she would whip away the shrouds—presto!—and show the disbelieving world her, well, whatever it was.

Max did not play to the drama of the moment; in fact, he seemed unaware of it. He simply peered at the sphere and snapped off a long series of questions: "What did you measure? How accurate are these numbers? What sources of error might there be?" Only then did he tap the sphere thoughtfully and nod.

"You've ruled out everything ordinary, so . . ."

"Yes?" she asked quietly.

"So it's extraordinary." He grinned. "Just as you said. That doesn't mean it's significant, just that it's interesting."

"I hope there isn't something simple I've forgotten."

"Doubt it. What's that smell?"

"Oh, the ozone. I forgot to mention that."

She told him and he leaned in between the magnet poles, looking closely at the sphere. "That ultraviolet you're detecting, it's very weak. And this thing"—he rapped on the sphere—"it feels hard, like glass. So whatever's giving off the ultraviolet isn't heating it up."

"No, the sphere is the same temperature as the lab."

"Damned funny. Notice how the air, well, feels different right next to it?"

She leaned in from the other side. "How so?"

"I don't know, just a sensation, like a . . . well, a rippling, as I do this.'' He passed his hand over the sphere.

She moved her right hand carefully in the space and moved it slowly between the big magnet poles. She did feel something, a faint tug as she pulled her hand away. ''I hadn't noticed that before.''

''Maybe it's new.''

''I would have felt it before.''

''How long has it been since you stuck your hand in there?''

She realized it had been at least a week, maybe more. The strangeness of the thing had made her wary, she suddenly saw. Brad and Zak, too, used distant diagnostics to study the sphere, careful not to disturb the photodetectors and electronics once they were set up. Controlled experiments led to detachment. Had they all missed this small deviation?

She frowned. If this thing were changing, all her measurements might alter, too. ''The high temperature, we found that weeks after the first UV measurements.''

Max looked blank. ''Yes?''

''What if it wasn't there before?''

He grinned. ''Experimenters hate things that won't sit still. But the world doesn't, usually.''

She was thinking this through when he started for the door, calling back to her, ''I think best in the library.''

''Me, the lab.''

''Good. See you later in your office, okay?''

This result she had not expected: very nearly a brush-off. She policed up the lab a bit, irked, straightening the usual tossed-aside tools and clearing the working surfaces of trash. This was automatic—therapy.

Max had annoyed her with his usual theorist's mannerisms. Most theorists were pavement people, city types, and experimenters were more outdoorsy. He dressed to type, favoring the classic tight button-down look. (And herself? At home she had to make herself get out of jeans every month or two. Without Jill as Fashion Cop, she would give way utterly, wearing clothes mostly because nudity was illegal.) Theorists gained status young, like genius musicians—noted as wizards at the blackboard, advancing in the field with collaborations that changed faster than movie stars divorced. Experimenters were more monogamous, working in long-lived teams clustered around their detectors. Not true of her, though; she was a loner and knew it.

Among the particle theorists the highest status attached to the field theorists who developed new models to bring more order to the particle zoo. Below them came the even more mathematical types, whose work often seemed abstruse and not intuitive, to her; it lacked the Right Stuff of gut-sure physics. Below them came the phenomenologists, which merely meant those who tried to fit existing theory to the bewildering thicket of experimenters' data. Max was of that tribe, as nearly as she could gather.

Experimenters usually avoided theorists and vice versa. "Theorists believe anything on graph paper" was a common putdown. If an experiment's data contradicted an existing theory, usually experimenters thought that probably something was wrong with the experiment. Theorists would think the error lay in the theory. But only if left in their own groups; put members of both tribes in the same room and they would act as if the reverse were true.

There were odd little tribal patterns, too; experimenters' daughters often married theorists, for example. Nobody could explain this, but nobody thought it remarkable, either.

She shook her head, glanced again at the sphere, and turned off the lab lights. Max was a waste of time, she was suddenly sure of it.

She went back to her office in the gathering gray twilight. The telephone was ringing as she fidgeted open the sticky lock on her door. It was Dave Rucker from Brookhaven. She glanced at her wristwatch; nearly 9 P.M. there.

"Alicia, Hugh Alcott wanted me to make this call." Tight, controlled, no preliminaries. "His review panel just finished. It's pretty late here, but I wanted to get to you about a serious problem. Hugh's panel thinks you took something important out of the accident area."

"Sure, just broken—"

"No, more than that. I've looked at the tapes and I have to

say I agree with him. There was something in that magnet assembly, wasn't there?''

"Uh, well, yes. We're studying it. I don't really think it was the cause—"

"That's for Hugh's guys to decide."

"I thought it was just an interesting piece of debris."

"Debris? A ball?"

"What else could it be?"

"That's for Hugh to decide."

"Look, Dave, I have to admit you're right—the thing is odd. When I took it, I had no idea how odd." That much at least was quite true.

"Even more reason why—"

"I figure we won't understand why the pipe blew, or why the uranium counts started dropping off, without understanding this thing first."

"Exactly why we want it here."

"We're right in the middle of extensive studies to—"

"Whatever it is, it's Laboratory-owned. Alicia, I can't block for you on this."

She thought furiously. Counterpunch. "How about my data?"

"What?"

"Remember? The uranium data must be partially processed by now. I want to see it."

"I'm not sure it's done."

"Then make sure."

"Stick to the point. The rules, our contract, they make it clear. Whatever that object is, it's Lab property."

"I'm afraid we can't give it up right now, Dave. I'll be happy to confer with you guys—"

"The hell with that. I can't let you walk off with—"

"The Core Element is UCI property, and this thing was smack in the middle of the wreckage."

"That doesn't matter a damn. It's vital to figuring out—"

"Can't we compromise on this? I'll share data—"

"You aren't on an equal footing here, Alicia. There's the earlier violation of the safety review procedures."

She bit her lip. "Okay, maybe I forgot to fill in all the paperwork."

"It's a lot worse than that. Hugh says your calculations, the numerical simulation of radioactive decay products, the charts—it's all bogus."

First rule: admit nothing. "That's his view. Look, even a back of the envelope calculation shows that there won't be enough residual radioactivity to fry a fly."

"I know, we all know—but the lawyers don't. That's why we go through these motions, Alicia. But you endanger the entire process if you, well"—she could hear him teeter on the verge of the next word—"*fake* the safety analysis."

"I'll stand behind the final result."

"Safety reviews aren't about final results, they're about the process."

"I'm a results type, Dave."

"Look, Alicia, I'm trying to be the diplomat here. Hugh, he wants your scalp."

"I'm willing to cooperate on scientific issues. But I must finish my own study."

"Hugh's climbing the walls."

"Let him. Maybe build a spiderweb while he's up there."

"Sarcasm isn't the way to—"

"And pressure tactics aren't, either. I'm in the middle of delicate experiments here right now and I don't have time for—"

"I'm instructed, then"—his voice had suddenly turned stiff, cold—"to inform you that we shall go through your superiors."

"Let me know when you find some," she said and hung up.

10

The safety review. She had forgotten to get back to it.

She sat at her desk as night fell outside, the soft yellow glow of the coastline seeping through the ivory haze. She fumed at herself for forgetting her simple paperwork dodge, the damned safety forms, allowing Hugh a handy lever to pry up the lid on this. After all, a vague blur on a videotape was suggestive, no more. But to the heart of a true bureaucrat, a paper infraction was raw meat.

She played over in her mind the possible avenues Brookhaven would use to get at her and did not hear the first knock at the door. She opened it and was startled to see Max, beaming happily. She had completely forgotten him.

"You found something," she guessed to cover her surprise.

"A long shot, but a shot. I saw a talk about something like this a few years ago and tracked down the author. Turns out he has a whole book on the subject."

"Huh? People have seen this before?"

"No no, this was all theory. I think"—he paused for effect, half-sitting on her desk, arms folded, head tilted up at a rakish angle—"you've got an Einstein-Rosen bridge."

"What's that?"

"In popular culture it's a wormhole. But the class is more general. Any deformation in space-time that is Lorentzian— that is, transforms like special relativity—fits the bill. I think you've found a stable form."

"Wormholes are shortcuts through space and time. This isn't a hole, it's solid."

He nodded happily. "That's what makes it even better. I got the idea from that funny ripple effect, when you slide your hand around. That's a *tidal* effect."

"What? How could it be? The thing's small, weighs maybe a hundred kilograms."

"Whatever holds it together is strong stuff. It curves the space-time around it."

"That's crazy." Her hopes for this guy were fading. Nonsense stuff about wormholes wasn't what she wanted.

"I looked around in the literature. There's a good book, *Lorentzian Wormholes* by Matt Visser. Theorems, discussion, everything. He doesn't know how to make them, of course— that's your department. They *might* be formed in regions of intense gravitational fields, since there the highly curved space-time manifold *might* allow nontrivial topologies to form."

"Might," she said soberly. No stopping a theorist on the wing, so she let him run while she kept her thoughts to herself. He went on about how the uncertainties in all this came from the crucial crackup of Twen Cen physics: attempts to merge the century's two great theories, Einstein's relativity and quantum mechanics, yielded a tantalizing, trackless wasteland of puzzles, messy inconsistencies, and flat-out incalculables. But Visser showed that to hold up at all—and be of reasonable size—the bridges envisioned by Einstein and Rosen had to have exotic building materials. Matter with negative energy density, whereas ordinary matter had positive energy.

When she sniffed with disdain, Max said quickly, "But negative energy density *exists*. You know the Casimir effect?"

"No." More theoretical hand-waving? She should have thoroughly checked out this guy first.

"It shows that if you have a small metal box, the space inside can have a net negative energy density."

"That's crazy."

"Not so," he said, cheerily oblivious to her expression. "The metal keeps out electromagnetic waves, right? Make the box small enough, the effect gets large. The missing waves depress the effective energy density inside the box. Do it enough, you get a negative energy.''

''How small a box?''

She had to admire how casually he tossed off, ''Oh, maybe as big as a proton.''

''A proton!''

''Sure, but that's just an in-principle argument, proof of principle. Point is, there's nothing crazy about making a bridge that can hold itself together and sit there in your lab.''

''That's another question. You're talking about holes in space-time, but this thing is a solid.''

''Stuff made of negative energy density might feel solid, too.'' He jabbed a finger at her. ''You can't say it's made of ordinary atoms, can you?''

''No, but—''

''No atomic line emission, no lattice like a crystal?''

''No, but—''

''Then that question's open. Nobody, but *nobody*, has any idea what such stuff looks like, feels like.''

''Look, I appreciate your coming down here and having a try, but—''

''I know, I know.'' He held both hands up, palms out. ''But I can make a prediction. Try a stress meter test and you'll measure that tidal force.''

She blinked. ''How so?''

''It should drop off fast, as the inverse cube of the distance from the sphere.''

''That's . . .'' She stopped to ponder how the experiment might work.

''Crazy?'' He gave her the grin again, which was starting to get irritating. ''Maybe just crazy enough to do the job.''

''Just crazy enough to waste a lot of my time.''

''You have another appointment?''

Yeah, she thought, *with Brookhaven's lawyers.* ''You know, when I brought you down here, I thought you'd look over the data, think of some exotic material it could be made of—''

"I did," he said brightly. "Just more exotic than you planned on."

After he left, she sat in the lab and thought over his remarks. It was early evening and her stomach rumbled, but things had moved so fast she felt a need to sit still and work the ideas around in her mind.

She was more convinced than ever that Max was a waste, his ideas fanciful. But if there was a definitive experiment, she would do it. Data always overruled theory. She might learn something new, anyway.

It took nearly a week to set up the stress analysis and then a full week to get it to work. Brad and Zak pitched in. Zak delayed for a few days the vacation to Mexico he had planned with his parents. To her surprise, they had dutifully agreed and visited the lab, seeming awed at how far their son had come from their tailor shop.

The undergraduates kept plugging away at restoring the Core Element, and she had to shepherd that, as well as keep up with her 3-B lectures, the homework, office hours, the usual. The department chairman, Onell, was after her again to show up for the excruciating Minority Mentorship committee meetings. She didn't answer her e-mail and managed to dodge him in the corridors. Hiding out in her lab helped. She came in early and stayed late and ignored Jill's calls. Their last outing had been a farce and she was not willing to brave the social gauntlet quite yet.

Particle experimenters learned skills in the three big areas: designing experiments, building detectors, and sifting data. Specialize, sure, but know all three—that she had learned early. Versatile physicists rose; "desk types" or "floor physicists" stayed where they were. Most of them, she suspected, wanted it that way.

Adaptability came in handy now. She had never thought about how to measure a gravitational stress before and learned a lot by talking to Riley Newman, a senior professor who had made a high-accuracy measurement of the gravitational constant, G. His method used delicate, tiny torsional pendulums.

Their periods fell the farther they were from a mass, an effect she would only have to measure to one part in a thousand to check Max's assertion. Newman's gear was portable and could do the job.

The task looked easy and proved otherwise. Alicia kept Max informed, asking just how precise a measurement he thought would be decisive. She was busy with Physics 3-B and would have handed the project off to Zak Nguyen, but he had delayed his family's long-planned vacation as long as their tickets would allow, so he took off for two weeks. This was just as well; he and Brad had rubbed each other the wrong way several times in the last week. Quick, assertive, Brad kept intruding on Zak's patient methods. Worse, Brad shortcut to get a quick feel for results, whereas Zak carefully framed every move, so there were few surprises. Brad wanted to spend more time on the sphere, less on the Core Element. When he left, Alicia could tell Zak was glad to get a break both from the lab and from Brad. Still, she found it odd not to have his steady presence.

His absence sent Brad into high gear. She used him as a general gofer while setting up Newman's rig. As usual, there were plenty of vexing details to go wrong. The magnetic field complicated matters, but late one afternoon she and Brad pieced together the data and plotted it on the blackboard. The gravitational tidal force around the sphere dropped off cleanly, inversely as the distance cubed.

"What the hell can it mean?" Brad asked.

"That we've found a very odd object indeed. It's spherical, but gives us a tidal force that means it has a lopsided mass distributed inside somehow." She was tired but strangely happy. She had not seen Max since his visit, though they had talked by telephone and exchanged terse e-mail queries. This would be fun to tell him.

"That theory guy, he predicted this?" Brad asked skeptically.

"He did indeed" came a voice from the distant shadows of the lab.

Max. She was startled as he walked into the lab spotlights

illuminating the U-magnet. "I came in half an hour ago, but I wanted to see you at work," he said. "I just sat in the back."

"How did you know—"

"You said you were nearly done. I'm due to give a seminar at UCSD tomorrow, thought I'd drop by."

For all the rivalry between theorists and experimenters, she derived an unclouded pleasure in stepping him through the experiment, showing the sharp, clear data. In a world beset by people and their endlessly warring opinions, their heartfelt passions, a firm foundation in fact, scrupulous fact, was welcome.

She could see the lines of concern deepen in his face as she led up to the final result. A theorist awaiting a test of his prediction was vaguely like a prisoner on trial with the jury out. The prisoner knew whether she was guilty, so she hoped the jury would get it wrong if guilty and get it right if she was innocent. In science the jury of Nature was always right, though one had to be careful to ask it exactly the right question. The predicter had to await a verdict, not knowing whether she was innocent or guilty, so there was genuine suspense as the foreman of the jury rose to speak—

"By damn!" Max grinned. "A lopsided mass inside, all right—internal structure we can't see." They all beamed and Max asked a few questions about details, breaking off to say, "No chance this is just some coincidence?"

She laughed. "This is much too clear an effect. Anyway, coincidence is God's way of remaining anonymous."

"Great." Max's unalloyed joy was a pleasure in itself.

"A prediction fulfilled—rather a rarity," Alicia said.

"I don't get it," Brad said, arms folded, leaning skeptically forward to peer at the data. "We've spent days checking this out, fine. It's a pretty peculiar thing we got here. But a *wormhole*?"

"Exotic objects require exotic explanations," Max said.

"It's spitting UV! What's at the other end?"

"A star, I'd say," Max answered blithely.

Alicia smiled. This was a classic theorist's casual lure, tossing off a snap judgment. Extra points if it was, like this one, particularly outrageous.

"An ultraviolet star?" Brad said dubiously.

"Not ultraviolet seen from outside. This wormhole could be inside a star, where it's hotter."

"Why?"

"Most of the galaxy's mass is tied up in stars. If this wormhole opened up near one, it could fall in."

"Seems unlikely," Brad said. Alicia wondered if he was trying to make his mark by being hard to convince. His chance to shine, since Zak was off on vacation. Indeed, he had been working quite hard recently, too.

"It is, you're right. Or maybe somehow a wormhole wants to open up where there's a local depression in the gravitational potential. Stars fit the bill."

"Sounds like a lot of guessing to me," Brad sniffed.

Max gave Brad a thin, tolerant smile that quickly sank from view. "Granted, but to figure this out, we need to make leaps."

Alicia had to respect Brad's indifference to Max's position; a good sign in a student, though often a quick route to a momentary humiliation. "We're all guessing here anyway," she said.

Max sketched some numbers on the blackboard. "Say it's a star like ours, pretty typical as stars go. Then it's got lots of light rattling around in it . . ."

He jotted down symbols Alicia vaguely recalled from her few courses in astronomy. She knew that light took decades to make its way from the sun's core out to the surface, bouncing around among the compressed atoms. Max rearranged his equation, then turned to Brad. "How many photons are you guys getting out of that sphere, per second?"

Brad had to look up the number and while he did Max went through his steps on the blackboard, ending up with an expression for how many photons of UV would have to come through the other end of the wormhole. It was a simple idea, really. If the wormhole opened in the blue-hot interior of a star, then light would shine through. "But we can't even *see* the light," Alicia said.

"Yeah, that bothered me," Max said. "But suppose the

other end's not the same size as this. Nothing says it has to be."

Brad came back with the number, a bit less than a million photons per second. Max put this number in his equation and wrote $\sim 10^{-4}$ CM. on the blackboard. "Tiny," he reflected. "No bigger than a dust mote."

Alicia shook her head. "So it's a speck on the other side, but a bowling ball here?"

"Ummm, I guess so," Max said.

"Calculations like this don't prove much," Brad said, echoing Alicia's thoughts.

"Particularly because," she said slowly, "you've skipped the obvious. If this is a wormhole, how come we can't go through it? Or the star's hot interior—why isn't it spewing out here?"

Max nodded, tossing his chalk into the tray. "Must be the stuff it's made of. All we know is that *if* a wormhole can exist, pretty exotic material has to hold it open. That's what's giving us this tidal force. Could be, such stuff doesn't let ordinary matter pass through it, but does let light through."

"Ummm," Alicia said, trying to be polite. "Still sounds like we're just making this up as we go along."

"We are." Max grinned. "Invent, then check. It's really the only way to make progress."

Brad scowled. "Doesn't explain much."

"I'm wondering if that's also a gravitational shift," Max said, still seeming unbothered by Brad's acerbic tone. "You mentioned early on that you had thought maybe you were seeing a red shift, rather than something cooling off."

"We abandoned that idea. I think it's cooling," Alicia said cautiously. Ideas were winging around a bit too fast.

She vaguely recalled that light, climbing up from the Earth to the moon, got redder. The effect had been measured using lasers. She thought of it as light getting sort of tired out and knew that was wrong, but that was a handy way to remember it. If the other end of the wormhole were buried deep in a star, then in getting here it would climb a steep gravitational hill and look weaker to their instruments. She tried to get a picture of this in her mind and failed.

"Could be, could be . . . though I'll admit"—Max crisply jotted more symbols on the board—"that doesn't work too well, either. It turns out, see, that to get that big a gravitational shift, you'd have to be near a black hole. Something that's really compressed, at the bottom of a steep gravitational well. Ordinary stars won't do."

"Why in the world should we have any faith in this idea, then?" Alicia asked.

Max shrugged. "Theory doesn't have to be right. It just has to be interesting."

Alicia had always hated this it's-just-artistic-taste way of looking at science, but she could see why he was making light of his troubles. "Give us the number, then," she said. "What's it take to make a gravitational red shift of—what was Zak's number?"

"Two percent of the speed of light," Brad said. "One hell of a shift."

"That requires . . . ummmm . . . about ten thousand times the mass of the sun," Max said, writing out the relation and underlining the result.

"Isn't there supposed to be a black hole at the center of our galaxy?" Alicia asked.

"It's supposed to be maybe a few million times a sun's mass," Max said. "So our wormhole pops out there?"

"Sounds pretty shaky," Brad said.

"Yeah." Max tossed the chalk into the tray again, snapping it in two. "Big problems we've got."

Alicia pointed to a sign she had nearly forgotten sticking to a spot on the wall above a chugging vacuum pump. It was copied from the Cavendish Laboratories of Cambridge. In archaic type, it said:

1. Do not choose the topics for scientific investigation simply because they are fashionable.
2. Never fear the scorn of theorists.

3. To see what has not been seen before, look where no one has looked before.

"Nearly a century old, but these rules still work." She looked at Brad. "In reverse, too—never scorn theorists just because they can't explain everything."

"Ummm, thanks." Max glanced at the sphere. "It seems stable . . ."

"But?"

"The exotic matter needed to build a traversable wormhole of that size is pretty big, about a Jupiter mass."

"Good grief!"

"But the total mass of the wormhole can be close to zero." He addressed this to Brad, taking pains to be cordial. "Y'see, the negative energy density walls offset the mass of the rest of the wormhole. The sum leaves just a little residue mass."

"Of 100 kilograms? That fine a balance, it sounds unstable."

"Not particularly. Not like a pencil balanced on end, anyway. No reason an equilibrium can't be robust and rugged. You've moved it from New York to here without it blowing apart."

"Ummm." Still, if this idea were remotely right, she felt foolish for taking risks. "And all this is because you want it to be a wormhole," Alicia smiled skeptically. "Suppose it isn't?"

"Then we couldn't explain the big tidal effect," Max said. "That's key."

Massive objects produced stresses in nearby objects, just as Earth's moon pulled water around in the oceans. For an apparently spherical bowling ball to do it meant that it had some asymmetric masses inside.

She shook her head. "You *think* it's key," Alicia said sardonically. She had a headache. Was it just from thinking?

11

Her headache started going away when Max asked her out to dinner. They went to a place near UCI, a long chilly hangar affair with enough bare concrete and ribbed ducts and stark lighting to be a Franz Kafka theme bar.

They settled into a booth and Max started chuckling. She was distracted. On the ride over she had started mentally replaying her telephone scrap with Dave Rucker. She looked at Max, puzzled, and he said, "I love it. Listen to this: 'A mellow, tempting blend of our hand-rolled angel hair pasta, smothered in a saffron-laced sauce of aged fromage, served on blue-white china with complete, authentic silverware.' Priceless; even worse than L.A."

"Law of the universe," she said. "The longer the menu description, the worse the food."

"I usually skip singles' watering holes like this." He gazed around speculatively. She noticed that the bar commanded most of the restaurant and was half-filled with various sleek animals in their hunting garb: molded jackets, tight skirts, big hair, even some show-off, in-your-face hats.

"Me, too," she said a little guiltily, thinking of Jill.

"I like Orange County, though. It's like L.A. without caffeine."

"Actually, I was surprised when you immediately jumped in your car and came down here to look at the sphere," she said.

"I'm curious. Also . . ." He gave her a veiled glance, eyelids hooding an assessing gaze. "I had a girlfriend down here, thought I might surprise her."

She felt a mild surprise herself. "And . . . ?"

"She was having a little dinner party for two."

"You 'had' a girlfriend?"

"Right, past tense."

Reassuring, somehow, to find that someone else was striking out in the social world. They ordered drinks and then she said lightly, "The search eternal," casting a sliver of bait.

"Tough for us, I suspect. Physicists, scientists generally, are a difficult lot to get along with."

"The way I look at it," she said, deciding to trot out one of her set pieces, "in your emotional life empathy is important, what I call the *Ah!* response. In humor you're going for the *Ha-ha!* In science we seek the *Aha!* moment."

She had found this a useful litmus test, whether a stranger would fall into the oblique angle of view she offered. Max's half-smile grew, one corner turning down in a quizzical curve. "The eureka experience? A sudden flashing insight into territories never seen before? The surge that had sent Archimedes running naked from his bath and through the streets, ecstatically driven and taking ancient dress codes to their limit?"

"You *do* like to talk."

"I keep in practice."

"Most women don't fit with . . . people like us."

"She was young and needed lots of attention," he said soberly, gazing off at the bar. "But if you were tired or busy, she wouldn't count that for much. She loved well and truly when she was in that mood, but was oblivious when her mind was on something else."

Alicia wondered if this rather pretty speech was prepared, but the look on his face said otherwise. Unless he was an exceptional actor. He seemed to feel her gaze, blinked, and said quickly, "Looked great, though."

"Vogue on the outside, vague on the inside?"

"Dead on. Maybe I wasn't the right romantic type."

Alicia shook her head. Usually people would say, *I'm kind of a romantic*, with a half-embarrassed yet subtly superior air.

"I've never understood romantic love, really. It's like a list of depressive symptoms, as if missing someone makes you feel really alive. So it's wonderful to cling, highly moral to be dependent."

He looked askance at her but nodded, egging her on with "Self-inflicted misery is so enormously self-improving."

"Right. Suffering, generally, makes life seem ultimately worthwhile. Madness!"

"Let's see. Is there any other sacred idea we could trash in a singles' bar?"

"Plenty. We were teenagers in the Nineties and now we have to get through the Noughts—"

"Or the Oh-Ohs, as some prefer."

"—and we've got far too much freedom."

His brow wrinkled. "Now that's one I haven't heard before."

"You haven't lived it. Women today have more freedom than many of them can handle." She felt a diatribe coming on, maybe a full-fledged "Alicia rant," as her father called them. But she didn't want to stop. *Let him have both barrels*, part of her said, *see if it spooks him*. "Take work, for example. How important should our careers be? Hardly any men ever had any freedom of choice there."

"Ummm," he said judiciously, watching her face.

With most men this was a danger signal, the full-bore skeptical gaze, but she plunged on. "Sleeping with somebody? Or somebodies? Or nobody? Few guys were ever pestered with *that* problem; they didn't get to do the choosing. How about marriage? Who, when, why—in the old days those got decided by the offers that came in."

"Always shadowed by the prospect of becoming a crabby spinster," he added.

She conceded this with a curt nod and plunged on, words ricocheting out. "Divorce? That's a really fresh freedom, available now just if you want it. No need to prove cause. The cafeteria of love. Any way you cut it, today a woman has to make up her mind about every major area. Every one! Society stands mute—"

"Though maybe frowning a little."

"Okay, some. But look at the *weight* of all that. Happy? Contented? No?—it's your responsibility, gal. Freud asked what women wanted; now women have to ask that, and often we don't know. We don't even recognize how to know when we do know. We're on our own."

He cradled his face in both hands, giving her a slow, understanding smile. "You're facing a lot, aren't you?"

He looked so disarmed, she found it disarming. "It shows, huh?"

"In spades."

"No pun intended?"

His mouth twisted, startled, and she had to laugh, quickly adding, "Sorry, it just came to me."

"I don't think of you as black," he said tentatively.

"I don't either. Not into identity politics. It's enough trouble just being me."

"Indeed, a full-time job."

She relaxed a bit and pretty soon was surprised to find herself telling him about the call from Brookhaven, wondering out loud what it might mean. "Brookhaven will go to the UCI administration, right away," she finished.

Max took another sip of merlot and thought a moment. The restaurant had filled, but neither of them noticed the rising noise level. Alicia was feeling much better. "And being bureaucrats," he finally said, "they'll appoint a committee to advise them."

"Why not make a decision at the top?"

"The best strategy when you're unsure is basic CYA— Cover Your Ass. You might need a panel of experts to point to if things get dicey."

"I don't like review panels and the like. They usually try to cut an issue both ways."

"I don't doubt you'll tough your way through them."

"How come?"

"You've got an edge on you. If you get pushed, you shove back, correct?"

She canted her mouth to one side, reluctant to concede the point. "I stick to essentials. You have to run your own life."

"Our lives are the exhalations and inhalations of the gods," he said loftily, sipping more wine. "All else is folly."

12

She was working on some new diagnostics with Brad when the knock came at the lab door. Students never did that, just barged in, so she went to answer it. Her back muscles conversed with her, protesting how long she had been working in a fixed position. *Should go snorkeling,* she reminded herself. *Why live on the ocean if you never go in?* She had been working solid, fourteen-hour days longer than she wanted to remember.

A secretary from her department waited at the door, nervously shifting from one foot to another. "Sorry to bother you, Professor Butterworth, but Dean Lattimer has been trying to reach you by telephone. She needs to see you."

"Okay, I'll finish up here and—"

"She said, uh, right away."

A small alarm went off way in the back of her mind. "Lattimer, she's dean of research, right?"

"Yes." She seemed anxious to get away. In the language of hierarchy sending a human messenger was part of the message.

Alicia closed the door. Some women on the staff still felt uncomfortable dealing with professors who happened to be women, slipping either into we're-just-nobodies camaraderie or a stiff formality.

She shrugged and said to Brad, "I'll be back soon. I hope."

He glanced up, hunched over a tangle of gear. His speed and understanding were remarkable; she had to keep reminding herself that he was a student. Did she expect him to be a bit less ambitious because he looked easygoing and dressed in the casual SoCal mode? "Uh, okay. I'm getting more photons than ever out of this UV counter."

"Have you changed anything? Reseated those light pipes?"

"No, I was going to do that next."

"But results are better?" She hesitated, not wanting to walk away from a puzzle like this. "Maybe it's changing."

"Like that tidal effect?" Brad nodded, adjusting some dials on an oscilloscope. "That was sure weird. We would've noticed it earlier if it had been there, for sure."

"Maybe." She kept being blindsided by events, it seemed, making her feel unsure about everything. "And now you're getting more counts in the photodetectors."

"Yeah, going up all the time. If it had been emitting like this before, I could've gotten that spectrum in a day, not a week."

"Ummm. Suppose Max is right about—"

"Wormholes?" Brad made a rude noise.

She blinked. Making fun of a Caltech professor's ideas was not typical student behavior; Brad had more confidence than sense. "Just suppose, okay? Then more light coming through could mean that the other end is getting bigger."

"This end isn't."

"Are you sure? How long has it been since we measured it?"

"Here," Brad said, getting up and grabbing a large pair of calipers. They both walked from the 'scope room into the bay. Carefully they folded back the blankets of light shielding around the U-magnet. Alicia had not been inside here for days; Physics 3-B was taking a lot of her time with office hours and homework grading. The sphere was nearly buried behind photodetector leads and lenses. Brad leaned through and with some grunting measured the diameter.

"Looks like 38.3 centimeters," he read out.

"Do it again."

His mouth twisted but he did it. "Same: 38.3."

"That's bigger, not the same," she said, pulling back a flap of the light blanket. "See?" On the board was DIAMETER 37.8 CM. She thought again about erasing it to keep casual inquiries down.

Brad frowned. "Now, how in hell . . . ?"

"Otherwise it looks the same." She felt a cold spike of unease. If it grew further . . .

"Yeah, but look, a little expansion can't explain how we're getting more than an order of magnitude more light out of this thing."

"Granted. Look, check your other baseline measurements. We can't assume anything holds steady."

"I guess not."

A glance at her watch. "I'm needed across campus. Let me get this out of the way and we'll check some of the other early measurements."

He stood transfixed by the sphere. "It's changing. Growing."

She saw him then more deeply, and at the core of him was a drive very much like hers, the engine of her life. For the first time she felt that she knew him. "Yes. So much for a controlled experiment."

Another odd result, straight out of the blue; blindsided again. They should set up a continuous measurement of its size, maybe with a laser beam reflected from the surface . . .

"Something big is going on here." Brad seemed a little uneasy and she wondered if he was being completely straight with her. He was gifted, able to keep up with this experiment as a mere grad student, though of course just as a data-taker. He would do very well indeed, once he knew more; his innate understanding of electronics was a marvel. But his quick-developing rivalry with Zak might have some side effects, she thought. Competitive types could easily rub each other the wrong way.

And was Brad telling her everything? Well, she would go through it all when she got back.

She deliberately put the whole issue out of her mind as she walked quickly through Aldrich Park, grateful for its calming trees and lawns. *Focus, focus. Research after politics.*

The receptionist outside Lattimer's suite was formal to the point of severity, a precursor of Lattimer herself. Tall and tweedy, Rebecca Lattimer had risen swiftly from molecular biology after only a few years of mediocre research, making the momentous movement two years before *across the circle*, over the green glade of UCI's central park to the ramparts of the Admin building.

Alicia had noticed two major styles of female professors at UCI: Frowsy and Brisk. Frowsy was easy, with its wild hair, clomping shoes, and shapeless dresses, often preferred in the schools of humanities and biology, with ropy ethnic jewelry in the social sciences. The Brisks, on the other hand, suggested Radcliffe, with tailored dress-for-success severity, usually softened with pearl earrings or a lacy touch. They always returned phone calls and e-mail and could be ruthless without anybody noticing.

Lattimer was a full-bore Brisk. Well-cut gray suit, eggshell blue blouse, turquoise pin to match her eyes, hair bunched to highlight the high cheekbones. Her office was startling after the fluorescents and shiny enameled surfaces in the rest of UCI, the Light of Scrutiny look. Here an ivory carpet lapped at the base of well-oiled paneling of tongue-in-groove cedar. An ample modernist couch sectioned the spacious preserve into a conversation area and a more official, desk-dominated realm. Several windows slanted afternoon sunlight into the hushed space, bringing out the polished mahogany of the scrupulously bare desk. Or nearly so, for the deep tones enhanced the effect of a single stack of paper. Alicia eyed those pages as she passed by them, ushered in with the usual cordialities to the couch area.

In this textured, welcoming space the afternoon sun cast a buttery radiance on Lattimer's face as she sat in a posture that looked studied, leaning casually back into an ebony leather chair, putting the papers in her lap, saying, "I'm glad you could come right over," without looking glad at all. A quick intelligence showed itself in the guarded set of her mouth, which bore only a trace of lipstick; Alicia wondered if this were deliberate, or whether she did not bother to replace the lipstick lost eating lunch; though, come to think of it, she probably didn't eat lunch at all. Alicia crossed her legs, now quite aware that she wore a gray jogging suit and heavy lab shoes.

"I've gotten some disturbing letters from the Brookhaven National Laboratory, and have appointed a committee to look into them."

"My, that was quick." Alicia knew that one of her own irritating mannerisms was a curt inability to smooth conversations along when plainly the other person was trying to, so she added, "I didn't know Brookhaven had done anything."

"Umm, they have, they have." Lattimer gave her a long flat stare, probably intended to sober the recipient.

"I promised to share data with Brookhaven as soon as I have a good result."

"I decided to convene a panel from the physics department—just advisory and completely confidential—to advise on, well, let us call them 'property rights' in your subculture."

Be diplomatic. "I'm surprised you didn't tell me anything about this."

"That was to avoid stirring up the issue more than it had to be." Lattimer tented her fingers and studied them intently, a strikingly judicious gesture.

"I could have told you, everything in an accelerator experiment generally belongs to the host body. A blanket organization, Associated Universities Incorporated, holds title. Brookhaven controls that, so they can decide matters."

"Quite so." Lattimer got up and stood behind her chair, grasping its back, peering down at Alicia, then slowly leaning forward. "I should have thought you would have informed them of your discovery."

"It wasn't a discovery then, just a depressing accident. I collected the wreckage of my detector and left."

"Are you *sure*?"

Piercing gaze, hands tightening on the chair back. Alicia made herself breathe in slowly. She had learned to beware anyone who dramatically leaned in toward her in conversation, or who pushed things back across the desk at her, or sat back and struck poses, or dressed a bit too carefully or adjusted the lighting to favor them, or who even had their chair placed higher than hers. Usually this revealed a phony more concerned with appearance than accomplishment. But the better bureaucrats combined all that with rhetoric and delivery, plus telling arguments.

"I was pretty torn up about the failure. We just hauled everything home. My students and I did not get a good idea of how strange this sphere was until we studied it." All true, too.

"Ummm." More narrow-eyed scrutiny, though slacking off a bit. "I could not help but notice that your colleagues do not even know you have this object."

Couldn't help it, see. Somebody forced me to convene this special panel, see . . . "No reason they should." No, too curt. Try some self-confession, maybe. "I—I've been pretty scarce around the department lately. Getting my students enthused about repairing our detector takes plenty of time."

"I had another call from the assistant director at Brookhaven just this morning—"

"Brookhaven didn't make it. It was in my detector debris. So why's it theirs?"

Lattimer blinked. Deans spent their energies managing underlings' appetites and getting money, not sipping from the heady wine of research reports; perhaps Lattimer had forgotten that scientists could get passionate. She blinked and seemed taken aback by Alicia's sudden gumption.

Carefully Lattimer said, "We must rise above feelings of ownership in such matters," using a tone which Alicia realized probably came in quite handy at fund-raisers, usually at the conclusion of a speech titled "Whither Science?"

Seeing no point in descending to the level of principle, Alicia said flatly, "What are you going to do?"

The dean steepled her hands again and peered at her over them, her mouth becoming a stern, flat line. Her excellent cheekbones caught the yellow sunlight which was slanting lower, reaching into the hushed recesses of the room. "I shall retain my informal committee to keep track of your progress.

Your argument, that this thing was in your detector, seems to have some minor merit.''

''I appreciate that.''

''Have you considered safety?''

''Uh, yes. There's no apparent cause for concern.''

''Good. I expect my panel will rule that you retain this object for study but share results with others in timely fashion.'' She had a concluding tone, nodding.

Alicia felt that she could probably not have done any better than this; Lattimer's panel seemed to be a tame animal, rendering whatever verdict she liked. Soon enough Alicia was crossing back through the circular park, mulling over matters. There was a difference of attitude here she could not quite fathom. Sure enough, she had stretched the rules all along. But she had stayed inside them—or thought she had—and that was what mattered.

Once in grade school she and some friends had wanted some bauble, long-forgotten, but the way they decided who would get it had stuck in her memory. A boy proposed that they each pick a number between zero and 100, and he would compare with one he had already chosen. Her best friend picked 66, another 78. Everyone seemed irked when Alicia naturally chose 65. ''You shouldn't get so close to my number!'' her best friend insisted. But to Alicia the point was to maximize her chances, so she captured the biggest fraction of the numbers. ''It's not *fair*,'' another said. When the boy revealed his number, 88, everyone seemed to feel that Alicia had been dealt a stinging rebuke, another reaction she could not fathom.

She shrugged, feeling a sharp desire to be quick, lean, sure. At the heart of all this lay the Riddle, and everything else was just packing material for it.

To work along precise lines with hard facts, after the muggy evasions of Lattimer's soft office, would be a genuine pleasure. But first she had some political scores to settle. She strode energetically back to the physics department through the late-afternoon light.

13

Martin Onell was in his corner office and not busy, the Management Services Officer assured Alicia, ushering her in. Onell wore his usual three-piece suit, brown today, with a sunset yellow button-down shirt and muted red tie.

"Alicia! I've been hoping I would hear back from you about the Minority Mentorship Program."

"Uh, I'm behind in—"

"The vice chancellor has been e-mailing me *every day* about getting you to show up for their meetings." He got up and came around his large desk, careful not to knock over a pile of physics journals.

"Those meetings, they're endless. I can't stand them. That Gender Education director is so boring—"

"It's an obligation we all share, though, I think you'll agree." He smiled warmly and crinkled his eyes, his let-us-reason-together mode. Best to cut this off before he got too sincere. "Of course, some more than others."

Here came the packaged minilecture on her obligation to other "minorities," especially since she embodied two for the price of one. (She sometimes suspected the administration would have been overjoyed if she had turned out to be a lesbian, thus making her a three-in-one recruiting bonanza.) She had to get this conversation off this well-worn track.

Deep breath, steely stare. "I'm here to ask why you set up a panel about my research and didn't even tell me."

The sincerity vanished and his face went blank. "I had to, of course."

"Why 'of course'?"

"The vice chancellor for research thought there might be, well, considerable liability for UCI. If you had in fact stolen valuable—"

"Stolen? I took—"

"—which *was* the way it was presented by Brookhaven, you must concede. Well, when I heard that, I decided that just asking a few of your colleagues from the particle physics faculty to render an informal opinion about how such disputes are handled was a good idea."

"I don't like you operating behind my back."

He fingered his tie. "I have to protect the department."

In the mid-1990s UCI had suffered through an interminable scandal when some women's eggs had been mishandled in a medical school fertility clinic. Starting as a minor paperwork problem, in the hands of lawyers the whole mess had ballooned into a many-megabucks payout, often to people who had suffered no real injury beyond "psychological damage." Since then, every administrator had tiptoed past anything that smelled of litigation. Alicia remembered all this as she watched Onell's face turn from wary distance to solicitude. She had intended to give him a thorough working over, but somehow her heart was not in gear for more confrontation. "I . . . see," she said lamely.

"I'm sure it will all work out," he said.

She knew that once he retreated into platitudes she would get no more from him. His managerial style was defensive, usually operating behind an armor of documentation; nothing truly happened unless it got written down, or so any investigating body would find. A predictable mode, if rather tedious.

"I'll be in touch, then," she said, her minimal-trouble exit line. She left the chairman's office only mildly irked, which in turn surprised her. *Maybe, God help us, I'm getting used to this stuff.*

* * *

The lab was dark when she finally got there. Dusk was settling and little light spilled across the concrete floor from the side doorway. Better not flip on the lights, though, she thought; probably Brad was taking more optical data.

By feel she found her way along a line of cabinets. "Brad?" No answer. Maybe he had gone out for something, leaving the diagnostics running. She could make out tiny red running lights on the computer monitors, like distant red stars.

The undergraduates would have knocked off their assembly work on the Core Element an hour before, she knew. Her left foot kicked some metal part lying in the way. It clattered loudly in the strange silence. She was used to some bustle and movement here and the hush was odd in the big bay space. Further along the cabinets she felt for a tool rack mounted on the wall. She was a bug about putting tools back and was rewarded when her hand closed on one of their narrow-beam flashlights. She went toward the red monitor lights, but Brad was not in the 'scope room. She listened for his stirring. Maybe he was inside the light blanket, which was closed. Probably he was making some fine adjustments or measuring the diameter again.

"Brad?" No answer. But then, he had a total concentration and often didn't respond when he was intent on a task. She liked such absorption; the best experimenters often had it. Carefully she moved through the gloom.

She had allowed herself to start puzzling over the diameter on the walk back over. The damned thing changed, as if it were alive. Certainly the mystery kept deepening, deepening wonderfully. There really was something going on here—something big—and she felt it intuitively in her bones. But what? She was still trying to decide whether she thought Max's wormhole idea made any sense. The tidal effect measurement gave him credibility.

The flashlight's watery light cast moving shadows amid the racks of gear; they would have to straighten up in here or else they'd be tripping over themselves.

She drew back a flap on the light blanket and stepped into the narrow enclosure. Her flashlight beam showed the clusters of light pipes tied in bunches along the top of the makeshift steel rod framework. The area had gotten jammed with more and more diagnostic leads, cables snaking everywhere.

There was a curious singed smell that made her wrinkle her nose. Ozone? No, different.

Some of the wiring looked out of place. In the flashlight's pale tunnel of light the sphere reflected her beam back at her. The smell was strong, cutting, as though some electronics component had fried itself. She felt alarm. What had happened? Where was Brad?

She stepped forward and her right foot struck something soft. She nearly lost her balance, shot out a hand to a steel brace to steady herself, and looked down. What equipment was supposed to be here—?

A black mask stared up at her. She gasped. Eyelids burned away so that the too-white eyes gazed at the ceiling.

She staggered, her breath coming in quick pants. The top half of the body was a charred mass, clothes plastered into a dark layer. She recognized the faded blue jeans and big Western belt. Brad. Or rather, what had been Brad.

His right hand clutched an electrical probe. The face was a swollen, scorched blob, as if it had been licked by a flamethrower. The cheeks puffed out like fleshy balloons. Lips like burst sausages.

She had to make herself breathe in, but the air seemed suddenly thick and putrid with oily, dense fumes. The dark gathered around her head and she felt woozy, teetering, and when her flashlight beam tilted crazily up, it caught the sphere's gleam again, a sharp hard reflected glare once more, like the fixed stare of an angry eye.

PART III

IMPOSSIBLE THINGS

Treiman's Theorem: Impossible things usually don't happen.

—SAM TREIMAN, PRINCETON UNIVERSITY PHYSICIST

1

The hospital was imposing, crisp and bright in its metallic sheen. She had come from the damp night outside into frosty brilliance and enameled warrens. The effect was surrealistic, jarring, quite in keeping with her own inner dislocations.

The waiting room was designed to soften tensions, she noted abstractly. Modern paintings highlighted by concealed spotlights made big subdued, calming blotches on the dusty rose walls. A big leather armchair dominated a cozy arrangement of two couches and a cheery flower arrangement, which proved to be artificial. Indirect lighting, satin-finished birch, lots of muted fabrics. None of this worked for her; she fidgeted and paced.

A physician came and asked if she were a relative. *From the black branch of his family tree?* she thought, then realized this was a purely formal question. "No, his thesis professor. How is he doing?"

The doctor said carefully, "Not good. He is in a coma and we are trying to reduce the serious swelling in his braincase."

She studied his face as if looking for answers. "His vitals . . . ?"

He showed her a clipboard holding a sheet covered in dot matrix type, a diagnostic printout. "No skull fractures. Proteins abnormal from the cerebral hemorrhage. The CAT scan shows massive swelling. Then, of course, the burns."

She remembered the chilling sight of the team lifting Brad. A clean line down his neck divided his blasted face from white skin. The front half of his hair was scorched away, the back still combed. "I don't understand, the way he looked . . ."

"If he lives, he will need extensive facial reconstruction."

She nodded vigorously. "They've been doing so much with that." Empty, automatic optimism. "Why . . . why is he in a coma?"

"Not concussion. The head sustained some substantial heating throughout, I believe. His burns are not superficial."

She was grateful for something more than smooth, meaningless phrases. Better, the man had not reverted to the hedged-in, minimize-possible-damage style. *And the first of all the commandments shall be: Cover Thy Ass.*

"Will he . . . make it?"

"I honestly cannot tell."

That was all there was to say. She spent the next hour pacing. University figures arrived, but they scarcely registered through her haze. When Martin Onell appeared, she answered his questions just as she had those of various police. "How did it happen?" Onell asked, but she had no answers. The sphere, of course, but *how*?

She found herself responding to Onell's questions with the soothing sentences that women were supposed to be better at than men. But she could not seem to get anything to come out right, to make her sentences hang together.

Onell had the proper team sent to secure the lab scene. People came and went, faces sliding by behind glass. A Detective Sturges, homicide, was persistent. "This was an accident," she said and he nodded, said nothing.

Brad's parents could not be reached. She called Max and somehow got out the essentials. Her throat was tight and she could not think of what to say. Max said he would drive down from Pasadena. More people, questions, the stale cool air stretched thin and tight around her. Brad, Brad . . .

Then the physician came in again and told them that Brad was dead. Just like that, no warning, and she was sitting in the big leather armchair with talk going by her and nothing registering. Onell said things and people came and went, but she could not get a grip on the sliding events at all, at all.

*   *   *

She was standing in the same waiting room with her arms around Max in a sympathetic hug. He had just arrived.

"Professor Butterworth?"

It was Detective Sturges, eyes slightly averted, seeming a little embarrassed to approach them. She and Max let their arms drop and she caught a closing in Sturges's face. He had seen a lot of mayhem in his line of work, but maybe not much affection. Or was it the mixed races?

"Yes?" She put on her best business voice.

"I've got some preliminary results here from the coroner. Wondered if you could add anything further." Sturges held out a clipboard. "These three-sheets are a mess to read—"

"Three-sheets?" she asked.

"The third carbon copy of the arriving officers' reports and the technical team reports. Like reading chicken scratches. Anyway, the radiological and CAT scan data show cause of death was cerebral swelling. It looks like his head just got cooked."

Alicia winced at the detective's words, opened her mouth, could say nothing.

"What about the rest?" Max asked sharply, stepping forward a bit, between her and Sturges.

Sturges paused just long enough for Alicia to see him resolve to not get irked, a professional reflex. She introduced Max and Sturges said, "The drug screen shows nothing, if that's what you mean."

"What went wrong in the lab?" Max asked.

Sturges glanced at her and said carefully, "I don't have to conclude anything just yet, but Professor Butterworth, you said something earlier about an object you were studying?"

She could not shake off her numb, stark disbelief. "A high-energy physics experiment."

"Well, accidents we still have to look into. I'll visit the lab and hand off on it as soon as I get the final coroner's."

Then he just went away. Alicia felt a wave of relief, as if the matter-of-fact detective had been her judge. But he had not banished the guilt she carried like a leaden weight in the pit of her stomach, an almost physical pain.

In the car back to UCI she abruptly said, "Times like this, I wish I was religious."

"Oh?" Max glanced at her, his tone cautious.

Did she seem obviously shaky? She tried to relax, found that her hands were clenched white. Keep talking, that might help. "I'd . . . I'd sure like to believe that Brad is off somewhere else, not just a bunch of fried neurons."

He nodded. "It would be better . . ."

She made herself keep going. "I was a teenage atheist. A big change from the good Baptist girl of twelve."

"Church was just going through the motions for me. Lutheran."

"I was quite proud of myself, liberated from dogma and all."

He chuckled. "Me too. If it's any consolation, your opinion doesn't change anything. Heaven and God exist, or don't, no matter what you think."

"Yeah, and even that doesn't make me feel any better. When I'm at my grandparents' and they drag me to a service, it's beautiful and nostalgic, like pictures in your high school annual. You know that hollow feeling? Like there's a young woman back there, sweetly naive, and that's the only way I can visit her now."

He smiled wanly. "She's still there. I can see her peeking out sometimes."

This took her off-balance. He looked at her almost shyly, as if to gauge her reaction. She said hesitantly, "There was more to her than what I am now, just getting nostalgic for her early faith."

"Don't beat yourself up about it."

"You too, Max."

He shot her a glance, said nothing, so she plunged on. "You were in the right ballpark with that wormhole idea, but it didn't give us anything to anticipate this."

He sighed. "Yeah."

"Don't blame yourself."

"Ummm." It was a grudging, hedgehog sound.

"It's pointless. I was in charge of the lab, not you."

"Ummmm." He reached over and patted her hand.

Irvine's neon consumer gumbo slid by beyond Max's dirty window. Relentlessly cheery colors brimmed beneath a sky of stars. The world seemed inky and impenetrable, dark with something more than night.

2

"**N**ow we have to run the gauntlet," she said dourly, slamming the door of Max's car too hard.

"You're sure it was the sphere?" Max asked, voice guarded in the thick fog.

"Must be." They walked through shadows toward the lab building. The big bay doors yawned and glaring blue-white light speared out through the misty gloom.

"How could it be? The sphere was giving off very weak UV."

"It was getting larger, though."

"Oh? When did you discover that?"

She glanced at her watch. "Four hours ago." How could it be so little?

"Grew how much?"

"Half a centimeter in diameter."

"Um. That couldn't make much diff—"

"How do we know?" She rounded on him suddenly as they reached the polished concrete of the dock. "*How?*"

"Well, sure we don't, but there wasn't much coming in . . ."

She blinked rapidly. "I'm . . . sorry."

"You weren't responsible. When you're studying something completely new—"

"You take precautions."

"Against what? You don't know, that's the point."

"At least you warn people."

"Again, you don't know what to warn them against."

She sighed and sagged against the steel frame of the bay doors. "You're going to keep on being the voice of sweet reason, aren't you?"

"My job." He looked into her eyes, his own lined with worry. "They're going to ask some nasty questions in there. Feel up to it?"

"I hope so."

"Maybe you should go home, leave it for tomorrow."

"I won't sleep anyway. I'd rather get through this."

"Us. We get through it."

"You're not involved."

"The hell I'm not. I can't let you walk in there and get shredded."

She studied his face. His eyes seemed large and luminous, peering into her confusion. "You can stay clear of this."

His lips compressed into a thin line. "No way."

"Sure?"

"Sure."

"You can't just Gary Cooper your way through this next part, y'know."

He smiled. "You've sure got a smart mouth on you."

"Not that it's done me a whole lot of good."

He peered deeply into her eyes. "It's a cover, of course."

"For?" She was flustered and automatically came back with a question.

"I wonder."

She opened her mouth, closed it, her mind awhirl.

He stepped back as if to give her room and his face reverted to his crisp, sharp-eyed expression. "Sorry, I shouldn't do things like that."

"Well, I . . . I . . ."

"One thing at a time. For now, just give them the facts. We don't have to speculate out loud."

"I wouldn't know how to."

"I wouldn't either. I just know not to try."

* * *

They were all there: safety personnel summoned from their dinners, police, Detective Sturges, Executive Vice Chancellor for Research Lattimer, Chairman Onell. They all milled around as both UCI and Sturges's team took photographs. Nobody seemed worried about the sphere as a threat; it looked as before, a shiny ball. Not much obvious menace there.

Alicia spent her first minutes getting people out of her equipment. A fat, mournful-looking man was taking fingerprints and complained to her that it was hard to get anything off the oscilloscope knobs. Another climbed halfway up the bay and took vertical photos. Others milled around, many just watching, more people than made any sense.

To her surprise, Brad's experiment was still running, the 'scopes and detectors showing tiny red ON lights. She had left it in the rush to get Brad into the ambulance. Now the milling crowd edged gingerly around the bunches of light pipe, cabling, and struts, looking uncomfortable. Something had killed a man here and nobody knew what it was. But training died hard and the lab looked so innocuous that nobody seemed threatened.

At least they had not fooled around with the U-magnet, though the cloak was drawn back. Some of Sturges's people were taking tiny samples of the cloak and wrinkling their foreheads. They spread the absorbent cover out on the concrete. It was scorched everywhere except for an odd blob. She studied it and suddenly saw the distorted shape of Brad, his shadow. Her head swam and she breathed deeply to clear it. The burnt smell swarmed up into her nostrils and she bent over in a wracking cough.

The buzz of conversations around her was lost in the tall, chilly bay, whose stark lighting bleached out the scene. She steadied herself, got her breath. The police lamps gave a clinical sharpness to the U-magnet. The sphere reflected the glare into their eyes, so few looked directly at it.

Then came the questions.

After she had arrived, most of the crowd had just shuffled back. Now they watched as she explained to a crescent arc of frowning faces how the experiment was set up and where Brad had been. By unspoken agreement they let Sturges set the tone.

"Professor Jalon, what is your role in this?"

"I'm a theorist from Caltech. I was helping Dr. Butterworth and her students understand what they had."

"But not actively conducting experiments?"

"No, I just think."

"Think what?"

"For a living."

Sturges gave Max a sharp look, seemed to decide there was no point, and started asking Alicia quick, detailed questions about where Brad usually stood, where she had found him, what the parts of the experiment did. "Any chance he was playing with something inflammable?"

"There's nothing here of that sort." She gazed at him steadily.

"The sprinkler system didn't go on. No signs of a fire, except the scorching on the inside of this 'light blanket' you've got here." Sturges stooped and fingered the material, which someone on the technical team had spread out for close inspection.

"The sprinklers respond to soot in the air of a particular particle size," she said tensely, just to be saying something. A quick pulse of radiation would not set it off at all.

Sturges ignored her digression and gestured at the U-magnet, where bundles of optical pipe diagnostics nearly concealed the sphere. "That thing you're studying, what is it?"

"We don't know. It seemed to us to be an unusual product of an accident at the Brookhaven National Laboratory. We were trying to fit it into understanding why our experiment there failed."

"Looks like a metal ball," Sturges said, peering between the magnet poles.

"Perhaps it is," Alicia said and instantly regretted it. "But it doesn't have many properties we understand." *None, actually.* "We do know that it emits light in the far ultraviolet. Very little, though, so we had placed this array"—a gesture at the photoreceptors—"to pick up its spectrum."

"So you figured right away it was radioactive?" Sturges asked.

"Not at all. No particle emission comes from the sphere. None. So far we had seen only very weak, invisible, ultraviolet emission."

"Except that something roasted your student and this seems to you to be the likely source." Sturges watched her carefully along with all the other eyes in the bay.

"I . . . believe so. I can't think of any other way he could have . . . been in danger."

"What can you tell us from all this"—his hand swept in the diagnostics in their steel frames—"about what happened?"

"Give me time to look at the data. I was gone well over an hour and the electronics are still compiling what Brad did."

"You can figure out what went on here?"

"Uh, perhaps." She was grateful for this chance to get away from the audience of eyes. She and Max went into the screening room. It was a plywood box with sheets of webbed steel that sheltered the optical and microwave detectors from outside emissions. Max shut the door and they looked at each other, both faces drained. A small pocket of privacy.

She sighed and sat before a computer keyboard with a big, flat screen. It was chugging away, still collecting data from the photoreceptors around the sphere. No damage evident to the system, not a single light pipe gone dead.

She called up the running data file and found that Brad had been doing the reduction in real time, smoothing out the statistical jitters. The incoming photon counts got batched and handed off to a separate program, running on another computer, which sorted and displayed the spectrum. She had expected the familiar blackbody spectrum they had seen before and indeed, early in Brad's run there were plenty of the curves. The cooling had continued, she saw, slewing peaks of the curves to the left, as compared with days ago.

She hit keys and quickly flashed through a dozen spectra. "My God, the spectra are coming closer together in time."

"So?" Max asked.

"We've got the system almost on automatic. It collects light long enough to make a reliable, smooth spectrum, then compiles it. A week or so ago, we took data for days to get one spectrum. These last few, though, have been shaping up in less than an hour of data collecting."

"So the intensity was climbing."

She typed furiously, her eyes widening. "Yes. Climbing through today, particularly. While I was busy and Brad was registering all this and saying nothing."

"Up by a couple orders of magnitude, looks like."

Max was leaning over her shoulder, reading numbers off the vertical axis of the spectra. She did not like people doing that but suppressed her annoyance; he was right about the increase, too. "Why didn't Brad tell me? *Damn.*"

"His discovery, he figured?"

"That would fit the Brad I know. He was competing with Zak Nguyen, some issue between them."

"Ambitious grad students go with the territory."

"He must have known this for days. I was working on other stuff—"

"Don't start blaming yourself," he said emphatically.

"Right, just do the data." She sat up straight, smoothed her hair back from her forehead.

"Let me have that intensity data, though. I want to look it over."

She quickly printed out the spectra; let him get whatever he liked from them. She felt herself veering away from all this, her thoughts shooting off in all directions to escape somehow from what had happened. A long watery sigh escaped and Max gave her a worried look. *Get a grip,* she told herself fiercely.

"Let's . . . let's follow these spectra forward," she muttered. There was trouble with the data files as she stepped them forward in time. Those from this afternoon were much more powerful and the program had trouble accommodating the huge increases. The smooth spectra also showed a thin, jagged peak.

"This looks wrong," she said.

"Or maybe it's not a blackbody anymore," Max said.

She studied the peak in what had been the expected blackbody curves, thinking. As an emitter became transparent, it lost the simple blackbody emission form. Instead, the radiation began breaking through, light no longer captured and reemitted. Sharper, distinctive lines could begin to poke their heads above the smoothness.

"The intensity's going up fast, too," Max pointed out.

"Ummm." She jumped through the late-afternoon collection bin; the peak got bigger, jutting out. "Don't know if I trust any of this."

"Is there any more?"

She checked the compilation lag. "Incomplete collection in the next run, seems to be." She told the program to display the spectrum anyway, narrowed to the odd peak. The software ground around as the hard disks buzzed, trading information, and then the screen filled with a ragged spike, a classic atomic radiation line.

"Very energetic emission," Max said.

"Look at the intensity!"

"Up orders of magnitude."

"Bright and sharp." She checked the time log. "This would be right around when Brad . . ."

"Yeah. The smoking gun."

"What line is that?"

"Let me look up something . . ." Somewhere in the software menu, she recalled, there was a finder routine that matched an observed line with candidate frequencies of various atoms and molecules. She found it and pulled down the appropriate menus, the usual pointing and clicking that still reminded her of kids' games. In less than a minute she said, "It's hydrogen."

"Can't be."

"It fits the basic recombination line."

"You're sure?" Max was leaning over her shoulder again.

"Of course I'm not. That's just the closest comparison."

"That's the line emitted when an electron falls into the lowest hydrogen orbit?"

"The lowest Lyman line, yes."

"So whatever's on the other side of this has changed from being a hot plasma into hydrogen gas."

"I thought there was a star at the other end of this wormhole."

He shrugged. "The star part was a guess. Whatever the hot plasma is on the other end, it's cooling off."

"Cooling fast. But why the huge flash of this Lyman radiation?"

"Suppose the other end of the wormhole is growing. If it opened up suddenly, letting a lot more light come in—"

"Why should it?"

"You said yourself that the size of this end is changing."

She waved a dismissive hand. "Grew by half a centimeter."

"It's growing. That's the point. On the other side the mouth could suddenly open up—"

"Why?" she persisted.

"I don't know. We'll have to be led by the facts here."

She sank lower in her chair. "The fact is that the thing killed Brad." *Flash-fried him,* she thought but did not say.

"True." Max himself sagged into a roller chair and they sat looking at the bright, cheery colors of the graphics display.

"Let's look at all the data sets together," she said numbly.

It compiled quickly. She typed in instructions which dropped away the spectral pictures and just gave the total intensity of the emission. These she plotted versus time. "Wow, look at what happens after 1 P.M.," she said. The curve rose steadily from 13:00 on, then really took off. A sharp spike of emission had occurred at 18:07, the time register said.

"Off the chart," Max whispered.

"That's the burst, all right," she said. "Many orders of magnitude brighter than we were getting before. See, the system saturated in self-defense."

The electronics had shut down the detectors, or else they would have been swamped. Max said, "It must have started glowing."

She saw his point. "Brad would've noticed it, even if he was in here just looking at the digitized images. So he ducked under the light blankets to have a look."

"Probably stuck his head up to it, curious," Max said.

"Rather than call me."

She understood completely. In research there came enchanted moments when one seemed to be peering into the heart of reality. Often they came to the solitary gaze, in gliding quiet times of concentration. She had experienced moments like that and remembered them clearly. Brad had been admiring something strange and lustrous in his last moments. He had died as a scientist, not out of accident, but out of the irreducible danger that went with the unknown. A strange chill ran through her.

They sat there for a long moment. Max finally stood and whispered, "What'll you—ah, we—tell them outside? They're waiting."

She sighed. The hushed moment had slipped away. The physics puzzle had mercifully taken her attention, given her some rest of a sort. Now she had to go out there and answer more questions from Onell and Lattimer and Detective Sturges—

"Wait a minute. Why is everybody letting that detective ask all the questions?"

"Homicide investigation comes first," he said somberly.

"They think . . . ?"

"They suspect. So they nose around."

"Am I a suspect?"

He shrugged. "It's your lab."

"That's crazy!"

"Sure, but these guys are methodical. They have their routines."

"I wonder what they'll think of this hydrogen line business."

"Pass it off as some technical accident," he said confidently, then added, "I hope."

She took off her clothes and threw them into the hamper. As she groggily took down her hair, she suddenly smelled it: a singed acid tang, thick in her hair.

She went straight to the shower and washed it, but after she blow-dried it out, the damned hair still smelled. It took leaving the scented shampoo on for ten minutes and two more showers before she was sure the smell was gone. It was hard to be sure because in straining she was trying not to remember the smell at all.

It was far past midnight and she made herself not review the last few hours. The only good advice she had gotten after emerging from the screening room with Max came from a UCI lawyer, summoned by Vice Chancellor Lattimer. He had whispered, "Say nothing and make it sound convincing."

She took two pills from a prescription a guy had gotten for her, a face only vaguely remembered now, though she had gone out with him several times four years ago. She had not realized until him that you could meet a man and like him and just as fast, say in a nasty hour in a restaurant, it could all go wrong. Well, at least she had gotten these pills out of it, which was rather more than she had to show for the others—a few, very few, other men.

The pills did not work at all and she was afraid to take any more. The guy four years ago had warned her about that.

3

The next day was pure hell of a kind she had never imagined.

First her introductory physics class, which felt like swimming through mud. Then the campus safety review board came to inspect the lab. After that, delegations from several other appendages of the campus bureaucracy, each probing her with questions for which she had pitifully few answers. Each wanted copies of lab notebooks, computer files, printouts; the urge to document, amass files, show that you were doing something concrete.

Next, a meeting with Chairman Onell and Executive Vice Chancellor Lattimer, each acting as though they had become their titles.

All through this she tried to figure out what had happened. She stared at the graphs on the flat, multicolored computer screen. The intensity of light coming from the sphere had risen rapidly in the hour she was over in Lattimer's office.

Brad would have seen it. Though the emission was at high frequencies beyond sight, there was weak radiation in the high, visible blue. Brad would have watched the sphere, wondering why it was lighting up, looking closer—

Then the flash. The spectra hinted that there was emission all the way up into the X ray. That alone might have killed him, but there was plenty of ultraviolet to do the job, too.

Then the emission fell. She plotted out the time dependence. Exponential. The hydrogen recombination line began to slide down in frequency, and the temperature of the overall spectrum dropped.

She pulled the light blanket aside and stepped into the close, cloaked blackness. The safety people had added layers, making sure that if any burst of emission came from the sphere, it would be muffled by nonflammable layers. They were already talking about erecting lead-concrete walls around it.

The sphere was invisible in the dark. The intensity was dropping steadily and had been already below visibility when she came back into the lab and found Brad, about thirty minutes after the flash. She leaned into the U-magnet and sniffed. No tang of ozone, either.

She thought about Max's ideas. Plenty of maybes, no real answers.

Max came down the next day and helped her get through Brad's funeral. Jill volunteered, too, but Alicia believed the day would be awkward enough and did not want to complicate matters.

Brad Douglas had been from a small town that was now just an off-ramp, swallowed by the expansion east of Riverside. Brad's parents were quiet and worn-looking and she could find no way to get through the silences that surrounded them. They were stiff and polite and asked her nothing. Somehow that was worse than anything she had anticipated.

The service was in the Gremlich Funeral Home, five blocks from the 55 freeway. It seemed an odd choice to her, until later at the reception she had helped Mrs. Douglas with the food in the kitchen and saw the calendar on the wall. "Oh yes," Mrs. Douglas said, "they send us one every year." It was from the funeral home; all those free calendars had finally paid off for Mr. Gremlich.

And Gremlich knew his business. The reception line led straight by the coffin, so everyone got a full view of Gremlich's craft. She had a terrible moment imagining Brad even after, as the doctor at the hospital had put it, *a lot of reconstruction work was needed*. Without wanting to, she was looking down at him from a great height, and she saw a giant version of those dolls people make out of dried apples . . .

Then she turned away, suddenly realizing that she had been standing there—how long?—and absurdly, how the metallic blue coffin made her recall a 1950 Mercury.

A minister spoke for a long time—or it seemed long. He started with compliments to the corpse and then moved on to the higher ramifications and meanings of it all. A lot of moral implications, rules for living, lessons to be drawn. He had an unnerving way of smiling after every few sentences. She folded her arms and reflected that death was one of the few biological functions that this kind of religion seemed to approve of.

When she tried to recall Brad, how he lived, all she could remember was his work, his ambitions. Ruefully she saw that she had not really known him at all. Perhaps if she had, she would have picked up on how much of a rivalry he felt toward Zak, and then guessed about his keeping the data to himself. Then maybe she would have been there when the hard blue glare came, could have gotten him away . . .

The deceased had indeed displayed several of the duller virtues, to hear the minister tell it, but to Alicia they paled to nothing in the wild glare of her own vices.

They had no place to go after the service. On the way back along the 55 freeway they stopped in the lab at UCI, drawn somehow without ever saying why. Yet they both understood; Max hauled in his briefcase from his trunk, a full overnight bag stuffed with papers and his laptop.

She showed him what she had learned. He waited her out, scratching his chin absently, seemingly off in a world by himself. He was a handsome man in a compact sort of way, features chiseled from a face that did not seem to have met much dismay in its passage through life. Devotees of theory were often like that, childlike in their fascination with the intricate play of ideas, oblivious to the rude rub of the real.

When she was through and thinking about leaving, maybe calling Jill and going out somewhere, Max said cautiously, "I've been doing some thinking of my own . . ."

"Why am I not surprised?" More theory . . .

He grinned. "You hated the wormhole idea so much . . ."

"So did Brad, remember."

"So he did. I'll miss his skepticism; we're going to need it."

"Sounds like I'm going to need some right now."

To his credit, he grinned again. They sat in the cool, bleached light of the bay for a long moment, staring at each other forlornly. Then he began cautiously to circle around his own thoughts. The ship of theory could set sail on tides of mathematical grandeur and hope alone, but only data could fill its sails. Now Max had more information about the sphere than he could fathom. Like meteorologists, more reliable at foreseeing the climate than at predicting tomorrow's weather, he began with what had been done before.

"I looked for precursor ideas," Max said. "I ran a quick database search on key words—'Macroparticle,' 'Quark-gluon,' 'Plasma'—and got nothing useful." He looked almost apologetic, mouth drooping at one corner in self-parody, drawn and tired; she realized that she was probably worse. "So I went back to my own thinking. I've got another crazy idea."

"I need real answers," she said, trying to draw some strength out of somewhere. "Is this crazy enough to be right?"

"It's probably impossible. That close enough?"

"It'll do." She had to smile, but it was a bleak one. "Shoot."

"I think it's *like* a wormhole, but not to another place in our space-time."

"I still don't buy the wormhole idea, and now you want to tack on—"

"A whole new space-time."

"How?"

Max brought a sheaf of photocopied sheets out of his brief-case. "I looked back at papers Alan Guth wrote with a bunch of other guys in the 1990s. Strange stuff, but it might fit."

"A separated space-time?"

"Look, suppose we think back to one second after the Big

Bang. To make it, you'd need about 10^{89} of the basics—protons, electrons, neutrons, photons, neutrinos. A lot. But now think about an earlier time, before the universe inflated, before it really took off. All you need there is a region of false vacuum.''

She knew all this, the standard early universe scenario from grad school, furniture supplied by particle physicists to the field of cosmology decades before. It had become as conventional as the story of how rock 'n' roll evolved from American pop to British invasion to psychedelic and then into slow decline. A minute region begins—never mind why—excited to a higher energy state. The Grand Unified Theories of a generation before demanded only a speck of false vacuum 10^{-28} centimeters across with a mere gram of mass packed into it. Close to nothing, in other words. But that matter was compressed to a density 10^{80} times that of water. Beyond the range of any conceivable techno-trick.

''—so if a false vacuum *can* form,'' Max was saying, ''it should neck off from ours in an instant.''

''Uh, 'neck'?'' Her lips puckered skeptically.

She could just barely keep up with his terminology, a frequent problem she had with theorists. He had already generated some computer sketches and printed them out with hand-lettered labels. She tried to follow the way the false vacuum formed a ''bubble wall'' within ordinary space, which was the ''true vacuum'' where everybody lived.

''Yeah, a neck is an indentation in our space-time—which is the 'true' vacuum. This dent represents a false vacuum, a dip which deepens very fast. This drawing tells the geometric truth, too. Once the bubble of false vacuum''—he shaded in the bulb at the base of the space-time funnel—''has room to move, it can grow *without* taking up volume in our space-time.''

The best way to follow a theory, she knew from long experience, was to break it into pieces and worry each until she got some physical feel for it. ''So the false vacuum makes a new space as it expands.''

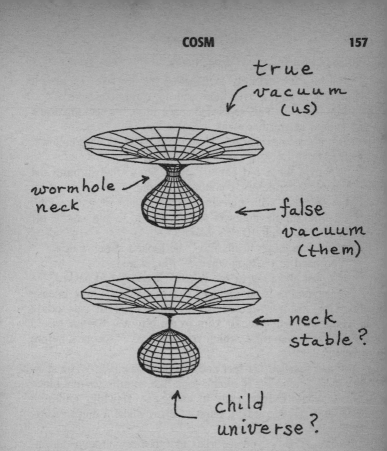

true vacuum (us)

wormhole neck

false vacuum (them)

neck stable?

child universe?

"Right, *new*. Very important. It doesn't have to expand at our expense."

"That cord connecting us to the bubble, you mean it's—"

"One end of it is a sphere, in our space-time. A class of wormhole nobody really analyzed before."

"Why is it solid?" Back to the earlier questions.

"Because the special compressed space-time that makes this cord, it's like an inconceivably hard substance. Light goes through it, nothing else."

"You said something like that before." *To Brad*, she thought, then deflected her mind away from the memory with

"Why should I believe that now?"

"Because it's the only explanation for how we can have a stable sphere sitting over there and not a tiny black hole."

"I don't get it. This separated space-time, it's necking down and should get farther away, right?"

"But it's also expanding. How those effects counterbalance, I don't know."

"What do these old papers say?" She riffled through the photocopies skeptically, catching titles that made no sense.

Max fidgeted with his chalk, a sure sign of uncertainty. "Well, the simple analysis shows that it should choke off rather fast, in about 10^{-37} seconds."

Rather than laugh in his face, she looked at her watch.

"You need to be somewhere?" Max asked.

"No, just checking to see if 10^{-37} seconds had passed."

He laughed explosively and she saw that he was uneasy about this theory, wanted her to approve. That was oddly touching in itself, but she kept to the physics. "What would it look like in that time, which you say is 10^{-37} seconds, before it was gone?"

He still shuffled his feet and fidgeted his chalk. "The standard calculation says it *should* look like an infinitesimal black hole. It would radiate away its energy by Hawking emission in about 10^{-23} seconds, a burst of energy like a megaton explosion."

"Whoosh! Boy, you theorists like to throw around the impossibilities."

She smiled to herself. So even if God made a universe this way, theory showed that it should gurgle down the drain in 10^{-37} seconds, gone forever. It reminded her of a line from an old Woody Allen movie, that if it turned out that there was a God, at least He wasn't evil. The worst one could say was that He was an underachiever.

Max went on, undaunted. "Ah, but! That result leaves out the possibility of 'miracle struts,' the kind of negative energy density regions I talked about before. If they're in place, then the black hole doesn't form. We get instead a new class of wormhole, held open by the tension in those struts of negative energy density.''

''Why not just say they're held open by angels?''

He sighed, nodding ruefully. ''I know this sounds like so much hot air. But we've got a *real object* to describe here, something made in a quark-gluon plasma. Nobody has *proved* that a negative energy density zone of the right size—as big as that sphere over there—is impossible.''

''How could the RHIC uranium collisions lead to *this*?'' she demanded.

''Quantum tunneling,'' Max said.

She blinked. A quantum system could make a jump from one state to another totally different configuration, even when the usual classical rules of energy conservation didn't allow it. The textbook case she had done as an undergraduate: calculate how often a prisoner, running at a wall, could quantum-mechanically ''tunnel'' through the wall and escape. This was where the popular press got the term *quantum leap*, used without understanding, as usual.

She recalled solving that problem and being intrigued by the simple form of the result. It turned out that his chances depended exponentially on the thickness of the wall and so was infinitesimally small unless the wall were so thin that he could poke a finger through it anyway. Still, in principle, if he kept running at it, eventually he could escape through any thickness of wall. It might take a billion years, but in principle . . .

''Look at it this way,'' Max said. ''Quantum tunneling means that a system can 'explore' energetically not-allowed regions of the classical configuration space. If a tiny false vacuum starts, it can tunnel through to another space-time, a very different one, as long as that final state is also allowed by general relativity.''

''To believe anything so far-fetched, I'd have to see a solid calculation.'' She sat on a lab bench, grateful for a moment of speculation, but pretty sure they were going nowhere. Her old doubts about Max were returning, though in the last few days he had been a valuable friend.

He shook his head vigorously, hair waving from a cowlick. "Impossible. That demands a complete theory of quantum gravity, which nobody has. The closest is a slung-together guess by three guys at MIT."

He tossed her a thick paper titled "Is it Possible to Create a Universe in the Laboratory by Quantum Tunneling?" by Edward Farhi, Alan Guth, and Jemal Guven from *Nuclear Physics*, a respected journal, dated 1990. Weighty evidence, but she was seldom impressed by long theory papers; her gut feeling was that a really good idea could be expressed simply and briefly—and had better be, if a theorist expected an audience beyond her fellow pencil pushers.

She frowned doubtfully. "You believe this?"

"I believe the calculation leaves a lot of possibilities open. Look at this—" Another paper, this time by Alan Guth alone. "See? A direct quote: 'If there exists a false vacuum with an energy density near the Planck scale, which is certainly not excluded by anything we know, then the tunneling probability would be of order *one*.' That's the last line of the calculation."

In a tiny sliver of time just after the Big Bang, she knew, matter was thickly packed at the Planck density. For that instant, gravity and the other forces were all one great metaforce, and Creation had a free hand. The Planck energy was the chemical energy of a car's full tank of gasoline—all concentrated in a single particle. A quantum state like that might be possible, she supposed, but . . . "So what? That doesn't prove an accident at RHIC could conceivably—"

"No, something else does." He stopped leaning against the blackboard and came toward her. "Your data."

"How?"

"That hydrogen recombination line. Your detectors saw the moment when electrons and protons settled down into marriage, making hydrogen."

"Meaning what?"

"The sphere is a window into a whole other universe—one just created."

Alicia frowned. "A whole universe . . . ?"

"This 'Mini Bang' of yours made a separate, tiny space-time. Not vacant, but with mass, just like ours. Then it expanded. That's why you kept getting that spectrum of a hot blackbody. The mini-universe was expanding, cooling, but the radiation was still getting reabsorbed by the matter. That's what gave the simple spectrum. When the mini-universe got big enough, the matter thinned out, the radiation cooled. As soon as things were mild enough, the electrons found the protons, they got hitched, and the wedding announcement was a burst of photons.''

She saw it now. ''That's what we detect now in our night sky? The relic radiation. It's been rattling around the universe ever since the atoms formed.''

''Exactly. When it was emitted, it was hot stuff: 3,000 degrees. It's been cooling off ever since, so now it's just weak microwaves in our sky. The hydrogen recombination line, that we can't see at all anymore. It's masked by infrared from dust clouds. But *you* saw it, right here, coming from that sphere.''

''Look, I don't remember much of the cosmology course I took, but I do recall that matter combined into hydrogen *long* after the Big Bang.''

He nodded. ''For us, yes. You're right about the era when hydrogen formed; I looked it up. A lot of things were suspiciously going on then. For example, the energy density of light was about equal to the energy density of mass then. When light lost out to matter and the atoms were free to form, well, that might affect the other end of this window we have here.''

She didn't let him dodge her question. ''When did it happen?''

Grudgingly he said, ''In our universe, the relic radiation came from about four hundred thousand years after the Big Bang.''

She could always smell a theorist ducking a crucial point. ''Doesn't that kill your theory? The sphere is only weeks old.''

''True.'' He tossed his chalk into the tray. ''There's more to learn, then. If that sphere is a peephole into a universe, then time is running faster on the other side.''

She waved away the time issue; the main idea was still dawning on her. ''A whole universe?'' She stared at the sphere, gleaming innocuously. "And we have a window on it?"

"Yeah, a window held open by negative energy density tension. It's recapitulating our whole history, but faster."

"How much?" She was having trouble with all this. "How fast?"

"Uh, I'll have to work on that." His fragile air of certainty collapsed; he shrugged. Theory in such rarefied realms was as fragile as a butterfly's wing, its flight sustained by bravado.

"We'd better be sure we even know what we're talking about," she said uncertainly.

He gave her a wobbly grin. "Can't go to the experts—there aren't any."

She glimpsed in his face something she knew all too well: what it was like to work on hard problems and have them take up all the space in you, leaving nothing for the soft word of people and pleasantries. You had to live with an awful uncertainty, not just the obvious nugget problem but the suspicion that you were wrong all down the line, asking the wrong question of reality, and would get from Mother Nature the nonreply you deserved.

Something in the swing of his shoulders, an unthinking confidence, moved her. Could he possibly be right? She was bone-tired and ready to clutch at straws, maybe, but—she *wanted* it to be right. So that the tragedy of Brad's death—*in Creation's sunburn*, she thought unsteadily—was offset a bit by the birth of a whole new . . .

"A cosmos . . . should we call it that?" She stared at the shrouded sphere and felt a mingling of wonder and fear: awe.

"No, we should have a different name for it. The cosmos is big. This is little, a toy." He gazed over at the silent, deadly thing. "Its hardness . . . maybe we're seeing a kind of durable event horizon here? One that lets very little through, except stray photons. Maybe the UV got scattered enough to slip through a tiny little trajectory-space . . ."

She sighed. "We're just guessing."

"When you have a Ph.D., you call them hypotheses, not guesses."

She smiled, said nothing, just looked at the U-magnet and what lay within, cloaked and latent and suddenly, strangely chilling.

Max continued gamely, "It lets through nothing solid, anyway, so we can literally rap on it with our knuckles."

"Only it doesn't sound hollow. It just absorbs acoustic waves. Maybe we should try to measure that?"

"Sure, measure everything. It might all matter. Maybe we should borrow from gravitational theory, call it a new kind of event horizon?"

"A theorists' name."

"Ummm, right." He followed her gaze, peering at the shielding around the sphere. "A pocket-sized space-time that nonetheless, in its own geometry, opens onto all the structure ours does."

"Yeah, but 'cosmos' seems a little grand."

"Maybe something that claims a little less than everything?" he said uncertainly.

"Let's shorten it. How about 'Cosm'?"

"Ummm." He narrowed his puffy eyes, nodded. "Better than any of the mathematical words I've been fooling with . . ."

"Cosm, then," she said. It seemed right somehow.

4

"**D**ad? I'm in trouble." Not the sort of telephone call one wanted to make, but Jill had browbeaten her into it.

"Honey, I heard." His voice was slow and careful, deeper than she remembered. "Friend spotted the piece in the *Register,* faxed it to me."

"I wish the university hadn't said anything to the newspapers."

"A medium-sized piece on the first page of the Metro section, factual, no speculation on cause of death. I think you got off pretty well."

His quick rattle of professional assessment reassured her. "We really don't know cause of death, Dad," she said guardedly.

"But you've got ideas," he said, tone rising, his drawing-her-out voice.

"Look, could you come down for dinner or something?" There, out in the open. She had gone to him before, out of the blue, with troubles far smaller than this.

"How about tonight?"

"Could you?" Her heart leaped into her voice.

"I'll e-mail from the San Jose Airport, let you know when I'll be coming in."

So she had gotten through the rest of the day, dividing her time between office hours for her Physics 3-B class, talking to Max in the lab, and dealing with the safety office. She picked Dad up at John Wayne Airport just before the rush hour. He came out of the terminal in a trim gray suit that framed his bronzed head well, gracefully swinging his flight bag, looking more rawboned than usual. He wore a tie she had given him years ago for a birthday and wondered if that was deliberate, a sweet gesture; then she thought better of asking.

"You look great!" He grinned at her, getting in the passenger seat, giving her cheek a quick peck. His diction was precise, even prissy at times. She could remember him doing imitations of educated blacks trying to do streetspeak, the "mutha" for mother, "livin' large, girl," "What dey gone set bail at?" jive. He was the opposite, controlled and exact, comfortable with his repute. She recalled that she had been so insecure during her college years, she hoped that some of the gold of her father's fame would rub off on her, a sort of gilt by association. Now she needed some of his calm to rub off, too.

They got into the usual catching up, asking about relatives, who was where doing what. She had long ago learned that from her father's pinnacle, one wing of his family was trash, people who learned only at the toe end of somebody's boot. These he ignored, while the suitable wing got meticulous attention; he regaled her with stories. In that wing you never missed a day of school unless you were bleeding from your eye sockets, wore demure clothes with orderly hair, and not only kept your eyes on the prize—you *were* the prize.

On the drive down Laguna Canyon she ventured a question about Maria, his wife of two years, and he said, "I still think it's best that you two not see each other for a year or so."

"It's been two," she said. He expressed surprise and she knew that nothing had changed. She and Maria had gotten off on the wrong foot and they had never put it right. Maria had a compulsion to verbally rearrange the world to fit her tight specifications; in practice this meant that she had plenty of theories about how black women should be, too many for Alicia.

"Well, Aleix, this'll take time," he said in a studied tone. She had changed her name from the African Aleix to Alicia when she went away to college, fresh beginnings and all. Her parents had been into black roots and the rest of it when she was born, then had rapidly backed away. Her father's political evolution had followed a trajectory away from what he termed in one of his op-ed pieces "the narcissism of minor differences." He had approved her abandoning the Africa-nodding of Aleix, remarking only that his thinking in those days had been mere mulling over food and folktales.

She had been surprised when he wrote a series of columns on his emergence, his recovery from her mother's death in an auto accident, and one entirely about her. This was on his long march abandoning, in his phrase, "obligatory blackitude," so he had folded it into a thesis about the hollowness of hauling out costumes and traditional foods from lands you had never even visited. He had taken a stand against a black group insisting on carrying their "cultural weapons" to political rallies, on grounds that they stood for a precious cultural inheritance which should be beyond criticism. Tom Butterworth ("Uncle Tom" to his enemies, of course) then argued that a ban on spears was scarcely an attack on their culture, since none of them knew much more about real spears than which was the business end. The entire series in book form won a Pulitzer. A man of the new libertarian left (an oxymoron, but he let it stand), social critic, occasional maven to the mighty, he made judgments for a living; she needed some.

All that shadowed her mood until they were walking on the beach near her apartment. It was hard to concentrate against the sunny splendor of the place. The lazy crescent beaches, despite their lazy sun worshippers, were battlegrounds. Roving eyes compared slim thighs, bunched pecs, ribbed bellies. Bodies sought audiences. All around them stirred restless devotees of the new narcissism, the conspicuous consumption of health as a brightly packaged commodity: plastic surgery and diet for the skin's pesky folds and wrinkles; lasers to clear blurred vision; pills galore to erase pain, amplify energy; clever genetic engineering to tailor away chronic ailments and create defect-free children. Stay slim, live right, last forever. And she kept thinking about the ruined face she had found on the lab floor . . .

She took some deep breaths and grasped her father's hand. In halting phrases she told the whole messy story and he nodded and made sympathetic murmurs but nothing more. She had expected him to be riveted by the key idea, the universe in a hatbox, but he accepted this without blinking. His calm was unnerving.

They had long since left the long main beach and mounted the rise to Heisler Park. Along the scooped-out rocky arches of its coast they strolled, Dad with his head back, taking in the palm trees and vistas, she with her head down, as if suspecting the footing ahead. He watched some surfers getting slammed against the rocks below in a white froth, winced at the punishment they took, and then said calmly, "You'll need Bernie Ross."

"Who is?"

"Attorney, good one, knows this sort of stuff."

"And what sort of stuff is this?"

"Media management. If you're ten percent right about what this thing is"—hand held up, palm out, quick flash of even teeth in a dead-white smile—"not that I'm doubting your professional judgment, girl—well, then, you can't keep it quiet."

"Of course I can. Until we have better results, a chance to thoroughly—"

"You'll get no chance."

"I don't plan to publish or even give a talk until—"

"Two weeks, tops."

She felt a spurt of irritation at him and caught herself before she let her mouth run away. "It's my research. Nobody, not Brookhaven or UCI or—"

"UCI will do it. You'll have to tell them something."

"Maybe a confidential committee. That's all."

"Remember that egg scandal at UCI a decade back? How long did that stay confidential?"

"Okay, but that was a scandal, as I remember."

"This has a death in it already."

"An accidental one," she said, voice rickety.

"Information wants to be free—remember that old saw? Some truth to it, only it's backward. This isn't an information economy—we're drowning in *that*—it's an attention economy. That's what everybody's vying for. Me, I've got a li'l piece of the public's attention, they read my column. So I know the territory. Any of my esteemed colleagues sniff what you got here, they'll be all over you.''

''I don't want attention.''

''No, *they* do. So they use you.''

''You're exaggerating.''

''I want a good lawyer to look after you. I wouldn't put it past UCI to go after you. That's what they did with the egg scandal doctors, even though nobody really proved a case.''

She understood now; he was rushing in with a solution, classic male pattern, before he knew what she wanted. ''Okay, have this Mr. Ross call me.'' Her classic easy-exit settlement.

He nodded contentedly. ''Then we've got to talk about what the hell this all means. And how my li'l girl gets through it.''

''Let's,'' she said happily. He kissed her lightly, smiled, and they walked back toward the south. He admired the golden coast spreading into the filmy blue distance, the south coast's offhand splendor, and she saw trouble coming toward them, in the form of Max. Waving, he walked quickly along the concrete path, oblivious to the beauty.

''Hello, sorry to interrupt,'' he said rapidly as he neared them. ''I missed you at UCI, wanted to look at some of that old data. The apartment manager said you'd gone for a walk.''

''You checked the notebooks in the lab?'' she shot back, somehow disturbed at his sudden appearance.

''There aren't many. What's there doesn't cover much of your work, as far as I can see.''

''I've got the rest in my apartment,'' she said. ''Oh, Dad, this is Max Jalon.''

''I'm Tom.'' The two men shook hands a bit stiffly, each eyeing the other, murmuring the usual. Max complimented Tom on his suit, the first sign of fashion awareness she had ever seen from him, and Tom took it with a skeptical drawing down of his mouth. Was Max trying to get on Tom's good side? Impressed with his minor celebrity? The thought bemused her.

Max made a few more casually companionable remarks as they all walked back toward the center of town, seagulls squawking overhead at the brimming sunset. They stopped to watch the sun's circle warp into a refracted orange oval and Max kept talking through the whole thing, explaining in needless detail how he had searched the lab, even though the UCI safety people were there making measurements of some kind.

"What measurements? They told me they were just placing a seal on the room."

"They didn't let me in until their boss came by and gave me an okay. It looked like they were checking the hard disks on your diagnostics computers."

"Taking my data!"

"Looked like. I asked them, but they wouldn't say anything, brushed me off really, referred me to somebody across the campus. I came here instead."

Alicia nodded, chagrined that she had left UCI without thinking of Max, who had been working in the library. Her father asked with his well-honed formality, "Mr. Jalon, may I ask your interest in all this?"

"I'm a friend of your daughter."

"What sort of friend?"

"A colleague," Max said, blinking with surprise.

"I see," he said with the fine-edged disbelief she had seen the public Tom Butterworth use in debates. "Then you'll understand her need to keep this matter as closely held as possible."

"Sure I do. I just need to see—"

"I think she can decide when to show her results," Tom said, aloof and smooth.

"I can, Dad, and Max is one of the few I trust," she intervened.

What was going so quickly wrong here? She tried to figure it out as she guided them both on a shortcut along by the art museum and across Coast Highway. Traffic muttered in the early stages of the daily snarl and the fumes wrinkled her nose. She studied her father's face and as they reached Lower Cliff Drive she guessed: he thought Max was her boyfriend. She almost laughed and then wondered what her father had seen that made him think so. Or was it the *white* boyfriend angle? She tried to recall, and yes—her father had never seen her going out with any of the half dozen white or Asian men she had favored in her early twenties. The two of them had been distant then, at odds; then came Maria. The last boyfriend material he had seen had been black—by pure accident, no calculation on her part—half a dozen years ago. She could not suppress a smile. Imagine!

The three of them reached her apartment and Dad looked around uncomfortably at the general clutter. He was a Neat, she was a Sprawler; genetics had failed again. Alicia went into the kitchen and opened the 1960s-style oven, fetching out six lab books, thick with taped-in printouts. "The oven?" Dad asked.

"Not as though I'm going to bake a cake or anything."

"They'd look there pretty early, though," Tom Butterworth said.

"Who?"

Deadpan: "UCI, once they get a writ to come after materials you've withheld from their investigation."

"They wouldn't do that," she protested, plopping down on the living room sofa.

"Never underestimate lawyers on a roll," Tom said.

"Ummm, can I keep these overnight?" Max said quietly, his tone tiptoeing by.

"I'd rather not let them out of my sight," Alicia said.

"I'm interested in tracking all the spectra you measured—and the exact time of observation," Max said, sitting down and stacking the bulky notebooks on her Danish coffee table. Three promptly toppled onto the carpet, which exhaled a cloud of dust in reply to the assault.

"Why?" she asked.

"Just a hunch. Prowling the data, y'know."

"Look at them here," she said.

"Looks like a lot of work," he said. "I can't do it in a hour or two."

"Stay overnight, then," she said, not wanting to dissuade

him from doing anything that might help. "Tomorrow you can finish here. I'm still not going to take them back to UCI."

When she glanced over at her father, she was surprised to see his face grim, narrow-eyed. "You should not involve others in what may be illegal."

"Illegal?"

"Or, at the very least, cause for dismissal."

"What? They can't fire me—"

"Of course they can! Do you imagine faculty are dismissed only for fornication with undergraduates?"

"In the humanities not even for that," she said, trying to let a little air into the suddenly heated tone.

"You don't have tenure yet, honey."

"No, but . . ."

Max stood. "Look, I can come back tomorrow—"

"No, you can stay here." Alicia stood up and paced, the silence in the room growing longer, then she put her hands on her hips and marched over to the window, glanced at the mire of cars on the Coast Highway, turned, walked back to the kitchen, then whirled and said to her father, "You don't want him to stay here overnight, is that it?"

"No no, I just—"

"That *is* it! And I'm thirty-one years old."

"Not at all, not at all." Stiff now, the public voice back. "I think you should look to the legal ramifications of all this. If UCI suspects you of withholding data which bears on an investigation, one which has criminal possibilities, even if only from negligence, then you cannot involve others—"

"You think I'm guilty of negligence?"

"I only hold out the possibility. Try to look at it the way an attorney—"

"No, you try to look at it *my* way!"

Max said tentatively, "Look, I really can come back tomorrow—"

"Stay there," she said fiercely, putting a palm on his chest when Max started to take a step. "Dad, all you can think about is legal-eagle crap!"

Tom shrugged. "That's my training."

"How about the . . . the *enormity* of this?"

"Plenty things look important when you're up close, honey, but—"

"It really *is* important."

He tipped his chin up and assumed a look of tolerant patience. A warning bell went off in the back of her mind and she made herself take a long breath. Abruptly she remembered how, when she was a teenager, she had stormed to her bedroom and slammed the door so hard it reverberated through the house. Her father had said not a word, just took a screwdriver and removed the door of her room. She lived that way for several days until the lack of privacy and the sheer unnerving feel of living that way made her apologize. Her father just nodded, kissed her, and put the door back up.

Anger wasn't going to work here. She expelled a long sigh and said, "We've created something new and, well, maybe awesome."

Tom nodded hesitantly. "I didn't really follow all that. The important thing is to see how UCI's going to play this, not that it's a new particle gizmo—"

"Gizmo? It's fundamentally *strange*."

"I understand that it's important to you—"

"And to the world," Max said softly. "If we're right."

Tom gave Max a quizzical glance, ridgelines of surprise rising on his brow. "It's that important?"

She realized in this quick shift that though her dad had listened to her go on about the sphere—the Cosm, as she thought of it now—he had simply blanked out on the physics, including the implications. Instead, he jumped to the bureaucratic, the political. Classic Dad demeanor; whatever problem pops up, if you own a hammer, look for nails.

Max said, "It could be a fundamental advance. A window into another universe."

"I thought there was only one universe."

Max sat back down and quickly began trying to explain. He was a lot better at it than she, and she let herself relax, sitting on the other end of the sofa from her father and wondering why she had gotten so provoked. What business of his was it if Max stayed here overnight? There was nothing between them. Could it be because Max was white, after all? Incredible.

But was that what set her off? She could not see through her own fog of emotion and so pushed it out of her mind. Better, far better, the cool abstractions of physics.

"See, these wormholes could connect different parts of our universe," Max was saying earnestly, drawing on a yellow pad, "or even hollow through to another universe entirely."

Tom gazed skeptically at the pad and Alicia felt a spark of affection for that rugged face. She had seen the same expression of puzzled concern through her tough teenage years, when he had played both Mom and Dad, nurturing one moment and sternly setting boundaries the next. Then came the tricky parting when she went off to college, exploring fields he never understood. Had they ever had an easy time? She couldn't recall one. Maria had been just another jarring jolt along an already bumpy road.

"It appears that in that other universe events are proceeding at an accelerated pace. It is cooling off faster than we did."

"How fast?" She recognized one of Tom's verbal tactics; even though barely hanging on to the drift of a conversation, he would shoot back a question about a detail. He had told her once that this created the impression of more understanding than you had, without actually making a claim.

"Millions of times faster, looks like."

"What in the world could make that happen?" Classic Tom, probing now.

"Uh, I don't know."

"Ummm-hummm." Polite frown. "How can you be so sure it isn't dangerous anymore, then?"

"Because it's cooling off."

"Uh-huh. But you say it's growing."

"Its expansion is into its *own* space, not ours. The sphere in her lab isn't going to swell, swallowing everything—or it would have already done so by now. But this other universe we can see *through* that sphere, that will evolve—and faster than ours did."

"How come?" Tom asked.

"I don't know." Max sat back, his hands making a neat little helpless gesture.

"Something about the, uh, wormhole connection itself?" Tom asked, this time not as a maneuver, she could see. Alicia blinked. He had never before ventured an idea when discussing physics with her. Not that they talked physics all that often.

Max nodded. "Could be, could be. We have no theory to guide us here, Mr. Butterworth."

"Tom. So . . . this is really important." He seemed impressed, gravely scrutinizing Max's sketches of drooping space-times. "And killing that boy, it was an accident? Can't happen again?"

Max said awkwardly, "Well, nothing's ever for sure . . ."

Tom chuckled. "Don't ever tell that to a judge."

"Look," Max counterattacked, "this other universe is cooling off very fast. No danger it'll be hot again."

Tom looked at her. "You've really tied into something here, Aleix."

Max asked about her name and Tom told his usual story about it. She had heard this approximately a thousand times, of course, and he did a funny version, so she used the moments to think about why Max had excited Dad's interest in the sphere while she had not. The outside expert syndrome? Somebody from Caltech who isn't your own daughter? A man?

Yet this same graying dad had also ushered her along the path to this moment, into fields he could not glimpse. She had always wondered why a whirling top slowly nodded, as if thinking to itself like an old wise man, rather than toppling over, like a child. Why soap bubbles made wobbly spheres, what the sun was burning all the time (and where was the smoke?), why chalk squeaked on blackboards, did the stars go on forever beyond what she could see, why did clouds sail high and not fall to the ground—all these were huge, consuming puzzles. And few adults, not even her dad, had seemed to have more than a vague guess about the answers. But he had seen to it that she found out.

She gave up and said, "Say, don't you guys ever get hungry?"

This was the right move. When guys were finally starting to get along, feed them and matters will improve. They would hunker down around the campfire and gnaw on seared meat and laugh and tell lies and forget whatever had gone awry before. She had Jill come over—calling Dad had been her idea, after all—and they went to a steak place. It was the usual upscale Orange County: glossy touches to the familiar pricey carved woods, leather wing chairs, cut glass, glazed lacquer, glints and glows highlighting the tastefully understated money. It worked out just fine.

5

The next day she knew it was trouble when Onell asked her to come up to his office on the fourth floor. The chairman's lair commanded a sweeping view of the inner park, now burgeoning in late spring. UCI recycled its water and had plenty to spare for grounds; already the surrounding hills were turning a seared tan, but the campus would be green all summer.

Onell wore a gray suit with blue shirt and a somber muddy brown tie, not a great combination. He looked pained, fiddling with his pen as he got through the preliminaries about how the UCI safety review people had made their recommendations, and he had conferred of course with Executive Vice Chancellor Lattimer, and everybody understood that serious precautions were needed, so "We believe you above all understand this and will therefore cooperate fully in what must be done."

Something impish in her made her reply to Onell's dour tone with "Sure. What's up?"

"Safety—that is, Environmental Health and Safety—feels that until the cause of Brad's death is clear, your lab should be isolated."

She had expected this, of course. "I'm pretty sure the sphere was the cause. If our ideas are right, it's safe now."

"I'm going to have to appoint an *ad hoc* department committee to consider the physics aspects of the issue," he said gravely. "For the moment, Safety has to be satisfied that the lab is not a threat."

"What's their idea of a precaution?"

"A concrete barrier around the sphere."

"Pointless."

"If you cannot be sure of the cause—"

"Also, a lot of time-consuming trouble."

"Time is not of the essence. Preventing another death is."

"Listen, we all feel badly about Brad's death. But I have to follow my own professional instincts in investigating what is a bizarre object—"

"Which you have not controlled thus far. And whose origin is, shall we say, problematical."

She had always been amused by this particular nugget of academic jargon, but here "problematical" seemed to veil something else. "You've been talking to Brookhaven?"

Onell kept his stiff, sober face, but his hands fingered his pen with renewed ardor. "They heard; it was in the news back in New York."

"And they put two and two together."

"The executive vice chancellor tells me that they are taking legal action to retrieve what they feel to be their property."

"Will UCI defend me?"

"That remains to be seen. First we must react to Safety."

"I hate the concrete bunker approach. How long would that take?"

"A month, perhaps. Time is not the—"

"Issue. I heard. Only I think it is."

Onell blinked. "Why?"

"The sphere is changing. We're not sure why, but it is. What killed Brad won't happen again, if our thinking is correct, but something more might—" To Onell's raised eyebrows she held up a palm. "Nothing dangerous, I assure you."

His eyes took on a canny look. "What do you want? Remember that you have no power here, that safety is all-important. The university has received undesirable publicity from this incident and there will undoubtedly be further inquiry into culpability and liability. Certainly Brad's parents will sue. We must—"

"Counterpropose to Safety. Let's move the sphere out of that lab entirely, to an isolated location."

"Ummm, possible, I suppose. Where?"

"The observatory."

She had plucked that out of the air, but it might work. Anything to stop safety minions from clomping around her lab and interrupting work for weeks.

Onell stopped fondling his pen. "It's an active research site. Others—"

"They use it by remote." The astronomy group ran the observatory by computer, taking data in the infrared, as per design; background light from Orange County loused up optical seeing. The observatory dome sat on the hill above the campus, hundreds of meters from anything else. "The best shielding is one over r squared."

This was a typical physics joke, referring to the falloff of intensity of anything, from light to explosions, with the square of the distance. Onell looked wary, not cracking even a diplomatic smile. "I doubt that's good enough."

"Okay, we'll put sandbags around it, too. They're quick, easy to move, cheap."

"How can you move the sphere itself?"

"Keep it in the magnet, haul the whole assembly up the hill."

"Ummm. I can speak to Safety, but—"

"This is a fast solution. If they're worried about risk, getting the sphere off to a remote site should come first."

His lips twisted in a lopsided ironic curve. "You think quickly."

"I'd better. I want to keep working on that thing, Martin."

"I understand. If something good can come out of this . . ."

"Yes." She just nodded.

Onell rose, his usual signal that a meeting was over, and then snapped his fingers. "Oh yes, I forgot to mention—Detective Sturges called. He is passing the case as an accident."

"Really?" A tremor of relief ran through her, surprising in its strength. "What . . . what took them so long?"

Onell shrugged. "It's an odd death, burning with no obvious source. They asked a lot of questions in the department and looked at the physical evidence and thought it over—"

"What sort of questions?"

"About Brad, his friends, you, the lab."

"Looking for a murder motive?"

"I wouldn't put it that harshly. They were polite when they questioned me and did not seem to have any particular line of inquiry."

She had known the police must be doing something and now realized she had simply not let herself think about it. Instead, she had focused on the physics. It had worked; Sturges had not even crossed her mind in days. The subconscious had its own methods, she was discovering.

6

The safety people were fumbling around near the apparatus and there was no one else allowed in the lab, by edict of the local Safety Nazi. They were taking elaborate pictures, working with some people from the legal office; more of their endless documentation. Alicia had been polite and distant and had gotten away from them as fast as possible when Max appeared. She had to argue with the legal types just to get him into the facility.

"The good news," Max said, "is that your assurance to Onell was okay. If I'm right, there is nothing further to worry about from the sphere."

"And the bad news?" she asked automatically, settling into a lab chair.

He looked puzzled and a bit bedraggled, in black jeans and a blue cotton work shirt. "Not much bad news, except that we're going to have to work fast to check out any of this."

"What's the scoop?" She was resolutely keeping matters light today. She did not want another sleepless night like the last one. No need to spiral down into a self-inspired depression.

Max was reluctant to discuss further his speculations of the night before, but she could see which way his thinking was going. He seemed a bit timid, maybe still rankled by how the wormhole idea had been received by her and Brad. And certainly he must feel some contrition for not having guessed what was coming. Pointless guilt, but she felt it in him. They had spoken of it in halting phrases, she unable to deal with hers, just as he was with his.

"Here. This says it all." He plunked down some graph paper.

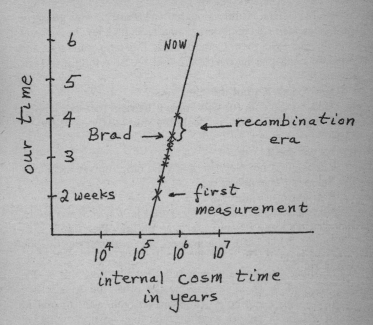

The vertical axis showed OUR TIME in units of weeks. The bottom axis was INTERNAL COSM TIME in units of YEARS. The diagonal line cutting across the page had points labeled RE-COMBINATION ERA and NOW and then kept going up. "Explain," she said, though a suspicion was forming.

"The trick here is to buy our assumption—that at the other end of that sphere over there, is another universe. One that formed at the Brookhaven Collider."

"So it's a little over five weeks old, right? This data point here, marked 'now.' "

"Exactly. We have the blackbody spectra from the last few

weeks, so I went to standard cosmology and asked a simple question. If that universe on the other side behaves like ours, at what age would it be the temperature we observe here?"

She thought quickly. "By looking up how fast we think our own early universe cooled off."

"Right!" His enthusiasm hid insecurity, she guessed; maybe his idea was really crazy and even he knew it. He went quickly on, "So then I could track the temperature of the expanding hot plasma over there and see how long it took as *we* see it."

"How come it's not the same time?"

"Stick to the data for now, okay? I found that the temperature you guys found is declining fast—exponentially, in fact."

"As we see it."

"Check—but now let's suppose the other universe isn't really behaving exponentially."

"But you just said it is."

"No, the temperature you measured is *how it seems to us*. That doesn't mean it looks that way on the other side."

She shook her head. Yes indeed, this was starting to look crazy, all right.

Her silence only made him talk faster. "See, this is the simplest way to go at it. Assume the other universe is like ours, only this wormhole—or whatever you want to call it, tunnel or tube or pipe or anything you like—distorts what we see."

"Why should I want to look at it that way? Makes no sense."

"Simplicity, as you'll see. Also, I've got some theory that says it should."

She much preferred talking about real data, not more mathematical abstractions. "Okay, simplicity."

"Occam's razor, y'know."

She froze, a sudden memory: explaining to Brad why there probably weren't any more of the spheres in the debris back at Brookhaven. *Occam's razor—prefer the least hypothesis,* she had trotted out the maxim with professorial superiority, never guessing what was coming . . .

"Alicia?"

She was gazing off into the distance and had to haul herself back into real time. "Uh, yeah."

"Suppose instead that the light from it is coming to us in a time-accelerated fashion. That lets us keep the same Big Bang model we already have for our own universe and apply it to what happens on the other side. The simplest approach."

"What distorts how we see the time on the other side?"

"I'll get to the theory later. I went to the data first, so let's follow my own fumbling, okay?"

He seemed to be urging her along and she realized that she must seem distracted, moody. She made herself concentrate. "Fair enough."

"So I took the temperatures you and Brad and Zak found, and I assumed those temperatures occurred in the other universe at the same time they did in ours. That gave me a mapping from your measured black body temperatures to the time on the other side. I just plotted it up on this lower axis."

She traced along the axis from left to right. "That's our first measurement: 5.2?"

"I didn't label this real well; that axis is the logarithm of time on the other side, expressed in years."

"Then the first time we took a spectrum, the other universe was already . . ."

"It's a log scale, see? So the universe on the other side was $10^{5.2}$ years old."

"But that's over a hundred thousand years!"

He spread his hands, palms up. "That's the way it works out."

"It's absurd." Relativity theory was full of time distortions and the like, she thought, but *this* . . .

"That's what the data leads to, Alicia. Stick with me."

"Impossible."

"As ol' Sam Treiman at Princeton used to say, 'Impossible things usually don't happen.' It's important to keep the 'usually' part in mind. You've got to be prepared to be surprised."

"Isn't that a contradiction?"

"I suppose so." He was eager to go on.

She chuckled despite herself. "Okay, show me some more impossible stuff."

"You're over the hump, believe me." He went on to explain the graph. The data points were all crowded down in the lower left hand of the plot. The straight line carved out the logarithmic relationship between time in their lab and time at the other end of the connecting tunnel. "See, recombination into hydrogen starts here, at about four hundred thousand years in the Cosm's history—that's a bit over four weeks, for us."

"Ah . . ." Best not to laugh at him anymore; he was looking fragile. "Very interesting."

She had learned to drop such empty praise whenever she read one of her father's columns in his presence. At least it was better than one time when she was a teenager and he had proudly shown her his first collection of essays; she had looked it over and said, "Nice paper."

"I plotted all the data you've got, to determine the slope of this line. I can write it out as an equation, too."

He neatly wrote on the board:

$$\text{COSM TIME} = 64,800 \text{ YEARS } [\text{EXP(OUR TIME/2 WEEKS)} - 1]$$

He had a figure printed out and hand-labeled, as was his habit. A smooth exponential curve rose.

He had crosses for data points in the third and fourth week of LAB TIME, with BRAD marked. At the top were questions, GALAXIES? STARS? The vertical axis was Cosm time in years, most multiplied by 10^6, a million.

He stood there beaming at her while realization dawned. "So . . . in the first two weeks the Cosm aged by . . . good grief, over a hundred thousand years."

"Right! So by now it's really taking off, maturing. The clocks in the Cosm run faster all the time. They exponentiate every two of our weeks."

"*If* they form. How do we know this universe is like ours?"

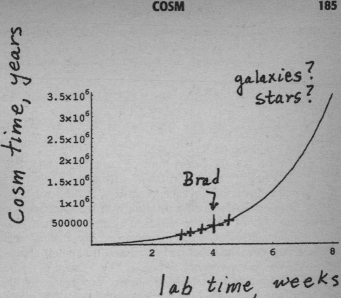

"We don't," he said cheerfully. "But we'll be able to find out."

"How?"

"Look for enhanced visible light while this UV we've recorded goes away."

"That visible light would come from stars, if they form," she guessed.

"Right!"

"Um." She stalled. Seldom was it a good idea to agree with a theorist; best to cultivate a skeptical reserve, bordering on disdain. "This exponential scaling you found, it comes out of the theory? I want to see the calculation."

He started to show her and very quickly she saw it was the kind of argument she did not like. He started from some symmetry principles in a twenty-three-dimensional space, which then caused all but five dimensions to collapse into regions of space-time so small they could never be measured. She asked him how that could happen physically and he showed her some more scaling relations which she could not see any physics in at all. It went downhill from there.

"So how can you put much trust in that?" she asked abruptly.

"It's one plausible model."

"How many other models are possible?"

"Let's confine it to plausible; the possibilities seem unbounded, provided that space-time is unbounded as well."

"I don't understand that, either."

He went on but she began thinking of a story about Paul Dirac, the English field theorist who had in the early 1930s formulated a theory of elegance, describing the electron beautifully. From it he deduced a solution with the same mass as the electron but of opposite electrical charge; all other quantum numbers they had were identical. He knew of no such particle but speculated that perhaps it was the proton, though the mass was conspicuously wrong, off by a factor of 1,836. Thus his failure of trust had led him to miss predicting the positron, which was discovered shortly afterward. But she respected a theory like that, a mathematical mind trying to forge its airy truths into concrete terms. Maybe, she realized as Max kept speaking, this could be like the Dirac case. Hold to the vision, hope to be vindicated. Maybe he should simply run with it.

"Okay, okay," she said. "What can you predict with this exponential curve of yours?"

"That inside that other universe, visible through the little window of this Cosm, galaxies should start clumping together within a short while."

"How long?"

He ran his finger along the straight line of expansion and squinted at the time axis. "About nine weeks from now, we could see galaxies form."

Well, at least he wasn't afraid to make a prediction.

"This really is a leap."

"Yeah." He sat down at last, relaxing from the tight, semi-fighter's stance he had adopted. "But it *smells* right, y'know?"

She could see the lines of anticipation in his face, deepened by fatigue. He had been frustrated and now thought he saw a solution, so he was following it.

Fair enough. Physicists often discovered things by getting frustrated. As a boy, Einstein thought of seeing himself in a mirror as he sped ever-faster, approaching the speed of light. He sensed that as he reached light speed his reflection would not vanish, that light would still be able to reflect from the mirror and reach his eye—and so discovered special relativity.

Nineteenth-century physicists thought about building perpetual motion machines and so devised the Second Law of Thermodynamics. Trying to pin down a particle's position and velocity simultaneously led Heisenberg to the uncertainty principle of quantum mechanics.

So now apparently physicists had made something out of nothing—made a whole universe, in fact. An accident, of course. But she had laid vehement claim to it all along, skirting the boundaries of scientific ethics. Would history judge that she had done it out of some deep, restless vexation she did not know?

She slept reasonably well for a few hours that night but as usual woke up and brooded about Brad and all the rest of it. She tossed and sweated as she listened to the traffic come booming in from the canyon and rumble to a stop at Coast Highway, the rustle of insect energies beneath the steady pale stars. Finally she mulled over Max's theory and then Max himself and what he had said there outside the bay, before she had gone in to face the detectives about Brad. Something about her having a smart mouth and "It's a cover, of course." "For?" she had shot back and he had said, "I wonder."

He had seen how close to the edge she was and his words had been sharp, cutting through her inner fog. It had seemed to make a lot of sense she could not quite describe, which meant that she could not explain it to herself, not even now.

She wondered if that meant that he had seen the Big Problem. Was it that obvious? The jagged nature of so many of her collisions with men implied that, even for a standard-issue obsessional neurotic, she was hard to get along with. Men rebounded from her as though from some unseen repulsive force. Or most men, anyway, though she did not get on famously with women, either. Most women had too much small talk and too little of everything else. She was perfectly aware that many of the physicists she knew felt something like that toward women as well. This had not been a happy fact to discover.

She had heard a lot of maxims for women scientists: Tenure Before Children; Marry a Fellow Workaholic; Smile but Dress Severely; Lace Underwear for the Inner You, but Jeans Outside. All these helped within the university but hobbled her outside.

The catalog of lovers scattered away by that strong, negative force was sobering.

Jonathan, a man of burnt pecan complexion which became caffè latte when he got irked, as he had after going through the obligatory Black Bourgeoisie dating code, following his ritual peacocking around: three dates got you to "heavy petting" (and where did that awkward term come from, somebody's mother?), then screwing on the fourth or fifth, usually on a weekend getaway to an upscale bed-and-breakfast (in New England for the East Coasters, Catalina for the West; definitely not Vegas). Somehow that weekend did not jell.

Frank, who lived up to his name in their last fight, calling her a "dick lick," and while she could scarcely deny the charge, clearly in his conceptual universe it was not a compliment.

Jonathan had just faded like a red dwarf star guttering out, certainly no supernova food-fight blowup in a restaurant, as with Ruben the Red. Ruben—she had left him with her virtue intact, but it was quite a struggle; she had almost won.

In all these collisions her difficulties rotated around sex, that alleged road to love. Jill had once said while only mildly drunk, so she might have meant it, that Alicia maybe had more personality than needed for one person; too intense. True enough; wasn't that what these late-night self-seminars were about? Even her self-doubt was overdone. She had waited in vain after adolescence for this pattern to abate: one mood was the swell dinner, the next mood was the bill.

Friends told her she had to understand herself better, which meant more talk, but she preferred to define herself by *doing* something. Chat she found claustrophobic. She thought of analysis as cutting off your head and counting the rings from all past years and the occasional forest fire. No, she would just tuck her head down and butt her way through her problems.

At college the predictable white sympathizers had ascribed most of her troubles to refracted racism, but Alicia had never bought that victimology, tempting though it was. Sure, if you're blonde and blue-eyed and lanky, things just showed up on your plate. But ugly black women of minimal talents made it to the top, too, or else how to explain Maya Angelou? Not that she was whining about being large of ass and bust and thighs and especially mouth. No victim, she; her defects were self-made.

So all right, maybe Max did see the Big Problem, or at least some version of it viewed from outside—and wasn't that what she was trying to do, find a way to see herself objectively?

Max the observant. She had made a crack to him about Gary Cooper quite automatically, an old line for her, really, and he had said that bit about her mouth being her cover, or something like that; it was getting sort of mixed up now. She wondered why, and then about Max again, something odd about that man, and suddenly felt the weight of all the rest of the empty night fall upon her yet again.

PART IV
A KING
OF INFINITE SPACE

I could be bounded in a nutshell,
and count myself a king of infinite space,
were it not that I have bad dreams.

—HAMLET

1

Moving the Cosm to the observatory seemed simple but took over four weeks in all. Alicia told Jill it was like swimming through mud, except that mud might help get rid of wrinkles; paperwork added them.

Bureaucratic measures sopped up a week all on their own. Safety wanted lots of time-consuming measures, of course. There were plenty of electronic diagnostic devices to pack up and redeploy in the more crowded floor of the observatory, with all their cables and cases.

Then came the moment when a crane lifted the U-magnet and Alicia held her breath as the Cosm seemed to wobble for just a moment in its magnetic trap. But then the crane whined away and took the massive assembly out to the loading dock and onto the back of a special UCI flatbed truck. The transfer took a whole day in which she did not eat or take phone calls or do anything except nervously triple-check every detail. When the U-magnet finally sat in its niche, surrounded by a cohort of electronic diagnostics like a fat king at court, she collapsed. Jill and Max took her out to dinner and they all went a bit giddy together.

She and Jill fell into reminiscence, regaling Max with tales of long-dead fashions; sitcoms whose characters they still remembered by name and felt that they knew better than their own classmates; ludicrous haircuts they had tried and then hoped would grow out over a weekend; dweebs who chewed tobacco or bubble gum; girls who slept around and got pregnant and then suddenly became sanctimonious about abortion; strapless gowns that gouged them unmercifully; Helen, who affected a walk with her nose in the air and paid for it by falling into a swimming pool at a big party; pulling all-nighters and wasting most of it going out for food and giggling from sheer fatigue. All these elements seemed in retrospect soft and warm and far funnier than they could possibly have been.

Max bore up under it well, throwing in some of his own. Yet beneath it all they knew that these weeks had been a hiatus; she and Max were saying goodbye to the UCI-imposed pause in their work. If they were right and the Cosm was some kind of window, then there would be so much more to see in the coming weeks, with no time to relax.

She did her best on her Physics 3-B lecture the next morning and then faced the day. Her office displayed the disarray that was almost a style, Basic Working Scientist: all horizontal surfaces were fair game for conversion to informal filing space, using the classic fossil-bed ordering, and no matter how computerized, there was always too much paper. She had not opened her mail for weeks, much less answered it. Still, the embossed Brookhaven National Laboratory stationery got her attention.

> *Professor Butterworth:*
> *We are proceeding against you in the matter of the missing portions of the experiment you recently performed here, April 24–30, using uranium isotope 238 . . .*
> *Yours sincerely,*
> *Jessica Farbis*
> *Legal Division, BNL*

There was a lot of legalese. A big battle was going on up in the levels where everybody dressed for success and had offices with carpeting, but she heard surprisingly little of it. She made a mental note to call the lawyer her dad had urged her to get, knowing that she would just put it off again. To submerge such thoughts she filed the letter, knowing she was going to hear from Lattimer about it. She turned to e-mail.

Over eighty messages were waiting, but most were UCI's ZOT Mail internal memos or other forgettable stuff. One of the reassuring aspects of being Out of It for a while was the realization that so much of the day-to-day routine was utterly pointless, plus the less-reassuring awareness that the world went on perfectly well without her. When she saw Rucker on the list, though, she immediately looked:

> Dear Alicia:
>
> The legal types don't want me to talk to you anymore, but they said nothing about e-mail. We've got several hotshots here who want to run with uranium again to see if they can produce what you made off with. There's a lot of anger over this in the Lab, I suppose I don't need to tell you. Your staying out of touch hasn't helped. So the admin types are behind the uranium guys and there's nothing I can do to stop them.
>
> The upshot is plain. If you don't give it up, they're going to start running uranium and specifically at BRAHMS.
>
> I don't like this and I appeal to you one last time.
>
> Dave Rucker

She liked Dave, but it was far too late to consider handing the sphere over to Brookhaven. They would take a month or two to ponder matters, giving it the full bureaucratic scrutiny with committees and the like, while the Cosm developed, unobserved.

But this bit about running with uranium again. Hadn't her damaged Core Element been enough of a warning? She hit REPLY.

> Dave:
>
> We're following up some exciting physics here, really a sensational discovery, we believe. I'll try to get something written down soon and off to you, including latest data.
>
> The sphere we took away is some kind of space-time closed geometry, utterly crazy, but you can rap your knuckles on it. And we can get tiny bits of radiation out of it, which seems

to say it is looking at *another* space-time. I really think this is the true scoop.

But it came about by accident. We think something made it stable, but it has expanded a centimeter or so since we started measuring.

That's why you *shouldn't* do anything right away attempting to make another. We don't know beans about this thing. It could be dangerous.

You heard about my student who got killed. Doesn't that make a strong point? You have *got* to stop them from running with U-238 again. Wait until I get a summary to you. Please?

Alicia

She didn't like the pleading question mark, but it might be effective; this was a male/female negotiation, after all. For long minutes she stared at the glowing words. Probably there was some way to make a big noise here and have the upper echelons at UCI wave to their counterparts at Brookhaven, but something told her that would be slower and less convincing. Physicists should clean up their own messes.

She made a hard copy of Dave's e-mail and her own, then punched SEND and hoped for the best.

Finals were coming, coming, then suddenly they were upon her. And upon Max, who retreated to Caltech for a week.

She had to take time out to make up an elaborate exam for Physics 3-B, with three different versions photocopied on differently colored paper. It was by now routinely canny to write exams so similarly that students copying from each other would be unable to tell what the other was doing. She took this further, arranging several problems that looked the same but had vastly different answers to penalize cheaters. This also thwarted ringers, who would take exams and write another student's name on them. The usual defense against this was to demand a photo ID with the turned-in exam. There were many Asian students at UCI, adding a twist: supposedly Caucasians couldn't tell Oriental faces apart, and some ringers advertised their services based on this. To counter this Alicia had specifically asked for Asian teaching assistants to proctor the exams. Coaching her teaching assistant proctors, judging the proper balance between written-out problems and multiple choice—it all took time.

At the end of the two-hour final, students came up to her asking about a new science fiction film that was doing big box office, wanting to know how much truth there was behind its fantasies. As nearly as she could tell from their descriptions, very little. She had not even heard of the movie.

Indeed, she had tried to follow books and films about science, but they featured rugged, style-conscious folk who transacted their work in ornate bars, atmospheric dens thickly mired in a high-contrast noir underworld future where bizarre ornamentation passed for any sense of newness. She had never known anybody who could design an experiment or do a calculation on table napkins, sipping hip drinks while guitar riffs wailed in the smoky background, but in movies and TV this was standard, apparently to make matters more interesting to a weary public with the attention span of a commercial. Scientists were either aggressively hip, often clad in tight leather, or else pitiful, hopeless nerds, obsessional neurotics nobody would trust for a moment with the discoveries they had, quite implausibly, ushered into the world while anxiously trying to get laid.

She had Zak making measurements on the Cosm, and Max was off at a conference, so she threw herself into getting the final exam graded immediately. On one of the simple qualitative questions in thermodynamics a student explained: *Water is melted steam.* Another wrote: *You can listen to thunder after lightning and tell how close you came to getting hit. If you don't hear it, you got hit, so never mind.* These the teaching assistants read out with glee around the grading table. Another related how a student had come to him, exasperated, saying, "My calculator keeps making the *same mistake*." At least the job had a few laughs along the way.

*   *   *

She left her office at sunset, having filed her grades by e-mail well before the deadline. There was a feeling of quiet satisfaction in it, she found. Certainly having momentarily drained the energies of the brightest of their generation, in pursuit of some solid knowledge, was an attainment.

Graffiti of the Hispanic regional cause marred a wall in the physics quad: a poorly drawn map of the Western United States sectioned off and united with Mexico to form a free territory for the flow of dollars and pesos and people. She stared at it and the ideas seemed light-years away.

See the scenic photons fall, she thought and realized that she was woozy with fatigue. But she biked up to the observatory to check on Zak. He was his usual quietly earnest self, never happier than when he could slug away at a tough experimental measurement. "What've you found?" she asked.

"Not much," he said. "The flux is dying fast."

She studied the curves of light intensity, descending by the hour. The trickle of light that fought its way out of the Cosm had shifted steadily down from the UV into the visible frequencies. They had caught images with the weak photons that came through, but got only a dim, uniform haze, no structure. Now the emission frequencies were sliding into the infrared and she and Zak had been forced to go scavenge more gear from Walter Bron to stay on the trail of the pale fading glow.

She wished Max had given them more guidance about what to look for. She knew the famous Enrico Fermi quotation: "Experimental confirmation of a prediction is merely a measurement. An experiment disproving a prediction is a discovery." But even such matters were minor, compared with what was at stake here. They were sailing utterly unknown waters.

"Nothing in the visible?"

Zak had shrouded the sphere carefully and mounted a whole new battery of optical sensors around it. "Still nothing. Peak's definitely in the IR now."

She fretted. It was easy to let your experimental acumen blind you. In the 1930s experimenters who bombarded elements with neutrons thoughtfully designed their experiment so that their Geiger counters switched off when the neutron beam did, to minimize sources of error. They missed the striking aftereffect; some elements gave off radiation as they then decayed, rendered unstable by the neutrons. This artificial radioactivity soon earned a Nobel for a less-fastidious experimenter.

"Let's look at this on-screen," she said. It was a simple matter to take some elementary cosmology, which she had been learning at breakneck pace lately, and apply it to Zak's measurements of the waning UV flux.

"Here." She used a simple plotting routine to take his data and turn it into a graph. "I translated the temperature of your UV counts into Cosm time."

"Time seen inside, you mean?" Zak was still having trouble following all this, not because he was not bright but because it was so bizarre. "How do you get time from temperature?"

"Using standard Big Bang cosmology. It says that temperature drops with time—in fact, inversely with the two-thirds power. I just transform that into our time, and—no surprise—we should see the temperature decline exponentially."

Zak nodded. "Because the two-thirds root of an exponential is still an exponential, just a slower one."

"Check. See?" His temperature data dropped exponentially. "The idea that the Cosm's time runs exponentially faster than ours still works."

"Y'know, the temperature we're getting now is about 300 K."

"Room temperature?"

The thought made her shiver. Inside the opaque sphere Creation's strange engines were speeding ever-faster toward a shadowy destination. The rate of time difference itself between the two increased exponentially, a cosmic roller coaster plunging for the bottom. Already the light that had fried Brad was no warmer than this observatory.

"Yeah, I'm getting counts only in the infrared. Even that's getting hard."

"You have to take longer and longer to get enough counts to measure?"

"Yeah. I'm integrating for about two hours a go now."

"It'll get worse, too. Weaker."

The photons inside the Cosm were still acting like a gas trapped in an expanding box—the prison of the Cosm universe. The walls in there drew apart steadily in time, just as they did in the "real" universe—she still thought of the Cosm that way—an effect that we saw as the Hubble shift, galaxies seeming to speed away from each other. Yet each galaxy was fixed in its own local space-time. Space-time *itself* was stretching like a rubber sheet.

She had always found this a bit hard to follow. The universe kept growing larger and photons responded to this by losing their energy, red-shifting down. The "gas" of light then cooled, its once-blazing glory now eroded to an ember's dull red.

In our universe the sole ancient remnant of the time when light dominated the universe was now the sputter of microwave photons spread across the sky, the 2.7 degree radiation which proved that an earlier, hotter era had in fact once held sway. The chill of that low temperature was a measure of how much the universe had swollen since it was a brawling newborn.

The universe at the other end of the Cosm "tunnel" was stretching itself, too. She tried to envision it spreading into an unimaginable separate direction that she and Zak could not see; it was literally beyond their ken.

Or so went her still rather amateur understanding of cosmology. She was paying for her single-minded concentration on particle physics as a student. In the required cosmology course she had dozed off pretty regularly.

Still, she was rather happy that the temperature data came out exponential, just as Max's time-shift equation said it would. Fermi wasn't quite right; it felt reassuring to find something that checked.

"What'll I do next?"

"Measure the diameter lately?"

"Yeah—looks to be about two millimeters smaller."

She raised her eyebrows. "Really? Smaller?"

"Looks like."

"So it's growing like crazy in its *own* space-time, but it can even shrink a little in ours," she said wonderingly.

"Funny, huh?"

"Ours is not to reason why, ours is to measure and report—the experimenter's credo."

Zak grinned. "Yes, ma'am. Your orders, ma'am?"

"Keep at it" was all she could say.

"Y'know, you kind of look like you could use a break."

"Could be."

"I can look after things here."

She felt a warm thankfulness at his concerned expression. She had steeled herself to plunge back into work, but part of her *was* worn down. She needed time to sleep, sure, but more important, to think. She nodded mutely and left.

Since the rig they had assembled in the observatory was nearly automatic now, she left Zak in charge and allowed herself an escape. The next morning she climbed into the Miata and zoomed up to Idylwild in the mountains for two days of hiking. She had been a team sports fanatic in high school and college, playing basketball and volleyball pretty well. But as her social isolation increased and she burrowed into physics, she took up loner sports: swimming, hiking, even workouts on the exercise machines that made her feel like a lab rat in somebody's perpetual experiment.

Hiking suited her perfectly now. She climbed Mount San Jacinto and ate heartily in a steak restaurant and slept as though in a coma. She kept to herself and thought about the Cosm and did not even read a newspaper.

2

She sat sipping coffee in Espresso Yourself on Forest Avenue, the morning after her late-night return, and casually flipped over the *Los Angeles Times*. Her eyes flicked down through the usual scandal, gossip, and politics, noting that there didn't seem to be much difference between them anymore. The item that snagged her attention ran below the fold on the front page. Not important enough for the headline.

EXPLOSION AT LONG ISLAND LABORATORY

(AP) A large blast at the Brookhaven National Laboratory has damaged the nation's newest high energy physics facility. The accident occurred during experiments involving uranium moving at very high energies. Though there is no report of radioactivity at the site, environmental groups demanded the right to send in their own teams, officials said.

An entire segment of the ring-shaped particle accelerator appears to be split. Helicopter observers reported a "shiny substance" visible through the upthrust beams and girders of the ruptured ring structure. The site is being searched, with one staff member reported missing.

The cause of this devastating accident, already estimated as costing tens of millions of dollars to repair, appears unknown . . .

She got up and ran out, leaving her corn pancakes steaming where they had just been served.

*   *   *

Warm summer rain ran off the gleaming silver dome. It shone under the arc lights in early evening as rivulets snaked across the pure smooth curve beneath fitful gusts of a sea breeze. She had grabbed a flight bag and a windbreaker at home and gone straight to John Wayne Airport, catching the first available flight for JFK. All her fidgeting worry on the way had not prepared her for this.

"Anybody hurt?" she asked.

"One technician killed, head crushed in," Dave Rucker said at her elbow. "We were damn lucky nobody else was. It blew a hell of a lot of steel around."

She felt a sickening lurch in her stomach. Brad first, now another . . . "Let me see it up close." She started up the berm of the RHIC ring.

"Ah, Safety doesn't want anybody—"

"Tell them I'll sign a release."

There were Brookhaven Lab guards and chicken-wire fencing all around it, but with a nod from Dave they let her pass. Soggy mud made the way tricky. The chrome globe protruded from the ruins of the accelerator ring, a skirt of broken concrete and girders rimming it.

"How big?"

"About sixteen meters across. As nearly as we can tell, it pushed everything out of the way—the beam line, BRAHMS detectors, the works."

"It didn't absorb anything in the lab?"

"Apparently not." Dave sighed. "Just pushed everything aside—*wham*—sounded like a bomb."

"Just like ours, only bigger."

"I'm glad you came right away. When you didn't call—"

"I didn't check in at UCI," she said, distracted. The rain was coming harder now and she peered at the object with narrowed eyes. "It's a sphere all the way around?"

"Seems to be. A team went into the tunnel and said it looks that way."

"Turn off the spotlights."

"Why?"

"Just do it."

"I need to know why."

"I'm not sure. Just a hunch." She waited, then said, "Please."

He took a while to get permission from some men in yellow slickers standing over by some hastily erected tents. Without asking permission anymore, Alicia walked right up to the dome. No steam where the rain fell on it. She touched the hard unyielding skin of it, no warmer than the ground. The spots winked off then and she let her eyes adjust to the gathering darkness. The globe was as dark as the night. The talking below had stopped, so she heard only the dripping of soft rain from branches and the patter of drops on her hood. Everyone seemed to be waiting for something to happen.

Dave came squishing up the slope behind her. "They said okay, just for a minute—"

"See anything?"

"Uh, no. Should I?"

"It's not emitting anything visible. Do you have UV detectors here?"

"Getting a whole battery of gear set up. The director ordered it. No radioactivity, we know that. First thing we checked."

"When did you measure for it?"

"Within an hour of the blast."

"There were plenty of nuclear processes going on in the early universe. I thought maybe some particles would come through and leave residual decaying nuclei here, induced radioactivity."

"None that we found," Dave's voice sounded worried in the wet blackness.

"That'll help with the environmentalists."

Dave chuckled without mirth. "Guess so."

"How far into the run did it happen?"

"Two days."

"The uranium fluence was good?"

"Yeah, it was a fine run."

"You were lucky," she said, running her hands over the

smooth surface she could not see. "I don't know what sets the size of the thing, how it appears in our space-time, but evidently it's fairly sensitive. You could've gotten an even bigger one."

"What the hell *is* it?"

He had been holding back, she sensed, not knowing how to treat her. Obviously the Lab people disliked her, but now she was the expert and they had egg all over their faces.

"A universe, I think."

"Huh?"

"Obviously the precise manifestation of it in our space-time depends sensitively on conditions in the quark-gluon state," she mused in a whisper. "Details like how big it looks in our frame of reference. Maybe in the time shift . . ."

"I don't follow."

"Ours is ten weeks older than this, but there's probably no reason to expect this one's evolution to march along just the same."

"That student of yours—"

"Exactly. Better clear this area."

"You think—"

"I don't know. On the other side of this—hell, that's not the right term, maybe I should say at the other *end* of it— there's a hot plasma of elementary particles, expanding and cooling and deadly as hell. The evolution of this thing might let some of it through at any time."

"Any . . . ?"

"There's something special about the recombination time, when atoms form, but we don't know why."

"You think it's going to blow?"

"I'm guessing. Let's get out of here."

She walked quickly down the slope of the ring berm, slipping once in the mud and falling solidly on her rump, feeling the presence of the massive silvery sphere at her back like an aimed weapon.

She stayed at Brookhaven just long enough to talk to an assembly of physicists and managers—no press or media. She owed them that much, but she did not want to pretend to be an oracle. Nor endure the glares and mutterings of people who didn't even know her but plainly had heard a lot of rumors.

So be it. Particle physicists did not consider themselves so much an elite as a priesthood. The director introduced her with minimal formality, citing only her UCI connection to BRAHMS. "Perhaps Dr. Butterworth can cast some light on our accident," he said and sat down. Gentlemen of the jury, be seated.

She stood before the jammed crowd in the Lab's biggest auditorium and told them everything she could, clearly and directly, as it happened, skipping nothing about her own actions at Brookhaven. Her taking it away, her slow-dawning perceptions, the works.

Mutters drifted up from the crowd, sour talk, but she continued steadily, through the first experiments, sketching the same list of mysterious traits she had drawn for Zak. Their first work now seemed a long time ago. From this point on the audience received her testimony as if from a pilgrim, back from a hitherto unknown land.

Suddenly she had stepped into a limelight cast by an unimaginable event, a revolution that arrived without the slightest warning, and many did not know whether to cheer her or scorn her. She had to admit that she probably would not have known, either.

The auditorium was utterly silent as she got to the UV blackbody spectrum and then the recombination emission. Brad's death was merely another data point. The time-shift effect she now regarded as a pretty solid idea, so she then had to sum up Max's ideas about what the spheres might be, and this got her into the theorists' arena. She gave them nuggets from her understanding, all the while protesting that this was not her area of expertise. The continued rapid cooling of the infrared emission from the sphere got her back on solid ground again, so she finished with that. Her sphere was now ten million years old, give or take a million.

Silence. Then tentative clapping, others joining in, and the issue finally decided as the whole room rang with it. She recalled some famous wit remarking that applause was the echo of a platitude, but no, this was the real thing, and suddenly it felt *good*.

Then came questions.

Why had uranium collisions done this, and not gold?

"Well, maybe the greater total energy matters? And perhaps something about uranium's oblong nuclei, so they occasionally slam into each other along their extended axes."

How come cosmic rays, which collided in outer space all the time, didn't make such spheres? There were uranium nuclei in the cosmic rays.

"First of all, how would we know? But maybe something about the RHIC conditions, especially aligned uranium nuclei, made the spheres stable. Random impacts in interstellar space might make unstable spheres, too, so they would not survive."

A voice from the back called out that even stable spheres could be coasting around between the stars and we would never know. If one fell into our atmosphere, it might very well not survive impact at 10 km./sec. She nodded, adding, "This stuff is out of my ballpark." Smiles; she would have to remember using sports talk more often.

Did she seriously think this thing was some portal to another space-time?

"Well, yes. Other ideas would be welcome. I am sure the theorists will have plenty more by tomorrow morning." That got a laugh.

Okay, if this sphere was a passageway, into what *kind* of universe? Einstein–de Sitter? Minkowski?

She had no idea. "Dr. Jalon spoke of modeling the first sphere, assuming it had close to the critical density, which would cause it to eventually stop expanding and then contract. As I understand it, that's one of the Einstein–de Sitter class of models."

This seemed to satisfy them; she was going to have to brush up on this cosmology stuff. A noted theorist stood up and made a long rambling statement about how a real space-time deformation would look like a black hole and vanish, so these spheres must be something else.

"I read some of the theory on wormholes, and I believe you're neglecting the possibility that exotic materials could hold open a space-time throat." Max had made her read the papers, though they had put her to sleep; now she was grateful. "There's even a book by Matt Visser." Always good to end with a pointer to the literature, implying that your questioner was less informed.

Alicia was getting tired, edgy. The next question asked her to describe the exact properties of her sphere.

She sighed with relief, able to simply recount her measurements and their results, free of the carapace of hobbling theory. She wished she had thought to make up some viewgraphs for an overhead projector. The details popped into her head anyway and she got them down on a big green blackboard; she had no trouble remembering the numbers. She sketched the UV temperature changes with time and the recombination era with quick, deft moves. It felt good to deal in concrete matters, not the airy issues of interpretation.

She had worn her professional persona through the whole ordeal. Like many, she had gotten ahead by displaying the required attitudes: competent, slightly daring, a touch haughty. The standard joke was that a particle physicist had to "act British, think Yiddish, but not the other way around." Be a blunt, bright bastard—or, in her case, bitch. This paid off well when the questions started, sometimes shouted from the back of the auditorium in sharp voices hoarse with barely controlled anger. Taking criticism, deflecting it, and especially dishing it out were admired. You had to show that you would expose inferior work no matter who did it. Subtlety was wasted; she had fathomed early how to highlight her own work, distract attention from others', and coax senior figures to advocate her side.

After the first two hours, they called a coffee break. She refused to go out into the foyer, not wanting to be confronted one on one; there were bound to be people angry that she had taken the first sphere away from here. Only then did she realize that nobody had denounced her for that from the audience. Were they being polite? Or was it that, now they had their very own sphere, they could treat her cordially again?

Certainly the director had not been more than minimally cordial; the suits kept their distance even now, clustering around the coffee urns and leaving her alone. Fair enough, she supposed. But maybe the rank and file had an innate feeling for why she had done it, something conveyed by her voice and manner, an unspoken intuition of their tribe?

She retreated and sat silently in a back room and slurped coffee—it was midnight, she noted abstractly—and somehow her mind would not focus on the moment. She thought of Brad, and now the second life claimed here. Then there was more talk and she finally got away. The apartment they gave her to sleep in was a good deal better than the usual accommodations.

She had a small conference with the director and his pals the next morning, just before her flight. She could not add much to measures and measurements here, and meanwhile she had not seen her own Cosm for four days.

"Can you assure us that this globe will not grow, Dr. Butterworth?" the director wanted to know.

"Of course not. Ours has both grown and shrunk, with no apparent cause. I think it's adjusting to minor effects we don't know about."

"How much larger could this globe become?" the director asked.

"Ours varied in radius by a few percent. Yours? I have no idea whether it could swell to the size of Long Island in the next minute."

Everyone looked stunned. She said mildly, "The possibilities are inversely proportional to how much you know."

"Because we do not have a theory of strong gravity," the head of the theoretical division said.

She smiled very slightly. "I would say it was because we do not have enough experience with such objects. After all, you don't know that this is primarily a gravitational effect here."

"It must be. Curved space-time—"

"Is a model. I'd rather trust some hands-on experience."

"That is precisely what I do not want to acquire," the director said rather antiseptically. "Your own student died from exposure to the first one."

"And it was a lot smaller," she agreed. "We can't be sure its time coordinates correspond to ours the way"—she hesitated, about to say "my sphere," then said—"UCI's sphere does. It could start emitting a lot of UV or other stuff at any time."

The director looked as though he had not slept much the night before. "I suppose I will have to evacuate the area."

"If you don't have some people close enough to study it, you'll learn nothing," she said.

"We will have to ask for volunteers."

She did not envy the man his job. She hadn't mentioned to Dave or anybody else that she had warned them not to run uranium again; they had legitimate complaints about her, too.

"We will expect full access to your data," the director said stiffly.

"You'll get it," she said and left for JFK. The Lab guards fended off the media multitude, which had grown to be quite a mob. The rain helped keep them at bay. They gave her a staff car and Dave went with her. He was quite pleasant, considering. They discussed the speculations put forward by the head of the theoretical division, which sounded like Max's early work. It was all very preliminary, she said, and believed it. Physics had abandoned ideas like the corpuscular theory of light and the transmutability of elements, then had to go back and allow as how, yes, they could be resurrected. Theory lay at the mercy of experiment, which after all was just orderly experience.

A TV crew overhauled them on the way to the airport and tried to get shots of her through the sedan window. She turned away.

Well, here it was, the Big Time, nature red in tooth and claw. "You aimed for this, girl," she whispered to herself. "So don't come on all sorry about hitting it."

3

"**H**eddo, 'tranger,'' she said to Max through her stuffed sinuses.

"Ah, so the goddess has a cold."

"Hunh?"

"We have a name for entities of your sex who go around creating whole universes." Max sat on a lab bench and grinned.

"Goddedded don't ged culds."

"Well, this one does. I've been reading about you, too."

"What?"

"First page, *The New York Times*."

She caught the headline as he handed her the newspaper.

PHYSICS LAB ACCIDENT LINKED TO EARLIER DISCOVERY
California Professor 'Stole' Singular Sphere

"Oh noooo . . ." She sat down heavily on a makeshift desk she had jammed against the outer observatory wall, the only spot not squeezed with diagnostic equipment. The *Times* piece was reasonably fair, but it still made her angry. "There wad no press ad th' talk ah gave 'em!"

"Mouths move."

"The dire'tor said he wad goin' ta keep all dis udder wraps ta preven' a panic."

"Ummmm. I'll bet he approved the leak and even chose the word."

"Wha' woud?"

"Why, 'stole' of course."

"Etablushin' Brookhaden's rights?"

"Sure, Brookhaven wants to establish that they rightfully own both, then push blame off on you for not warning them."

"Ah did."

"Can you prove it?"

"Lemme see, where'd I pud dat . . ."

Neither Dave's nor her e-mail was on her hard disk. "Must've misfiled 'em," she said. Then she remembered that she had it in hard copy, stuck in the briefcase she had carried on the plane.

"Great," Max said, reading the messages carefully. "Now you get into action."

"Uh, how?" Her head had been stuffed with cotton since she got off the plane from JFK, slowing her thinking until she felt even more like a dunce.

"Let them know you have this." He waved the hard copy. "And that you don't appreciate their buddies erasing it from your hard disk."

She gaped, then looked dubious. Max shook his head in pity. "My my, such an innocent. There are several people here who might do a favor for an old friend back at poor Brookhaven, y'know. Especially if they think you committed a true breach of professional ethics."

"Mah files have a password . . ."

"Which any real keyboard weenie can get around within microseconds."

"Maybe ah erased th' files . . ."

"Maybe." Raised eyebrows, a grin.

"Ah'm . . . surprised."

"I'll bet my explanation is right. Y'know, you've had your nose pressed so close to the Cosm, you're not registering how this is going over. It's big, really big."

"I'm . . . naive?"

"Charmingly so. Next thing, you publish. Get out in front with physicists, post your discovery online."

"Uh, I don't feel like—"

"Point is, get there first. And if Brookhaven knows you can prove you warned them, they won't lean on you so hard in the media."

"The media aren't supposed to know!" Somehow her rising anger was clearing her sinuses.

A sardonic smile. "Yeah, right, Snow White."

Publish? It felt like somebody suggesting that you stop to take photographs while in a fistfight, but . . .

The time needed to publish a paper depended linearly on the number of hurdles put up by the anonymous referees. The journals were perhaps the last citadels of science as a meritocracy; even giants could find their precious papers shredded by dwarfs. Irksome duels with masked referees were a favorite genre of physics lunchtime tales. They could block her for months, even years.

She balanced this with the time it would take her to write up a complete description of the object, how it came to be, methods and failures, comparing theory and experiment, alternative explanations . . .

Too much; she was not a fast writer anyway, sharing the common affliction of those who had to read slowly to ferret out dense arguments in compact notation and acronym-choked jargon. Having tracked at such snail speeds, one could not then quickly write. In a way this was a blessing for the field—or else the journals would be even more fat.

"Y'know, you could follow a riskier strategy," Max pointed out. "Go the 'oral publication' route. Fly around to a half-dozen places, give seminars, gotta be the fastest way to publicize results."

"And take me away from doing any experiments."

"Well, yeah."

No, the answer was to get out a terse description of "discovering" the object and a list of its properties. Period. No speculations, maybe a few graphs of data, some numbers.

Leave 'em with their tongues lolling out for more. Send it to *Physical Review Letters*, the linchpin of the profession? Most likely it would get jammed up. She knew an editor at *Physics Letters*; why not there?

Then there was Max. She had leaned so heavily on him for so long it seemed he had been around from the beginning. Could he write up the theory?

No, and he didn't want his name on the paper, either. She was surprised; he "set her straight," as he put it: Data first, theory a distant second.

"But you gave me ideas of what to measure," she countered. "The tidal stress—"

"We'll publish later. Right now, you're at bat."

"Why do men always resort to sports analogies?"

"Why do women always make a big deal about our doing it?"

"Look, sticking your nose into things is pretty easy. Pointing the nose the right way, that's hard."

He grinned. "Gee, this is the first fight I've ever seen over *not* taking credit."

She laughed. "Okay, sport."

Somehow it came out easily. She sat down at her laptop and started to write, using the basics: no passive voice, simple declarative statements, linear logic. Only a few times did she even need to consult her lab notebooks; the numbers were seared into her memory. To her surprise, she got it all down in a few hours.

She asked Jim in the department staff to send out the colloquium announcement with merely her name and, as a title, "Topic to Be Announced." Lesser lights never used this ploy, lest they speak to an empty room. But she knew the rumor mill would summon the entire department, while probably spreading slowly enough to bring few from other campuses, and if lucky, no press at all.

Zak had the latest data on the Cosm in good shape, so she could end her meticulous, many-viewgraphed talk with a smooth curve showing the cooling of the background photon emission. The *relic radiation*, cosmologists had called it, yet she could not forget that it had killed Brad only seven weeks before. She had opened the colloquium by dedicating it to him. She had made Brad and Zak coauthors on the paper. At the conclusion she asked for a moment's silence for Brad and left the cooling curve for an entire universe on the projector, his death marked in red.

It all went well, though a senior figure in the particle physics group asked several stinging questions about the propriety of taking the sphere from Brookhaven. Suddenly she felt that Max had been right about her warning to Brookhaven, mysteriously missing from her computer. Could this older man be the hard disk scrubber? She eyed her esteemed colleague and wondered. Quite probably she would never know.

She had expected e-mail about the spheres but had forgotten that the final exam was only a few days in the past, and students were now getting their grades. She was unprepared for the messages from her Physics 3-B students that had stacked up.

"I'm looking for a break here," one said. "I *really need* a B in this course for med school." Another pleaded, "If I don't get at least a C from you, UCI will kill my scholarship!" Since mostly biology students took the course, and most bio majors were thinly disguised med school candidates, she got a lot of "My life is over unless I can get a full letter grade increase!" Several had left phone messages asking her to call them; no explaining message, of course, but she recognized their names.

Still, they weren't as bad as the sad-eyed types who showed up at her office door. "Professor Butterfield? I was in your 3-B? I, uh, got a B and wondered is there anything I can do to raise it?"

She was tempted to respond, "Isn't it a little too late? Do you fear declarative sentences?" Perhaps so, for the grade-seekers all shared a dislike of definitive statements, of grades that wouldn't budge, of fulcrum moments which, once pivoted about, were forever gone. Instead, they believed that the esteem-building smiley faces of grade school carried over to the university; artful begging should bring a higher grade, right? Final grades, done and posted, simply announced a last chance to whine for more. Just asking should count for something, shouldn't it? Points could be added to a score, like freebie burgers or T-shirts. After all, out in the big world fame and wealth often went to those with no love of knowledge at all; why should the world of academia be different? They wanted to do extra credit after the course was over or partial credit instead of taking the exams. Getting a right answer was, after all, only part of the learning process.

But bridges fell down if you calculated the stresses wrong, people died on the operating table if a med school graduate miscalculated a dosage. Such possibilities did not affect their quaint feeling that they should be doing better, so something was wrong with the system. Only about ten percent of the class acted this way, but they roused her ire. They wanted to be judged on their "potential" and wondered why the world didn't see it that way.

She laid low for a few days, resting and getting over her cold. That helped a lot, because the media were perking up to the news.

The photographer from *Newsweek* bobbed and clicked around the observatory lab, apparently trying for a sort of still-shot cinema verité effect. There was a journalist with him who kept slipping in insinuating questions. An anxious UCI publicist accompanied them, torn between her joy at having a national print medium team here and the fact that UCI had not had time to figure out how to put the right spin on Alicia's actions.

She let them all fidget and work around her. The journalist wore a severe black suit, very New York, with thinning black hair dulled by a dye job, combed straight back and plastered to his skull. Between his oily questions and the photographer's "Coudja turn a little this way," she made her routine measurements, wishing she had worn something better than an old blouse and black jeans.

Then she took a telephone call on her private cellular—she

never used her university number anymore and didn't check for messages there, either—which proved to be somebody from *Scientific American*. "I already have a subscription," she said and had nearly hung up before the voice blurted out that she was an editor.

"Just checking some background facts. I mean, you haven't published very much—"

"None, actually."

"But we hear from a little bird that you're about to."

"So why not wait until I do?"

"Coming with the Brookhaven disaster, your invention has so stimulated debate—"

"Discovery, not invention."

"Well, of course, though some say you are not interpreting what you've found correctly—"

"So I'm 'inventing' it?"

"Uh, I wondered if you would comment on several quotations in the piece we're doing—"

"Read them."

"We're devoting nearly two full pages to the issue in the 'Science and the Citizen' section. Here is one professor who says, 'I'll believe it when I see it.' And—"

"Sounds like he wants into the lab, is all."

"Yes, doesn't it?" she said cheerily.

"Who said that?"

"Uh, that's one of our not-for-attributions. Sorry. The next critic—"

"And you want me to respond to anonymous insults?"

"I realize this is not—"

"Just print this, okay? Dogs bark and the parade moves on."

"What?"

She repeated it, knowing it would sound more than a bit arrogant and not giving a damn.

"I'm not sure I can use that."

"That's all you're getting." She hung up. Shaking her head, she went back to work, putting it all out of mind as well as she could.

*   *   *

During the colloquium and in her paper, she had followed an unconscious pattern that only slowly came to the surface of her mind.

She had referred to the Cosm as "it," or "anomaly," partly because the name still felt a bit odd in her mouth, but also, she ruefully recognized, out of a small-minded impulse: maybe they would name it after her. Butterworth's Object? The thought was petty and she shoved it aside the moment it came to mind, but then it returned. Astronomers named asteroids after those who spotted them in the skies, though bigger objects like planets and stars had appellations from mythology. In science notable results could carry a scientist into immortality: Avogadro's Number, Planck's constant, Boyle's Law. There was even Millikan's Falling Oil Drop Experiment, though that skirted close to the modern danger of a term so long that the effect became named for its acronym: the *laser* stood for *L*ight *A*mplified by *S*timulated *E*mission of *R*adiation, and only professionals knew the men who had invented it.

Finally she realized that her saying "it" all the time was making her feel guilty, so she quit. It might as well come to be known as the Butterworth-Jalon Object, anyway, since he had been rash enough to figure out what the hell it was . . . if, in fact, he was right. And there was an outside chance that, given her own dimensions, some would term it the Butterworth Ball.

4

Alicia:

We've followed your procedures for observing the globe and have picked up the UV radiation. The distribution is blackbody and it's cooling off fast. We estimate the recombination will occur in about two weeks, so we're fairly close to your sphere's development.

Our theory group thinks maybe the big flash of emission at the recombination era is due to some adjustment of the sphere, so that more photons get through. We're wondering if this "neck," as you called it, is dynamically changing. Any further evidence from your end?

Dave Rucker

Dave:

We're seeing continued cooling. The sphere has contracted another three millimeters, too, so some minor adjustments are going on, all right.

Better be careful around the recombination time.

We've got to keep as much of this out of the media as possible.

Alicia

Alicia:

Our director feels that since this object has shut down the Laboratory indefinitely, we have suffered the most and should handle all relations with the press. We're negotiating with UCI right now.

The globe weighs well over a million kilograms! This we got from a combined study by geologists and engineers. It's resting on the bedrock. Nobody has a clue how to get it out of the way of RHIC.

Dave

Dave:

Wonderful. You face the media music all you want. I had a little negotiating session with Vice Chancellor Lattimer and other honchos here, who're doing the dance with your people, I gather. They want to manage developments, too. I propose that we let them fight it out, so long as they leave us alone with the physics.

Have you thought about rebuilding RHIC around your Cosm? Maybe alter the curve so the particles go around?

Is that possible?

Alicia

Alicia:

We've already engineered that one out. Pretty expensive, but the big problem is, who would work right next to the globe? The risk-based pay scale would kill us.

We're sitting and waiting for recombination here.

Getting demonstrators, too—threats, even.

Everybody's pretty depressed. RHIC is down and we may never get to rebuild it. If we do, it'll take a year or more. And while the experiments with gold worked well, we don't dare risk using uranium again.

Dave

Dave:

Remember, Magellan didn't actually make it all the way around the world, but it's his name we remember.

Alicia

This last message was a weak salute, but she could not think of anything more to say.

Decades before, an important result that eventually won a Nobel was nearly rejected by *Physical Review Letters* because a piece about it had run in the local university newspaper. Only after the student journalist owned up to cobbling his story together from gossip did the journal editor relent and allow rapid publication. Alicia worried about such tiny matters and anxiously awaited the judgment of *Physics Letters*, a rather easier journal.

Not that journals were so important, she told herself, especially since the Net pervaded all physics. Research was what got talked about; anything written down and published in hard copy was by definition done, uncontested, boring.

She had posted her paper at the usual watering holes for the particle and cosmological species. The Net was mostly a hunting ground. If an interesting paper turned up, physicists would e-mail or waylay its author at a meeting to get the real dope. Where was the work going? Who was in on it? What did Big Authority X or Y think? Particle physics was genuinely international (more so since the waning of the Americans), but it followed the patterns of a dispersed village. It was like photons exchanged between interacting particles, nourishing sandwiches of information establishing that one knew enough to *give good gossip*.

Gossiping and staking claims, particle physicists in person rarely credited others. In their publications, though, tradition demanded a spare ledger of credits. Building on past work, one had to pay royalties of credit and even homage by citing. This had been the hardest part of writing her letter, so she had resorted to general works on cosmology, Alan Guth's papers with collaborators, and other papers whose abstracts she could scarcely comprehend: protective coloration.

Refereeing resembled the body's immune system. Science could defend itself against small assaults on conventional wisdom, but major events, like Heisenberg's invention of quantum mechanics in 1925 or Watson and Crick's discovery of

DNA's double helix in 1952, overwhelmed the lethargy of any establishment.

So when she finally got her three referee reports, none challenged the importance or basic authenticity of the work; all asked for a few extra references, though. This gave away more about the probable referees than the paper; hitching a ride on a gaudy bandwagon about to depart.

The letter would go into print immediately. This unleashed the media managers of both UCI and Brookhaven and Alicia hunkered down.

Once installed in the observatory, she seldom noticed the bare rectangular austerities and eye-jarring clutter of her new lab; to her it was all one instrument, shaped by a supple logic to ask questions of the physical world.

She had a mild affection for this big integrated tool; running a measurement, she mentally donned the lab the way she put on a jacket. She knew the point of this room down to the last cable and moved through it vigilant for any difference between the diagram in her mind and the never-perfect reality. Yet she felt a tension here, too, a vexed irritation at a universe that withheld its secrets. Theorists faced thickets of intractable mathematics; experimenters struggled with balky gear, their dirty hands a badge of hard-won honor.

She and Zak reviewed their data, but there was little new. Zak went off to get some more supplies. The UCI security guard knocked on the observatory's side door: a visitor.

"Max!" She brightened. "Where have you been?"

"Hermit time." He was in jeans and a sweatshirt, but looked rested. "I went off to do some calculating."

"I need some moral support here."

He studied her face and she remembered the penetrating gaze when they had been outside the lab, about to confront the police, several thousand years ago. "Looks more like you need immoral support. A weekend of relapsation."

"I had that. I went to the mountains. By the time I got back, Brookhaven had fallen on their sword."

"It's going to get worse. Be sure you stay rested."

Abruptly she hugged him. "Boy, don't I wish."

They stood that way, he making no move one way or the other, and eventually she took her arms back and gave him what she hoped was an unreadable smile. Not that she would have known quite what to write into it, she thought, not at all.

She told him about *Physics Letters* accepting her paper and he nodded, as though the outcome were obvious all along. "You have fresh marching orders for us, the experimenter infantry?"

He grimaced and inched his way around her gear, now arrayed in metal racks to conserve space. "I think we ought to start looking for stars."

"Uh, how?"

"Looking very small and very fast."

"Explain?"

Max settled back in the one comfortable chair in the place. "There's really no choice in good physics between beauty and utility, y'know. Anything really useful had better be simple, though God knows it may be hard as hell to work out the consequences, just because the math is tough and often quite new—but not because it's complicated. In fact, it's elegant, usually in ways we haven't seen before."

"Ummm, sounds like an introduction to a lecture."

"I burrowed into string theory, came up with some better solutions."

"They're still time-shifted, as before?"

"Definitely. That comes out of some beautiful math, but it ran into a wall. See, the local physics near a wormhole throat doesn't tell us much, so I decided to take a more engineering approach."

"You? Mr. Math Equals Truth?"

He tipped his head in confession. "Thing is, we can measure the Cosm's mass and tidal force, so start there. If it's changing in time, that'll tell us something basic. From that, I can calculate the curvature of space-time required. From that, calculate the stress energy and ask if it is physically possible."

"It has to be possible—it exists!"

"Sure, but I'm trying to find out what field theory will give us a Cosm, see?"

"How about the mass we already measured?"

"I used that. The answer is that near the throat the stress energy is peculiar but not obviously incompatible with known physics. It demands a negative energy density, of course—the exotic stuff that holds this throat open. Then I realized that we know one more important fact—you're still alive."

She blinked. "Say what?"

"You were the first person to touch it, right? It didn't kill you—or me or Zak later—so whatever weird stuff holds that throat open, it isn't going to come apart when ordinary matter touches it. But it can repulse matter, and nearly all radiation, or otherwise we'd have been flooded with hot plasma."

"Same for Brookhaven's globe, too."

"Exactly! Once might be a miracle, but two's a statistic. That means there's a whole class of equilibria for these things. How come? Maybe something about slamming uranium together, polarized just right—I dunno. But I used that fact to select out the kind of theory that would give me rock-solid spheres, and now I trust the work."

"So? How do we see stars?" She smiled. Typical theorist, he had gotten so carried away with the sublime beauties of it all that he had forgotten his conclusion.

"Uh, this sphere, the solutions show that there's got to be a sphere on the other end, too. A chrome ball sitting in space, in that expanding universe. It gathers in light from nearby like a fish-eye lens. We see images, just as if we were there. Walking around the cosm is just like craning your neck. But already that universe is thinning out, matter getting separated. So odds are, there's nothing interesting nearby. So we need a telescope to survey the sky near that point."

"I've got to become an astronomer."

"Yes. But in a universe that's moving at a rate millions of times faster than we are. So even distant stars will move while you're looking."

"They'll look like smears of visible light?"

Max shrugged, in the irksome way theorists did when dismissing a minor detail. "I suppose so."

I suppose so. His idea made sense but implied that she had to look sharp and fast to make out anything. This meant more gear:

- Framing camera, 5 ns/shot, 50 ns pause, 3-shot capability
- Streak camera, gives one shot 10 ns long
- X-ray framing camera (?)

She took this list to Onell, the department chairman. Her Department of Energy grant was bone-dry already and to continue she needed a quick infusion of funds. Onell told her she could have it, pending the dean's approval, but she should "be a good campus citizen, too." She asked what this meant and Onell started in again about serving on the "mentoring" team and she walked out of his office and went straight to the dean. Not the politic thing to do, but she was in a hurry and it was summer, a time which should, she reasoned, be free of academic prattle. What was that old adage? *Easy work drives out good work.* Committees and administration were simple and seductive. If you had nothing of pressing interest to do, they might even get to be fun, though she doubted it.

The dean listened soberly and gave her some of the same tut-tutting medicine, but then with brisk efficiency signed off on thirty thousand dollars that she could use immediately. The X-ray camera would cost fifty thousand dollars, so she forgot about it. Instead, she called up people at other institutions and after a day spent working the phones she got one on loan from Sandia Labs. This was doubly good, because this route would not arouse interest in the usual alleys of the particle physics community. For the rest of the gear, she located local suppliers. With Zak she drove a UCI van up to L.A. to get it right away.

Within two days of all work and no sleep, she had a makeshift observing rig mounted next to the Cosm, an array of optical readers and light pipes and lenses that could collect visible emission from a tiny patch of the sphere. Max thought that the Cosm acted like a spherical lens, dispelling images outward, so to get a real image of anything she had to study one small zone.

Of course, his expectations rested upon a bunch of airy mathematics scribbled into four or five yellow pads he carried around wherever he went, in classic nerd fashion. He did his calculations with a rather elegant silvery fountain pen, though, which redeemed the yellow pad stylistic flaw somewhat—but still, she reminded herself, his anticipations were gossamer stuff indeed. But she liked the chance to test one more possibility, even a tenuous one. Amid the rising hubbub of attention from the outside world, the rituals of thinking through the measurements, setting up, and tinkering were positive joys in themselves.

By now the Cosm was developing at a colossal rate. She worked it out from Max's exponential equation and had to check it twice to be sure she had not made a mistake.

Every second in her lab, twenty-three years passed in the Cosm.

She had to admit, the number made her gasp. It meant that nearby stars would smear out their images, if the sphere at the other end were rotating at all.

"Sure, it's not spinning around on our end—not in the lab frame, anyway," Max said. "But we're moving, too. The Earth's spinning, it's orbiting the sun—"

"So somebody looking from the other end could see us."

"Yes, but not the stars in the night sky. They sweep around every night."

"We don't know what the other end's doing, do we?"

"Nope. It's orbiting around whatever matter is near it."

"That's why I got the framing cameras."

"Uh, what do they frame?"

She had to chuckle. Max put up a good front but gear was not his area. "It takes a snapshot every five-billionths of a second."

He whistled. "So you can get a snapshot covering less than a second in *Cosm* time."

"Good enough?"

"Uh, hope so. No bets."

"I thought you were the brave theorist, voyaging on strange seas of imagination, bound for alien shores."

"I'm a theorist who hates to lose money."

She and Zak ran the framing cameras with the observatory utterly darkened. They chose a spot on the Cosm's surface and expanded it with an ordinary microscope, then took snaps only five nanoseconds long. The first day yielded absolutely blank negatives. Not actual photographic negatives, of course—all data was processed digitally from light pipes; hardly anybody used real film anymore.

The second day's work yielded the same. And the third.

On the fourth they got a tiny pip of light.

The fifth day gave them more of it, enough for Alicia to extract a spectrum.

"It's a K-star," she said confidently. "I'd guess it's about a light-year away."

"Goddamn," Max said and just stared at the spectrum, then back at the photo image: a red dot.

"I expected more eloquence, Magellan."

"Lay off the strange seas stuff. This is *real*."

"All my results are authentic, fresh off the reality griddle."

"A real star. In your universe."

"*My* universe? I don't own it. In fact, Brookhaven has lawyers getting ready to argue that it's theirs."

"Precedent is clear," Max said. "You made it, you own it."

"What precedent?"

"Genesis."

Zak coughed, as if embarrassed. Alicia wondered what tone she had been using. "I think there may be more of those, too," Zak said quietly.

"How come?" Alicia said.

"While you were processing that image, I shot two more."

Zak grinned. "Used longer exposure times. There are fainter dots nearby."

"Stars forming near each other," Max said decisively. "Let Brookhaven claim *those*, huh?"

5

*O*range County Register:

UCI PROF COULD COST
TAXPAYERS BILLIONS
Damage to Long Island Laboratory 'Colossal'

(AP) Officials at the Brookhaven National Laboratory revised upward their estimates of the eventual cost in money and lost time following from the mysterious accident there . . .

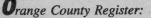

From: rubyt@aol.com

I know you don't know me and since you don't return phone calls (I have left SIX MESSAGES), I have to use e-mail. I feel I have to speak out for all those who are appalled at your behavior. I am a taxpayer tired of know it alls who think the laboratories we built for them are their playthings and steal what is not rightfully theirs from these labs. You may think taking this thing—which I don't for a moment believe is a "universe"—is okay since now you are famous but . . .

Dear Faculty Member:

I am responding to your communication regarding the recent events concerning a professor in our Physics Department and the Brookhaven National Laboratory. This matter must be kept in perspective. As Chancellor I have been close to the complex legal and ethical issues surrounding this controversial and still-evolving case.

229

I am sending this letter to all those who have privately inquired into the circumstances of this issue and wish to reassure you that I am following the advice of the Chancellor's Special Committee on all issues in the disagreement between UCI and the Brookhaven National Laboratory. UCI shall not condone any irregular or illegal actions by its own faculty in the conducting of scientific research. Indeed, UCI has historically been vigilant in assisting the prosecution of any faculty accused of wrongdoing. Nor shall we allow this dispute to reflect badly upon our growing reputation as a leader in cutting-edge research in the fields of physics, medicine, biology, and engineering . . .

Professor:
The Bible has cases similar to yours, foretelling of those who would usurp the power and dignity of God to further their own ends, which are the same as those of the Fallen. If you will turn to Scripture in this dire hour, you will find succor in the following passages: . . .

Los Angeles Times, unsigned editorial:

GODLIKE GAFFES

Recent events in the abstruse world of nuclear physics have cast UC–Irvine and the Brookhaven National Laboratory into the glaring light of national publicity, exposing a human drama of sobering short-sightedness. Considering the implications of this work, involving the accidental production of what appear to be a wholly unanticipated class of physical objects, the physics community has displayed little understanding of its responsibilities. We feel, for reasons outlined below, that a special national committee should be appointed, perhaps at the Federal level (since funding came from that level), to provide oversight and wise counsel in the further studies of these objects. Already vast damage has occurred, life lost, and much rancor fills the news columns as the two institutions confront each other—all over shiny spheres of inexplicable meaning . . .

To: Butter@uci.edu
From: advocat@okedoke.gov
Like all profs you don;t think anymore about your own student
do you? Remember the one who DIED IN YOUR PLACE and
all because you stole something wasn;t yours? Its students pay
your salary and you treat them like dogs or worse, we hear
nothing about THEM do we? Now there's a bigger one of
these things and you℞ damn lucky it didn;t kill anybody. Your
meddling with WHOLE UNIVERSES is the ultimate grossout
arrogantt prof experiment and you should be ASHAMED.

After a largely fruitless day in the lab, she beat the traffic
down the Pacific Coast Highway, avoiding the toll road, and
went for a walk along the beach at dusk before her Dad-
planned rendezvous at a new downtown Laguna restaurant.
After the crash and tang of the waves, the halogen lights had
an electric leer, their promises licking out of the gloom that
had swallowed the sunset.

Orange County, with its signature long lines of tall palm
trees, was working toward being "max-frilled," as the slang
had it, but at least it didn't have the touches of L.A. The post
office didn't offer valet parking yet. On rainy days parking
tickets weren't slipped inside protective envelopes, as in Bev-
erly Hills. There were no water bars, with fifty chilled varieties
at two bucks a glass, with no ice because it would erase the
regional subtleties. And when you called the police department
and got put on hold, no classical music played.

She left the beach and went along Ocean Avenue. Outside
the Sea Lounge were ranks of motorcycles, mostly Harleys.
Through the open windows she could see a jammed crowd
raising beer glasses to the monotonous thump of the live band.
Being Harley guys, they were of course rebels, rugged lone
wolves, individual spirits, as was obvious because they were
all wearing the same jackets and jeans, bandannas and sunglasses, big brass belt buckles and tattoos, probably even the
same underwear. (Boxers or Jockeys? she wondered. Her social intuition was not precise enough to guess.) She walked
on, feeling the tiny sliver of self-consciousness that always

came when she was far from the academic context and immersed in a thoroughly white crowd. Biker gangs were the stuff of cartoons now, most of them with graying, fast-receding forelocks and bulging bellies, but the tiny voice didn't care about that.

Summer's vagrant breezes stirred the lush shrubbery, exciting the birds. A tiny mote still darted after the sweet water residents left out. Beneath the actinic streetlights coming on the hummingbirds were eerie, like moths with beaks.

"Hey, gal! Wait up."

Jill was overtaking her at the corner of Ocean and Beach. "You're looking great."

"I met a guy, became beautiful," Jill said breathlessly.

"Who?"

"Then we broke up, but I kept my looks."

"Well, at least you didn't keep him around for cosmetic reasons."

"And you? What about this guy you've been working with?"

"Max? Great guy, not my type."

"He's what? Gay? Dead?"

Alicia had to laugh. Jill never let her get away with a brush-off. "He's a good man, just doesn't do it for me."

"At least not right away."

"Which means?"

Jill stopped outside the buffed steelwork façade of the restaurant, No Strangers, her face tilted sideways in the way she had of showing concern. "You're never going to fall for a man in a microsecond. Me either, come to think of it, though I try to."

"Max, well, we've been working together a lot lately . . ."

"And that's an antiaphrodisiac?"

"No, but I have a lot on my plate right now."

"You need to get out of your head a little more."

"It's enough just to get out of the lab. This is the first time we've had a chance to talk in what . . . a month? And we're doing it on the sidewalk."

"Gives me a chance to look over the bikers. Gives you a

chance to calm down before you meet this lawyer.''

"Lawyers I can deal with. My dad's something else.''

Jill had been a good gal-buddy through all this, unlike her more distant pals from the academic world. Alicia's friends didn't call that often, and she didn't either. They just moseyed along, knowing they would take in a movie or have dinner once a month or so to catch up; by unspoken agreement, they did not remember birthdays. Jill's friends were different. They called every few days, gave full-packed parties (with games, even), had nicknames for each other which they *always* used, all looked good and slim and shared similar tastes in clothes (this year was slim but casual). They all had intriguing little quirks, like Jill's carrying her "special tools" to pick locks. In short, they were a television show. Alicia was sure there were identical tribes among the Black Bourgeoisie, but she had never gotten along with them, probably because she was a bit dull; yet Jill seemed to accept Alicia as a fellow tribeswoman without comment.

"No stalling," Jill said, giving her a mock push through the yawning restaurant door, which resembled a mouth with polished metal teeth. Inside, the place had enough bare concrete and ribbed ducts and stark lighting to be a surrealist theme bar. Very hip but still just another joint where luncheon was lunch for six bucks extra.

"Dad!" He was sitting with a thin black man who would be Bernie Ross. Jill always made her father's face light up and that gave her time to explain to Mr. Ross that she had been bedeviled by events, which was why they had gotten into a perpetual game of phone tag, and even e-mail just got buried—

"Hey, not your fault," he said affably, holding up both hands, palms out. "People been on your case. And it's Bernie."

Maybe it was Bernie's personality or just possibly an ever so slight loosening that came from having not one but two solid black men around; somehow the effect worked. She had a gin and tonic and traded jokes and do-you-knows with Bernie, classic Black Bourgeois Network stuff. Against the razor-angst metallic styling of the restaurant she had to admit that Bernie's cozy bear look was vaguely out of place, like a cowboy wearing glasses. But so was she, and always would be, in a place whose menu featured drinks that faked absinthe, a twenty-seven-item coffee menu, and had a special on a Spicy Tower of Jicama.

"I resisted following Dad's advice, of course, and now I'm in pretty deep," Alicia said.

Bernie nodded. "We're playing catch-up ball here."

"Sounds like my girl's not even in the game yet," her dad kibitzed from the side.

Alicia gave her father a pursed-mouth expression that said, in family code, *I'm doing all right here by myself, thank you.* "I think UCI is cutting a deal with Brookhaven over my head."

"As long as you just lie there and do nothing, they'll do that," Bernie said guardedly.

"I know, I know. I should've had my own representation. I thought UCI would protect my interests."

"UCI protects UCI," Bernie said, and Dad nodded.

"Well, I sent you my version of events."

She had written up a chronology of her actions, figuring her memory was getting filled up with the rush of events. This habit she had picked up from keeping good lab notebooks; she had even kept diaries about her relations with men, coding their names by number in case anyone found the notebook (as one guy did, later; the coding worked).

"I have some questions"—Bernie's hands came up again, deflecting her worried, tight-brow expression—"but we don't have to do that this evening."

"I got a call from the vice chancellor's office today informing me that the Department of Energy has come into the matter," Alicia said.

The table got quiet. An espresso machine shrieked its mournful moist wail somewhere. "That's serious," Dad said.

"Very." Bernie frowned. "They have police powers, where matters of property are concerned."

"Translation?" Jill put in.

"The Feds can confiscate property," Dad said.

"Stolen property," Bernie added.

"The Cosm isn't stolen," Alicia said, offended.

"It was made in a federal lab," Bernie said. "Powers of reclamation have expanded steadily, partially driven by the War on Drugs legislation. I checked into the statutes—"

"It's not theirs!" Alicia spat back.

"How can it be?" Jill demanded loyally.

"It was made within and by use of their facilities," Bernie said.

"But *I* made it, not them," Alicia shot back.

Bernie shook his head. "The statutes are clear."

"I don't like the sound of this." Dad glowered at his salad as it arrived, an oily anthology of virtuous veggies.

"I expect the university does not want to get caught in the middle on this," Bernie said. "I've used some contacts of mine to feel them out, just informally, and it's a solid gray wall."

"Contacts?" Alicia asked.

"Informants," Dad said. "Don't ask for names."

"They say the administration is trying to distance themselves as much as possible from you," Bernie said soberly, "on advice of counsel and of the Department of Energy."

"Translation?" Alicia said, feeling weak. She raised a finger and ordered another gin and tonic.

"The Feds will go easy on UCI if they get what they want," Dad said.

"Which is?" Jill asked.

"My head, roast-suckling-pig-style, with an apple in my mouth."

Bernie said gently, "You're overdramatizing."

"Privilege of the condemned, isn't it?"

"Not so fast," Dad said. "We haven't even gotten our ball on the field yet."

"No fair switching to sports analogies," Jill said. "Let's stick to food imagery."

"I'd rather have the food itself." Alicia was feeling the gin working like an emulsifying fluid on the air. This was a cliché trendy spot in the all-hard-surfaces mode, every voice sharpening under the reflections from concrete, marble, and steel. The usual instability was at work, in which every table finds that it must talk louder to overcome the noise, which then builds nonlinearly as fresh customers arrive and more alcohol reaches tired workday brains. The lights dimmed about every twenty minutes, momentarily suppressing the chatter.

Their waiter took their order as if he knew secrets but wasn't telling. His pseudo-tux was cut to enhance his shoulder blades, which gave the impression that he had swallowed a coat hanger. She found herself looking at him and somehow, also nonlinearly, thinking of Max. This transition she could not explain and put it down to the gin. Bernie stirred her out of her reflection by bringing up details of UCI's position, what the vice chancellor had said, and similar matters of High Gossip that she could never remember. Alicia tried to answer his barrage of questions, grateful for Jill taking up her father's energy. Dad had been calling and e-mailing furiously and finally "just happened" to be in the area, so he had arranged this dinner to get Bernie "on the team." Alicia watched Jill charm Dad and wondered at her fluidity, an innate social grace that made Alicia feel like the ugly duckling in a performance of *Swan Lake*.

Then they got back to Topic A and Alicia was at stage center.

Dad opened with, "Now, honey, let me ask a dumb question—"

"Your questions are never dumb, merely ignorant."

"Thanks. That's reassuring, I guess."

—and they were off, with Alicia having to provide show-and-tell descriptions, like minilectures in a course titled Universe Building 101.

Already she knew to start very simply. Suppose two masses were far from each other, she began. They attracted each other gravitationally, so they each fell toward the other and collided; kinetic energy was created. Yet their gravitational fields were superimposed once they collided, so there was more gravitational energy in the end, too. The only way this made sense was if the kinetic energy gain was positive and the gravitational energy gain was negative.

She had resorted to diagrams on napkins by that time, so intent that she barely noticed that they were good polished white cloth and the coat-hanger waiter was glaring at her.

"So the net sum is zero—no total energy has been created here, right? If absence of a gravitational field corresponds to no energy, then having a gravitational field means negative energy. What happened at RHIC—both times—was creation of an intense speck of matter with a gravitational energy just about equal to its kinetic energy. The Collider didn't have to provide the whole energy cost of making a universe, just the down payment, a compressed speck of mass. That meant that we could make a distortion in space-time with the properties of the early universe, at very little cost."

She went on about how compressing 10^{-5} grams of matter into a speck 10^{-33} cm. across could start a Big Bang. But one could also rely on quantum tunneling. This allowed a quantum state to move into a final state not allowed by pure energetic requirements. Then a bigger less-massive speck could tunnel into the Big Bang state. More diagrams here. She finished by noting that those mass and size numbers were called the Planck mass and size, named for the first physicist to think of energies on this scale.

"Honey, how much energy is that?"

"Ummm, it corresponds to a tank of gasoline."

"Make a universe in one pit stop," Bernie mused. "Jeez-us."

Dad whistled. He was really trying; she could see that. She was pleased that she had gotten the idea over. "I can explain more fully the implications of the quantum gravitational model—"

"Say no," Jill stage-whispered to Dad out of the corner of her mouth.

"Uh, no."

6

A classic story: a particle physicist went to a shopping mall with his wife and agreed to meet her at a store in half an hour. But while browsing in a bookstore, he met a stunning blonde and they hit it off and he went with her to her apartment. Two hours later he remembered and rushed back to the mall. Remorseful, facing up to the enormity of what he had done, he told his thoroughly steamed wife that he had met a woman and made love to her for two hours. Angrily, she said, "You're lying! You were in your lab!"

Alicia told Max this joke after she found him sleeping on the floor of the observatory the next morning. "I thought I'd beat the morning traffic," he said groggily over coffee. "Drove down at midnight."

"There are easier ways. I'll give you a key to my apartment. Just sack out in the side room when you need to."

"Uh, thanks." She let him recover slowly. Plainly, he was worried about something.

"What's up? You've been calculating a lot lately."

"I'm wondering if this thing of ours is at all predictable."

"Meaning, dangerous?"

"Well, yes."

He had been working on a plausible model, the same one that gave them the exponential time behavior. It showed that a *child universe* would expand at no cost to the parent. Thanks to the warping ability of the wormhole, the child grew into a space of its own. "Remember that old basic paper on making

238

child universes? It's studded with phrases like 'We cannot be decisive' and arguments where 'We have not excluded' and 'Our entire discussion has been in the context of classical general relativity.' And they're right.''

Alicia shrugged; theorists' worries were pretty far from her immediate concerns. Zak came into the lab and started making ready for more measurements. Zak reported that he had images of some more stars and diffuse, gassy patches. They were all moving away, as seen in steadily redder Doppler shifts.

''The other universe is expanding, so its stars are getting farther apart. At least, so far,'' Alicia said.

Zak had the data neatly computer-filed; she let Max worry by himself for a while as she checked everything. She and Zak would have a fantastic body of data when this was all over, in both senses of the word. When she came back to Max, he said earnestly, ''We have to check our assumptions.''

''Such as?''

''I've found some solutions that have the Cosm growing with time.''

''In size?''

''Yes, and mass.''

She stood up, stretching. If Max's math led down a path, well, there were worse reasons to follow. Theorists avoided being seen as too mathematical and lacking a gut physics feeling. Experimenters took pains to evade seeming to be routine engineers or gadget jockeys. But they had to find common ground.

The fact that you could attack a problem without worrying about making up lecture notes in the next ten minutes was the best part of working in the summer. ''Zak, let's try something new.''

They took two days to be sure: the Cosm now weighed half of its original 100 kilograms. They checked the measurement three times; it was difficult weighing something suspended in a magnetic grip.

''How the hell can that be?'' Zak said, the ''hell'' an index of his fatigue. ''How come we didn't notice?''

"No way to tell, was there?" Max asked.

"It's also two millimeters smaller," Alicia said. "So its radius is utterly unrelated to its mass."

"*Apparent* mass," Max said. "The balance between positive mass energy and negative gravitational potential energy must be readjusting all the time. That's disquieting."

"Why?" Zak asked, his black hair unruly. He needed a haircut and looked as though he had not seen a mirror for days. Maybe he hadn't, she mused.

"As the universe on the other end of this neck ages, the connection gets, well, stretched. Fluctuations in the total energy of the connection—the Cosm we see—get bigger."

Alicia guessed, "And if it can get lighter, it can get heavier."

"Right. And big enough, it's dangerous."

Zak said wonderingly, "If it goes up by a factor of ten—"

"Or a hundred, say"—Max nodded—"it could get out of control, sink into the Earth."

"This is just theory," Alicia said uncertainly.

"Your measurement isn't," Max countered.

"You're worried about danger, but what if it keeps getting smaller?" Zak asked.

"Then it will dwindle away. End of experiment."

Alicia sat up, alarmed. "How can we stop that?"

"We can't." Max shrugged—almost guiltily, she thought. "I found solutions that also have the mass shrinking in time. Apparently that's what this one is doing. But the steadiness of the total energy is very tricky, like a pencil balanced on its point."

Alicia felt a spark of irritation, for which she then chastised herself. To physicists the universe was particles and waves, or more deeply, the interplay of fields. To a theorist it was deeper still, the unfolding of symmetries that God the Mathematician ordained would be obeyed, or broken, at various inscrutable energy levels. They shared a rather chilly vision of an abstract seethe, prickled by radiation, space-time warped and puckered by blunt mass. But she felt physics as a gut, hands-on experience, not an airy labyrinth of disembodied ideas.

Zak nodded earnestly, hiked up his fashionably oversized pants. "So we should be careful . . ."

"And alert," Max added. "I can't really predict much here, I'm afraid."

"Then let's study the hell out of it while we can," Alicia said.

Publication of their paper in *Physics Letters* unleashed a storm. It was as though the entire scientific community, primed by the disaster at Brookhaven, were in a metastable state, like a laser, ready to emit a burst of glossy light at the slightest resonant tickle.

Immediately theorists sent in papers explaining the spheres, posting to the high-display showcases on the Internet. The advantage of pseudo-publishing there were considerable: nailing down credit for an idea, while not waiting for the reviewing process. That came later, if ever; sometimes papers disappeared, their errors caught offstage.

Herbert Himmel of the University of Chicago then Net-published a paper interpreting the spheres as "a class of solutions in N-dimensional string theory." He did not even specify the number N—theorists worshipped at the altar of Greater Generality—but presented analytical solutions that cast doubt on Max's interpretation. Alicia could not follow more than two lines of the argument and quickly tuned it out. Max fought it out with Himmel, giving five seminars around the country in a single week to defend his ground. Academic trench warfare.

Her fellow experimenters followed quickly enough. Frank Lutricia of CERN in Geneva attacked her for "obviously incorrect" measurements; his argument seemed to be that the results were simply too, too incredible, and therefore wrong. She did not reply, but she steamed in silence.

The vice chancellor and then the chancellor himself asked her to "be cordial" to the media. Bernie Ross told her it was worthwhile doing, as a good-faith gesture. He had been stalling the legal issues.

"The bad news is that Brad's parents have filed a wrongful death suit," he told her one afternoon over coffee in the Phoenix Grill, her favorite eatery on campus. Here, at least, she did not get pointed out by strangers.

"They've got grounds," she admitted.

"Of course. But UCI isn't going to hang you out to dry."

"How'd you arrange that?"

He grinned. "Magic."

"Meaning, I'd better be nice to the press."

"Let's say there's no point in leading with your chin."

Despite the sports metaphor, she agreed. So she did the obvious interviews with the big newspapers and a little TV, provided they stayed away from Brad's death beyond a bare mention. The process was "enlightening," as she put it to Max.

"We're looking for human interest here, not just facts," the man from the *Los Angeles Times* said right away. His expression spoke volumes about what he thought of facts. At least UCI had arranged them in groups, so she did not have to repeat herself into catatonia. She "sat" for TV interviews, too. Max came in on some of them, to her relief. Often she had the feeling that they were really talking to each other, despite all the other people in the room. In the big PBS interview for *Nova,* she told herself she would give these people an hour and whispered to Max, "Already it's seeming like a long time." He glanced meaningfully at his watch. There were still forty-two minutes to go.

Worse were some who sneaked in. One woman began, "Just start with the five W's, you know, who, what, why ... uh, which ... you know." In this interview Alicia began to wonder when had it become acceptable to answer a "Thank you" with "No problem." Prolonged exposure to journalists made her distrust any news report; they got matters wrong so casually, even the simple ones. A supposedly major media figure she had never heard of came to ask scowling, abrasive questions focused on how she got the Cosm away from Brookhaven. The man had a tapered nose descending to a tight, pouting mouth, the combination a fleshy exclamation point.

He commanded TV Minicams that stared in cyclopean stupor at her, unwavering even when she blew her nose—or maybe because she did. She never watched the final product but heard enough to write a fuming letter of complaint—which nobody answered.

But these were mere passing irritants. Deeper were the systemic troubles. She stressed the many unknowns; the media wanted sharp answers to huge questions, preferably in a compact one-liner. She tried to emphasize the progressive questioning of her method and how all answers were provisional, awaiting confirmation; reporters liked zippy adventure and exciting guesses with, of course, striking visuals in primary colors.

As the results began appearing, she started to perceive by a sort of radarlike reflection how the vast audience beyond saw her world. The barely awake public, trained to the attention span of a commercial, thought that science had two children: either consumer yummies, served up by the handmaiden of technology, or else awesome wonders like the beauties of astronomy. The unsettling side they largely ignored, unless for the momentary shock value of, say, swollen insects doing disgusting things. But the root promise of science was of a world unshaped by humans. The expanses of time and space that stretched out from the human community were terrifying, and most avoided even thinking of them.

She recalled that polls showed over half the American population thought astrology had scientific principles undergirding it. Many believed in clairvoyants, faith healers, palm readers, and everyday parascientific notions like energy halos, mystical pyramids, UFOs, and ESP. The Cosm seemed like more of the same to them.

She was checking out at the Glenneyre Market when she saw the *National Enquirer*'s headline:

GIRL WHO MAKES GALAXIES
Is Shiny Bowling Ball A Universe?

She yanked all the copies out of their wire rack and stuffed them behind another tabloid. Two days later somebody sent her anonymously, through interdepartmental mail, an even worse rag:

THIEF OR GODDESS?
Is 'Brilliant But Driven' Scientist A Swindler?

"Ummm," Max said, finding the whole matter funny, while she fumed. "How come you can't be both?"

The melancholy clouds in her mind she increasingly dispelled with long walks with Max on the beaches north of Laguna. They were being swallowed by housing tracts from inland, an upscale fungus. She had not been at UCI long, but the feeling of constriction, even along the besieged beaches, alarmed her.

How did we lose all this? she wondered. By inches. The developers, the eager immigrants, the boundless plenty of sunlight and sharp air—all conspired to wedge in just one more condo, another street, a minimart to shave seconds of convenience from myriad lives. As the universe expanded, humanity seemed to outrace it, filling it with their numbers, with riotous life's unstoppable growth.

Her fame in the larger world rose exponentially. She even began getting invitations to receptions, evenings at the opera, dinner parties, and the like from people she did not know. She went to some, sometimes straight from the lab, not changing out of her work clothes. They reminded her of why she had never cultivated the usual university crowd and preferred people like Jill.

To Alicia it seemed that academics often tossed around political topics, showing no more understanding of them than any amateur would. Beneath the arch contempt for the powers in business and government, she sensed envy. Most professors had once been the brightest people on their horizons: valedictorians, scholarship students, honors graduates, fellows here and there. Now they saw the real power going to the sort of people they never even noticed; the world was run by B students, at best. This distorted their political views, which ill concealed a longing for power—at least to straighten things out, as if a tweak or two could do the job, administered by the right (their) hands. As a political commentator of the time put it, most real-world people she knew thought of Washington, D.C., as a whorehouse where every four years ordinary folk got to elect a new piano player. What they really wanted was somebody to set fire to the whorehouse. Academics wanted to run it.

To all this she said nothing. Her style was not theirs, she reminded herself, sitting at neatly arranged dinner tables. Even tiny matters differed. In the humanities buildings office doors stayed solidly closed, whereas in the sciences doors hung open on often deserted rooms, as if inviting casual ideas. Or perhaps both were advertising: the humanists, that they *might* be there, the scientists, that they certainly were but were probably off in the lab right now.

At a special reception presided over by the chancellor, she met a major figure from an avant-garde wing of the philosophy department. She had heard that he was behind a whispering campaign, complaining that UCI was handling her altogether too gently. He had sounded formidable, but the man himself had a big barrel chest that, in distracted moments, would slide down to reveal itself as a momentarily levitated stomach.

She knew he had maligned her to other faculty and yet here he was, cordial and loftily smiling, white wine held at port arms. She thought of saying very quickly something like "You duplicitous phony-pal, hiding behind etiquette when everyone knows you slandered me. What, exactly, are your standards of propriety that you lack even the convictions of your petty gossip and now dare address me with your insipid salutation?"

But she didn't. She deployed the Cold Hello Defense and turned away. It didn't help, though.

After came the doubt (*Why didn't I say . . . ?*), pathetic excuses (*I didn't want to give him the satisfaction*)—to which the doubter subprogram in her shot back: *Oh, I see, you didn't want anyone to know that you're a sensitive, feeling, open woman despite being a physicist, who has been gouged by negative, cheap-shot gossip . . . so you'll grow a tumor instead?* So she fumed and ate too much of the finger food and felt like an ugly piece of work, a hypocrite herself.

Her stress levels mounted. Jill had talked her into "seeing someone to talk all this through" a month before. She had to admit it was at least a relief to yammer on to someone who would not laugh in her face or repeat her more humiliating revelations, who might even smile and nod. She had even managed to get around to discussing Max, a major subject about whom she felt much but could say nothing, not even to loyal Jill.

So after the reception she called her therapist and unloaded. The therapist said very calmly, "You should *use* this anger. As long as you're sounding so out of control, ah, your insurance denied my billing because I forgot to preauthorize. It would really help if you called them right now while you're this upset and they could hear in your voice how much you need this therapy."

She slammed the receiver down, but that didn't do much good either.

Max said happily, "I beat the crap out of that guy Himmel."

"Literally, I hope?"

She scooted her rump up onto a lab bench, the only seating room left in the observatory since she and Zak had brought in more detection gear. They were gathering plenty of data, of stars simmering into ruby birth, great masses of inflamed gas swirling in grand gavottes, strange sprinklings of momentary light in the black immensities—all from the sphere, which continued to lose mass. They were working sixteen-hour days now, overlapping schedules so that every moment of the Cosm's development got logged into the stacked hard disks of big cylindrical hard drives.

Max grinned, nodded. "Seminar battles, real trench warfare."

If there was anything she disliked more than sports analogies, it was war metaphors. "How nasty?"

"He's shown up at all the biggies—MIT, Harvard, Berkeley, Princeton—and I've come along right behind him. I arranged it that way, quick rebuttals right down the line."

"Great. And . . . ?" She beamed at him, surprised at how pleased she was just to see him walking through the lab door again. It had been a lonely week.

Max was quietly proud, indeed, pumped up. "The tide's running my way. Every major figure in particle theory has jumped into the arena. There'll be more papers on this than you and I will have time to read—just you watch—within a month.''

"Even one is more than I want to read," she said wearily.

"You're going to have to do some selling yourself, too," he said gently.

"Huh?"

"This guy at CERN, Lutricia, he's going around saying this is all bad experimental technique.''

"What!''

"I know, I know. But he's saying it. Part of it's personal ambition—he's notorious for walking over people—and part is CERN's rivalry with the United States generally.''

There was no lasting class system in science unless there was a lasting, convincing upper class. The particle physicists had for so long assumed that they were the natural candidates, the obvious Brahmins, that to find themselves suddenly part of the unruly mob vying for research bucks was a profound shock. Manners were changing.

"He says right out that I'm wrong?''

Max reached out and held her hand and she felt both a tingling from the touch and a rising dread. "He's hinting that maybe you're faking some points for the publicity.''

"What!''

She made herself count to ten, a well-worn trick her father had taught her when she was eight years old; but it did work. Scientific integrity demanded little things, like not misleading funding agencies about how likely your research was to yield useful results, and publishing data even if they didn't support your pet theory, and giving the government advice they might rather not hear—day-to-day matters, proceeding on up to the crucial matter of not fooling yourself about whether you had designed your experiment to give truly unambiguous results. Making *doubt* primary, not just proof, was the essential. Learning how to not deceive yourself was never specifically taught in courses; physicists just assumed students absorbed it by osmosis. But *this*—

"The son of a—''

"He's being delicate about it. Hints, little remarks about how much press you're getting, no more."

She groaned. "He can't do this!"

"He is."

"I'm being honest, scrupulously—"

"I know. But you'll have to go out there and slug it out with him. And with others. There's a lot of skepticism."

"Why?"

"Well, it's pretty damn fantastic. And you haven't let anybody come here and see the thing."

"We've been too busy—"

"Sure, sure." Placating hands, palms out, a warm smile. "But people wonder why you're stuck up here on a hill like a hermit."

"The safety people—"

"I know, I know. Still, see how it looks?"

"I don't want a lot of visitors in here." She swept the cramped dome of the observatory in a grand gesture. "Look around. How many could we wedge in?"

"You're right, of course. But—"

"You *know* I'm no diplomat."

"Uh, yes."

"Well, hell, you didn't have to agree so fast."

They both laughed suddenly, pressures equilibrating.

She knew he was right. She was not tactful or smooth. What had her therapist said? "Well, you're not a *classic* monomaniac, but . . ."

"This CERN guy, tell me what to do."

Fundamental physics drew smart, strong personalities; milder types faltered and left the field. Such personalities saw physics differently, of course, and were not shy about saying so. Through half a century of increasingly sharp competition— and especially since the budget cuts started—the community had learned a basic rule: when food gets short, table manners change. The particle physicists developed a social method to make decisions when strong personalities disagreed: the slugfest.

To win a slugfest meant digging through the library, marshaling all the lore surrounding the subject, and using it to shore up support for your views. Then prepare viewgraphs and slides, using the latest full-color technology—not old-style pie charts and flow diagrams, but 3-D exploded views and over-layered sections. Rehearse the talk carefully. Show the audience implications they hadn't thought of, presented in razor-sharp detail. Come back fast and decisively to hostile questions. Make doubters look preposterous if you can, but avoid making fun in any way. Remain solid and factual; avoid rhetoric. The best practitioners could draw a laugh from an audience while responding with an absolutely deadpan, factual remark.

Then take your polished act on the road and sell, sell, sell it for a month.

She sighed. "I don't feel up to a big campaign."

"You've got to do something."

"The truth will out. We'll keep taking data."

"Well, at least do something to gain sympathy."

"What?"

"Um . . . I'll think about it."

"Max, this is getting away from me."

"From us. We're in this together." He got up and angled sideways past tall metal racks of electronics gear, nearly trip-ping over cables. He reached into the yawning U-magnet and touched the sphere, nearly buried beneath light pipes and other diagnostics. "It's all about this interesting, freakish object, in the end. And I've been doing some more thinking . . ."

She settled back, ready to listen. His presence had kindled something warm in her and she allowed herself to simply en-joy his company. His tailored slacks even fit well and weren't perpetually wrinkled, a common scientists' signature. For a theorist, he wasn't half bad.

It took her half an hour to see what he was driving at. "So this isn't just an 'interesting freak'—good to hear. But then how do we use it?"

"Not to escape into another universe, if that's what you're wondering."

"Good, I was thinking you were *National Enquirer* material."

"Huh?"

He had missed the two-week tabloid blitz. She filled him in and he grimaced. "Nope, nothing so moneymaking."

"Glad to hear it."

"All I'm saying is, a better model of quantum gravity can reveal itself through failures of the Standard Model."

"Sort of, footprints of the Theory of Everything."

"Check. Say, in the decay of the proton, which the Standard Model says shouldn't happen. Well, the Cosm isn't just a footprint—it's the real thing, a direct quantum-gravity artifact sitting still in the lab, big enough to put your hands on. We're taking fundamental physics back to a human scale!"

"Bravo." She was happy to see him so delighted, and of course he was right. This shiny sphere was plain evidence for a universe that still held mystery and enormous implication, not buried down in infinitesimal particles no eye could ever see, but smack in your face, obvious.

To theorists Nature was a text to be read. If the Bible was the word of God, then Nature was God's worked-out Examples. Nature was Data in a fine cloth, laced with a mathematical beauty. But in the hands of modern science, reality had descended to the infinitesimal. Where was the gritty feel of the real in abstruse mathematical symmetries and a swarm of unseen particles?

"All we had was an abstract, microscopic world," Max said with sudden vehemence. "Until the Cosm."

8

She realized something was wrong only when the air bag hit her in the face.

Whump! Then the bang and crunch of the gray car smashing into her left front side penetrated, and the thump of the air bag against her. She had been pulling out of a UCI parking lot, after saying good night to Zak. Max had left at midnight and she was thinking about him in a distracted way as she pulled onto a side road. Events compressed.

Now she could not see the gray car because the windshield was mysteriously starred. She sucked in air and tried to reach around the air bag to turn off the ignition. She could not do it. Tight-pressed, with her right hand she popped her emergency belt open. At the same instant the clatter and metallic grind of the collision struck her, and the sudden reek of oil, another bit of delayed perception that unsettled her. Her door popped open. She turned her head and glass tinkled on the concrete and a man's head wearing a broad-lipped hat was there, his hands grabbing her by her collar.

"I can get . . . get out—"

Powerfully, he yanked her out of her seat and she was stumbling on the concrete, trying to get her footing—a very important point, must keep her footing. But it was hard, since the man was big and had strong hands and was hauling her along, forcing her steps away from her car. Another man was pushing her from the side and here came another car—black.

The gray car was buried in the side of her beloved Miata and there was no one in it.

"Hey there—" she started, and a third man in a hat opened the trunk of the black car as they came around to it.

"Wait, who're . . . ?" They grabbed her without a word and tossed her like a garbage bag into the trunk. The lid slammed down.

She gasped and rolled over onto her back. The car took off with a surge, but no roar and squealing of brakes. Smart; don't attract attention. Let people at a distance go back to their business.

She rolled and thumped against the left side of the trunk as the car accelerated along a long curve. The circular road around campus, she guessed.

Panic leaped in her throat. Her strangled cry was thin, weak. Her palms slapped against the metal above her face.

Who *were* they? Rapists? Ancient horrors rose in her mind; gang assaults in the woods, brutality, front-page stories of bodies found. Dread filled her. She pounded against the trunk lid until her hands hurt.

Then she lay in the dark and took a long steadying breath.

Okay, some idiots were kidnapping her. *Think.* Don't give way to fears or worries. Yes.

Try to get away. Fast. Don't waste time figuring out who they are. She envisioned her dad saying that to her and knew it was right.

Should she wait until they stopped at a light and then make noise? If a pedestrian heard and reported her shouts, maybe the police would come.

No, that was stupid. Not very likely a good citizen would try to make the car stop or anything. And if she made a nuisance of herself, they might just open the trunk and rap her soundly in the head. Besides, it was two in the morning—who would be around to hear?

The car hit a bump and surged ahead again. She lay uncomfortably across the length of the trunk, her head tilted up against what felt like the spare tire. *Get your bearings.*

She had gotten only a glance at this car. As she remem-

bered, many cars of this size had a compartment connecting
the trunk to the backseat, for carrying things like skis. Could
she use that?

They were slowing and as road noise lessened she heard a
murmur of talk from the men. One was louder, closer: in the
backseat. Thoughts of kicking out the panel separating her
from the backseat crossed her mind, but she saw no point in
joining the man in the backseat.

They stopped, turned right, and she tried to figure out which
way the car was pointed now. Out along University, maybe
headed for the freeway? Once they got on a fast highway and
put away the miles, then even if she could somehow escape,
she would be in unfamiliar territory. *Hurry.*

She felt along the top of the cramped volume to the latch
assembly that sealed the trunk. She had never looked at one
in detail and in utter blackness had to translate her fingertip
impressions into images.

Fumbling, feeling. Here was a steel bar and something fas-
tened around it. The something turned out to feel like a thin,
smooth metal lobster claw. The jaws of the lock, yes, mounted
on the inside of the trunk lid.

From feel alone she tried to see how it worked. Slam the
lid, the jaws locked on to the bend of a U-shaped steel bar.
Heavy springs held the lobster claws in place, once secured,
she guessed. Her fingers could not reach the springs to check
this. Not much hope of forcing them free, since they were
somewhere inside the claw's steel casing.

Where? She ran her fingers around the rectangular edge of
a plate. Probably the springs were behind it.

Okay—think about the bar, then. It met the body of the car
at the lip of the trunk. Her fingers felt around where the U
met the car body. There were bolts there. Unscrew them? That
way the U-shaped bar would come loose and the lock's jaws
would swing up, carrying the bar still in its grasp.

But for that she needed a wrench. She tried turning the bolts,
hoping they would have some give in them. Rattling around
on the roads shakes a car loose . . .

No luck; they were tight. Their edges cut into her fingertips.

She tried to see the whole assembly again, sense some vulnerability. The car slowed, rolling her slightly toward the backseat. More murmurs from the men. Who the hell *were* they? Their speed, their unnerving skill, not a word said while they got her out of her car and into theirs—

They had left the gray car behind. Were they not worried about it being traced to them? Maybe it was stolen anyway. Maybe—

She made herself stop speculating. *The lock. Think about the lock. Jill can pick locks, so I can, too.*

She ran her hands over the assembly, making mind pictures from her fingertips. Her left hand skipped as it passed over a small hole. Her little finger found it. She could get the tip of the finger in, no more. Not much hope there, either. But it was in the plate that concealed the springs, she was sure of that.

She felt around and realized that the hole was near the plate edge, only inches away from the latch itself. The latch had to have a release somewhere. Some cars had a button the driver pushed to pop the trunk open, she remembered. Not her Miata, though.

Think. That button probably connected to a cable that tripped the release. Not electronically, no; pointless to have a servo that would wear out when simple mechanical pull could do the job.

Okay, enough theory. This lock's release was probably somewhere under the few inches of steel between the claw and the small hole. She tried her little finger again, got it maybe an inch in. It touched nothing. Okay, then, stick something in there, wiggle it around.

But what? She felt around the trunk, but it was bare. They had thoughtfully cleaned it out for her ride. No cushions, though; comfort wasn't their motivation. Not even the jack . . .

She felt in her pockets. Keys, but all far too thick to get through the hole. Something slender . . .

Her pen. She found it in the vest pocket of her work shirt. It was a fairly lean job, a cheap ballpoint from the physics department storeroom. She took the cap off and placed it back in her vest pocket.

The car hit a bump and picked up speed. The surge rolled her into the trunk housing. She rolled herself back and found the plate and hole by feel. It was easy to get disoriented in the utter darkness.

Their speed increased. Going out along University, there was a fair distance without lights. Or were they on the freeway? Not yet; not enough tire noise.

Still, there couldn't be much time. She found the hole by feel and slid the pen in. Not much freedom of movement. She angled it toward the claws. The latch would be in the middle of the assembly, she guessed.

The pen touched something. She pushed the pen as far sideways as it would go. No give at all. Try again. Nothing.

Okay, maybe she was pushing in the wrong direction. Which way would a latch operate? Up or down? No time to figure it out; just try. She worked the pen around some, losing contact with whatever had stopped it before.

The car slowed, rocking her away again. *Damn!* She got back in position and worked the pen around in the hole. There wasn't much angle of attack available.

She dropped the pen. It slipped away and her heart leaped. Why hadn't it fallen on her chest? She felt toward her right and it was not there, either. How in hell could a pen get away—

Her left hand found it. It had hit and rolled a few inches.

Back it went into the hole. The car slowed some more. Suddenly, as she swiveled the pen around, she wondered if the latch would make much noise even if she could trip it. Enough for them to hear? Then best to do it before they stopped, let road noise cover it.

The pen met resistance. She held it carefully and probed. Firm, felt solid. She pushed hard—and a *spang!* came from near her ear. Hard blue-tinged light flooded through a thin crack. The lid had popped up an inch and stopped.

She felt the brakes bite in. She slipped the pen into her pants pocket and wriggled around. They were nearly stopped. She shoved upward and the trunk lifted. No shouts. She sat fully up, hooked a leg over the trunk lip. Streetlights glared.

She lowered her foot to the pavement as the car stopped. Carefully she eased her weight onto that leg, so her load did not leave the car suddenly. Her shoes scraped on the rough concrete.

She was crouching right behind the bumper and could not see the men for the lid. But they would notice it pretty soon, if they hadn't already. She put both hands on the lid and lowered it to within an inch of the lip.

A quick glance. The three heads in the passenger compartment did not turn. She looked around as she crouched. No other cars in the intersection. This was the intersection of Michaelson and University, she recognized, a red light, and as she registered this the yellow flashed on Michaelson, about to change.

She fought the urge to run. Instead, she stayed put. The light went green and the car burned rubber getting away. The freeway on-ramp was in the next block and the driver probably was impatient. They roared off. She stayed in her crouch. The driver might glance in his rearview and a figure running away would draw his eyes. She watched the car, ready to spring up and run if the brake lights went on.

But they didn't. The car zoomed smoothly out of sight around the curve and she gasped, choked, gasped again, gulped in lungfuls of chilly air. She had been holding her breath.

PART V
SOCIAL TEXTS

If you ask what is needed to work out the full consequences of the laws of physics...the answer is: Nothing less than the whole Universe. It is not too much of a guess to say that this is just what the Universe is. This explains a problem that has puzzled theologians, philosophers, and scientists alike: Why is there a universe at all? The theologian, with his belief in an all-powerful God, wonders why God didn't simply perceive the Universe. Why bother actually to have it? The answer is that the Universe *is* the simplest way of perceiving it.

—FRED HOYLE, 1994

"Why can't they *find* these guys?'' Max demanded.

"No clues. The car they rammed me with was stolen.''

"Hard to believe. Somebody pulls off a crime like this and the police just go through the *motions*?''

She shrugged, still tired though it was midmorning. She had tried to sleep late, after all the endless run-throughs with the cops, but her unconscious wasn't having any.

The police had been polite, but what did she have to give them? There she stood, none the worse for wear, at a pay phone with her odd story. She had been a little hysterical and that had gotten her what she interpreted as some men-only, sidewise wry glances, eyebrows lowered, not arched. They seemed to have a protocol for even so outlandish an incident. As they carefully inspected her car, they gave her tips on avoiding collisions, which at the time struck her as throwing a drowning swimmer a strand of barbed wire. A team took fingerprints. Various campus officials were notified and came and spoke quite reasonably and it all had seemed to happen behind a pane of glass.

That mood had persisted when she finally got home and, unable to sleep, watched some TV. It was as usual, a cacophony, which combined with the other audio media gave a disposable pop culture that made every moment but the present seem quaint, bloodless, dead. She had wanly hoped that the matter did not get into the news.

In morning's glow she had realized that was impossible, as

she worked before the mirror, painting the suitcases out from under her eyes. Max was waiting in her office when she slouched in. She had given him keys to both her apartment and office, since he was down from Caltech all the time now, but still it was a bit startling to find him busily running a Mathematica program at her desk; he had stopped immediately, though. He had heard and did not waste time asking her to tell her side.

"How could anyone *do* this and just get to walk away?" Max went on.

She roused enough to say in a flat tone, "More precisely, why in the name of fuck?"

"You mean they were nuts, but what brand?"

"I've gotten coverage all the way from *Nova* to throwaway rags."

"Yeah, that *Nova* crowd can be rough." Max grinned, rather obviously trying to shake her out of her mood.

She summoned up a smile, which quickly lapsed. "I can't really figure a motive unless they just wanted to do some weird hostage thing."

"Thing about crazies is, they're crazy. You can't even understand them in retrospect."

"I don't want to understand them. Ever."

"Must be they are out on the *National Enquirer* end of the spectrum."

"Ummm. I wonder if my father would be any help."

Her dad had just published a column analyzing the media response to the Cosm—without telling her, of course. She mentioned this and Max encouraged her to call, which she did a bit guiltily, since Dad predictably went into hyper mode, aghast that she hadn't called him immediately. Trying to explain that she had gone into some sort of passive withdrawal did no good. He revisited the same territory she and Max had and said he would look into the media end and she finally got to the lab that afternoon, with some relief.

"I've been looking into that increase in IR and visible emission," Zak told her once she had settled in.

"Oh yes, I forgot." It seemed like a long time ago.

"We used to strain to catch photons; now they're flooding out. Look what I got."

Zak showed her images of great shimmering red masses, incandescent in the infrared. She was impressed. Spokes of yellow radiance poked through the thick banks, where young suns fought back the dark pressures.

"Dust clouds, stars condensing out—no sign of galaxies yet, though?"

Zak shook his head, long hair falling across his eyes. "Looks like the astrophysicists who say stars come first, then galaxies, are right."

This was an old issue, whether the great billowing bulks of dust congealed into galaxies before making stars, or the reverse. The sort of issue that mattered to astronomers and few else, but Alicia felt a pleasurable surge to *see* the answer, uncover a secret for the first time. They had been measuring infrared emission from dust for weeks now, first cooling as the Cosm universe expanded, now heated again by the birth of blazing blue-white stars. The Cosm was waking to its possibilities.

"Thing is," Zak said, "it's dead easy to see things now."

"The dust is condensing, clearing the way?"

"No, we're just plain getting a hell of a lot more light, straight across the spectrum."

"Ummm. The Cosm is brighter?"

"I think more light is coming through."

Careful study of the flux measurements showed that Zak was right. The visible emission was still too faint for eyes to make out, but quite enough for their instruments. Carefully they went over everything that could be wrong, but Zak had made no apparent errors.

She nodded. "Good work. Somehow the stuff that holds the Cosm neck open is letting more electromagnetic waves through."

Zak nodded. "I've never really understood that part of Max's theory. The exotic matter, negative energy density and all, that's hard enough to get a feel for—"

"No kidding."

"But why does it let through some light, but not matter?"

She shrugged, smiling wanly. "Why is it losing mass? The super-stuff that holds the neck open is thinning out, so more light gets through? But matter, no; it's still a window."

"Sounds reasonable . . ."

"Max has some involved picture, but I don't follow it. Let's just measure and let the theorists worry about how to make models, okay?"

"Yeah." Zak grinned, punching in commands for more data-taking.

She felt a burst of affection for Zak, his tenacity and quiet support. The bonding between people who worked long hours on hard problems was one of the unspoken emotional struts of any science. She remembered how her advisor had taken her and the other students and postdocs out for a few beers, following the customary mode: he told tales of past glory and mirth; they joked with him, but respectfully, often throwing in a note of self-deprecation. Scientists learned how to work hard under men and women for whom it was the true center of their lives. Students copied the advisor's role and ended by reproducing the person they wanted to be, a collaboration between mentor and self.

There was a steady traffic in students and especially postdocs between the major experimental groups, resembling the exchange of brides among tribes, fostering kinship networks. Not that the exchange was always among equals. The maxim was: knowledge trickles down; students percolate up. The best people got to the best places, so low rank meant low merit. Such was the faith of the field. UCI's reputation would rise because of the Cosm work; she was already receiving inquiries about postdoc positions, and visitors who wanted to get into what would probably become a whole subfield.

"Say, did you see the piece in *The New York Times* about Brookhaven?" Zak interrupted her thinking.

A sinking feeling. "Uh, no."

"They saw the recombination flash. It lasted about ten minutes, started fires, burned up some trees."

"They didn't *tell* us?"

"It was on the TV news this morning. I figured you saw."

She was irked but just said, "Ummmm."

"They're calling it a 'micro-universe,' too, saying they're doing the first 'systematic' work on it."

"Oh really. And what are we? Chopped liver?"

She and Zak exchanged lopsided smiles. "They sure do want to beat us in the media arena."

Getting the jump on your competitors was an old game in particle physics, the most competitive and time-sensitive science of all. In the 1970s, she recalled, a Brookhaven group led by Sam Ting had named their newly discovered particle the J. A rival group at Stanford had found the same particle and named it for the Greek letter *psi* because their computer graphics produced a pattern resembling that character. Which symbol one used in later papers implied a position on which group was the true first discoverer. Eventually, given the choice between a symbol for a pattern and one for a man, the diplomatic used J-*psi* and let it go at that. With delight the Stanford group pointed out that J resembles the Chinese character for *ting*, so Ting had covertly named the particle for himself.

"We're ahead of them in the Cosm's development," she said. "No way they can—wait . . ."

A few minutes' calculation showed that the Brookhaven recombination era had taken a week less than their Cosm's. "Theirs is running at a different time shift," Alicia said.

"Faster. They'll catch up."

"If our Cosm is even around by then. It's losing mass steadily."

Zak frowned. "I wonder if that's related to our getting more light from it."

"Probably."

Zak went to check some details among the diagnostics. The day had slipped away and she did not look forward to a night poring over their results at home. Her thoughts drifted back to her time in grad school when she had felt this way, exhausted by the work yet strung so tight she could not truly rest. That was probably why she had gotten through with her thesis work more quickly than her cohorts. All around her the male graduate students had married and settled down, supported in their late nights and drudgery weekends by sympathetic wives whom they would certainly, the field's traditions taught, never divorce. Did they make damned sure their prospective wives were suitably impressed with the importance of particle physics and would not expect too much of their husbands' time? Those men unmarried by the postdoc phase could expect a perpetual probing interest; a successful physicist was a married physicist. Once she had heard a postdoc remark that he wanted to get married so that he would not have to bother with a distracting social life.

Zak came back and they finished a few details. "Come on, Zakster," she said, hugging him, "I'll buy you a beer."

2

The kidnapping haunted her. She glanced around warily whenever she left a building. At night she avoided going out at all. Approaching her parked rental car, she kept her key poised in hand for stabbing if someone should grab her. Strangers she eyed suspiciously. Hang-up phone calls left her a seethe of anxiety, unable to concentrate for hours afterward. Once she actually jumped at her own shadow.

Zak noticed and in his own quiet way did what he could. Max's method was more systematic, making sure to escort her around campus whenever he was down from Caltech. Jill sat and listened to her endless river of talk, which helped a lot. She had a few nights of heavy drinking and paid for them with wracking headaches.

The police "hit a wall," as one of them put it. The kidnappers had been careful and left few clues. Her work was well known and the suspects many, in principle.

She thought about getting a gun and rejected it; they spooked her, too. After a few days of free-floating anxiety, the effect seemed to wear off somewhat, but she was never again to be unconscious of her exposure.

UCI had put an armed security guard outside the observatory. This helped a lot. Matters calmed down and she got some solid work in. Still, she gasped in fear when she came in early one morning and found a lanky, smiling man standing inside the observatory.

"What? Who're you?"

"Just a member of the public. Wanted to look around."

"How did you get in?"

He grinned. "Ever'body gotta sleep."

Images from her kidnapping sprang to mind, tightening her throat. This man did not seem threatening, but her heart was thumping hard. The awful black moments in the trunk—Some of the stored anger from that now came to her aid. She slammed down her briefcase and gestured at the door. "Well, you can just get—"

"The secret is your mass here, right?"

"What?"

"No, hey, I understand this, see? You don't have to hand me the line you give the TV."

He was big but did not look dangerous. She tried to think of a quick way to get him out of there. "Sir, you can see—"

"Your thingy in there, it's got a lot of extra mass, right? But your trick is, you've squeezed it into that ball. Smart! Only, I"—a canny wink—"know how you did it."

"Really?" She edged casually away from him, getting some gear between them.

"Magnetics, is how. Am I right?"

"Magnetic fields don't affect mass—"

"So you say! But you've trapped this thing and I say you know more than you're telling."

"Such as?"

"It's not a space-time thingy at all, right? Look at it!" He whirled so fast that she thought he would trip over himself. Instead, he jabbed a finger between the magnetic poles. "It's all shiny. A spaceship, that's what it is."

How could she get him away from the Cosm without herself getting close to him? "Look, the reflection of light is—"

"It's a UFO. No need to be covering it up, miss. You've finally captured one of the aliens."

"I'd appreciate it if you would simply leave us alone to—"

"Perfesser, you'll be famous! Think! The aliens, they're

trapped in there. They'll pay you anything if you'll just let them out."

She backed toward the door, her anger dampened by this burst of looniness. He didn't seem threatening anymore, just pathetic. "I've had enough. I'll call Security unless you—"

"Oh, I see. You want to keep the aliens for yourself, just snow the rest of us, is it? Well, we been working on this UFO problem a lot longer than you have, Perfesser. We won't let you just walk in and take over, even if you have got a magnetic trap here—"

The man's face congested with words and ideas he seemed unable to get out through his tight, angry mouth. It took several more minutes to call the guard, get the man outside, and close the door. The click of the lock brought a shuddering sigh of relief from her.

He was merely the first.

In a way, the cranks were the comic relief her anxieties needed. It was hard to be fearful of intruders when they so often were laughable.

They thronged to the physics department office, which resolutely refused to direct them to her office or lab. Since the downstairs directory gave her office number, it quickly became a bad idea to hang around there. Her lab was a bit harder to find, but the more shrewd found her in the bay. She took to locking the lab doors, which helped all but the truly crafty. One of them even got in carrying a pizza delivery. She and Zak—and eventually Max too—developed economical methods of brushing them off, up to and definitely including a stick she had sharpened.

Many brought their own manuscripts, which would explain, if she would just spare them a few minutes, all that she had discovered. She fell for this once, while distracted, only to find that what the particular character wanted was a chance to lecture her on his overall theory of the universe, or rather, the "megaworlds" of which ours was but one rather minor example. He had cobbled together enough terms from newspaper articles on cosmology to unspool an almost-plausible line of science chat. Many excoriated Einstein to her face, maybe believing this brave stance would intrigue her. Those she successfully drove away sent her their ideas printed in pamphlets or even bound books, all published by private presses, usually sent in thick packaging, as though the ideas inside were fragile, and by overnight delivery, for time (or maybe space-time) was of the essence. Somehow she did not have the heart to throw these away; they spoke of a twisted earnestness that resembled the true scientific impulse. She gladly turned them over to anybody who noticed the growing stack in a corner of the lab. Inside their stiff covers were jargon-choked claims, equations of odd symbols, but none of the worked-out examples that a real theory could be judged by. Indeed, highblown rhetoric plus uncheckable consequences were the two sure signatures of the crank. They claimed to have a complete theory that could explain everything—and if you read far enough, just about anything. Their theories were ramshackle edifices, some several hundreds of pages long in monograph form.

Humor was wasted on them, subtlety impossible. The earnest religious types at first tried to sidle up to the topic, but if joshed at all would quickly shift to accusations of hubris (though none of them seemed to know that specific word) and atheist arrogance. These she used the stick on.

A subspecies of the generic crank interpreted her quick dismissal as evidence that she would somehow steal their ideas. A bulky man from Encinitas proudly presented her with his red-leather-bound "Treatise on the Giga-Universe," then quickly snatched it back, sputtering that she was just the sort who would publish this wonderful stuff without giving him due credit.

Most tried to reach her by telephone—so many that she finally gave up answering it, except in the lab. Visitors got screened by the valiant department staff; Jim, who manned the front desk, got into a fistfight with a particularly ardent sort.

She took him to lunch in apology. "There're so *many*," he said wonderingly. "And they all read the tabloids." Indeed, they believed in a sort of eyewitness truth, the dominance of the odd event, which they took the Cosm to be. They were innocent of the scientist's worldview, founded on a web of interconnected logic and experience.

Most amusing to her were those who tried repeatedly to reach her, and if successful, usually began with a sober, sad expression and the dignified announcement that if she did not give them the necessary time to discuss their ideas and, of course, tour the experiment, they would have to unleash their secret weapon: they would denounce her on television. Since TV was to them the ultimate arbiter, and they had seen her exalted momentarily by it, surely she would not risk losing it all before the piercing gaze of the cameras.

Her colleagues in the department found the traffic of wandering pilgrims at first amusing, the stuff of afternoon coffee jokes, and then, irritating. She regaled a few with stories of the odd theories and twitchy behavior of her unwanted visitors, but after a few weeks the joke soured. The more traditional faculty disliked attracting such attention, their unblinking scowls holding her responsible.

3

The next afternoon, in the middle of routine work, she noticed something different about the Cosm. She and Zak were changing some of the optical diagnostics and she reached in to adjust some of the feeds and saw that the sphere was black.

"Good grief," she said.

"It's gone transparent," Zak whispered.

It also seemed a little smaller. Zak's eyes bulged. Instead of metallic reflection, the surface seemed obsidian black, with grainy smudges here and there. They spent several minutes carefully pulling back the equipment beneath which the sphere was nearly hidden. Peering into the deep black, she saw faint streaks and gleams.

"Time-blurring," Zak said. "We're seeing into it!"

"Why?"

"Like you said before, the mass loss may mean it's weakening."

She calculated quickly in her head. "If Max's time-rate equation still applies . . . Wow, with every second here, centuries are passing by on the other side."

That was a continuing problem. After the dying away of the primordial light as the Cosm's space-time expanded, there was no reliable clock on the other side. Max had tried to figure out a way to use the complicated Doppler shifts they kept getting, in the spectra of the stars they could make out on the other side. But there seemed to be nothing like a simple Hubble shift, the rate from a universal expansion. Max thought this was because the neck connecting them was getting stretched, adding a red shift all its own. More complication.

Such deliberations did not detain them. Zak started swinging their optical array back into place. She understood without a word. The IR and other gear could come later; right now they wanted to *see*.

Within half an hour, they were watching framing camera photos. Ruddy blurs that seemed to be glowing reefs of dust in the distance. Traceries that resolved into handfuls of crystalline points in sapphire and orange—globular clusters of stars like bee swarms.

They turned out all the lights and sat in the darkened observatory. Absolute silence descended. The Cosm worked with quick, darting turquoise incandescences against background ruby glows. The intimate workings of stars. Labors of millennia. In all the tangle of equipment, in their indirect ways of study, there had never come a moment like this, when they saw directly and cleanly into the living abyss of another entire Creation and felt it in their bones.

"Alicia?" It was Onell, the department chairman, one of the few who had the number of her portable phone. "I was wondering if you could stop by?"

"I'm pretty busy. What is it?"

"Something I would rather not discuss this way." Onell's voice was a bit stiff, guarded.

"Wait'll I finish an observing run."

"Anything new?" Even Onell could not disguise his curiosity. She had long since decided against issuing bulletins.

"We're still gathering." She liked using that phrase, because it could also imply "gather" in the sense of infer or conclude, which was certainly true.

She got back up to her office by midafternoon of a simmering hot day, grateful for the deeper chill of the building compared with the cramped observatory. She had not seen her desk for a week and indeed could not see it now; letters and packages covered it. In the wake of her aborted kidnapping, UCI had taken to checking all packages in case they might be bombs. The physics department no longer accepted phone messages, since she never answered them anyway. She had quickly discovered that the latest generation of new, hip journalists did no homework and believed their most important research tool to be the telephone. She had changed her e-mail address, giving the new one only to Brookhaven, Max, Dad, and Bernie Ross; not that she checked there very often, either.

Not that she had kept entirely out of the line of fire. Bernie handled most things, but she had to meet with some committees and explain herself, just to get more resources. The vice chancellor for research had given her help, including the armed guard. To get this, with Dad's teaching she had learned a few moves in the academic meeting game, such as slowing to breathe in the middle of her sentences. This let her rush past her last words and plunge into the next sentence, so that those waiting to pounce did not know where to smoothly interrupt. That was actually fun, in a way, but like going to a sporting event just because you liked to eat hot dogs.

She went into the chairman's office and Onell asked again about what they were measuring. When she put him off and again brushed away the old bit about serving on committees, Onell settled back and his face closed off, eyelids drooping. His smooth jowls bulged against the restraint of a tony cotton broadcloth shirt, she noted abstractly, setting off nicely against a gray worsted jacket; he was as sleek as a beaver, even when slouched in an executive chair.

He began with a rather airy generalization about how physicists liked those who did the conventional sort of lab work. She wondered what this had to do with her until she saw that, of course, he meant the Cosm. Onell implied that the "controversy" would only count against her in the short run, but unfortunately, the short run was where they were all currently living. All this was a run-up to his news: she had been denied the merit increase that she had applied for last winter.

She had been an assistant professor, II, for two years now and wanted the usual merit increase move up to III. In principle she could be promoted to tenure and become an associate professor by now, but the waiting periods and protocols were time-honored, hardening like arteries as the University of California aged. Not getting the routine merit increase did not bode well for the coming, crucial vault to tenure.

She used her command of language by remaining silent. Certainly among some other faculty this would seem a ripe comeuppance, principally for those for whom the university was mostly like a chat show with more guests. As she walked out of Onell's office, still without a word, she was surprised to find that not getting a step up the ladder did not even measure on her emotional scale. A year before it would have been rattling. Now it was like reading about a flood in China; bad news, no doubt, but for somebody else.

4

"This is *great*," Max said. He had braved the freeway traffic to get down here as soon as he heard. After Onell, she had been okay for a few hours, but then found she needed cheering up.

She wished she could watch his face, but they sat in the utter blackness of the observatory, watching the swirl of color from the Cosm. "A cosmic light show," he murmured slowly.

"Not a show. The real thing."

"Yes," he whispered, "the real thing."

As if he still did not quite believe it, she thought. And yet she knew what he felt. They had been throwing every diagnostic at a metallic bowling ball, behaving like good scientists, reasoning all around it, but until now there was no direct, firm confirmation that made you *feel* the presence of a whole other space-time. The grand dance of radiant dust and stars, wheeling in gravitational gavottes, finally did it for her. And him, she could sense.

"I still don't understand why we can see it," she said.

"Me either. The neck is stretching, getting thinner."

"Will we lose it?"

"Well, it's held this long, through the rough first stages of its expansion."

"In other words . . ."

"Right. I haven't a clue."

They sat and watched and an odd, warm sensation of intimacy crept into her. Max knew when to say nothing, to be humble before the huge facts of the world; maybe that was essential to being a true scientist. Pleasant, very.

"It's accelerating," he said, voice distant in the dark. "Running faster all the time."

"I wish we could measure time on the other side, get some—"

"Can't you feel it?" he said suddenly. "I almost think I can *see* the globular clusters swooping through space."

She knew what he meant, some gut-level perception she had when the masses of luminous raw gas gave way to spinning crowds of pearly stars, only to be swept away moments later by tides of dark dust that blotted out the furious luminosities of Creation. Speed. The spectacle on the other side moved almost with . . . "Haste."

"Yeah, impatience." He sighed. "To be born."

"It was born over four months ago."

In the utter blackness, their eyes never leaving the swirl and rhapsody before them, she could read his mood from tone alone. "I mean life. Struggling to be born."

She blinked. "Already?" Stellar evolution was one thing, but—

"There's an old saying in popular astronomy courses," Max said remotely. "Why was the Earth 4.5 billion years old? Because it took that long to find that out."

"With everything else changing, the mass and so on, is your first fit to the time shift still good?"

He turned to his laptop and updated the curve with the new measurements Zak had made of the background radiation temperature, the cooling haze of the emission that had killed Brad. He printed out the new curve and added his hand-drawn labels and axes. On this scale the early weeks were squashed into the bottom axis. All that remained was the remorseless steep curve, taking the Cosm time frame into an accelerating future. Brad and the recombination era were far down, where the slope met the axis. QUASARS marked where the bright cores of galaxies burned, then had quickly ebbed away. NOW showed the present, with the Cosm aged about 4.5 billion years. His graph was now a steep exponential in coordinates of lab time versus Cosm time.

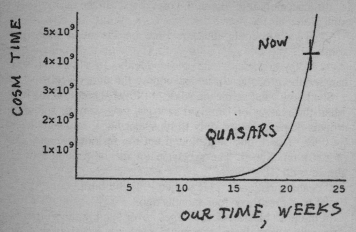

"Ummm. A billion years in the Cosm—"

"Took about twenty weeks for us to reach. But now, for the Cosm to add a billion takes just a week or so. The Cosm's clocks are running away from us."

"Can we be sure of that?"

To her surprise, he gave a dry laugh. "Of course we can't. There's really no other way to calibrate their time rate. Things like galaxy formation are coming in at just about when astronomers think they should, though. Y'see, we don't have a reliable hold on what kind of cosmological model fits their universe—"

"Their?"

"If it isn't inhabited yet, it could be within weeks. *If*'—a finger jab at the Cosm's swirl—"it's a universe built like ours."

She whispered, "How would we know?"

"Impossible. We'll never know."

Again to her surprise, she felt relief at this. "We're getting all this down, Zak and I. Miles of data storage, canisters—"

"You're doing a great job. Generations of cosmologists and astronomers will pore over every jot of it, spectra and images and Dopplers. So much . . ."

She could tell he was smiling in the blackness, though she did not know how she knew. A long silence passed between them as the streaming, shimmering violence went on in the face of the sphere.

Then Max's voice carried a note of analytic distance, as though he too had passed through a stretching moment where words were useless and now wanted to come back to the comforting human world of discourse, of method.

"Look, there's plenty we don't even know about our own cosmology. For us to be here at all demands a hell of a lot of fine-tuned coincidences. *If* there had not been a one part in a billion inequality between matter and antimatter, all coming somehow out of the Big Bang, then there would be nothing but light buzzing around. And *if* nuclei weren't much massier than the electrons weaving about them to make atoms, then there'd be no stable structures. *Sploosh!* Same result *if* the electron charge didn't exactly balance the proton charge. And that's all atomic stuff! Add to that: *if* the expansion of the universe wasn't nearly exactly equal to the gravitational attraction of the matter that happened to be in it, so that even though the whole universe expands, local gravity still manages to hold things together—"

She had to laugh. "You're getting carried away."

A rueful chuckle in the dark answered her. "Yeah, well, the arguments go on, right down to prosaic points such as ice floating in water, so that unlike every other common fluid, it makes a protective skin of ice. Beneath winter ice in lakes, life can ride out a cold season. Even *that* might be basic to making any life survive in even *this* universe."

"I see . . ." Let him talk it out.

"Fine-tuning, everywhere you look! For weeks I've been trying to find ways of telling what sort of thing the Cosm is, and I keep coming back to the basic facts that we don't even know what makes *our* universe work so well."

He was agitated over an entirely abstract point, which

meant, she judged, that he had been putting in a lot of time and getting nowhere. She patted his arm, still keeping her eyes on the endlessly moving radiance of the sphere. "Well, then, a universe that didn't satisfy these *ifs* could exist, but with nobody with a brain to witness it."

"Which makes a cosmologist wonder why ours seems so well designed. Some great designer at work? Cosmologists talk about God a lot, but we can't invoke Him to solve our problems. I've tried to figure out some general way of attacking this . . ." His voice trailed away in quiet frustration.

"So what's our little Cosm going to do?"

"Hard to say. You can scarcely find out if ice floats in there. Hell, we were lucky to see stars."

"Lucky how?"

"Well, not really, uh . . ."

Silence in the blackness.

"There's something you're not telling me," she said.

"I . . . I figured out why Brad died."

"The recombination radiation . . . ? Why was it suddenly so strong?"

"Same reason we're seeing globular clusters, stars, dust. There was plenty of matter near the other end of the Cosm's neck. It recombined and gave us a burst of radiation. The other end of the Cosm's neck somehow flared open, too, letting lots more through. It fried Brad."

"Why?"

"Remember, right about that time in our universe, matter and light were on nearly equal footing. When mass got the upper hand, I think the Cosm's other end suddenly grew."

"You're sure?"

He sighed. "It checks out with the equations, if I assume a universe expanding pretty much the way ours did. There were mass concentrations by that time in our universe, too, with spaces in between. The Cosm's other end must've been swept up in one of them."

"A galaxy starting to form?"

"Probably. We'll wait and see."

"Then if the Cosm had been in one of the voids between concentrations . . ."

"There wouldn't have been so much radiation. Brad might've lived."

"And the Cosm would be in an empty, uninteresting place. So that we wouldn't be seeing stars and clusters nearby now."

"Right." His voice was heavy, slow. "The Cosm gives and the Cosm takes away."

5

She got ready for Dinner with Dad by playing the radio and working on her ensemble. It always paid to dress up for him. And she enjoyed it, had always gotten a warm feeling from the preparations. She had the conversation with Max to think over, too, and let herself spend an hour trying on different combinations of outfits, skirts and blouses piling up on the bed. Like a rummage sale—though, of course, for people with exquisite taste.

She opened a bottle of merlot and wished for a cigarette. One of the better aspects of aging was that she no longer practiced dragging on cigarettes before the mirror, striving to get the right dissipated look, or tried on sunglasses until she found the kind the latest hip singer wore. Had she really worn those mirrorshades? Perfect holdovers from the Me Decade, because they let the viewer watch himself.

What else had she gained with the piling on of years, just as she was now piling up clothes to find the mythical perfect combo? No more looking for the perfect man, *homo sensitivus*. Good riddance! And after the Clinton years, an indifference to politics. The 1990s had taught some useful lessons, most of them inadvertent. Given a choice between existential despair and rapt religious fervor, her crowd chose marijuana.

All through the years while she had worked on her physics, she had nonetheless cocked an ear for the baying of the social hounds. Her twenties had been a time when women didn't have affairs, they sported "sexual friendships," during which they didn't fall in love but rather built relationships. She had devised a smooth carapace of detachment and beneath it a rickety emotional scaffolding. On odd-numbered days love was a disease looking for a cure, and on even-numbered ones she longed for it.

"Been there, done that," she summed up matters brightly to herself, then added, "Or maybe, Been done to."

But now, she reminded herself, she was on a roll. Mistress of Universes! "Fine," she said aloud, "but why does it make you uneasy, girl?"

She burned off some of her anxiety with a flurry of straightening up, on the way to finding her pearl pin, just perfect for the azure blouse she had picked out. Of course it was not where she remembered putting it.

She spun around the apartment, singing, twirling, finishing off another glass of the merlot; quite good stuff, actually. She thumbed the radio to an AM "soul station" and hummed along to an ancient classic, "Annie Had a Baby," hips swinging, getting into the Black Thang.

While she picked up her bedroom (Dad would frown if he saw it), the show gave way to a collection of rap crap and she turned it off. Time to meet the Dad . . .

Which turned into a heavy-duty session, just as she had feared. Dad had flown down and seen Bernie Ross and was full of advice. There were legalities: Brad's parents' lawsuit, which named about half of UCI, just to be complete; a suit from Brookhaven, plus a separate but equal suit by the Department of Energy; a nuisance suit by a church of some sort, claiming that the Cosm was a violation of—

"Church and state?" Alicia asked disbelievingly.

"They claim through you the U.S. government usurped God's laws. Forget that one; it's crazy."

"And Bernie can handle the others without my being there?"

"For now. But not forever, girl." Dad reached out a big hand and laid it on hers.

"I don't want to lose a second to this . . . stuff."

"It's okay, you can say 'shit' in front of me."

"No shit?" she asked wonderingly.

His crinkly-eyed smile. "You're all grown up."

"And getting in big-time trouble proves it?"

"No, keeping your head up and proud does."

A long moment during which she took refuge in her vodka collins. "Ummm. How much is this costing me?"

"Don't worry. That'll come later."

"I didn't even pay Bernie a retainer."

"Okay, so I did. You can't afford him right now."

"I'll never be able to."

"Once you write your bestseller about this, you'll sleep in thousand-dollar bills."

"Bestseller?"

"You've been sticking your head so far into the sand, you can't feel the hurricane blowing your tail feathers around?"

"I have to tune out the noise right now."

"I know. How much longer will you need?"

She told him about the accelerating pace of the Cosm, of seeing into it, of what might be coming.

"Then the religious people who're writing all these opinion pieces about the Cosm, the ones I answered for you—"

"Oh yes, thanks a lot for doing that."

"They've got a case."

"What kind of case?"

He spread his hands, palms out, a familar gesture to mollify her hard tone. "There are really big issues here. If this Cosm spawns life, intelligence—"

"We'll never know that. The Cosm neck's other end is at one isolated point in a whole universe. If it passes near a livable planet, that'll be a miracle."

"Could happen, couldn't it?"

"No. The Cosm neck's other end is way out in the middle of nowhere, not even a star closer than a few light-years."

He frowned. "You're sure?"

"I'd stake my reputation as a goddess on it."

She got the laugh she hoped for. Then Dad sobered, hesitating. They were in an Italian joint with so many ceramic surfaces inside, great acoustic reflectors, that sitting at tiny tables outside on Broadway was quieter. Headlight glows skated across the ebony facets of his broad, troubled face. "Thing is, honey, we were never very religious—"

"Not since I was in grade school, actually."

Baptist fundamentalism had dominated the other wing of the family, the sort of people of whom her father once said, "When a relative buys a new house, you go over to help take the wheels off." But he had relented, and she had dim memories of going to church in a crisp white dress, sporting a wrist corsage at Easter.

"Not since your mother . . ." His face went carefully blank and she guessed that he knew that would get them back on the dangerous territory of his remarriage. He took a sip of red wine and began again. "See, I get a feeling for these things, just listening to people in the trade."

She let herself smirk. "Journalists? For theological insights?"

"Okay, but they do have a sense of how people think. They're edgy about this Cosm of yours."

She allowed herself a long pull on her vodka collins; Dad was watching how much she drank, she noted; better take it easy. "Edgy? Yes, I can feel it, too. Even at the university."

"See, people don't want some remote God who set the universe going and walked away on other business. They want an interested God. But all you scientists work in the opposite way, toward a downright chilling vision."

"Ummm. The impersonality in nature's laws."

"Honey, religion—Holy Roller or High Church, it doesn't matter—didn't just occur to men and women musing about infinitely removed first causes and all that. It came from heartfelt longings, girl. From people who wanted continued intervention by a God who thought we were important."

She listened, his points striking resonances in her she had not voiced to anyone. Well, this was what dads were for: saying the unsayable when you needed it.

She was enough of an outdoorswoman to feel that nature

seemed far more beautiful than called for by evolution. Jays and hawks and pelicans and yellow-rumped warblers darted and wheeled outside her window every day, dazzling in their grace. It would be hugely satisfying to believe that all such splendor was here for our appreciation. But the God of beauty also had to own up to cruelty, ugliness, and death. And that God had certainly gone to much trouble to conceal any overt concern for humans.

"Sure," she said. "Scientists hardly ever discuss religion. Most aren't even interested enough to own up to being practicing atheists."

"And comments by some of your colleagues have made it pretty clear that they think of religion as a mildly interesting tribal ritual."

"Ummm, something to keep in the closet to be trotted out for weddings and funerals," she said, thinking of Brad's family.

Yet there had been real comfort in that awkward service, she now realized. More than one got with religious liberals, who were an odd bunch indeed, saying that they believed because it made them happy or at least contented. They calmly accepted that people could swallow mutually contradictory "truths" so long as the beliefs worked to benefit the holders. This piety without content was not even wrong, in the physics sense, because it didn't really care about the truth, not even as a goal. She suspected that most people didn't think God and heaven and all the rest of it was important, because they could not really admit that they did not believe any of it.

"Still, Dad, we can't compromise *science*."

He listened dutifully while she went through the standard counterargument: how the conservatives did the real damage: holy wars, oppression, all born of a deep longing for certainty. Science lived on uncertainty, the idea that a fresh experiment could unseat a revered theory. "Part of growing up, for me, was realizing that men and women were not playing a starring role in a grand cosmic drama. Physics—"

"And now you've disproved that," he said mildly.

"Huh?"

"You've shown that a bright woman can make a whole universe. *That* uproots a lot of beliefs." He grinned, springing the trap. "Including yours."

6

The worst part of being black lay in having your attention jerked back to it. No media piece mentioned the Cosm without bringing up her race. All very politely, they made their point that a bright woman had apparently made a universe, and did we mention that she was black?

Not that this was new. Anything you did, she had long ago learned, from simply asking a question, to Rollerblading to rock music on your way to the mall, somehow manifested differently. She had played reasonably good basketball in high school, profiting from her beefy height, only to find her classmates pigeonholing her as vaguely inferior. Black athletes had skills with no real function in the modern world, beyond passing entertainment, so in their eyes she was what a psych text termed the "Freudian primitive," just another proof that blacks were good at things that didn't matter much in the bigger consequential world. That she was the best in high school math and physics and aced exams had come as rather a shock even to her friends.

All the way up through the academic world she had spent a lot of energy fending off the blandly patronizing efforts to enter her in what she termed the Oppression Sweepstakes. Now that she had done something worth noting, blackness attached itself to her like a lamprey. The speed of the knee-jerk electronic world compressed everything, especially fame. She got appeals to speak to groups, letters proudly announcing that she had been selected for awards, inquiries about whether she would accept fellowships. Alicia gave her secretary a form letter to answer all these.

"But a *form* letter?" the shocked secretary asked, eyes wide. Alicia just grinned and went back to work.

Luckily, and with some relief, she found that she could go to Max with her worries. They talked while she worked with Zak in the lab, the cramped quarters always astir now with the taking of more data, reams and spools and slabs of it.

"Sure," Max said offhand, "there are plenty of archbishops wringing their hands, mumbling philosophers and New Age gab pouring out in the media, but so what?"

She laughed. He said New Age as one word, "newage," rhyming with "sewage."

"I . . . wonder what long-term effect this is going to have."

"Not our department, m'girl. We just explore."

"And then just let others move in, put up their Fast Faith Franchises?"

He gave her a learned piece he had run across in a leading national magazine, titled "Creation by Amateurs." She immediately riposted, "Who're the professionals?" And then read it. There were the usual anxieties, starkly revealing the uneasiness that ordinary intellectuals had with science.

After all, she shared some of them herself. She always thought of herself as a seat-of-the-pants gal, and that physics was similarly grounded. But to theorists nature was a text to be read.

Descartes felt that it took God Himself to ensure that the world men saw was real, not illusion. Physicists had abandoned God long ago and hoped that firing repeated questions at nature would get to the truth. What scientists really believed in was that the think-check-think-again style of scientific method would yield some species of Truth.

She digested this, then turned the same arguments on her own style. What about experimenters? In the end their detectors shielded them from error and, in turn, shielded nature from human contamination. Nature was *out there*, its laws commanded by mathematics.

Theorists, experimenters, they were all in the same existential boat. All their work pursued a world outside human space and time, eternal. Laws that were *laws*, damn it.

And now she and Zak and Max—yes, and Brookhaven, blundering in—had upset all that. Universes could be made by nasty little primates that picked their noses, farted, and did not pick the laws that governed the universe they had made.

"Who did choose the laws?" she asked Max.

Max shrugged, giving her a wobbly smile. But she could see that the questions, mounting higher all the while, bothered him, too.

"I've got a real surprise for you," Onell said breathlessly.

"I'm hard to surprise these days," Alicia said, slumping into a chair in the chairman's office. She was spending all day in the lab, eating pizza with Zak, puzzling with Max, even sleeping on the floor some nights. And still jumpy from the kidnapping, alas.

"This will do the trick," Onell said happily. "With the lawsuits and all—"

"They've called them off?"

"Uh, no."

"Rats." She had been talking to Bernie Ross and now she knew how lawyers made so much money.

"The White House just called. The President wants to come and see your, uh, sphere."

She sat without speaking and realized that she had no reaction. None. Was she that tired? "I, uh, don't have the time."

"What? This is—"

"I know, the President."

"It's quite an honor, Alicia. The chancellor is ecstatic. After all the bad publicity, he feels this puts a sort of seal of approval on UCI's role in the matter of your, ah—"

"I see. It couldn't be that the President is just curious about the Cosm and wants to have a look?"

"Well, we feel it is a great honor—"

"Yes, of course." Already she had a feeling of inevitability about it all.

"And, after all, if you had followed my advice, let the media people take the pictures they wanted—"

"And lose data."

"Only a few hours, is that so much?"

"Now that it means a million years of cosmic development lost, yes."

"I don't follow."

"Never mind. I'll go along with it, okay?"

Onell sprang up, actually rubbing his hands—a cliché she had never seen anyone actually perform. "We'll arrange everything, don't worry. There will be a big party to receive him and—"

"But nobody else."

"What?"

"Nobody else comes in the lab."

"But surely this means that the principal reporters and those who cover the President, the White House, they will want—"

"Nope. Just him."

For reasons she could not fathom, she became more popular among her own community. Criticism had waned a bit. Brookhaven had stopped taking "off the record" potshots at her; they were busy enough managing their own sphere, announcing to the press that they "had inaugurated the study of 'cosmo-metrics' in a rigorous manner." The ugly term *cosmo-metrics* sank immediately, and now even the Brookhaven press people referred to their sphere as a Cosm—though the name, leaked by someone at UCI to the national media, still had not appeared in the formal scientific literature. The Net was another matter entirely; she never eavesdropped there anymore, where there were hundreds of theoretical papers alone.

Others, far from the fray, saw that huge possibilities were opening. Over the last decade funding for physics had gotten more and more applied, as the U.S. and European budget problems steadily worsened. But in which areas should federal funding place their bets? The approved technique was to convene a panel of senior experts to pick the most promising areas. Older scientists tended to not see much farther down the paths of the future than their own careers would plausibly carry them and so favored the quicker payoffs. Fundamental physics inevitably suffered, though invariably the bureaucrats described this as "sharpening" their efforts. Alicia reflected that knives also are sharpened, but by making them narrower. Some areas seemed to have been sharpened into oblivion.

The Cosm was undoubtedly fundamental and had no plausible application. This did not prevent newspaper articles wondering about the possibility of tapping resources from other universes. Her fellow nuclear and particle physicists were overjoyed at the sudden possibility of studying quantum gravity using objects the size of basketballs, as Max had predicted.

Their about-face she discovered first by a card, slipped under the observatory door, carrying a T. S. Eliot quotation: "The Nobel is a ticket to one's funeral. No one has ever done anything after he got it."

"Ummm," she murmured to Max. "Somebody being subtle."

"I'll bet it's from a colleague who's nominated you to the Swedish Academy."

She blinked. "There are nominations?"

"The Academy doesn't like their nominators to mention it to anyone, especially the nominees. This is a quiet way of letting you know."

"This is entirely premature. We published one letter, haven't even sorted our data—"

"Sure, you won't get it anytime soon. But you're in line."

"Nonsense."

UCI had its own Nobelists, but Alicia had never thought about the selection process itself. The academic world was choked with people who should've gotten a Nobel but wouldn't. The whole Nobel system distorted perceptions of science, she thought, turning it into an annual horse race. Unlike the arts, where giants of unique style could dominate, science was built up mostly by the small persistent efforts of the many. Scientific giants proposed new theories of gravity or evolution, but they stood on a firm ground provided by those who measured the constants, worked out the detailed implications, or scanned the myriad special cases of the natural world, all in search of the telltale clue that existing ideas were not quite adequate. And this army of patient laborers worked because they had curiosity and a sense of wonder and just plain liked solving puzzles—not because they wanted to win a prize at the end of it all.

Zak came over, smiled at the card. "Hey, right." She reflected that Zak was just the sort of patient laborer who made science work, far more than types such as herself. He had great loyalty to the scientific worldview and to Alicia. She had to admit that she did not honestly feel that she deserved such unstinting help.

She shook her head impatiently. This was all too fast, too downright off-the-wall. "I don't think they'd give it to somebody who accidentally—"

"Remember, the Nobel is biased toward discovery, not mere explanation."

"Without your 'mere explanation,' Zak and I would have gotten nowhere."

"There's the 'genius of the moment' in accidents, too," Max said gently.

"Genius does what it must. Talent does what it can. Me, I'm a drudge."

Max just chuckled.

7

A presidential visit was a logistic lummox that amazed those
who saw it for the first time at ground level. Hotel managers
found their inns remade overnight into workable White
Houses. Beat police found themselves drafted into an army
large enough to take Guatemala. UCI parking lots were trans-
formed into sound stages for the networks.

Secret Service staff trickled into town. Would the expected
crowd be big enough? Diverse enough? White House staff
liked UCI's large Asian presence, the highest percentage in
the country, even though Asians weren't an "official" minority, and fretted about not having enough black and Hispanic
faces in the crowd for the daily TV photo-op. The Secret Service liked UCI's easy terrain and simple perimeters. Advance
teams started arriving in waves, all coordinated by the White
House Communications Agency. Cost was no object. After all,
Air Force One cost forty thousand dollars an hour to fly.
Bomb-sniffing dogs prowled the physical sciences complex
and, of course, her lab. "Crowd-builders" bloomed in the
parking lot, movable walls that shaped the spectators into a
big-looking backdrop in case not enough students showed up;
classes had not started yet.

Technicians rewired a wing of the Four Seasons, where the
President would spend the night after a political dinner. An
outsized gray van pulled into the physical sciences complex
parking lot, packed with secure telephone lines and festooned
with microwave dishes. Barriers and press platforms went up

overnight. The John Wayne Airport was shut down for Air Force One's arrival. Agents scoured the campus and approach route, securing manhole covers, showing around pictures of shadowy men perhaps seen in the vicinity, introducing themselves politely and wondering if anything odd had happened in the last few days.

The right picture was everything. The President peering seriously at the Cosm, then speaking to students and scientists gathered like children at his feet. Worth maybe thirty to forty-five seconds on national television, all four networks plus CNN, so go for a few striking images.

On the big day Alicia stood with the array of notables, just outside the observatory. Well-corralled spectators were growing restless; they had been instructed to arrive two hours ago and the sun was bleaching away their good mood. She kept smiling and sweating in her best marine suit, as selected by UCI publicity advisors.

Basic TV Age thinking seemed brisk and heartless to those who took such events at face value, as simple chances to see a President and hear a message. Usually the crowd saw mostly the rear ends of reporters, cops, and cameramen. Logistical magic worked for the lens, not the eye.

The Secret Service men, at least those Alicia could spot, wore the cliché dark suits that seemed to be sausage-tight casings for bodies of slab brawn. They dealt only with the higher UCI figures, nodding to her as if to a figurine. Stage directions: "Ma'am, the President will come in this way, you'll greet him, we'll go on into the cars and then up to your laboratory, fifteen minutes there, then the press, then"—a memorized phrase, delivered at maximum speed—"I'm-afraid-that's-all-we-have-time-for-sorry."

The local police were out in full panoply, masses riding on their hips: holsters, blackjacks, phones, billy clubs in black, handcuffs, ammo, citation books, cameras. A knot of reporters and TV crewmen sat or milled restlessly in jeans, rough shirts, clodhopper shoes, and velvet zipper jackets with splashy logos on the back. Then the limos pulled up and the moment had arrived.

The President seemed somehow smaller than he should. He coasted through the crowd like a homecoming float, his passive grandeur defined by the onlookers. Taller politicians fared better at the polls than short ones, but Alicia was surprised to find him shorter than her five-eleven. Amid the whine of rewind motors in cameras and gimlet lens eyes peering like extra appendages from the TV crews, they all exchanged handshakes and homilies.

Among the UCI hierarchy, his presence brought a visible tremble, like trees feeling the first brush of the hurricane, as power far greater than theirs coasted by, oblivious. In their everyday lives they could coax and reward faculty, who in turn presided over students, but *this* . . . Alicia saw in the chancellor's throat a swallow of something—awe? fright?—at the passing of more raw power than any of them had ever felt, potent pressure like a massive weather pattern shifting, blunt and lordly.

"Great work you've done here," the President said to her as she ushered him into the pathway cleared among her gear.

"Our work is still at a preliminary stage," Alicia said carefully.

"I thought maybe I'd visit the Long Island one, but it might be dangerous, my people said. And you were the first, right?"

"Yes, sir. Here it is."

She and Zak had hauled the U-magnet out, with Max helping with the grunt labor, to reveal the Cosm to its best advantage. They cut the lights and the President, with two Secret Service men in the background, stood transfixed as his eyes adjusted and the glowing sphere seemed to swell out of the dark. He made appreciative sounds and asked the usual questions. He seemed to think the Cosm was an entire universe, just one he could, if he liked, hold in his hands. It took a while to get over the fact that they were looking through a three-dimensional window at a real enormous universe that lived in another space-time. She was surprised that he had been so little briefed. True, this was just one of five stops today, but—

"You think it'll be like us?" the President asked.

"Support life? We can't tell and probably won't be able to."

"But you can study the stars, can't you?"

"Yes, we can," she could not resist adding, "sir." She showed him the fast-photography pictures of cherry-red nebulae illuminated by the hot spikes of young stars.

"It certainly is a wonderful thing."

"We want to see how far it develops. I'm afraid our connection to it may be slipping away."

He looked at her in the Cosm's pink radiance. "We can't let that happen."

"I'm afraid there's not much we can do about it."

He gestured briskly at the U-magnet. "Hold on to it."

"I'm afraid it isn't that simple—"

"I have every respect for your abilities, Professor Butterfield, but this is a national asset now, not just a research object. My advisors tell me we have stolen a march on all the rest of the world with this."

"So we have, sir. We simply know so little—"

"I'm sure I speak for all Americans when I say that we want to see *more*, Professor." He grinned broadly. "Thanks for finding it for us."

This last sentence rang oddly in her mind as the President left, shaking hands with Zak and Max and a half dozen UCI suits. She had to admire the way he gave each person an intense ten seconds, then smoothly passed on. Within minutes, even with the ritual handshaking in the crowd, they were all back in the parking lot and she was standing beside the President on a raised platform and the media moment was at hand: a quick, punchy speech with three lines honed to get on TV. The networks had an hour's clear window left to get it onto the East Coast nightly news. Then the entourage began its melancholy withdrawing roar.

She waved goodbye with all the rest, grinned at Max, shook hands with the knots of local officialdom, and greeted Zak's parents, who beamed at everyone, speechless at the splendor. *Wow.*

* * *

UCI's publicists could not resist a big clambake press conference after the President's departure. Alicia let Max do most of the talking, and when the crowd seemed to want data—"Let's *see* this thing," a voice called from the crowd sitting on fold-out chairs, and others swiftly echoed it—she gave them Zak. Far from selflessness, she distrusted her own ability to withstand their probing. Zak did well, a dispassionate rendering of "Just the facts, ma'am."

But finally she had to go forward and face the blinding lights, then the popping of flashes. She stuck to what Max termed the High Church strategy: a brief statement that the Cosm was developing with ever-increasing rapidity, that theory suggested the connection might not persist for long, and therefore, with the greatest respect, they would decline further interviews or press "opportunities" until they were through with "the crucial phases of the study." Then, thanks to several evenings' ferreting, she ended with a grand historical perspective note.

"Around the turn of the century, the French scientist Henri Poincaré worried about the conflict between his Catholic faith and the hard laws of my field: physics. Miracles bothered him. He argued that we scientists can't treat phenomena that occur only once, since science could not test itself by reproducing the event. And Creation itself was a one-time-only event. There were plenty of aftereffects, like galaxies and girls, all worthy of study, but the essential moment came but once."

She liked the alliteration of galaxies and girls, and was enough of a feminist to no longer bridle at the term when it was useful. She gazed out over the heads of the crowd and was thrilled to see her father there. Into her voice, rehearsed and modulated so far, came a wobbly, proud note she could not control.

"But now we know that Poincaré was wrong. We can reproduce even our universe's origins. The implications of this I leave to others. The reality of it we shall continue to explore, with care and humility."

To her genuine surprise, a storm of applause followed her

from the rostrum. But as it died, she saw people at the back carrying signs with Biblical quotations on them, plus some from the Koran, and heard shouts of derision and genuine anger hammering in the hall.

8

"I don't feel like going out."

"You have to."

"Why?"

"To capitalize on your fame," Jill explained.

"Ugh."

"Also, you've got cobwebs in your brain, silly."

"Ummm." Alicia stretched out on her sofa, trying to hear the comforting crunch of the waves through her open window. Maybe a long walk on the beach . . .

"Not to mention cobwebs elsewhere."

"Oooof, a low blow."

"I can hear your ovaries shrinking from here."

"Hey, girl, I feel like vegging out. Catch one of those sitcoms, y'know, middlebrow wisecracks by bone-thin women with big firm knockers, living in an apartment in some fab city?"

"Sure, and eat popcorn and chocolate while we do it." Jill made a gargoyle face. She had been waiting when Alicia got home, having performed her usual trick of picking the lock.

"Listen, I was at that reception over at the chancellor's last night, right on top of the President's visit, and today I worked in the lab straight through—"

"I signed you up three weeks ago."

"Against my will."

"I have twenty bucks invested in your having grandchildren."

Alicia smiled, feeling helpless. "All so I can meet guys who use seductive tongue gestures?"

"Hey, that was *one* guy, and he was in a leisure suit."

"He said they were coming back in."

"All the better." Jill bustled her into the bedroom, threw open her closet. "We'll know how to spot the species now. My God, you haven't been shopping in ages, have you?"

"Who has time?"

"You seem to have forgotten about those other pesky little necessities, like eating and sleeping."

"Listen, lately my philosophy has been 'I endure, therefore I am.' "

"True, but sad. Me, it's more like 'I flirt, therefore I am.' "

She couldn't hear the waves breaking on the shoreline beyond Pacific Coast Highway. Maybe that was a sign; her world was shrunken, self-involved. With a sinking feeling, she realized that she wanted to go out socializing in an entirely theoretical way, without the zest she used to feel. How come? Max had stayed behind at UCI, working on some insight he wouldn't discuss, not just yet.

"You game?" Jill persisted.

"I have a choice?"

The social Jill hauled her to was inland, at the outer reaches of the town that called itself Lake Forest and had no lake and no forest. They voyaged past strip malls and "condo communities" perched smack up against a bleak prairie of prefab electronics assembly plants and industrial park bland tilt-ups, metallic and windowless and crouched down, as if ashamed. Like insect colonies, lines of stucco houses squatted beigely in their land of "sunburst" linoleum.

Alicia was getting by with a rental car, still dithering over replacing her Miata, which the kidnappers had totaled. Jill curled a lip at the rental, so they took her "more spiffy wheels." Jill drove them under a flapping NOW RENTING banner caked with dust, past already cracking aggregate-concrete steps with flimsy railings, into a basement parking garage guarded by grinning steel street teeth. Inside the "suite" apartment complex the reception ran in rooms that echoed with a cultural emptiness, the walls without pictures or books, the marble-veneer fireplaces with antiseptic gas instead of logs. Furniture attempted to fill these spaces, but even the mandatory oversized sectional couch seemed dwarfed by the austere, automatic geometry of sameness. Dress was "casual elegant," which apparently included rumpled wide-legged, button-fly, stone-washed pale jeans, looking like a phony effect when worn with a black leather jacket. In the first half hour of trawling the crowd, which had spread throughout the ground floor and probably ran over three hundred of what Jill termed the Tribe of Assessing Gazes, they saw tackiness galore: mixed florals and stripes, plastic piercings, avocado green with pink, a sheer blouse over plaid pants, even a parka vest with bare midriff and a diamond in the navel.

By adroit word of mouth this singles' arena had drawn more blacks, and she circulated among them without anybody, thank God, recognizing her from the news. She saw a tall, loose-jointed man drifting among the chattering crowds. Named Jerome, Jill soon ferreted out, mid-level executive, marketing. He had that certain homecoming-float quality, like the President, of latent grandeur. Good-looking black men had a strike against them, to be sure, just by being black, but in the sexual sweepstakes they had two strikes for them, too: an ebony prince elegance and the sheer scarcity of suitable black men.

She sipped her drink, waited him out, circulated, had another drink while pretending to be interested in local politics. Late-night lectures to herself asserted themselves: *Don't just sit at home in your head*, she reprimanded herself. *Don't live* for *the moment. Live* into *the moment, on your toes, eyes bright.*

The dancing started. Jill prompted, "You go first."

"Ask him to dance?" Pure terror.

"Listen, there are plenty worse out there. A guy just told me a joke: 'Why are mononucleosis and herpes opposites? Because you get mono when you snatch a kiss.' And he thought I'd be charmed."

"You talked me into it." So she went over to more-ebony-than-thou Jerome and croaked out a weak hello. He smiled, was kind, they danced, and everything worked, the room going around a little but her smile staying in place.

"You hear about the new black restaurant?" Jerome said.

"Uh, no—"

"It's called Chez What."

She rewarded this sally with a muffled guffaw. Jill gave her a thumbs-up and Alicia wondered what she was doing here, really, her classic avoidance symptom. Jerome talked about the usual things, leading off with the obligatory career history, not asking about hers. After the first hour, things were going more than well and the room was indeed going around unless she sat down. When he finally asked what she did anyhow, girl, she said she worked for the state, which was technically true.

A little later in the proceedings, dancing again after some reconstruction work in the ladies' room, he whispered, "Honey, it's good ol' love makes the world go round."

"Actually, it's inertia."

Back to the table where Jill was entertaining five others with a description of a recent night at Rubber Gotham, a new club, quasi-hip, with B-list celebs on opening night, Chardonnay and warmed-over chicken wings (exactly what she skipped as a girl, now heading for deserved oblivion as an appetizer), women lurching around on heels they couldn't manage ("sexy evening columns" as Frederick's termed them)—further proof yet again that money can't buy a clue. Jill was good at it, just the right details in the story, all haute-style. Alicia tried to think of an amusing way to bring up how Jill had been that first year at Berkeley when she was their dorm's Queen of Gross, giving darkened-room demos of fart-lighting, using big kitchen matches to ignite astonishing blue and orange plumes a foot long, "a scientific feat extraordinaire." On the other hand, she was far too gone to bring anything off very lightly. She had a fresh drink and Jill said with her trademark uneasy delicacy, "You're doing a lot of that tonight."

"You're the one wanted me to come on out."

"True, but not all the way out."

"Y'know, when I was a tomboy I asked my dad what it

was like to be drunk. He said, 'See those two men sitting over there? When you see four men, you're drunk.' So I said, 'But, Dad, there's only one man there.' My father's expression was worth it. And''—a slow, pointed look at Jill—''he never bugged me about it again.''

"Just checking," Jill said. "Time to go home, I think."

"C'mon, girl, not *yet*."

She got Jill to do her best set piece, a takeoff on a woman from the '60s on an acid trip, trying to eat dinner with friends: "Have I already chewed this food in my mouth three hundred times? Are they on to me? Wow, how *wet* this water feels. Is this the same lump of burger I was just wondering about? Or was that half an hour ago? And what is food anyway, really?"

It was all funny now and she was only vaguely conscious of Jerome taking her home, with Jill supervising. As Jerome went around to get in the driver's seat, Jill whispered, "Careful with this one," and they were off.

As lights streaked by on the windshield, she told herself very solemnly that she was not taking a guy home with her from a singles' meat market, not at all, he was taking *her* home was all. Misgivings she brushed away like a pesky insect.

Into Laguna, out of the car, the world going very fast now. Time jumped forward, accelerating like the Cosm, she said, but Jerome didn't understand. Into her apartment, stomach lurching, hall light on, Jerome against her, the smell of him warm and rosy, his hands starting up and going down. His tongue in her mouth cut off her breathing and her head cleared as his hands started hurting suddenly, his body wedged hard into hers against the closet door, the apartment too hot and his face too close, "No, I'm not . . . No, I don't . . . Please, not that—''

And Jerome was chuckling, sweet-talking low and threatening, forcing her stumbling into the living room, somehow her blouse off now, her arms coming up protectively as she lurched away from him in the sudden blaring light coming through the archway and there was Max.

"Hey, back off!" Max said.

"Who the hell're you?" Jerome said.

"Get away from her."

"You some kind of *peeper* or somethin', man—"

"Beat it, fella."

"—sneakin' in here—"

"I can handle this," Alicia said firmly, then tripped and fell on the couch, face in a pillow.

She watched dimly as Max came forward and Jerome swore at him and pushed Max back. Then it was very fast and she felt very sick. Max and Jerome tangled together and then there was just Max in the air over her and she closed her eyes just to straighten things out a little, a rest, then it would all be clear.

PART VI

FLAWED GODS
LATE FALL 2005

It is not from space that I must seek my dignity,
but from the government of my thought.
I shall have no more if I possess worlds. By space
the universe encompasses and swallows me
up like an atom; by thought I comprehend the
world.

—BLAISE PASCAL

Dimly she realized hangovers were like the Japanese language: no articles, no "the" or "a." Head hurt, hurt, hurt. Waves crunching in distance, traffic swishing. In bedroom articles strewn everywhere. How got there? She remembered nothing. Up, groaning. Out, teetering on wooden feet, living room painted in tiger stripes by venetian blinds. Clock told time. Most morning gone, where? Scratched head; that hurt, too. Ice, yes. No, too much work; she lay down. Room settled into place. Ceiling was vast plain. Moving? Unfolding geometry of swelling universe or else swelling head.

After a while, she got all her head to operate together and though the pain was there, it did not pound on the front door and demand attention. Basic question: Do I need to hurl? No. Do I want to? Yes. A little later both answers switched and then at least she was through that and feeling a bit better.

Smell of coffee? Sounds? Front door opening. Alarm, panic, something about last night—

Max appeared in the doorway. "I went out for pastry."

Then she remembered the awful all of it. "Oh God."

"I threw him out."

"You were . . . ?"

"You gave me your key, remember? In case I wanted to work late at UCI, then crash here."

"Ah. Jerome . . ."

"A hard man to convince."

"He was . . . okay at the party."

"Lacked a little technique, seemed to me."

"I'm so . . . embarrassed."

"None of it your fault. Guy went too far. You're just hung over, that's all."

She nursed the coffee he brought and then showered and dressed and repaired some of the damage to her face, bags under the eyes: the raccoon look. He had some eggs scrambled and the pastry crisp and she spoke little. He didn't ask why she had gotten so drunk and she didn't ask why he had come to her rescue, which didn't make them nearly even, but helped. Max did not seem puffed up about the incident and he didn't show those little signs of disapproval anyone else would have—Jill or Dad, say. Their talk drifted around and then a little pool of quiet formed between them and spread and filled up whole minutes, a void of silence she felt no need to fill with talk, like a warm bath of untroubled stillness. Neither moved. Insulated time ticked on. An invisible sphere enveloped them and he leaned over absolutely casually and kissed her.

Everything seemed to lead up to this first kiss, with all else leading away. Deep-sea kiss, cramming for the final kiss. She thought, *I'm going to remember this,* then didn't think any more for a blessedly long time.

Fingers through tangled hair, smells swarming up the air, his hardness insisting on her softness.

A long time later he said, looking at the ceiling, "First time I ever had a breakfast that worked like an aphrodisiac."

"Anglodisiac, in my case."

"Okay, A-F-R-O-disiac, for me."

"Boy, do I hate that term, African-American."

"I'll never use it."

"I wonder if we're different enough, though. Two physicists . . ."

"What, there should be miscegenation laws?"

"I always thought I should look for somebody more, uh, normal. Not a scientist. I'm a bit *yang,* maybe some *yin*—"

"Two *yang*s don't make a right?"

She punched him and giggled. "I'm *serious*. My therapist—"

He groaned, buried his face between her breasts.

"Well, she says people don't ever really change, not fundamentally, so—"

"So what's the point of going to a therapist, then?"

"I think you need to know your emotional posture, where you stand in the world—"

"Until we know where we stand, let's stay lying down."

"Gee, this seems a lot like the last time I had déjà vu."

He laughed. "That's a teenage joke."

"If you were a teenager, we could do it again right now."

"If I were a teenager, I'd have been finished an hour ago."

He seemed to definitely like the "ampleness" of her, as he put it. Even her "fantastic bottom," which she duly told him was "pronounced lordosis, like the !Ko tribeswomen"—and felt enormously embarrassed, then suddenly not at all. "I'm awful damned arrogant, aren't I?" she asked soberly. It was as if she could ask him all the questions now, all the parts of the Big Problem.

"More like grand."

"You're tense, the antisocial form of being not relaxed. I'm nervous, the social form."

"You pay a therapist for this sort of stuff?"

"My medical covers it," she said defensively.

"When you're dancing, don't look at the dance."

"What's that mean?"

"I'm being *yin*."

2

They drove into UCI and she had to keep remembering about the driving part. She wanted to look at him and talk and admire the fresh way the world kept looking outside the windows, all at the same time.

Zak had been working most of the night, improving the time resolution of the optical data-gathering. He was good at it and they were having to store so many gigs of raw images now, Zak was stacking boxes of high-speed digital tape outside the observatory simply for room. Months before they had set up storage in a secure room in the central files office of UCI. The data rate was so high now that she and Zak had to run tape disks over nearly every day.

Max stayed in her office to do some calculations. He was still being mysterious about his thinking. This had irked Alicia in the last few weeks, but now it was fine, just an oddity of his otherwise generally wonderful self. She did not puzzle at her emotional swerve of these last few hours; she basked in it, heart elated. Understanding, in matters of love, was inevitably the booby prize. Was that what he meant about not looking at the dance? The man was enticing.

The Cosm was alight and afroth with fire now, the churn of great galaxies visible to the eye. She used high-power binoculars on a secure mount to watch the specks of light. Spirals spun like luminous Frisbees, winging across the blackness.

They had tracked nearby stars as well. She replayed some of the data tapes with Zak, viewing time-chopped segments on a high-quality screen tucked into a corner of the observatory. Stars blazed as they arced, their immense reservoirs of energy dissipating as quickly as their bulk allowed. A few weeks before they had found a star that spectral lines said was over ten billion years old, nearing the end of its life span. Already it was beginning to burn heavier and heavier elements at its core, growing hotter. Its atmospheric envelope of already incandescent gas heated, swelling as they watched. From a mild-mannered, yellow-white star, it bloated within minutes into a reddened giant.

"If it has planets," Zak said, "they're being swallowed right now."

Alicia tried to imagine first Mercury, then Venus, then Earth beneath a glaring red sky, its crust roasting, its oceans and air boiled away by a huge angry sun.

Then the star whirled away, swept out of view by the rotation of its galaxy. If it had a solar system, then its planets, once a grand stage, would be withered relics beside a guttering campfire.

During the last week, the Cosm's point of view at its other end had slowly drifted down into the plane of a giant elliptical galaxy. An astrophysicist's career could be made with the data on that process alone, as the invisible frictions of dust and magnetic fields nudged matter into the bee-swarm blender of a thousand billion suns. Until now, astronomers had been able to take only snapshots of the stellar dance and from that had to deduce the music of the spheres. Now the Cosm's time acceleration gave entire concerts as masses swept together and apart, bristling with suns both fresh and dying in furious gulfs.

Zak loved to examine under high magnification the flaring of supernovae as giant stars blew bubbles in the surrounding dusty mist, returning heavy elements to the mix, where collapsing clouds would harvest such chemical riches to make the next generation of stars.

Watching these matchheads flare amid sheets of luminous gas, he said, "Until now, doing cosmology was like taking a picture halfway through a fistfight and figuring out who must've started it."

"And why," Alicia said.

Far above the teeming throng of stars and burning nebulae, she and Zak could witness the stabbing lances of jets that poked up and out from the galactic nucleus. These apparently came from a black hole abuilding at the very center of the entire bee-swarm rotation. They saw violet beams jut into the spaces between galaxies and carve paths for later ruby flows of hot plasma.

Her grandmother had always termed God Providence. There was even a Baptist hymn about that, which she had learned one summer when forced to go to Sunday school. Now Alicia wondered about an entity that spattered the night sky with endless stars, gaudy gaseous nebulae, whole long chains and superclusters of pale galaxies, all silent and glowing without apparent purpose, and thought a better name was Improvidence: extravagant impulse lavishing its abundance in wasteful display.

Alicia:
    You're impossible to reach by phone, and I can figure why, but I have to warn you about the attitude of people here. We're seeing plenty of development in what we can see in our Cosm. I'll try to compile it and get you a summary, but what the director is insisting on here is *your* data. We need it to guide us.

                                                            Dave

Dave:
    I've just been too busy to organize our work. Your Cosm is still exponentiating in time, right? Our rate is still slower than yours, but we're further along in the exponential. If our numbers and yours are still right, you should overtake us in a few weeks. But by then ours will be really old.

    As ours speeds up more and more, our data flow rate is taking off, nearly beyond our capabilities, gigabytes per minute. I'll try to get some to you within a day.

    If only we could do the physics and forget everything else! At least you have a lab staff and admin types to insulate you.

                                                            A

Alicia:

Thanks. Yes, the exponential time shift continues. Ours has a different mean growing time, though, close to 1.74 weeks. With yours holding steady at 2 weeks, we'll catch up to you eventually, I guess.

What we need right away is certain spectral line measurements; see the attachment document following, specifying lines.

As for politics, we're worse off than you. The Lab approach is to keep our work intradisciplinary, not inter-. A short way of saying nobody knows the whole story. They wanted it this way from the start because they can manage the news better that way. Nobody going off half-cocked. You're their horrible example, you'll be happy to hear.

Dave

Dave:

I checked your numbers on the carbon, oxygen, and nitrogen lines. I measured these pretty carefully when we first started getting enough light through to make the numbers reliable. I see the same frequencies that anyone can get out of the CRC handbook. In other words, our Cosm is looking at stars with exactly the same atoms in them as our own.

What I take your data to mean is that you aren't. Your carbon frequencies are all shifted down, relative to the nitrogen, for example. What gives?

A

Alicia:

That's what I wanted to hear. Forgive me for being mysterious, but I didn't believe our own results and wondered if you saw the same. Those carbon lines clinched it. Since all these spectra are all from the same star, the differences can't be due to some Doppler shift. The carbon atoms really are different!

How can that be? I was sure we'd made some dumb mistake, but it's not that. We burned a lot of time rechecking, believe me.

The shift is only a tenth of a percent, but it's not an error. We're checking other elements now, too. The conclusion is clear, though. This universe we're looking into has different physical constants.

How can it? This is crazy. Any ideas? What's that guy I saw talk at your press conference, Max Jalon, say about this?

                                                                    Dave

Dave:

I haven't got a clue. Our Cosm seems to have ordinary elements in it; their spectral lines are ok. I'll look again, but I'll bet this is still true, even though our Cosm is billions of years older than when I last looked at details like that. Thanks for the warning!

We can see very rapid cosmological and stellar evolution here now. Has your Cosm gone transparent yet? It's quite a show. Be prepared. If it does, you'll be scrambling like we did. I'll attach a list of the diagnostics you'll need.

                                                                       A

Alicia:

Thanks for the suggestions. We'll follow them right away. The exponential rate is holding and our going transparent might come pretty soon. That's assuming our Cosm (might as well use your term, though everybody here frowns if you do; hell, I'll even capitalize it, like you) is keeping to the exponential shift scaling. We check that against the cosmic microwave background, and it seems to hold.

There's something more, too. Your people at UCI are going to get a formal request, through the Department of Energy. We want to run tests on both Cosms. That will be much easier here. Start planning to bring yours here soon.

                                                                    Dave

ONLOOKERS CROWD BROOKHAVEN LAB SITE
Change in 'Cosm' Rumored Coming;
Thousands Flock to Long Island
Planes, Balloons, Hang Gliders Fly Over Object

"Professor Butterworth?"

She had opened the observatory door unwarily, thinking it was just the security guards notifying her that they were changing shift. The strange face brought back a sudden spike of fear, memories from the kidnapping, her throat tightening. Then she realized that the face was not strange; it was Detective Sturges.

"Oh. Ah, I'll come out."

She stepped into the brilliant sunshine, blinking. The observatory interior was utterly black and she had been in it for a long time, savoring the spectacle. The crisp, dry tang of the sage was bracing after the air-conditioned dark.

Sturges's face was angular in the strong sun, his brown suit out of place among the coastal scrub desert. His car in the gravel lot bore no official markings. "You're doing okay?"

"Oh, you mean putting the kidnapping behind me? I suppose so."

"It takes time, it does." He shuffled uncomfortably. "I came over to ask if you know of any connection between Brad's parents and some religious groups. People who might have been involved in your kidnapping."

"No. I only met them at the funeral."

"Brad never said anything about his religious views? Or theirs?"

"It's not the kind of thing physicists usually discuss."

Sturges lifted one side of his mouth in a wry gesture that instantly lapsed, like a formal gesture. "Some federal officers paid us a call, wondered if there was a link."

"Federal officers?"

"They said they were looking to see if the kidnapping had a religious motivation, maybe linked to Brad. The kidnappers' methods fit something done in other states, they said."

When she shrugged, he looked at her significantly. "They went through our files, got a lot of the background information on the place here."

Was there a veiled implication in his gaze? "About the observatory?"

"How you're conducting operations here, the whole thing."

"Why would they want that?"

Sturges gave her another long stare, as if his pauses told more than his words. "I'm sure I don't know. Thanks for your time."

Though it was just another interruption in another long day, she remembered his studied expression, as if trying to give something away.

3

"**W**ow," Max said, reading her e-mail on her laptop in her office. "This stuff from Dave is great."

"You mean about their carbon lines not fitting ours?" She had not been all that thrilled. Compared with the wealth of images flickering over the face of the Cosm, a dry number for a spectral line was forgettable, and she had barely remembered to bring it up.

"It means their Cosm, call it Cosm II, is fundamentally different from ours. There must be 'genetic' differences, variations, in the natural constants." He stared off into space. "Maybe some shift in an electromagnetic constant, so it shows up in carbon particularly . . ,"

"Wait." She wanted to kiss him, just on general principles, but it seemed the wrong moment. "Where do you get 'genetic'?"

"Think like a biologist. This universe of ours has now made two more. But its children aren't exactly like it—that's what Dave is saying, though he doesn't know it."

"In biology you get different children because both parents contrlbute genes."

He grinned. "Okay, so the analogy isn't exact. But look, you made the Cosm by exciting a fluctuation in space-time, and the quark-gluon plasma, it tunneled through to another equilibrium for matter—"

"But for matter in its own space-time, sure."

"—and Dave's spectral lines, they say that in this process

you can wind up with a slightly different universe on the other side.''

She sat on her desk, knocking off a tall stack of mail. ''Our Cosm, though, so far looks just like its . . . parent.''

Max had that distant look she had come to know in these months, his mind whirring along new paths. Even *this* trait, normally the sort of thing that drove women to distraction, seemed endearing. He had crept up on her, slipping under the defenses she had so long ago erected against men scientists. At the time, she remembered, she had described it to Jill as ''too much like, well, incest.'' Max's eyes snapped back into focus and he got up and came around the desk, taking her in his arms, kissing her expertly. ''Which means ours has an excellent chance of sustaining life.''

''So I'm going to be a grandmother.''

He pulled back an inch, blinked. ''Aaaahhh . . . yes.'' His eyes went distant again. Other women would feel insulted at this, but she understood. There was more than a little of her in him.

*   *   *

Saul Shriffer, Inc.

Dear Professor Butterworth:

I understand from repeated calls to your Physics Department that you are not currently represented in the fields of visual media. Certainly your astounding discoveries have excited the entire world, not least the world of entertainment and education. This avenue is the *most powerful* gateway for spreading the word of your work, and certainly can be the most profitable.

My agency represents many of the leading figures in modern science. I would like to speak with you about undertaking . . .

''Playing at Being God,'' cover article, November *Atlantic Monthly*:

... Science can be blind to moral and especially religious views, seeing them as mere noise. Indeed, many vast social movements have rejected rationalism, experimental checks, logic, and even facts. Objectivity, as a mode of thinking, only slowly integrated with older systems. As well, hasty imposition of technologies destroyed the fabric of meaning knitting together communities.

Human life can only be sustained afloat on a sea of meaning, not upon a network of spare information. Stir this sea with detached logic and unrooted data, and you are asking for trouble. Cast people into the cultural void—which the elite endure only by filling it with endless diversions—and you inevitably condemn everyone to a perpetual consumer culture. And that is if all works according to plan, and social unrest can be contained.

Meaning came only from the inner world. When technology intrudes upon this sanctum, its logically compelling face bares a grotesque, mechanical sneer. That is the principal lesson of the Cosm, like it or not.

... offer you a cohost position on *Saturday Night Lively*. Your cohost would be Roberta Lasky, hit comic. While a sense of the dignity of your work will be present, we hope you understand that this is not an educational show. Our offer is contingent upon your bringing on the air your discovery, the Cosm, so that for the first time the television audience can see just what ...

From: rachelm@pict.com
To: butter@uci.edu
"All nature is but art, unknown to thee,
All chance, direction which thou canst not see;
All discord, harmony not understood;
All partial evil, universal good;
And, spite of pride, in erring reason's spite,
One truth is clear, Whatever is, is right."

SETI INSTITUTE
Menlo Park, CA

. . . if life does emerge in your Cosm, this is an unprecedented opportunity to detect radio waves from civilizations emerging there. If, as rumors have it, the pace of time in your Cosm is accelerating, then soon we might be able to directly detect radio beacons from . . .

Northrup Grumman is proud of its role in the creation of your discovery. As the world's leading quality magnet makers, we wish to photo your Cosm with our magnets that "got the job done," and are willing to offer $20,000 . . .

Editorial, *Social Text*, Vol. 48, p. 81:

The recent "discovery" of a "Cosm" (plainly a calculated term, devised to gain the most respect for her findings by the "discoverer") has excited much comment. We remain to be convinced that in fact the talk of creating a portal or opening to another universe has any substance. Surely the members of the scientific establishment have noted the extreme secrecy and hermitlike seclusion of the "discoverer"? Her unwillingness to allow teams of disinterested observers to visit this "Cosm"?

Most astonishing is the lack of philosophical sophistication on the part of many physicists, who seem ready to accept mere publication of a paper—a textual event—as solid evidence, independent of interpretation. The central doctrine of our more modern view, emerging from scholars in science studies, is that society constructs its science in narratives peculiar to a time, place, and culture. Science's chief function is to create stories about the world consonant with dominant social and political values. They are no more "true" or even more reliable than any other culture-specific description. Independent reality is itself a recent, modern western social idea, one disputed by many other philosophies which challenge the intellectual hegemony and the familiar but impermissibly universal claims of western rationalism . . .

... as a leading "ghost" writer for several prominent scientists (names on request, of course under a confidentiality agreement), I can promise a completed draft within three months of our interview series. If needed, agenting services to major publishers may be discreetly arranged . . .

Council of Churches
5000 Riverside Drive
New York, New York 11054

... attend and address our annual national meeting, to give the keynote address, perhaps based upon your stimulating remarks to the press concerning the "reproducibility" of the creation of subuniverses . . .

Editorial from *The New York Times*, Sunday edition:

In the end, perhaps we are trying to be logical about a question that is not really susceptible to logical argument: the question of what should or should not engage our sense of wonder . . .

Letters to the Editor, the *Washington Post:*

The fatuousness of this and other similar "acceptable" uses for making universes in a laboratory, revealingly described as "a free lunch" by physicists, merely points out the lengths to which some scientists and science apologists will go to justify what is really just a desire to tinker, to fiddle around and then claim that a technology developed out of that desire satisfies some pressing human or societal need.

Gina Montebello
Miami Beach, FL

ARCHBISHOP SAYS 'COSM' PROVES GOD'S
BEHIND UNIVERSE
'We Must Talk Philosophy with Science'
(UPI) A prominent cleric has declared, in light of the recent claims of discovering an entire universe that fits into a labora-

tory, that "the 'reason within'—rational minds that conceived mathematics—had to be connected with the 'reason without'— the rational structure of the physical world—by an overarching cause, i.e., God."

Archbishop Erma Ehrlich of San Francisco believes this is a "more compelling proof that what these scientists are doing is in fact acting in the cause of God, not, as some believe, the reverse . . ."

Max tossed the printout aside. "Archbishop be damned."

Alicia was compiling data tapes and did not look up from her keyboard. "She's just trying to piggyback on the news."

Max circled in the confined space available in the observatory. Only computer screens lit the area.

"I know, I know, and true enough, Einstein said that the only incomprehensible thing about the universe was that it was comprehensible. But resorting to God forgets what biology says—that our minds came out of the physical world, y'know, through evolution of early brain stems and neural systems to higher levels of complexity."

Alicia looked up at last. He was agitated and she couldn't see why. "Hey, let this media rain run off your back, old duck."

"No, I'm working on an idea here . . ."

He paused, studying the wealth of color and movement flickering across the nearby face of the Cosm. It was brighter than ever, almost lurid in the view of stars wheeling across a lacy blue-white firmament. The Cosm was passing through a molecular cloud where banks of dust glowered with the irritations of young suns.

After a long moment, he said suddenly, "Boy, do I hate these holier-than-thou types."

"Clerics?"

"Anybody who tries to hem science in, tell it what it can and cannot do. Boundaries are best defined by pushing against them. Expanding our horizons, our sense of wonder."

She smiled. "There's nothing holier than *wow!*?"

He brightened, nodded. "Something like that. Look—somewhere in our past there was probably a primate who saw the curve of a rock thrown through the air as a complicated arc, a mess, tough to follow—''

"How can that be? It isn't a mess. It's just a parabola."

"To you and me, sure. But that primate, he got selected against. He wasn't good at bringing down game, so he starved—or his children did, in the end the same result."

Her thoughts leaped ahead. "So intuitions of order, symmetry, and even beauty came to have use in the world: they made it simpler."

"Right." Max paced eagerly and the Cosm glow played along his angular features. "Easier to control, to succeed. In the long run even the beauties we look for in math, they have this elegance and symmetry."

She said, "All that stuff about math being unreasonably good at describing the world, then that's because it came out of the world."

He beamed. "Damn right. It's as unremarkable as the fact that a glove, made by hand, then fit hands."

She enjoyed his harangues. He paced and muttered some more and she thought through the idea, too, wondering where he was going with it. In its search for aesthetic principles which could preside when selecting among candidate mathematical theories, science echoed the ancient shaping forces at work on African plains. So science's success did not need a God to explain it; the world was enough.

Something told her that Max would not stop there, however.

4

In its own time frame the Cosm's speeding spectacle was now approaching the age of our own universe. Events in the dark spherical lens sped ever-faster. The other side spent most of its time gliding between stars in the bulge of a giant elliptical galaxy. As the banks of dust thinned, collapsing into fierce young stars, the vault of night cleared and they could see farther with their telescopes. The swoop and gyre of galaxies they witnessed in real time. Stars stirred across the foreground like snowflakes in a blizzard, whipped by gravity's winds. Beyond, galaxies themselves glided like pale, coasting birds, orbiting in the cluster, which had this elliptical as its heart. Zak and Alicia measured the images of far more distant galaxies and found that they were receding. This was a stretching of space-time like the one found by Hubble eighty years before. Would it continue? Could this new universe's expansion ever reverse? A closed universe seemed the ultimate doom, all structure ultimately ending as an imploding fiery mass.

This was still the crucial unanswered riddle in our own cosmology. With enough matter, eventually gravitation would win out over the expansion. The new Cosm universe gave no clearer answer.

"They may have different fundamental constants," Max said, "but they could share our same fate—whatever that is."

"Implosion," she said, "or else a slow freezing as space-time expands forever and matter runs out of heat."

"Right. Either way, they're doomed. But then, so are we, when you think about it."

Which she tried not to, actually. Alicia shivered, watching the grand gavotte of galaxies. If the Cosm followed roughly the course of our universe, for its first fifty billion years it would brim with light. Gas and dust would still fold into fresh suns. For an equal span the stars would linger. Beside reddening suns, any planetary life would warm itself by the waning fires that herald stellar death. And within a few weeks, she could see it all play out.

Silently witnessing, she wondered if even now—well, wrong word, but "now" in Cosm time—something like an inquisitive chimpanzee, in mind though almost certainly not in body, was restlessly spreading over a green world, somewhere in this same storm of stars. Minds embodied in strange shapes would still find themselves sharpened against evolution's ceaseless whetstone.

What challenges would they face? In the end the universe as a whole was life's ultimate opponent.

She and Max met Bernie Ross for lunch at the Phoenix Grill on campus. Bernie looked uncomfortable sitting outside in the slanting autumn sunlight, on plastic chairs and eating a coconut curry, but he got right to the point.

"The UCI administration is coming under pressure from the Department of Energy. They're undertaking legal moves to reclaim the Cosm."

She stopped eating. Bernie was usually reassuringly jovial, but not now. "You can't block them?"

"This is federal to the hilt. They're going for injunctions against UCI, calling in other agencies to hit them from every angle. Inspecting the books on research, oversight visits on health and safety issues, invoking inspection of compliance with regs in the med school, the works."

Max said disbelievingly, "Just like that?"

Bernie allowed himself a narrow smile. "Government doesn't often move quickly, but when they do, it's like an elephant stampede."

"Don't be in its way," Alicia said, frowning down into her plate of red enchiladas. "You know this for sure?"

"I have my sources and they're reliable."

"Inside UCI?" Alicia asked.

"Not everybody is a total toady of the administration."

"They've been pretty good about giving me an umbrella so far."

"The Feds are another matter, believe me." Bernie stopped working on his curry and leaned across the table, taking Alicia's left hand.

"You really can't block them somehow?" she asked forlornly.

"I promised your father I would look after your interests. The best thing to do now is give it up while you still have a choice."

"We're at a crucial time!" Alicia cried. Heads turned at nearby tables. "It's losing mass, time is accelerating—"

"There's never a good time," Bernie said comfortingly. "You kept it as long as you could."

She looked plaintively at Max. He was visibly torn between supporting her and following the advice of someone who understood legal matters; to Max they were hieroglyphics, their needless complexity clear evidence of the underlying irrationality of mankind. He spread his hands and shrugged. "I remember your father saying to you, 'Hire the best people, then follow their advice.'"

"So he did . . ." Her voice trailed off.

"I believe I can get the right figures in the administration to handle this with discretion. No alerting of the press, no pictures, just a quiet transfer."

"Mighty decent of them," Max said sarcastically.

"An elephant stampede," Alicia said. "Don't be in its way."

Chairman Onell had not expected her outburst. Blinking, he sat back and stared and then noticed that his jaw was still hanging open and closed it.

She repeated, "No, I will *not* show the Cosm to a bunch of donors."

"They have all given a minimum of ten thousand—"

"And I don't give a—" She stopped, breathed deeply.

"Pressure from vice chancellor—"

"Look, I don't have her style. I'd like to be remote and subtle about this, too. I'd like to play this the way a cool analytical academic plays things. But nobody will let me—not Brookhaven or the Department of Energy or UCI. I try to keep some space between me and them. But I keep feeling I'm going to wake up next morning in an alley with the cats looking me over."

"You're self-dramatizing."

"I'm being metaphorical. That's a good academic word, isn't it?"

"I advise you to cool down."

"I've got a universe that's doing just that and I have to get back to it."

Jill said, "These big things are awfully hard to drive."

Alicia studied the bay of the Pathfinder. "I always wanted to drive one. Sit up high, four-wheel drive, go where you want."

"It's a lot of cash just to get a view of all the traffic." Jill looked around at the dealer's showroom. "I liked your Miata a lot better."

"Well, a few billion years have passed since then."

"Big-ticket items, these."

"That's why I'm going to get one used. This is just an educational visit." Alicia pointed to a meek little compact car across the lot. "I'm going to buy one of those."

Jill grimaced. "That? It's style-impaired."

"Cheap, though."

"Strictly transportation. Dykey, too."

"I'm tired of renting, and I just got my insurance money from the Miata. Thought I might take off with Max, camp out down in Baja." Her plans were still shaping in her mind, but it wouldn't hurt to throw out some false clues that could mislead people later.

Jill frowned. "He doesn't seem quite the type, but go ahead."

"You think I'm rushing into this too fast."

"You ask me, your whole life is moving too fast."

"Max and I have been working together for months—"

"Might be best to keep a little more distance."

Alicia grinned. "Think I'm overplaying my hand?"

"Clingy is *out*."

"You don't mean as in negligees."

"As in *needy*, speedy."

She kept to a narrow track, wary of crowds. No day went by without the kidnappers coming to mind. A stranger would approach her or an odd phone call would set her off, bring the panic reaction swarming back.

Detective Sturges called again; no progress there, but the religious angle was looking fruitful. His veiled tone made her impatient, but he would reveal nothing more.

The fourth floor of the physics department had a security guard just to keep away the curious. Whenever she happened by the department coffee and tea cart, somebody snagged her for news. She was the focus of much gossip and speculation, she knew, but there simply wasn't time to bring everybody up to date.

She noted a subtle shift in the attitude of her fellow high-energy experimenters, as well. She remembered her high school advanced physics text extolling particle physics, "the spearhead of our penetration into the unknown"; she had laughed at the metaphor. Particle physicists knew in their guts that the spearhead had a shaft following: engineering, chemistry, then biology, with (if they ever thought of it) social sciences and then humanities far back (though not, of course, the real balls of the matter). Math and fine arts shared traits with particle physics—imagination, rigor, grace—and so were not in the continuum. Particle physics was a very male arena, and she had entered it at breakneck pace, under a cloud.

Still, to make it in a dramatically different way, to open whole horizons through an accident, definitely made one a member of the club, though her methods definitely did not fit the clubby manner. By holding on to the Cosm and extracting some understanding from it, she had become both audacious pioneer and sacred monster. To herself, she had to admit that mostly she had been just plain lucky.

PRESIDENT ISSUES EXECUTIVE ORDER BANNING MORE 'COSM' PRODUCTION
Declares Ethics and Dangers Must Be Evaluated
Appoints Blue Ribbon Panel

"Dad, why would the President go on TV—"

"He's in trouble, honey, taking flak on the budget, the medical bankruptcy thing—"

"This hasn't got anything to do with those."

His warm chuckle came over the line and she could imagine him shaking his head at a daughter so out of it. "Sure, but he needs to be seen doing something."

"I hope it doesn't interfere with our experiments. Finding out about it is the only way to know what to do."

"He wanted to get out in front on the issue. Congress—"

"When he came here, he was so positive."

"That was ancient history, weeks ago. He's been reading the letters to the editor, op-ed pieces."

"Well, yours are good."

"And pretty lonely. Just check out the late-night TV talk shows, hon. They've got some pretty funny jokes, actually."

"I haven't got the time—"

"I'll tape 'em for you."

"—and don't need being laughed at just before bedtime."

His patented diplomatic pause, then, "You don't have any idea how strongly people feel about this, do you?"

"Not really. I'm too busy."

CONGRESSIONAL SUBPOENA

You are directed to appear before the House Committee on Science and Technology, Rep. Lois Friedman, chairman. This hearing shall require full documentation of your involvement with the Department of Energy Brookhaven National Laboratory, said documents to be presented two (2) weeks before your appearance date . . .

"Bernie?"

"Hey, thanks for getting back to me so fast. I can't delay this matter anymore, Alicia, I'm sorry."

"What's this subpoena thing?"

"They're trying to get our attention—"

"Well, it sure worked."

"Just a shot across our bow—and not even a close one." His tone was warm, casual, professionally reassuring. "Plenty more will happen before that House Committee can get organized. They're doing it to get before the cameras. The real negotiations with DoE and UCI, those I've been handling."

"You've done a great job. What do I have to do?"

"Surrender it."

"So I figured. A cop, a county detective, came by and hinted very strongly that federal agents were figuring out how to take it if I don't."

Bernie's voice was measured, resigned. "That would be consistent."

"I'm just finishing up what I really have to do. A few details—"

"They want it tomorrow morning."

"Wow, that soon?"

"They've got a federal district judge in their pocket, the usual one who blocks state ballot initiatives if the Feds don't like them. So this tame judge issued an order today giving them the Cosm, hands down. They can walk right in and seize it if they want."

"I'll need tomorrow. How about we meet in my office— 7 P.M.?"

"I'll try to set it up."

"No TV, no reporters."

"That's in the deal, yes."

"I do appreciate all your work. I'll send you a check—"

"Forget it. Do me a favor. Call your father. He's been riding me about this every hour on the hour."

"Will do."

"I think you might not want to be around later today, is all," she said to Max.

He bristled. "I'm in this legally just as much as you—"

"Nope, you're in the clear. I took the Cosm and this is my lab."

"But I—"

"Bernie's quite clear on this part, anyway."

"Damn it, let me finish!"

By the pale glow of the Cosm, she could see the irked twist of his mouth. "Fair enough."

"I want to be there because *I'm* with *you*."

She felt a pleasing warmth steal through her. "I . . . I know. But it's better if you go home and wait for me."

An adamant set mouth this time. "Why?"

"I can't tell you. I don't want you to have to deny anything."

"God *damn*, I hate it when you turn into a control freak."

"Goes with being a goddess."

His mouth relaxed, one tip inching up to grant her a point. "And lonely martyr. I don't like it this way."

"Neither do I, actually." She sighed, leaning against him. Some minutes passed that way. Usually she felt the need to fill silences, but not now.

"I have some obligations at Caltech anyway." Max peered somberly at the rippling vistas that flashed across the face of the Cosm. "I'll go this afternoon. What's all this moving around you and Zak are doing?"

"Last rites."

"How come I get the feeling there's something you're not saying."

She smiled. "I don't want to involve you if it doesn't come off. Just get some sleep tonight, is all."

He studied her for a long moment. "We aren't going to have any secrets, I thought."

"About us, about personal stuff, no."

He smiled grimly. "So this secret isn't of the squishy sort."

"You'll know within hours."

His mouth worked uneasily, but then he shrugged. "I heard some coalition of fundamentalists declared you 'an abomination.'"

"I think it was some of those who kidnapped me."

"Sturges giving you any more information?"

"No, it just feels right."

"I'm still irked that they can't find out who did it." He put an arm around her in a completely casual way that thrilled her. In silence they watched the sweep of events across the curved face of the Cosm, a shifting pearly light of the elliptical galaxy's densely packed stars. The other end was working through a matrix of glaring suns. The jets that once had stabbed out from the galactic nucleus had faded. Their viewpoint glided with discernible velocity along an arm of aging stars, their ruby glows pinwheeling in complex orbits. The brilliant hub of the galactic center rose like a mountain of light above the foreground, growing larger by the hour.

Alicia let herself just watch for a while, held by Max. It was quite enough, and the weight of what was coming momentarily slipped from her.

Max began speaking, not love talk but physics, and somehow it had the same effect on her. Through his words she got a feeling of how he saw all this, events piling upon each other with bewildering swiftness. He had a way of showing her how a theorist *felt*, which had always been hard for her. She had seen his neat calculations, the delicate tapestry of tensor notation, his face compressed with an inner energy, a sublime concentration she well understood. Hard work took you out of yourself. He loved the power of pure calculation, when airy mathematics could congeal into the iron fist of inevitable logic. Behind the laconic equations lay cold immensities of gas and stars, dead but furious mass laced with cutting radiation, all bending to the will of gravitation and the brute curvature of space-time, stars dying like matchheads exploding in an uncaring vacuum.

Compared with the supple weave of the equations, the pictures of the world that people formed were crude and hazy. To peer through the quick stubble of mathematics and see the wonders lurking behind was to momentarily live in the infinite, beyond the press of the ordinary world where everyone else dwelled in ignorance.

"Y'know, what we're seeing here is how the entire history of the universe is, in the end, the slow victory of gravity over all other forces." When he explained, she saw it better: how the nuclear fires that burned through the strong force, how the rhapsodies of light and lacy plasma that sang through the electromagnetic force—how finally all were finally humbled before gravity's blunt, relentless hammer.

With a sense of foreboding, she knew then why she was about to make a large number of enemies.

5

She gave herself plenty of time.

Everything was set by 6:15 P.M. Dusk had settled and she had her used compact car pulled up to the observatory, loading a few last things. She had bought it the day before from a newspaper ad, paying a hundred dollars more than she should have. She had the car nearly full when she saw the big fleet of vans coming onto the campus ring road a quarter mile away. They were big and conspicuous and when they stopped at the intersection below and turned uphill, she knew they were coming here. Of course; get in place early, be crisp and efficient.

They labored slowly up Gabrielino Drive, three of them, with escort cars. Her world tilted. *Move.* But in the car she would have to drive right by them, as obvious as a roach on a linen napkin.

She called to the security man, "Good night. I'm walking back to campus now."

"Yes, ma'am."

"Don't let anybody in, no matter what ID they have."

"Uh, yeah."

He frowned at this odd instruction, delivered in her patented nervous warble, but there was no time to make it more plausible, and it might buy her a few minutes. No Feds were going to be blocked by a rent-a-cop for long, though.

Quickly she walked into the darkness. The guard was a sleepy sort. She covered twenty meters along the gravel road, looked back; the guard was gazing off into the distance. Trot-

336

ting, she angled off through the dry grass away from the observatory. Down the back side of the hill, away from the straining of the trucks. She tried to think, but the trucks suddenly sounded very close and darting panic made her break into a run. They undoubtedly would call upon others as soon as they knew that the Cosm was gone and her with it.

Ah, if only she *were* with it! Then she could scram out of Laguna Beach, where she had parked the Pathfinder. But no, there were files and data she had wanted, so she had buzzed back to campus to load up the compact. She had imagined that two cars, both bought used and so harder to connect to her, would be enough; but it was tempting to cram in just a little bit more.

With Zak safely away and the Cosm in the Pathfinder, she should have been smart, not pressed her luck, left the additional diagnostics and data behind. But enough of the shoulda, woulda, coulda. Focus, girl.

She might still reach the Pathfinder just by getting a lift into Laguna. But there were only a few ways into Laguna and they certainly would cover those, and fast. For that matter, there were few roads around UCI. They would be patrolling them within moments.

She headed downhill amid low scrub brush in sandy soil, toward Bonita Canyon Road, away from the university. Irvine prided itself on its well-lit streets. Well, now she was on the other side of the law, and the bright avenues looked like traps.

Thinking hard, she ran straight into a big knot of artichoke thistles. The barbs jabbed her legs and arms. She stopped, rubbing the scratches, and saw that there was a large grove of them here. Carefully she crossed the last dark portion of the UCI grounds and saw barbed wire looming up between her and the long loop of Bonita Canyon Road.

She lifted the lowest strand and looked back; something symbolic about leaving the university grounds? Out into a hostile world. She could see several figures around the observatory's exterior lights: looking her way?

Gingerly, she slipped under the wire and loped toward the darker portion of the highway. Back on the hill, headlights went on, three sets. Leaving the observatory, broadening their search. She trotted across the darkest portion of the highway and plunged into some bushes. Crouched there, she thought anxiously. What next?

For a full minute she thought about giving up. They had her, after all. On foot at night, she might get to the home of a friend. But could she be sure they would jump at the chance to help her elude federal officers? And could she rightfully get them involved? Zak had readily assented, but her colleagues . . . And of course, they knew she was on foot on campus, so those faculty living on the hill near the observatory would be the first they would check.

She still had her portable phone clipped to her belt. Call someone for help? The Feds undoubtedly had her phone covered by now, just in case. This close to campus, they would nail her before any friend could get here.

Nope, face it.

Option one: give up and then lamely try to cover over why she had taken the Cosm away in the Pathfinder and parked it on a street in North Laguna.

Option two: try to get a lift to Laguna. Hitchhikers were conspicuous, and she had to cover the fifteen kilometers by road to Laguna faster than an energized officer would.

Two options: one disagreeable and the other impossible.

But there was an assumption here, she felt vaguely, one that itched at her. Something about hitchhiking, her forlornly trudging along a roadway. Everybody else on wheels, her on foot.

Once she stepped back from her assumptions, the answer seemed simple. She set off along Bonita Canyon Road, staying in the shadows and among the shrubbery lining the concrete block wall. Her long walks on the beach paid off; she kept a steady pace, devouring the three kilometers until the road turned left into a housing development. She was puffing but excited.

Then she had to confront her idea with the daunting reality. Above loomed the San Joaquin Hills, a brooding presence over the twinkling sprinkle of lights. Her pursuers would count on her using the easy ways, known streets. People trying to escape moved fast, after all. They used cars, ran lights. Who would think that she might hike her way out of the trap?

Instead she headed up Shady Canyon, past the darkened golf course. This was the only uninhabited way into the vast expanse of the Laguna Greenbelt, a preserve like a green moat around the sole remaining town with a real identity in the entire county. She had on a light jacket and had, of course, skipped dinner in the rush. She searched her pockets and found a Mars bar in a zipper compartment. At last, her hoarding habits paid off. She wolfed it down.

The dark did not bother her; in fact, its thick quiet was comforting. A crescent moon coasted behind thin, high silver clouds. She wished for more clouds, for darkness, and regretted missing the weather report that morning. She easily scaled an iron gate and quickly pressed on. The grade steepened and she began puffing, jogging and then just fast-walking along the single narrow path in the glow of faraway streetlights. Her night vision adjusted and she avoided more of the sharp-bladed artichoke thistles, the irksome by-product of grazing cattle. On the low ridge nearby million-dollar-an-acre lots were already marked off and she could catch the moist tang of raw earth ready for further editing by bulldozers.

Ever since moving to Laguna, she had hated the incessant pressure of the developers, had hiked in the Greenbelt with locals who felt the same way and knew the terrain, and now it was paying off. The distant city shine helped her navigate along the trails. Shady Canyon began to earn its name as the night darkened around her under the trees. A scrabbling in the bushes told of a pursuit, then high-pitched squeaks of a catch, then silence. Not a great metaphor for her tonight.

An owl hooted. Coyotes yipped in the hills to both sides, maybe talking about her. She had heard stories of campers out here surrounded by a pack of them. Fair enough, it was their territory; it would be a relief to confront predators with more than two legs.

Gasping, she reached the top of Shady Canyon at Four Corners and knew to turn right, heading toward the broad tollway's glaring lights and traffic buzz. Even if her pursuers were checking the tollway, the cars were below her here. She worked her way along a side road and got to the animal underpass, a muddy track peppered with the prints of coyotes, bobcat, deer, and roadrunners. Between north- and southbound lanes lay an open median. The divided four-lane segments cast a lot of light into the underpass. She reasoned that anyone looking for her would have to be in the fast lane, so the odds of being seen near the tollway—a slashing blemish that split the Greenbelt, isolating its animal populations—were small. But she felt eyes on her as she ran away from the eight-lane highway's glare, into the blessedly shrouded canyons.

It had been two hours since she left UCI. Not bad, maybe ten kilometers covered. Her excitement was gone and the energy with it. Sweating, she labored up onto the ridge beyond and began to wonder if she had the stamina for this. With help, the federal agents could scout every street in her neighborhood, find any suspicious vans. Or would they wait for her to fall into a traffic check somewhere? By now they might very well guess that she had found some other method around them. Would they think that a physics professor would go for an escape that depended on endurance? She hoped they'd imagine some technical trick instead.

She was panting hard now, a stitch developing in her side, wishing for another Mars bar. *A li'l ol' unexpected weight-loss program here,* she thought. At least the hard uphill parts were past.

Thinking about her weight somehow made her think of Jill. Of course—she should have called Jill back at the beginning. But the old argument worked for Jill, too: the Feds would have overheard and picked up both of them at their rendezvous. Unless . . .

On the fifth ring she heard, "Uh . . . this better be good."

"It is. Remember the pledge? Well, I'm in deep trouble and I need a girlfriend."

"I hope you're talking about breakfast tomorrow."

"Nope. Now."

"Ooooohhh . . ."

"Remember where the little boy is giving water to his dog?"

"What?" Silence. "Yeah."

"Meet me two blocks inland from there."

"Somebody's listening?"

"You bet. Let's say, in two hours."

"Oh great, I can go back to sleep easily now."

"Leave now, before a tail can get to your apartment."

A groan. "You're serious?"

"I really need it, girl."

She clicked off. Were phones that easy to tap? With the growth of federal police powers, probably so. She had watched a lot of cop movies, but she really had no idea.

A glance at her watch brought the incredible news that now nearly five hours had passed since she had seen the trucks coming up the hill. The hard exercise had focused her incessantly fidgety mind. Or maybe she was just tired. Dawn in maybe six hours. Surely they would be checking out the streets of North Laguna well before then. They should miss the Pathfinder; she had curtained off the back and dirtied up the paint. But trudging along, she would be conspicuous. Groggy, too.

She was trotting doggedly along the ridgeline toward Guna Peak when she heard the helicopter. It came up Bommer Canyon, low, just one ridgeline over from her path. Floodlights lit the ground beneath it in actinic blue-white. She froze; she had not even thought of this obvious move. Then she went crashing into a mass of lemonade berry, ignoring the slashes and stabs of dried branches.

Had they figured her out? Very bad news.

A brilliant dazzle passed overhead noisily as she cringed. The engine's hammering seemed to steepen and the hard incandescent stab of the searchlights played restlessly in the sky. For a long moment she thought that it was turning, coming back for her. She tried to burrow deeper, pulling shrubs over her head.

Its roar seemed right on top of her for an unbearably long time, a hovering weight. At last she felt from the rising whine of its engines that it was heading down one of the side canyons and away.

Probably checking each side route before returning to the exposed tops of the ridges. Not doubling back. Maybe.

She would keep her eyes and ears sharp after that—ready. The helicopter buzzed away, along the canyons leading to the sea in a repeating, systematic pattern. Probably a police chopper, called in. The Feds had all the men and time they needed.

She started running then. She was secondary here, the Cosm primary. If they suspected her route, they would cover the several ways she might get into the northern end of town. On the other hand, maybe they would drop the whole idea, since the helicopter had found nothing. That was her only real hope.

But where would they cover the exits from Laguna? There were only three roads out of town. Plans whirled in her head as she pumped along the ridgeline toward the town's soft ivory glow. Coyotes yipped and called into the bowl of night.

The last mile drew raw, ragged puffs from her and seemed to take hours. Her forehead was crusty with dried sweat. Well, at least she was losing weight and would look quite fetching in prisoner's garb.

She came down the long slope of the finger hills into Laguna. The city slept, cuddled against the black sweep of the ocean. She could see fifty miles down the coast as she at last padded onto Pinecrest Street. The big steel gate was formidable, with big locks, but an easy place to squeeze through the barbed wire. Asphalt felt easy beneath tired feet.

In the hush the usual deckologies and angular, slabby ensembles clung to the steep hillsides here and afforded her places to slip by in shadow, around the lawn lights of the wealthy. She avoided the streets where she could, cutting across yards heavy with acacias, eucalyptus, and bottle brush. Even through the dry summer, Lagunatics kept lush surroundings.

A helicopter rattled far to the north as she angled along a hedge and saw her Pathfinder on the street ahead. There didn't seem to be anyone watching it. She slipped alongside it and got the key in and with a long sigh slid into the driver's seat.

A quick check: the Cosm was there, glowing serenely in its iron magnet's jaws. She threw the tarp back over it and the gear all around it. Her jury-rigged diagnostics were recording it all. She gunned the engine and got out of there.

Now what? First, Jill.

She eased the Pathfinder toward her own apartment. The only landmark she could think to give Jill over the presumably tapped phone was a statue half a block from her apartment, a statue from the 1920s of a boy giving his dog a drink. Two blocks inland from there she parked the Pathfinder and slipped down an alley. Jill's car was parked in a driveway up the street. She could see Jill in it, so she came up on the car from the front and waved. Jill waved back; clear. Jill got out of her car and followed Alicia among the shadows. They got into the Pathfinder and Alicia finally let Jill speak.

"Thought you'd need these." Jill opened her backpack and service station food spilled out: moon pies, breakfast bars, chewy delights, and Dr Pepper (her fave).

"You're a genius." Alicia stuffed her mouth full without shame.

"Finally you notice. Now explain."

It seemed to take a long time. When she got to the lawyering part and her plans, Jill said, "Oh no."

"Oh yes."

"You're kidding."

"I wish."

By the time she was through, Jill was already nodding. "We have to plan. You're hoping this Pathfinder won't come to their attention right away, since you bought it in a private deal, used, right?"

"Yes. I'd hoped they'd be busy looking for the compact instead, at least to buy me—us—some distance and time. But they got the compact back at UCI." She smacked the steering wheel with her palm. "Dumb, dumb, dumb."

"So they know to look for something big enough to carry the Cosm. It has to be within walking distance of UCI or you wouldn't have tried to escape on foot. Not good." Jill munched a breakfast bar in the gloom. "They'll probably watch the roads out of Laguna."

"With only three, and plenty of choke points, that won't be hard."

"They'll count on your being worn-out, too."

"Not far wrong there," Alicia conceded, letting her head loll back against the headrest. Maybe if she just got an hour's nap . . .

"Hey!" Jill was punching her in the shoulder. "You nodded off."

She shook her head. "Doing my meditation. Got another Dr Pepper?"

"Ol' girl, I don't see a way out of this box."

"I don't either." *Was it me who said, "An elephant stampede, Don't be in its way?"* "I guess I thought once I got back here, something would come up. Funny, I get through miles of wilderness okay, but get trapped once I reach civilization."

Jill's head jerked up. "Hey, that's it."

"Civilization?"

"Sure. You got this Pathfinder because you wanted to hightail it out into the boonies, right? So let's just *go*."

Alicia gazed at Jill's indistinct profile, not following at all. Jill grinned and said, "We just go back out on that trail you followed."

"But there's a gate, locks—"

"This is Jill the lock genius, remember? And I brought my secret tools."

6

Through her fog of fatigue the next hour was ghostlike, filmy. Alicia drove back to the top of Pinecrest. Jill got through the gate locks in less than a minute. The Pathfinder found its way up the dirt path with ease, Jill driving. No headlights, of course; a helicopter patrolled to the north over Irvine but didn't head their way. "Anyway, they're prob'ly still looking for you heading away from Irvine, not back."

Lurching, creaking, they made their way along the ridge-lines. The Pathfinder earned its keep. Beyond the tollway there were several ways down to Laguna Canyon Road. Alicia got down in the back and Jill threw a plastic sacking over her. She lay next to the iron magnet, secured by bungee cords, and peered at the glow of the Cosm. Her optical gear was working fine, clicking away, the whole array drawing power for its batteries now from the Pathfinder. As a hasty kludge, she had to admit, it was amazing; Zak had done a lot of the tricky bits. The only creative part lay in realizing that the Cosm, now weighing less than five kilograms, could be transferred to a small portable magnetic trap.

They negotiated the ridge road, a bit hairy with no lights, just poking along. Eventually they came down onto Laguna Canyon, looking intently for any cars that might be surveying the road. Nothing; just the silence of predawn canyon. They barreled out toward the freeways and Jill said, "Where to now?"

"You've saved my ass. I'll drop you somewhere, then—"

"The hell you will."

"Look, this is going to involve multiple felonies—"

"Think you can hog all the infamy? C'mon, girl, this is *fun*."

"Look, I have some suspicions that this might get dangerous."

"Even better."

"I can't get you involved—"

"I *am* involved. Think I'll walk out on you now? Where to?"

Pasadena came like a sudden movie jump shot; she had gone to sleep as they hit the 57 freeway. Easing through streets pale with dawn, she wondered if she should stop for Max at all. That had always been her plan, involve him only if she successfully got away with the Cosm. Now the enormity of what she had done sank in.

But so did the necessity of handling this properly. Whatever happened, she at least would finish knowing she had done what she truly thought was right. Max had a right to be in on the end of it.

He lived in a morose pile built on an aging Douglas fur frame. Jill got them into the foyer of the apartment house with her "secret tools," which had turned out to be a strip of industrial plastic and a little metal pick.

"Doesn't look hard to do," Alicia said as the foyer lock clicked over.

"All in the wrist."

Alicia had never been here before, so she had to check the mailboxes to find Max's apartment. A sullen redbrick façade outside had tried to make the apartment house look like New England, but the cramped lobby had big-leafed plants in tubs, a dingy carpet, and air scented with Essence de Spray Can. Alicia pondered this and Jill saw her expression as they went up the stairs to the third floor. "Penny for . . ."

"I'm thinking, 'I'm in love—might as well admit it—with a guy who lives in a place like this.' "

"Style isn't everything."

"Here, style isn't anything."

"Isn't it a little early to start with the second thoughts?"

"Ummmm." Somehow the stairs were taking a lot out of her and then she remembered that she hadn't slept in several years. "I never thought I'd fall for a guy who blindsided me, coming up on my professional perimeter."

Jill said, "You mean he actually built a relationship first."

"Oh, maybe that's why I didn't recognize it. First time."

"You're riding a whirlwind, girl. Don't start second-guessing Max."

"Right, I'll need somebody to visit me in jail."

"Hey, you're famous. I'm an accomplice. You'll walk and I'll be in handcuffs."

"Well, you always said you'd get around to trying bondage."

Jill laughed. "And I'll be thinking of you as they roll me into a grave marked 'Nobody Special.' "

They knocked five times before Max opened the door, managing to yawn and look surprised at the same time. His living room seemed to be deliberately retro by three decades. The doorknobs were just enough off-round to be sure you noticed them and the thin drapes were trying to be lighthearted by letting you get some of the view of an even worse place across the street. At least the furniture was clean and dusted, but the air was telling her that he had take-out food for dinner, probably Mexican, but with fried stuff it was hard to tell.

"Funny, I had a call about you," he said, voice foggy.

"From?"

"Said he was some lawyer. About an hour ago. Asked if you were here."

Jill went into the kitchen and started opening cabinets. "Uh," Max said uncertainly, "can I get you something?"

"You can get dressed," Alicia said. "Pronto. You have a sleeping bag?"

"Sure. When do I hear what's going on?"

"About fifty miles from here, which better be inside half an hour."

*   *   *

Death Valley did not have the thin, stingy light of autumn, but rather a perpetual slanted glare. The highway wound through the rugged grandeur of the slopes, skirted by the usual bright strip of cheesy fast-food mills. They ordered in one of them, Alicia now feeling much the better for several hours' sleep.

"Burgers. Six. And throw in fries and onion rings," Alicia added in a devil-may-care, arteries-be-damned voice.

Zak grinned. "What are the rest of us going to eat?"

They had been headed for Badwater (ELE. −280 FT.) on Highway 178 when they spotted Zak pulled back on a side road but visible, just as he and Alicia had planned. Not that his U-Haul van was hard to spot; there was not too much distraction among the rutted hills and baking rock. She had gotten a truck from UCI yesterday and then hidden it on a street in Costa Mesa, hoping the Feds would then be looking for it still, but that dodge was probably quite dead by now.

Alicia gave him the first onion rings to arrive. He had been driving the slow van all night and looked worse than she did. "The Cosm riding okay?" he asked.

"Rock-solid," Alicia said. It was midafternoon, with few patrons in the fast-food joint. The burgers were tasty, or was she just pumped on adrenaline?

"I'd like to get set up soon, have a look," Max said. "I've been thinking about ways to check the evolution of the Cosm as it ages."

"Let's head for the Furnace Creek RV and tent camp," Jill said, tracing the map and consulting the AAA camping book with sticky fingers. "Toilets, but no showers. Oooh. Why can't we stay in the hotel there?"

Zak said, "We'd have to register."

"Camps register you, too," Max said.

"Our idea was that nobody will think we'd come here," Alicia said. "None of us has ever been here."

"How wide a net they cast depends on how important this is," Max said reasonably. "I doubt that even the Department of Energy can muster an all-out effort."

Jill said, "I'm just an ordinary citizen, but this doesn't sound like an agency wrangle."

"Why not?" Zak asked.

"The President. He's going to be embarrassed by this if we just skip off with a national treasure."

"Good point," Zak conceded. "He can even get on top of the issue, say it's a matter of safety."

"You've gotten politically savvy pretty fast," Max said.

"Part of his education," Alicia said lightly. Indeed, this canny Zak was a great change from the quiet prototypical good-immigrant persona he had projected not long ago. She had underestimated this one.

They all felt better leaving the place, fully fed if not well. As Alicia walked toward the Pathfinder, a cotton-top couple in caps and jeans and sneakers stopped in their tracks. For an instant she wondered if this was the shocked-to-see-a-nigga-here reaction she occasionally got, then saw something else in their open-mouthed wonder.

"You're the one!" the man said.

"On the TV," the woman said.

Everybody froze. The parking lot lay in bleached light for one long heartbeat in Alicia's ears.

"That's right," Alicia said, stepping forward with a smile. "Veronica of the Virginals, glad ta meecha, caught us on 'What's Hot' last night, didja?"

"Virginals?" the man said.

"How'd you like that new song of ours, huh? Wild or what?"

"Uh, I thought I saw you ... the news ..." the woman said.

"Great coverage, huh?"

The man hesitated, peering at Max and Jill and Zak in turn, then held out the road map in his hand. "It *is* her, Irma. Uh, can I get your autograph?"

The *Los Angeles Times* they bought from a vending machine had nothing about them. "Not enough time," Max said. "But you're on TV. That lets out the RV place."

"What's left?" Jill asked. They had driven quickly away from there and pulled into a rest stop ten miles farther along.

"Camping out. Run our gear from the generator Zak's got in the van," Alicia said.

"If that couple figures out that they've been bamboozled, they'll blow the whistle," Jill said.

Max said soberly, "And spot us from the air, no matter where we are out here."

"We'd be safer in the forests, up toward Lone Pine," Jill said.

"I need to go to fugitive school, gang," Alicia said. "But I thought out here there would be less at risk if something . . . happens."

Jill said, "We all chose to be here."

"I mean the Cosm."

"What could happen?" Jill asked. "I mean, as I understand you guys, the Cosm will just get older and older."

"Let's hope that's all," Max said. "The neck connecting us is, well, thinning out. If it snaps off in some way, I don't know what will happen at this end. There's a lot of potential energy stored in the exotic matter that keeps it open."

Jill's face wrinkled, puzzled. "So it was safety that made you do this?"

Alicia's face flickered with conflicting emotions. She realized that she was still tired, though adrenaline-driven; anyway, she should be straight with these three, who had given her so much. "Some, sure. But mostly, I want to see what comes next in there." She hooked a thumb toward the Pathfinder, where the Cosm rested under plastic sheeting. "Let's roll."

They went another fifteen miles and pulled off on a dirt road. Even in late autumn the temperature was in the high seventies. A few miles in, they found a box canyon and parked the two vehicles close together on a level area. Max found a news show at 5 P.M. that was full of excited talk about the "woman-hunt" on for Alicia.

"How come they don't mention any of us?" Jill asked.

"Disappointed?" Alicia ribbed her with an elbow. "We've covered ourselves pretty well, so they can't be sure you're with me."

Zak shook his head as he unloaded gear from the back of the van. "They know. They're just not saying."

At 6 P.M. one of the L.A. talk shows dedicated two hours to the "woman-hunt" and various loudmouths who called in to denounce her. Talk rapidly deteriorated to the playing-goddess clichés and they all laughed at some of the more outrageous callers as they grouped detection gear around the Cosm.

It sat at the center of a circle ten feet across. Deep in its ebony sheen were gauzy veils of gas roiling with fitful light. Setting up was actually easier than at the observatory because there was enough room.

Jill had stopped by the observatory weeks before to see the Cosm and now she was shocked to see how much it had changed. "It's . . . marvelous." After a long moment, she said, "So my goddess girlfriend here is just like most people's idea of God, huh?"

Puzzled, Alicia looked up from her work. "How so?"

"You made this, courtesy of taxpayer dollars, of course, but now you can't intervene in it. Nobody can. You don't even know if anything's alive in there."

Alicia said soberly, "I wouldn't know how to intervene. Or on what side."

"Most people I know figure God doesn't actually dip His finger into our lives."

"Maybe that's a good idea," Max said.

As darkness came, they sat and watched it, Zak's radio barking out its frothing-at-the-mouth voices in the background.

The Cosm now looked out on a reddening galaxy. In the cool desert dark Max said, "While we've been getting here, the universe on the other side has aged over fifty billion years."

Murmurs of astonishment. "That's how exponentials work. It's maturing at a rate that is taking off toward infinity."

He punched on his laptop and displayed the graph, using his hand-writer to scratch in labels.

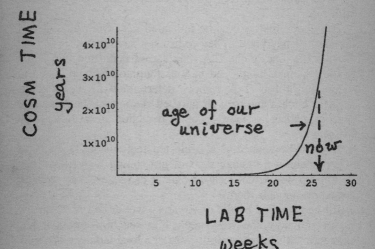

The curve of Cosm time was very nearly vertical. NOW lay beyond 25 WEEKS, so the Cosm age was around 4×10^{10} YEARS; forty billion was well past the age of our universe. Max nodded, taking the vast implications in stride; in a sense, these were just more points on the curve. "The elliptical galaxy is past its prime, reddening. See, no big bright blue ones left? Smaller stars will live longer, and they're dim and red and numerous. But even they're only good for a hundred billion years or so.''

Alicia thought of abodes for life-forms near stars that were guttering out. Such planets would orbit close enough to their stars to stay warm and so would also be tide-locked, one side baked and the other freezing. Still, such worlds might prove temporary abodes.

Did the sphere seem smaller now? Alicia could not tell.

Max said slowly, watching the churn of rosy radiance across the Cosm's face, ''But eventually, even with superengineering, nearly all the stellar hydrogen gets burned. New stars can form, but not many. See those faint red stars glowing? The great big dust banks we saw just a few weeks ago, they're trapped into stellar corpses now.''

Jill shivered. She had suggested building a fire, but they had no wood, and anyway that would be a giveaway. ''So the stars are mortal, same as us.''

Zak said, ''They just take longer.''

''I wonder if there's life in there,'' Jill said.

Max said, ''That galaxy we're watching ebb away is ten times older than ours. In an hour it'll be a few billion more.''

Alicia thought of life, sheltering closer and closer to star warmth. They would have to labor hard to capture light.

From Zak's radio came a long stream of invective against Alicia. She jumped up suddenly and swore back at it.

Max chuckled, not taking his eyes from the Cosm. ''Fools taking your name in vain? Now you know how God must feel.''

She glared at him. ''All this goddess stuff—so okay, I created this first universe, but plenty of people can now.''

He regarded her soberly, the planes of his face sharp in the luminosity of the Cosm. ''What makes you think you were the first?''

8

Jill swayed in the night, hoisting the bottle she had produced from her backpack.

"One tequila,
two tequila,
three tequila,
—*floor*."

A dramatic pratfall. Appreciative applause. They were getting cold but could not stop watching the unfolding drama written by radiance across the sphere's face. Jill's tequila came at just the right moment. It was like attending a wake, Alicia thought as she took a swig of the raw stuff straight from the bottle. A wake for a universe: hers. With one of her children, an elliptical galaxy, smoldering in the foreground.

She went to the Pathfinder and hauled out warmer clothing from her suitcase. She had been meticulously planning things when she packed it, thinking of nights spent in motels with Max. Right on top was a killer purple chemise, a reliable if predictable black lace teddy, plus her latest weapon in the passion arms race, a magenta front-hook demi-bra . . . all nestled beneath the baggy gray panties that she usually wore.

Her optimism seemed remote, odd, like a packet of your teenage love letters found in a drawer when you're clearing out after your second divorce.

Why? She had run faster and harder than she had ever imagined. Her implacable, unseen pursuers she had felt like a dark weight always at her back. Fatigue gnawed at her still.

But she had indeed gotten away. They were safe for at least this final night, here in the serene dry wastes. Why this drifting sense of melancholy?

The Cosm. She could not resist its ebbing drama. Brad had died to bring it to this point, death surrounding Creation, her Creation, that now itself must wane and perish. In a desert.

"Say, there are those jets again." Zak's voice came through the chilling night. She threw on a heavy jacket and hurried back.

The Cosm point of view was on an arc high above the somber masses of the elliptical galaxy. This gave it a penetrating view of the central core. Crimson crescents rimmed the smoldering inner regions, now swept clean of dust. At the dead center was true deadness: an immense black hole, growing by devouring the exhausted suns that orbited ever closer to its engulfing grip.

But above the inner black hung a lance of shimmering yellow. As she watched with the others, it grew, poking out into the empty void above the shrinking elliptical.

"Funny," Max said, "the theory says jets are a symptom of a black hole's early life, when there's plenty of dust around to get sucked in."

"So the theory's wrong," Jill said lightly.

She had been at the tequila. Alicia thought about having some more, but something told her she wasn't going to go that route again.

Max nodded ruefully. "Not exactly a big surprise."

"Pretty," Zak said. "And look, there's another on the other side of the galaxy, going the opposite way. They're forcing their way out, already bigger than the elliptical itself."

Max spoke slowly as they watched the jets work their way away from the growing blackness. Stars would inevitably meet and merge, he said. All the wisdom and order of planets and suns finally compressed into the marriage of many stars, plunging down the pit of gravity to become black holes. The fate of nearly all matter would be the dark pyre of collapse.

Galaxies are as mortal as stars. The elliptical was being devoured. Inky masses of smaller black holes blotted out whole zones of dim maroon. The central hole chewed visibly faster, a squatting appetite gnawing without end.

She tried to imagine the events he described; obviously Max had been brooding over this for some time, seeing what was coming.

Against an utterly black sky, shadowy cinders of stars glided. Planets might still orbit them, their atmospheres frozen out into waveless lakes of oxygen.

But the Cosm universe was no static lattice of stars. It grew and galaxies found themselves lonely in the gathering dark. The fabric of space stretched as time ticked on.

As they watched and the pace accelerated, the Cosm's viewpoint plunged back into the maelstrom of dying masses. Its orbit now arced through a long, toiling twilight. Grand operas of mass and energy played out their plots, their last arias sung. Nowhere in the chilly desolations could Alicia see any refuge for life, for any rickety assembly of water in tiny compartment cells, dangling on a lattice of moving calcium rods. Any life in there, she thought, would have to transform itself profoundly, remaking its basic structures from organic molecules to, say, animated crystalline sheets.

Witnessing such grandeur, she felt like an imposter, a derelict who had accidentally stumbled into a grand opera, a dog wearing clothes.

Something in the murky masses caught her eye. A glimmering line stretched away from the galactic hub. Its pale yellow lanced through shadowy swarms of spent stars. In the distance another long curve worked, structures growing with great speed, long and spindly and . . .

"Those . . . they're forming something," she whispered.

Max said, "Look, they're linking up."

"Circles around the whole galactic center," Zak said.

Jill said, "And spokes shooting outward, too, see?"

"Almost like a coordinate system, longitude and latitude . . ." Alicia's voice trailed off. Her breath was fog in the encroaching cold.

"Maybe magnetic?" Max said.

"Anybody's guess," Zak said.

Max pointed. "And growing so fast—look there."

From the concentric circles and the spokes came a brimming luminosity. Colors flickered where they intersected. Then the entire network—there was no other term for it, she thought hastily—began to throb with quick lightning strokes of brilliant gold and crimson. To Alicia the display crackled with energy, with . . .

"Purpose." Her word hung in the air.

"What's that?" Max got up and crouched closer to the sphere.

"Looks like thinner lines, poking up from the grid," Zak said.

"Like a root system spreading or something," Jill said. "What's going on, supernovas or something?"

"The supernovas are extinct," Max said. "All the stellar energy is burnt-out."

"Well, something's lighting up this thing," Jill said reasonably.

The Cosm's point of view veered then, swooping once more back toward the central hub of the dying galaxy. Against great ebony banks of dead suns, a few embers glowed. Yet the growing luminosity of the circles and grids cast a glow even into these somber, clotted clouds.

"Those 'roots' of yours, maybe that's not a bad term," Max said. "Something's growing. From what I don't know. But growing."

"Making structure in the face of oblivion," Alicia said with sudden energy.

"Looks like something alive to me," Jill said.

Max stayed rooted in his crouch for a long moment and then said softly, "I can't imagine anything else. Life! But where does it get the energy?"

"Not even the best theorists know everything," Alicia said lightly.

They sat and watched as fibers grew from the lattice that now spanned the entire giant elliptical galaxy. Against the cinder-dark bulk of dead and dying suns the pattern beamed its silent, persistent message.

Alicia could not take her eyes from the spreading luminescence. A part of her dearly wanted to believe that perhaps this was the final answer to the significance of it all. In principle, life and structure, hopes and dreams could persist—if it chose to and struggled. In the far future of her own universe, in a darkness beyond measure, something could dream fresh dreams.

In the Cosm's realm, did unimaginable entities now recall a distant, legendary era when matter brewed energy by crushing suns together, when boundless energy let life dwell in mere accidental assemblies of atoms, and paltry planets formed a stage?

9

"**W**hat's that?" Zak said suddenly.

They had been sitting silently for a while now. They watched the impossible fretwork grow in the darkening carcass of a seemingly deceased galaxy. Alicia dragged her attention from the vision.

She listened. "A car?"

"More like a plane."

"Damn! They'll see us in the infrared." Max jumped to his feet.

"Those people back at the restaurant. I sure didn't fool them for long." Alicia got up, her joints aching.

"Get inside," Zak said quickly. "We're the warmest things here and the vehicles have cooled off."

Alicia and Max tumbled into the Pathfinder, Zak and Jill into the van. She hated to leave the Cosm.

The buzzing came closer. The Pathfinder cab was warmer and Alicia lazed back, unable to resist her weary body's demands.

Max rolled down the window an inch. "Sounds like a plane."

"What did you mean back there, about my not being the first . . . goddess?"

"You're the only goddess for me, kid," he said in a quite passable Bogart imitation.

"No, seriously. As our comeuppance bears down upon us."

"I've been thinking about the larger picture here."

She chuckled. "What we just saw wasn't big enough?"

"Granted. I mean conceptually. Look, do you think the production of Cosms will stop here?"

She thought about Brookhaven, about the sociology of particle physics, of the personalities, of the entire horizon-pushing history of the cultures that had come out of Europe over five hundred years before. "No."

"And the Brookhaven Cosm, it's not quite like ours. It differs slightly in some fundamental parameter, apparently, though we don't know which one yet."

"So?" Lazy warmth, the buzzing slowly getting louder, then fainter, then louder again: a search pattern.

"Any future Cosms we meddlers make can also differ slightly in fundamental numbers. Some will be changes that make life impossible, some will be good for life. Maybe even better than this universe, though certainly ours looks very finely tuned to make life possible."

"Even enjoyable." She reached out in the dark and found his hand.

"Look at it this way. You've given this universe the ability to make copies of itself. But not perfect copies. We've just seen that life did incredibly well in your Cosm—it outlasted the death of stars!"

"Yeah, let's see goddamn Brookhaven do better than that." Had she had too much tequila? Well, write it off to fatigue.

"They may, they may not. Point is, pretty soon we'll have three elements. First, a population of self-reproducing universes. Second, small variations in the basic 'message' those daughter universes have."

"Daughters of the goddess," she said dreamily. Not that she ruled out having some flesh and blood ones someday, too. A little early to bring that up, though.

"Third element. Suppose your Cosm built its own RHIC. Then they made universes, too. Some will work out and support life. Others got the parameters too far from optimum and didn't make stars, maybe, or carbon that was stable. No life in those, then."

She caught a glimmer of what was coming in his argument

and then she caught another glimmer, a real light this time, sweeping over the ridgeline beyond.

The airplane circled them twice, sweeping the area with searchlights. Then it headed south and was gone.

"They spotted us for sure," Zak called from the van. "What'll we do?"

Alicia rolled down her window. "Nothing."

"But they'll catch us."

"They were always going to catch us. The only question was when." She started rolling up the window.

"Shouldn't we give them a run for their money?" Jill said.

"We did. Now we'd just be playing their game." She rolled up the window and looked at Max.

"You're right," he said.

"Tell me the rest of it."

"With even ordinary curiosity, intelligence in your Cosm is going to try out its own Cosm-making experiments, if only to check the theory. Maybe they even find a way to enter a daughter universe, to migrate there, who knows? Anyway, some of their daughters are hospitable to life, so those in turn evolve intelligence, and their daughter universes do the same . . ."

"Conceivably." On a night like this, damn near anything was conceivable.

"All the created universes that can't spawn intelligent life never reproduce. They're sterile. So in time—not our time, or even Cosm time, but a kind of meta-time that measures all this—you get more and more Cosms with life in them. Even if the odds of making a Cosm that's hospitable to life are small, eventually they prevail because they outbreed the sterile ones."

"There's a natural selection for universes with intelligence in them." She tried on the idea, breathing shallowly.

"Exactly. Only you weren't the first, of course."

"What?"

"A natural selection process explains why our universe's constants fit life so well. We're a daughter universe ourselves."

"No way."

"Think in the frame of meta-time, Alicia. There are plenty of Cosms with life in them, after a while. What are the odds that any single one, picked at random, was the original?"

She frowned. "I'm leery of statistical arguments."

He grinned, a pale profile. "Look, there are different kinds of scientific interest: the known, the unknown, and the flat-out unknowable. This idea falls in the unknowable. It's plausible, but how can we check it? Probably we can't. But we can still ask questions, invent explanations about what started it all."

"Then some experimenter in a lab . . ."

"Made us. Yes." He said it very mildly.

"Just like me."

"Except that experimenter had tentacles, yes."

"And all this . . . this wonder and glory, by *accident*?"

"That's what Darwin said about species. I'm just applying the same logic to universes."

"But that leaves out any *cause* to our whole universe."

"Unless accidents are God's way of dodging responsibility."

"And this isn't an infinite chain, right?" She bit her lip, seeing implications running in all directions. "All you've done is shift the beginning back some distance in, uh, meta-time."

"Right. I take no position on what god or goddess started this."

"I wonder if the idea of beginning actually fits any of this at all."

He murmured agreement. "Maybe not. Ever since St. Augustine in the fifth century A.D.—see, I've been reading up on this—Western thinkers saw time beginning with the creation of the universe. Nobody thought of it as like cell division, seeing it as just one more species coming into being from a parent."

She shrugged. "So okay, so I'm not the first goddess. Or the last. Just a member of the family."

"Sorry to steal some of your glory." His warm hand patted hers.

"Should I be blue about this? I don't feel that way."

"Because you're well balanced. Not many could have goddesshood snatched away and stay cheerful."

"Cheerful? I haven't got the energy for cheerful."

They all got out and walked back to the Cosm in the cold air. Alicia ate a crunchy breakfast bar beneath the sharp stars of a young universe.

"Hey!" Zak said. They stood in the cold and looked at the black mass that seemed to fill the Cosm's point of view. "We're getting closer to the central black hole."

"Looks like," Alicia said. "Max, what happens when we get there?"

He stood very still. "I have a feeling I don't want to find out."

The Cosm's viewpoint was speeding through torrents of dark clouds now. The circles and grid brimmed on the horizon as it plunged toward the swelling black ahead. Bee-swarm motes whipped past, were gone before anyone could comprehend what they were. The sense of time accelerating was like plunging down a steep slope.

"I wonder why the Cosm's other end has never gotten swallowed by a star?" Zak said dreamily. "I mean, the odds are it should have."

Max said, "Maybe the other end repulses other masses. There are still a lot of possibilities, all allowed by the equations."

His voice sounded worried and Alicia slipped an arm around him. But she did not stop staring at the quickening spectacle brimming at the center of their circle. Pale ivory radiance fizzed and fought in the surface of the Cosm. She remembered how it had sparkled with an eerie luminosity the first time she had seen it. When it was young. That speckled brilliance was returning now, when the universe on the other end of the space-time neck was vastly aged.

Max shifted uneasily. The Cosm's glow brightened and flecks of all colors raced across it. It was so dazzling that she became aware of the flat droning sound only gradually.

"What's that?" Zak glanced upward.

"That plane again," Jill said.

"Two of them," Zak said, looking up. "There."

The dots of light came bearing directly down on them. "One's a chopper," Zak called.

The airplane swept directly overhead, spotlights on. They all closed their eyes as it passed, to keep some of their night vision. Alicia was torn between watching the Cosm and the angry buzzing overhead.

Max didn't even look up. "I have no idea, no theory, to deal with what happens when a space-time nugget like this gets swallowed by a large-scale contortion . . ."

"It's gonna land!" Jill shouted against the gathering roar.

Searchlights swept the area in a hard glare. Alicia thought she would be unable to see anything in the Cosm at all now, but when she looked down, her hands shielding her face, the sphere was alive with working blue-green tendrils, like a strange standing lightning.

"Get away!" Max shouted against the hammering racket of the helicopter. It was landing a hundred meters away, blowing grit in their faces.

"We can't escape them," Jill said.

"Away from the Cosm!"

For a long moment she hesitated, gripped by the cascading, accelerating pace of events in the face of the Cosm. Dark clouds had blocked their view of the approaching black hole. Now those dissolved, blowing past. A yawning solid blackness rushed out of the distance. Fizzing white light burst from the surface of the Cosm.

"Come on!" He tugged her. She took a step, looked back, had to be led away.

In the Cosm's brilliant surface she saw seething brilliance collide with somber, growing black. Events compressed. Time raced as vast forces bore down.

She shook herself. Sucked in cold, dry air. Turned and ran with Max.

They all started directly away from the helicopter and then she yelled, "No, go right! Otherwise they'll run after us and right into the Cosm."

They veered right. Alicia looked back and saw men jumping out of the helicopter, a big one. They immediately began pursuit.

They all ran in silence for a full minute. Shouts in the distance. A bullhorn voice babbled.

Matters moved with a prolonged gravity, as if the entire scene were underwater, events unspooling at the bottom of a well-lit swimming pool. Jill and Zak ahead ran sluggishly. The bullhorn spoke so deeply that she could hear dragging spaces between the actual words, which in turn took stretched moments to come through the chilly air. Max's legs too were caught in the thick molasses air of the deep-sea scene. She was scarcely able to move in the heavy, unmeasurable time.

She stumbled over a stubby plant that jabbed her in the leg. The sudden jolt of pain brought back the speed of time and made her lose her stride. Max stopped, grabbed her arm to keep her from falling over. He glanced back. Behind them stabbing lights probed and his words came like the dry rustle of leaves.

"My God."

The others kept running. Flickering shadows chased them across the rough ground. She turned to look, still reluctant to leave. The Cosm now brimmed with an acid fire. It flared suddenly, blue-white and ferocious. The fierce brilliance of it expanded and blew her backward, head over heels.

EPILOGUE

If and when all the laws governing physical phenomena are finally discovered, and all the empirical constants occurring in these laws are finally expressed through the four independent basic constants, we will be able to say that physical science has reached its end, that no excitement is left in further explorations, and that all that remains to a physicist is either tedious work on minor details or the self-educational study and adoration of the magnificence of the completed system. At that stage physical science will enter from the epoch of Columbus and Magellan into the epoch of the *National Geographic Magazine*.

—GEORGE GAMOW, *PHYSICS TODAY*, 1949

EXPLOSION IN DESERT
'Cosm' Leaves Ten Yard Crater
Butterworth Among Casualties
No Trace of Remnants

'LIT UP SKY,' SAYS DESERT RAT

ACCOMPLICE CHARGES FILED AGAINST 'PHYSICS GANG'
Three Released from Hospital
Suffered No Radiation Exposure

UCI'S BUTTERWORTH LEAVES HOSPITAL
Placed Under Federal Arrest
Federal Marshal Accuses Her of Theft

LAWSUITS MOUNT IN DESERT 'COSM' EXPLOSION
State Police Officer Leaves Hospital
Helicopter 'Totaled' in Explosion

UCI WILL NOT PAY BUTTERWORTH LEGAL EXPENSES
Father Attacks UCI, Defends Daughter in Raucous Speech

BROOKHAVEN LAB VICINITY EVACUATED
Fears of Second 'Cosm' Explosion Mount
'Could Be Megatons,' Lab Head Says
'Amazing' Views Inside 'Cosm II' Rumored

PRESIDENT ATTACKS 'RECKLESS SCIENCE'
National Council of Churches Applauds
Finger-Jabbing Speech

ARRESTS MADE IN BUTTERWORTH KIDNAPPING CASE
'Foundation for God' Followers Traced to Arizona

CLAIMS AGAINST BUTTERWORTH DISMISSED
'No Control, So No Liability,' Judge Says
Surprise Move Angers Critics

BUTTERWORTH KIDNAPPERS CONFESS
'We Did Right,' Leader Claims

BROOKHAVEN 'COSM' 'EVAPORATES,' NO DAMAGE
'Cannot Explain,' Lab Head Admits
'Poof'—Gone; No Debris

CONGRESS TO INVESTIGATE PURSUIT OF 'COSM' DISCOVERER
Critics Call President 'Nervous Nellie'

BUTTERWORTH RETURNS TO TEACH AT UCI
Support Rally Scene of Violence
She Rejects UC 'Black Woman' Award

NOBEL LAUREATES CALL FOR FURTHER 'COSM' EXPERIMENTS
'Must Work at Frontier'
Technological Benefits Seen

SOCIAL ANNOUNCEMENTS
Dr. Thomas Butterworth of Palo Alto proudly announces the engagement of his daughter, Alicia, to Dr. Max Jalon, son of Mr. and Mrs. John Jalon, of Springfield, Maryland.

AFTERWORD

We are lucky to live in an age when grand questions arise, and one in which we just might find answers.

I began working on this novel in the late 1980s, spurred by papers by Alan Guth and collaborators. Alan was already famous, having constructed in the early 1980s a truly amazing new theory of our universe. I commend to you his excellent account of his invention, *The Inflationary Universe*. According to the inflationary model of cosmology, our universe grew out of less than ten kilograms starting in a region 10^{-24} cm. across. One could hold such an object in one hand.

More recently, Guth and his coworkers have made intricate calculations of the physics of universe-creation in the laboratory. This suggested a large theme, suitable to fictional treatment.

While I was at MIT on sabbatical leave, I enjoyed many delightful conversations with Alan Guth, whom I had met some years before. Ideas came readily, and I roughed out a plan for this novel. Marvin Minsky made several perceptive comments. A visit to the Brookhaven National Laboratory, hosted by old friends Lawrence and Marsha Littenberg, helped this germination along, as did conversations with Tom Ludlam, who showed me around RHIC, the Relativistic Heavy Ion Collider under construction.

The enormous, impressive accelerator abuilding there suggested to me a possible way that some of the ideas developed in those MIT papers might find expression in our time.

Others had been exploring such areas for quite serious reasons. When RHIC was being planned, theorists had worried about collisions in it creating "strange matter," a kind of lower-energy state for mass that would be more stable than the kind we know. That meant that in the tiny, compressed collisions of the RHIC, ordinary mass would convert into strange matter, given the opportunity of intense conditions, cashing in on the energetic advantage. This strange matter could then gobble up the Earth, converting everything to a new lower-energy state. Just incidentally, this would destroy all the structure invested in ordinary matter, erasing the entire slate of Creation. This would probably occur at speeds near that of light, leaving us not even time to regret our curiosity.

A theorist named Piet Hut put such fears to rest by showing that cosmic rays plunging through our atmosphere have already collided many times, creating conditions far more extreme than those in RHIC. The fact that we didn't see strange matter created every month or two from cosmic rays meant that RHIC was no threat.

Ah, I thought, but what about even more exotic accidental offspring?

Of course, the entire matter is a huge long shot. One must consider the relatively puny energies to be available even at RHIC, compared with the energy densities of the very early universe. Only if quantum mechanics works just right will this great gap be spanned. We do not in fact know how to do the calculation. A correct one awaits a better understanding. Further, there are the great uncertainties of our current rickety ideas about what a better, true theory of quantum gravity might look like. It could well be that a solid theory will rule out everything envisioned in this novel.

Still, they stir the imagination. In planning and writing this book, I had what seemed a good notion for rounding out the book's conceptual framework, but delayed writing the novel itself because of other obligations and other novels clamoring to be written. In early 1996 Arthur C. Clarke pointed out to me a striking paper by Edward Harrison, a noted cosmologist at the University of Massachusetts. It was the same idea I had vaguely worked out at MIT, better set out in Harrison's hands. In the *Quarterly Journal of the Royal Astronomical Society,* Volume 36, pages 193–203, he elegantly described the concept of natural selection of universes.

Harrison cites Isaiah 45:18, speaking of the "Lord . . . who created it not as a formless waste but as a place to be lived in," and thinks that perhaps many would prefer his vision, "if only because of Occam's razor, the concept of a [single] supreme being." In his conception, one needs only one Being who starts the ball rolling with a Grandaddy Universe that has fundamental parameters roughly suited to life. Evolving intelligence then takes over, making trouble, as it must. Harrison refers to Olaf Stapledon's classic *Star Maker,* in which a superior being keeps inventing universes of greater complexity, though none with the self-reproducing feature essential to explaining why we, a later generation, live in a universe admirably tuned to yield creatures at least as smart as we are. Harrison goes on to speculate that perhaps our mysterious ability to comprehend our universe arises because it was made by beings roughly resembling us. We are thus harmonized with the fine-tuned fundamental parameters we find. In this sense, we would then indeed be created in His (or Their) image.

I like audacious ideas, and this novel uses some in a context reflecting another of my repeating concerns: depicting scientists as they actually are, especially at work. Except for detectives and spies, seldom does fiction spend much time treating people at their work, yet it is a central aspect of life.

I hope that along with some intellectual excitement, I have made some aspects of the scientific enterprise and those who carry it forward at least a bit more understandable. All foreground characters herein are entirely invented. I have used the names of several actual people as background figures, for a note of authenticity.

For those who wish to trace some of the ideas further, I recommend "Is it Possible to Create a Universe in the Laboratory by Quantum Tunneling?" by Edward Farhi, Alan Guth, and Jemal Guven in *Nuclear Physics,* B 339, p. 417 (1990). A somewhat simpler summary by Guth alone is in

Physica Scripta, T36, 237 (1991). During the last drafting of this novel I came upon Lee Smolin's intriguing ideas in his *The Life of the Cosmos*, which treats some parallel ideas.

My thanks are due Alan Guth, Sidney Coleman, Riley Newman, Lawrence Littenberg, William Molson, John Cramer, and Virginia Trimble for scientific advice on the manuscript. Matt Visser provided wisdom and a figure. For insightful readings I am indebted to my wife, Joan, to Jennifer Brehl, Lawrence and Marsha Littenberg, Mark Martin, and David Brin.

—Gregory Benford
Laguna Beach,
June 1997

A LETTER TO MY READERS
From GREGORY BENFORD

Before anything else, thanks for reading my books!

I address you, readers of my fiction, because you may be interested in a swerve I shall take in my writing, along lines you may like.

Fiction strives to look long: to see ourselves from a perspective that permits reflection. The vastness of space helps us set the stage for our small human dramas, as I have attempted to show in this novel, *Cosm*.

But there is another vista we can use: the panoramas of time which modern science has opened to us. Though I have written much fiction about these ideas, I thought you might like to know that my next book, after twenty novels, is nonfiction. It is called *Deep Time: How Humanity Communicates Across Millennia*, and will appear in hardcover from Avon Bard in January 1999.

"Deep time" is that which bridges human cultures, outlasting the passions of the day. As an example, consider a visit to a Pleistocene cave in southern France. Paintings on the cave walls and ceiling show a pack of wild horses galloping along a ledge, while vivid antlered reindeer leap toward the viewer from nearby walls. Bison scratched into stone show fine-line features of nostrils, eyes and hair. Big-bellied horses lope toward us on short legs.

These are far from crude sketches. A big rocky bulge forms the muscular shoulder of a bison. A cow's body follows quite naturally a long, deep depression in one wall. Cleverly drawn animals blend, sharing a natural line in the wall. A ceiling frieze of small reindeer seem simply rendered under a flashlight's direct beam, but when the light angles away, the racks of their antlers follow the crests of slightly raised ridges in the rock.

Some prehistoric master saw the essence of these animals embedded in the chance curves of the cave. Then he called them forth to the eye, using negative space in ways we do not witness again until the work of the sixteenth century.

These signals across thousands of generations carry a heady sense of graceful intelligence. We know well enough what animals lived then, but only in such paintings can we delve into the cerebral wealth of our ancestors. Whether the artists intended them as such, these paintings then are the best sort of deep time messages, conveying wordless mastery and penetrating sensitivity across myriad millennia and staggeringly different cultures.

Many works about archeology, astronomy and evolution portray great stretches of time, but seldom do they confront our growing influence on events millennia hence. *Deep Time* treats several examples of the restless energies, which seek to reach across the ages.

It is sobering to contemplate that our distant heirs may know us best not by our Michelangelos or Einsteins or Shakespeares, but rather by the signposts we are busily erecting. *Deep Time* treats my own experiences while doing research as a professional physicist—explorations into our nuclear waste markers, our messages aboard space craft, our many signatures (and abuses) upon the soil and on other, fast-vanishing species.

One of my reasons for departing from fiction lies in our current cultural malaise. Our era can benefit from the vistas made possible by science. When hatred and technology can slaughter millions in minutes, such terrors deprive life of that quality made scarce and most precious to the modern mind: meaning. Deep time in its panoramas redeems this lack, rendering the human prospect again large and portentous. Continuity with both our past and our future summons up long perspectives, aligning our lives along an axis of common effort. We gain stature alongside such enormities.

If we let it, our past can loom large, as the pyramids do. We are much less aware of our reach into the future.

The Voyager probes of the 1970s carried plaques rhapsodizing over our culture, gestures at eternity cast into the interstellar abyss, possibly to be read billions of years from now. The high vacuum of space preserves well, but at the price of putting any message beyond ready human grasp.

Conversely, leaving messages close at hand runs great risks of obliteration. On Earth, until this century, the Pharaohs were the champions at knowingly reaching down to their posterity, a compass of less than 6,000 years.

Our twentieth-century cultures can do far better. *Deep Time* focuses on how our species has, in a single century, begun to have effects which shall ring down through many millennia in unprecedented ways. It moves from concrete cases to abstract proposals. Frankly, my agenda is to encourage a deep time outlook, arguing that it may help us with our most vexing problems as a civilization.

Increasingly, such perspectives emerge from the reach of our technology. Rockets can carry indelible plaques to the stars, and nuclear waste can demand that we mark sites for times longer than the age of our civilization. More important, our subtle impacts come from our inadvertent effects upon our planet itself. These now tower over our future, as the prospects for global climate change suggest.

Through the ages, we have tried to leave some testament to ourselves. Some are unconscious, others are nonverbal, and some are accidental or unintended. As soon as civilization appeared, the Egyptians and Chinese began erecting monuments to themselves. The impulse seems buried deep within us.

Such early testaments convey pride, even grandeur, but little more. Many ancient monuments are unmarked and mysterious, like the Sphinx, Stonehenge, and the American mounds. Probably most were not tributes to their builders, but religious sites or mausoleums. Deeper motives may have pervaded societies which we, at our great remove, can only dimly sense.

Why do we humans do this? Surely the global character of

this impulse tells us much about ourselves, in ways that the customary chronicles of history do not. I suspect that deep within all of us lies a need for continuity of the human enterprise, perhaps to offset our own mortality. This explains why so many deep time messages and monuments have religious elements or undertones.

A yearning for connection also explains why ancestor worship appears in so many cultures; one enters into a sense of progression, expecting to be included eventually in the company.

Somehow in the human psyche a longing for perpetuity has manifested itself powerfully, erecting vast edifices and burying considerable treasure—all to extend across time some lasting shadow of the present.

In *Deep Time* I have tried to outline what we know of how our ancestors tried to leave some record of themselves, and how well their strategies worked. Then I take up my own adventures covering a decade—in designing markers for long term monuments, from waste sites in salt flats to diamond disks riding aboard spacecraft.

It has been a grand pursuit, much of it sobering.

Readers of fiction about science, and science fiction, may find the perspectives I explored interesting. I certainly did! More, I learned a lot, and hope the trip will be fun for others.

Gregory Benford,
Summer, 1998